Job's Wife

Don Arey

Postmodern Publishing

Fitchburg · Massachusetts · U.S.A.

Table of Contents

ABOUT THIS BOOK 3

COPYRIGHT 5

DEDICATION 6

1 NADA 8

2 SLAVE GIRL 18

3 REDEMPTION 35

4 SAFEHAVEN 47

5 PROSTITUTE-PRIEST..59

6 HANDMAIDEN..73

7 BODYGUARD..83

8 MEET THE MASTER...95

9 CONFESSIONS..107

10 CONSPIRACY 121

11 PREMONITIONS 137

12 ENEMIES 152

13 PEACE 176

14 RUIN...185

15 ABANDONMENT..199

16 PURSUIT 213

17 MY FATHER'S HOUSE 233

18 SECRETS...252

19 RETRIBUTION...260

20 JUDGMENT 277

21 REUNION 295

EPILOGUE...313

ABOUT THE AUTHOR...321

CAST OF CHARACTERS 322

About This Book

There are only three verses in the Bible's Book of Job that refer to his wife:

1 - His wife said to him, "Are you still maintaining your integrity? Curse God and die!"
   - Job 2:9

2 - "My breath is offensive to my wife"
   - Job 19:17a

3 - "If my heart has been enticed by a woman, or if I have lurked at my neighbor's door, then may my wife grind another man's grain, and may other men sleep with her."
   - Job 31:9-10

The most well-known verse of course, is the first. Job's unnamed wife betrays him in his hour of greatest need and tells him he should give up. But Job's answer to his wife's curse is very interesting.

In a mild-mannered response, Job implores his wife to remain patient and faithful to the path of Godly wisdom. He says she is "talking like a foolish woman", implying that she is *not one of the foolish women*. I deduce from Job's response that he considers his wife's curse to be a surprising, temporary lapse in her normally good judgment.

The second reference in Job 19:17a, seems to be a euphemism about Job's general physical repulsiveness due to his illness. He was so sick that his wife and family could not stand to be around him. I extrapolated freely from this idea. Given all the other stresses going on in their lives, the final wedge between the couple may have been his physical pain and her withdrawal from it. She had stayed with him through everything else, but when Job broke out in ugly boils, it was more than she could bear.

The third verse seems to imply that Job and his wife had separated and that he was worried she would be unfaithful to him if he did not remain faithful to her and to his God. It is possible to deduce that Job's wife remained faithful to her husband because Job remained faithful throughout his trial. Job's wife may have been *faithless* for a time, she may have lost faith, but perhaps she was not *unfaithful*. After all, God blessed Job with ten more children after his trial ended. The Bible does not say where the new children came from.

And there you have the basis for this book:

> 1 - Job's wife is wise, but temporarily and foolishly fails in her devotion due to her passions.

> 2 - Part of her failure of devotion may have had something do to with Job's physical affliction - the terrible visual impact of his blistering boils.

> 3 - Job's wife may have strayed in her faith, but perhaps she did not go so far as adultery.

If paleontologists can reconstruct a dinosaur from a small scrap of fossilized bone, perhaps I can build a story from these three small pieces of evidence about an obscure, unnamed woman of ancient times – Job's Wife.

Copyright

Dedication

For Amie

There's a little bit of Nada and Frayda in you, my darlin' daughter.
No, wait! Reverse that.

1

Nada

"Have you ever given orders to the morning,
or shown the dawn its place,
that it might take the earth by the edges
and shake the wicked out of it?"

The Book of Job 38:12-13

-:--o--:-

Abel the thief spat contemptuously when his messenger rejoined their small den of thugs to shout news that Abel's woman would bear a child for him in the spring.

"Bah! Perhaps she will be strong enough to deliver a son to my knee like a good little ewe and not spill it prematurely dead and cold on the ground like last winter, eh?!" Cruel laughter echoed into the night throughout the narrow wadi where Abel and his band of thieves had paused around a campfire to divvy up their loot.

A scarred and bejeweled hand offered a brimming mug of bitter ale to Abel's leering grin. The firelight danced its demonic design in Abel's eyes as his partner proffered a vile toast, "Drink, friend for you are doubly blessed! You have broken the teeth of our enemy and reclaimed our honor from those accursed Sabean raiders! Harun's own treasure lies at our feet splattered with the blood of their whore women. Now we learn that by spring your own woman will bear you a son! I know it will be a son! I feel it, by the gods you are a man tonight! Drink! Everyone drink, to Abel the man!"

Hoarse shouts and laughter encouraged the revelry heedless of the darkness closing like a shroud around them. Their campfire's loud crackling seemed to join them in mock celebration, its noises masking the muffled snap of a twig breaking under a sandaled foot stealing its way toward their camp.

Abel accepted the mug and saluted his fellow thieves. He tipped back his head and quaffed the ale with great gusto, the foam running down his beard to glisten darkly in the firelight. He tipped the drink high for the last drop and staggered slightly. He dropped the mug to his side just in time to see the firelight briefly illuminate the gleaming bronze tip of a spear as it whistled its way out of the darkness and straight through the center of his chest.

He crumpled in gurgling death, the camp suddenly erupting in chaos as black-robed men seemed to spring from the desert's dust with arm-length sabers whirling in their gleaming death-dance. In less than a minute the plunderers lay plundered, the black-robed men leaving nothing but scattered bodies for jackals and vultures.

-:--o--:-

In early spring, Abel's wife, Miriam lay sweating and groaning on her side with the small of her back held tight against the wall of a mud-packed hut. Its rigid warmth gave her some relief from the terrible strain of labor and the comparative coolness of the desert night. Her sister squatted helpless at her feet murmuring, "Too soon, too soon... Ah, Miriam, why are we so cursed by the gods?"

Instinctively, Miriam knew her labor was a few weeks early, but the gods alone decided when a child would come. She was grateful for her sister's help and regretted that her husband Abel would not be here... Her thoughts exploded into chaos with a stab of excruciating pain that filled her world and mouth with screams. The baby erupted into her sister Anna's hands all mucous and blood. Anna stared horrified as more blood followed the child, so much blood...

As Anna wiped the birth fluids from the newborn she spared a glance at Miriam whose face had turned ashen, "A girl-child. Miriam, you have a daughter. She is hale."

Miriam managed a thin smile, "Abel would have been... disappointed."

Anna spat on the floor. "That worthless, god-cursed man! May Ba'al's demons chase him through Sheol forever!"

Just then Miriam shuddered as she delivered the afterbirth. Anna lowered her eyes with resignation as she saw the volume and color of fluid that followed. From experience she knew her sister had little time now. Indeed, Miriam's very life was leaking away with her every heartbeat.

"Miriam!" she could barely utter her sister's name as she attended to the child.

Miriam had already sunk into a twilight sleep where she was feeling no pain, only the blissful euphoria after the birthing labor – a soporific now amplified by her imminent death. She answered in dreamy sing-song, "Hmmm?"

"Miriam! This child must have a name. Have you given any thought to your daughter's name?"

Miriam was in shock and fast approaching delirium, beads of cold sweat, death-dew formed on her brow. Her eyes lolled aimlessly in her head as she struggled to stay in the world just a little while longer, to enjoy the presence of her sister and newborn daughter as long as she could -- her newborn daughter! With strength borne only of a mother, she discovered alertness and clarity with the thought of a daughter! From somewhere within her, vitality surged into her mind and body giving her the strength to shift position and face the opening of their mud hut.

The sun was rising, painting the sky with royal shades of red and purple. From her position on the floor, Miriam could see the morning dew sparkling like gems in dawn's light. The dew decorated every palm, fern, fence post, rock... everything except the desert sand and it looked to Miriam's blood-drained mind to be more beautiful than any king's palace. She wondered who could be the god that had placed such beauty in the world. Men spoke of "gods", but that did not ring true. She felt there must be One God above the other gods who was capable of such beauty and willing to share it with everyone. If this God existed, she would like to meet him someday...

"Miriam?" her sister prompted, snapping her thoughts back from the brink of the void. "Do you want to name the child or shall I?"

Miriam smiled languidly and thought of God's beauty, the God of gods and the hope of dawn. Her smile broadened and she said clearly, "Nada. It think it means 'Glistening with Dew'. That is a pretty name, is it not?"

Anna stroked the dew from her sister's forehead and drew her hand down to straighten her tousled hair. "Yes, Nada is a good name. She will be called Nada."

"You have been good to me, Anna. Take care of Nada for me won't you? For just awhile. I need to sleep now." Miriam sighed gently as she drifted away with the rising sun in her face to meet God.

Though her heart was filled with regret and loss, Anna was a leathery woman much older than her sister and toughened by years of desert life. She shed no tears for her sister as she busily finished cleaning Nada and then wrapped her sister Miriam in a blanket for burial.

At last she turned to the baby who had oddly remained silent throughout, "Well, little Nada, what's to become of you?"

-:--o--:-

Later that day, Anna handed Nada over to a wet-nurse in the village to be cared for until weaned. When the elders of the village met that evening with Anna's husband Abed, he begrudgingly committed payment of two female goats for the wet-nurse's services. The goats would be returned or replaced as soon as Nada was able to eat solid food. Abed was a harsh man who did not care much for family duties thrust upon him by his second wife Anna. To his mind, a girl-child was not worth the loss of two goats, even a temporary loss. During negotiations with the village elders, he made certain the contract contained a clause that ensured any kids his goats produced would be his and not the wet-nurse's. "Milk for milk!" he shouted at their meeting and made his point by pounding his fist into his palm.

The wet-nurse's husband, Amal reluctantly agreed to the deal because his large family was in need of extra goat milk and additional income obtained from cheese. After agreeing, he made certain the offspring of Abed's two goats mysteriously and regrettably, did not survive birth.

"How can I help it if you gave me the worst and weakest does of your herd?!" he complained when Abed confronted him and demanded payment for the lost kids. Village feuds were born in this manner and men often died as a result.

-:--o--:-

There are fortunate children who are born and *raised* in families. Other children simply grow up within a family because that is where they are fed. Nada's lot was cast with the unfortunate latter class. To make matters worse, she was the daughter of a murdered thief and a mother who had died in childbirth. Traditionally superstitious, her aunt and uncle considered her anathema, avoiding her suspiciously, raising her out of duty. They set her to work as soon as she could walk or hold any type of tool – a spoon to stir a pot, a broom to sweep, a knife to trim meat. If little Nada had cut herself and bled to death they would have thought it a fitting fate to their god-cursed burden.

But Nada turned out to be extremely intelligent, physically agile and socially observant -- a miracle of nature and a frustration to the superstitious. There is a common belief that the gods should not protect those whom the believers are certain the gods have cursed. The judgments of humanity are perpetually at odds with the divine.

Naturally thoughtful and silently philosophical due to the isolation imposed upon her, Nada threw her intelligence into amazingly astute observations. She learned that lying was not in her own best interest, but that telling the whole truth was not always so profitable either. If she lied, she was invariably caught and the punishment was much worse for having lied than confessing in the first place. She learned to confess with mitigations to lessen her punishment. This compromise served to preserve her sense of integrity and self-justification while saving her own skin to boot. She was a mere five years old when she began to figure this out.

For example, her aunt once asked her if she had eaten any of the dog's food. She tried lying with a simple "No" but her face betrayed her as did her cousin who had seen the malfeasance. The punishment was a severe beating. The next time this very same scenario occurred, her answer was different. "The dog had left it behind, he was no longer hungry and I was." That time, her punishment was only a scolding and ridicule for eating after the dog which did not matter to her at all since her aunt was wrong to leave her so hungry all the time.

Somehow, a sense of integrity formed within a child who was not taught integrity – some things in life are apparently caught, not taught.

By watching her aunt, uncle and cousins, Nada began to develop a sense of what was right and wrong with them. She came to believe that they were mostly wrong all the time. She did not have the experience to know just what made them 'wrong', it was more of an intuitive conclusion than deductive logic, but she knew that their constant curses and allusions to fate and blame on 'the gods' did not make sense. Every morning, the sun came up with such splendor and beauty it would fill her soul anew with hope for a bright new day. Her hopes always evaporated like dew by the harshness of each day's events, but somehow hope renewed with the dawn. Even Nada did not understand why she did not despair under the heavy burden of her life. She had little to sustain her, but the surpassing beauty of each dawn was apparently sufficient grace to explain the miracle that her soul did not wither.

-:--o--:-

Life ground on under the heavy millstone of the desert sun as it pressed its daily path over Nada's village. More sparks of life flashed anew among the hovels as children were born squalling into existence. Most sparks darkened again as they were snuffed out by diseases which claimed so many during their first year.

The laments of women and curses of men blended with the throaty complaints of sheep and goats into a cacophony of village noise that made human and animal voices barely distinguishable when heard from the distant hills or the heavens above.

Years passed wearily on. Abed's grudge with Amal, the husband of Nada's wet-nurse, mattered little now. Amal had been found with his throat slit, an apparent victim of thieves that constantly chewed the village edges. Abed's outrage and grief over the death of his 'friend' seemed a bit contrived and surprising, given his history with Amal. That he hurried to comfort Amal's grieving widow surprised no one. Within a year Abed added the woman as his third wife, conveniently expanding his herds. Whispers of foul play flared and passed because no one liked that goat herder Amal anyway. Small villages tolerated small scandals as their only entertainment.

In the spring of Nada's twelfth year she awoke on the flat roof of their small mud hut where she liked to sleep. The roof served as an escape from the stifling heat of the claustrophobic single room below as well as the resonant snoring of her uncle. As she stood to look east expecting her morning's infusion of dawn's light, her heart thumped once hard, in fear. A dust devil appeared to be coming over the horizon straight at her village! If a storm was headed their way, she must warn her family!

She nearly tripped over a chicken as she hustled down the steps built on the outside wall of their hut. The chicken fluttered away angrily which set a dog barking. She heard her uncle stirring inside as evidenced by his cursing.

"Uncle! Uncle! A storm is coming from the east!"

Her uncle Abed cursed all the more which elicited groans from his wives curled nearby. "Fool! No storm comes from the east! You are dreaming! Go away child or I swear if my head did not hurt so I would make you wish you had died with your god-cursed mother!" Abed had spent the previous night drinking with the village elders, as he did most nights now. His larger herds had made him considerably more notable among them, though in his case wealth did not equate to wisdom -- a proverb noted by few and ignored by all.

Frustrated by her uncle's scorn, Nada withdrew. She ran back to the rooftop for another look at the storm and was horrified to see it was no storm at all, for creatures were rising from the desert sand as if stirred up by the devil himself! There were men riding on these creatures of the storm! Men were riding toward her village on swift beasts which she had never seen before.

The beasts were smaller than camels but with shorter necks and much larger than donkeys and so much faster! The men wore black robes that fluttered behind them with the swiftness of their ride. There must have been more than a dozen! Before she could move to warn her uncle again, they were storming into the village waving long, curved swords that gleamed a golden bronze in the morning light.

She saw a neighbor run out of his house only to have his head severed from his shoulders with one swift stroke of the black raider's sword. Nada ducked down behind the low parapet that bordered the roof's edge. It served as scant shelter to the eyes of her enemies but not from the sounds. Screams, curses, rage and hideous laughter all found their way to her position on the roof as she shrank further and further within herself, hiding from the horror. She curled into a ball with her hands cupped over her ears, but her hearing still betrayed her. She could hear the sounds of her aunt and uncle in the room below as they were slaughtered. Her uncle's cries had been cut off abruptly, but her aunt's shrill screams had gone on much, much longer.

After an hour, Nada began to dehydrate in the morning sun as it baked her on the frying pan of the roof. She knew she must escape somehow, but as a child of only twelve, she realized her chances were slim if any chance existed at all. Maybe the black-robed men would not check the roof. She resigned herself to die and surrendered to her doom.

At twelve years old, Nada experienced the epiphany of peace that comes only with the certainty of impending death. To her own amazement, she discovered that she was not afraid.

She had witnessed death many times and many ways in her village. Accompanying her aunt Anna, she had been present when children had died and when babies had been stillborn. Working for her uncle Abed, she was intimately familiar with the slaughter of sheep, goats and cattle and had learned to help in the butchering. But she had never contemplated her own death until now, not in a real and personal way. To discover that she did not fear death, yet did not welcome it -- that she still wanted to live to see tomorrow's dawn -- was an exhilarating feeling!

She resolved to live if she could and die without fear if she could not.

Nada discovered amazing inner strength and self-control flowing within her stemming from the power of this decision. She did not know why or how, but she felt that a protective Hand other than 'fate' or 'the gods' was covering her even as she lay curled up on the roof. Whether she lived or died, she somehow knew she would be protected and alright.

This sense of protection caused her body to relax and unwind itself from her fetal position. She realized that the sounds from below had grown still. She opened her eyes, not remembering she had squeezed them shut. She found herself staring at a pair of sandaled feet.

Nada's agile brain made instant calculations and conclusions. *If he meant to kill me, I would already be dead. If he means to have sport with me, I will spoil his fun by jumping from the roof!* She almost chuckled to herself because the situation had become so clear there was no fear. She slowly stood up to face the black-robed man.

He was tall, very muscular and dark-skinned with a deep scar that ran from his right ear to chin. He smiled wickedly and shouted a question to the street below in a language she could not understand.

An abrupt answer returned and her captor smiled at her again but with seeming genuineness.

He spoke her language with a heavy accent, "You are in luck, young one. I shall not kill you today. Perhaps tomorrow." His laugh was also genuine but Nada scowled her rebuke at his poor taste.

"A caravan will pass near us soon. You will fetch a good price. Come." He grabbed a fistful of her hair and dragged her behind him with all the concern one would give a piece of luggage. Nada did not cry out, instead she grabbed his wrist with both hands to save herself from going prematurely bald and thought of several imaginative ways a twelve year old could kill a Sabean raider in his sleep.

-:--O--:-

2

Slave Girl

"Do not mortals have hard service on earth?
Are not their days like those of hired laborers?
Like a slave longing for the evening shadows,
or a hired laborer waiting to be paid,
so I have been allotted months of futility,
and nights of misery have been assigned to me."

The Book of Job 7:1-3

-:--o--:-

Nada's captor dragged her to a line of other children, mostly girls, a couple older boys but also a few young women. She recognized no one because her social life had been restricted to family only. Apparently none of her family had survived the raid, leaving her twice-orphaned. Shock anesthetized her mind. She felt no grief, no horror at the mangled and bloodied bodies strewn around her village. Instead she felt a heightened sense of awareness and keen clarity that she found extremely invigorating. She did not know if this was the same Hand of protection she had sensed before, but she decided to take full advantage of each opportunity that presented itself -- any opportunity to survive to tomorrow's dawn.

Her captor fitted a chain of stiff leather collars to each of them. The children's collars were too large, so a cloth was knotted uncomfortably inside to reduce its diameter. The black-robed man stood back to examine his work and shouted orders in his thickly accented voice, "You will walk behind the horses." *Horses, thought Nada. The beasts are called 'horses'.* "Any who fall will be left for jackal food." He paused to see if any dared complain, when there was silence he laughed long and loud. Nada decided to be both brave and foolish.

"Sir, may have some water?" she asked, looking at the tall man without blinking.

The raider snapped an angry look toward the source of this insolence. Nada returned the look with an expression that communicated nothing other than that she expected water. The raider grinned as he found a water pot, carried it to Nada and contemptuously threw it in her face, soaking her clothing.

Nada licked at the water dripping from her upper lip. "Thank you sir, I was very hot." This caused the entire coffle line to burst out laughing. The raider grabbed at his sword and had it half-drawn but another man barked an order.

"A'jin! Do not ruin this day by killing off our profits."

"Just this one, Harun. Surely we can spare one?" He glared at Nada, not sheathing his sword.

"Perhaps tomorrow, A'jin. Tomorrow is another day and we shall be rich enough for you to kill any one you want! We must be off!" Harun waved A'jin away.

A'jin slapped his sword back into its sheath with a snort and grumbled curses as he mounted his horse. Harun, apparently the leader of the raiders, turned his attention to Nada as his reined up his horse beside the line.

"You there!" Nada turned her eyes toward him, "Yes you. You have a keen mind, young one, and a sharp tongue. Where you are going they will be needing slaves with keen minds, but not tongues. If I hear you speak again, you shall find the sword of Harun is sharper than your tongue, do you understand?" Nada's eyes flared in fear and she nodded her understanding. "Good! Today you did not die. Tomorrow I may let A'jin kill you all, he would enjoy that." The entire line shuffled in fear. The man leaned back in his saddle and let loose the remorseless laugh of a strong man glorying in the trivial defeat of the weak.

-:--o--:-

Fortunately for everyone on the coffle line, the caravan they were to meet the next day had made unexpected progress in their direction so they were spared a tortuous walk in the sun. The rendezvous was an oasis with plenty of water. Nada's feet where burning from the journey, but not terribly burned as she was a desert child with almost leather-like skin on her soles. She found herself unconcerned for her future, simply curious about the next moment or hour. Almost anything would be an improvement over life with her uncle and aunt.

The girl in line next to her seemed very strange. She cried quietly but constantly. It irritated Nada because crying might bring the attention of A'jin or his boss again and that would never do.

"Stop crying!" she hissed when no one was around. "Why are you crying?!"

"Why are you not?" the girl whimpered. She seemed to be Nada's age, maybe a little older.

"I do not wish to have my tongue cut out! That is why, you fool!! Your constant crying could get us killed."

The girl was not mollified, but she did make a visible effort to control herself. "You are Nada, yes? I have seen you around the village. It is said your uncle killed Amal."

"I do not know. What if he did? What if he didn't? Does it matter now?" Nada thought this was a stupid thing to bring up, it was ancient history.

Her eyes watered up again and Nada groaned. "Amal was my uncle." She said.

"I am sorry for your uncle." She said without emotion. "Anyway, my uncle is dead now too. The desert is very hungry and swallows everyone eventually." She had heard her aunt say this many times and could think of nothing else to say.

The girl sniffed but remained thoughtful. "My mother said the desert is a place created by Elohim, 'God the Almighty' and that it is not a thing that can have an appetite."

Nada blinked confusion. She had never heard of any god named 'Elohim'. She asked, "What is this god named, 'Elohim'? He makes deserts? That does not seem to be a good thing for a god to make. The desert is very harsh, so Elohim must not be a very good god."

The girl almost laughed, "God does not have a name and he is not a 'what' he is a 'who'. 'Elohim' is something we use to talk about him, like calling him 'sir'. And he made everything, the whole world, not just the desert. He is very, very good and is known by many names." The girl appeared very weak-minded to Nada. Nada concluded this girl bragged about her god to compensate for her own weakness.

Nada stared at her for a bit longer and thought perhaps the many tragedies of this day had caused the poor girl to lose her mind. She had heard her aunt speak of such things – people driven to think crazy things by grief or fear. She determined that she would not let that happen to herself.

She was about to speak to the girl again but hissed them both to silence as A'jin's formidable figure appeared before them.

"Good news young ones! Harun says you will not have to wait until tomorrow to die! I get to kill you now!" The girl beside her shrank in fear, but Nada, risking everything pulled down her collar to expose her throat with a smile, calling A'jin's bluff. He grinned wickedly. "Ha! Ha! I like you young one! I would keep you for myself, but unfortunately I do not have the silver. And what would I do with you anyway? I already own a good horse and my dog bites everyone but me. I expect you would bite me if I gave you the chance, eh?" Nada relaxed, mission accomplished.

He spoke to Nada, "You have been sold to a master E'mat bin Jadal whose agents will fetch you momentarily. He lives by the sea so if you do not like to eat fish, I suggest you develop an appetite or you will starve. And as for you, young one," he glared at the girl cowering next to Nada, "you have been sold to A'dab Ben Hareb, the richest man of Edom. I pity you. He hates children and has probably purchased you for his breakfast." With his news delivered, A'jin left with a laugh, leaving Nada's new acquaintance whimpering in fear.

"Don't let A'jin bother you, he is a liar, I can tell." Nada said emphatically.

"Do you think so?" she sniffed.

"Of course, I am sure the man he spoke of does not want you for breakfast, he wants you for dinner." She stopped crying, clapped her hand over her mouth to laugh, her eyes dancing at Nada's rough joke. She decided that Nada could be her friend, whether Nada thought so or not.

"My name is Frayda. I would like you to be my friend, Nada." She said warmly.

Nada nodded, "I do not think I will ever see you again, but I like you too, Frayda. I have never had a friend." Frayda leaned to embrace Nada in a rattle of chains but the rough leather collars prevented anything more than a symbolic gesture. It made both girls smile.

"I have had many friends, Nada, but you are very different. We will meet again, I am sure of it." She seemed quite certain. Her confidence made Nada wonder again if Frayda was in her right mind.

Nada smiled indulgently, but she knew Frayda could not know the future. Just then a young man walked up with A'jin. He was very tall and young with sharp features. He seemed to be an uncertain boy attempting to be about the business of a man.

"Which of you is Frayda?" he spoke pompously with too much feigned authority. Frayda gestured and knelt in submission. A'jin unlocked her collar and the boy/man gestured that she follow. He locked eyes with Nada for a moment. Nada saw something there. For a moment his eyes softened in compassion, but then he turned away with

Frayda and disappeared into the dusk with her. He and Frayda were out of her life forever just like everyone else she had ever known.

A storm rose up in the desert over night; there was no sunrise to Nada's dismay. She would have taken it as an ill omen, but Nada had decided she did not believe in omens. She decided she believed only in Nada and in the dawning of each new day.

She was released from her collar, fed some rice with dried fruit and loaded onto a donkey cart with three other bedraggled, weeping young women. The others talked between themselves but said nothing to her the entire trip. Nada found herself wrapped in solipsistic isolation once again as the cart rattled its way along a road that grew more and more rocky and ever cooler. They traveled for many days.

-:--o--:-

E'mat bin Jadal was a well-to-do, rather than wealthy fish merchant. He lived in Haqal, a small village at the northern tip of the Aqaba Gulf which emptied into the Red Sea. E'mat owned three boats, but two were in such battered shape they were often pulled up on the beach for repair rather than out on the water making E'mat rich. Just when he thought he would go broke, the gods favored him with a good catch and just when he thought he would get rich, the fates broke the mast of his ship in a storm or tore his nets on a sunken boat or… E'mat sighed a heavy sigh. He could make a good living, but he could not make good money.

E'mat's wife, Leah, had turned sickly this past year – the latest of his misfortunes. She demanded he purchase more slaves to assist her with household chores which included cutting up the daily catch of fish. E'mat figured that if they had fewer slaves they would have less household chores, but his wife was beyond logic. More slaves represented status and that is what she seemed to want more than anything.

He had tried many times to reason with her, but Leah's father-in-law was a village elder and very influential in the fish markets. He dared not offend his wife or he would find his catches rotting in the sun waiting for someone to come inspect them. He groaned inwardly at his own frustrations. His doorman, Raziel looked quizzically in his direction, for apparently E'mat had groaned outwardly too. He turned sad, watery eyes to the doorman and shrugged off his question. Most of the staff was used to their master's morbid ways. E'mat acted as if he was in constant pain -- but it was not physical pain.

The caravan arrived yesterday and he hoped there would be one or two slaves who would be worth their silver. E'mat eyed his purchases with regret. He sighed again… The young women looked strong and the boy could serve on the boats, but that one young girl! She looked so spindly and… wild! She did not have the eyes of a slave. She had the eyes of a lioness hunting for its prey. He recognized that look for he had lived with it as long as he had been married to his wife. He waved her off with a gesture and told his agent, "Send her back, she is too young."

"What's this?!" his wife bellowed from behind him, "I have waited two months for our shipment to arrive and you are going to 'cull the herd' without consulting me?!"

"But Leah…" E'mat whined, but his wife cut him off with a dismissive wave of her hand. She had made up her mind and nothing he said made any difference. No further discussion was necessary in her mind. E'mat groaned and decided to check on his fishing boats. E'mat checked on his fishing boats often.

Leah was a short, stout woman only a little taller than the twelve year old Nada, but perhaps twice the mass. The two lioness predators sized each other up with professional precision. The elder, more experienced Leah won the staring contest as Nada's eyes dropped to the floor in submission.

-:--o--:-

Nada woke during the predawn darkness of the next morning but did not move. An early riser, she was used to the silence of a household with herself the only one awake. She stared at the dark ceiling while she considered her new environment. The strangeness of everything and the chaos of the last several days lay heavy on her like a sack of grain holding her to the floor. She felt as if she were sinking into the floor and the world was about to swallow her up. The walls of her new master's house loomed high around her with no apparent opening to the morning light.

Her aunt, uncle and all her cousins had been slain in the raid mere days ago. Yet the long journey to E'mat's house by the sea made the murdering rampage by the Sabean raiders twice-removed by time and distance. She tried, but she could not feel the pain of loss like the emotion so easily flowing from Frayda, the girl she met on her march from their village. She did not feel anything this morning except a nagging hollowness. She seemed like an empty clay pot and she felt there should be something to fill it, but what? Life had dumped her upside down and emptied her out. She felt nothing, understood nothing and saw nothing as she stared upward. There was so little light she could not tell if her eyes were open or closed.

Suddenly, abruptly, Nada's eyes filled with tears as she tried to fight her panic. It was a battle she lost. She dared not make a sound for fear of bringing unwanted attention. But her mouth stretched wide as if in the rictus of death as she silently screamed out her agony of loneliness and abandonment. Her chest heaved in wracking noiseless, secretive sobs, her fists clenched and body thrashing on the mat until she thought she would break -- but she did not break.

The attack persisted for a minute that seemed eternal. Her wrenching, silent sobs eventually subsided and became rhythmic as ocean waves in the gloom. Rational again, she began to examine her own mind and wondered what force had calmed her.

Nada realized she no longer felt alone in the room. It was not the other girls sleeping that she sensed, nor was she afraid of an invader. She felt a presence within her, beside her and especially under her, bearing her up. It was like the floor upon which she lay had become softer somehow and had become part of the whole world. She found the feeling to be amazingly wonderful and actually relaxed into it. She was not afraid.

She thought of something Frayda said at the oasis just a few days before, something about God the creator of all -- 'Elohim' she said. She wondered if Frayda's god could be real. Frayda said her god did not have a name and could not be seen. Questions bubbled into her mind, "*Does Frayda's God know my name? Can he see me?*"

In sudden answer, as if in a flash of intuitive brilliance, Nada could see herself lying on the floor of the room. More than that, she saw herself in relationship to the other slave girls, to her owners E'mat and Leah, she knew and felt herself a slave – bought with price. She could see herself as part of the small town, and though only a child, still an integral part of the town's life and function. She could see the fishing boats and the sea that she'd only glanced as she rode by in the donkey cart the day before. She saw herself in her new role as a child slave in the household of a fish merchant, working daily as part of life in the fishing village and all the interconnecting lives as threads that bound all lives together in intricate patterns. She saw all this in an instant that seared its image on her mind and then vanished leaving behind only its emotional imprint of calm assurance – she would be alright. Her mind felt as if it had been caressed.

Somehow Nada knew her mind was not playing tricks on her. Her flash of intuition, her insight of understanding her place and role for here and now was a gift from the God Frayda had called 'Elohim'. He must be the presence in the room she felt but could not see. There were words floating in Nada's mind, an emotional imprint that was linked to her insight. The words seemed to fill her with confident assurance as she heard them repeated in her mind, "*I see you.*"

Nada discovered that her body was growing tingly with the onset of sleep. Her brain felt incredibly weary yet she was still awake. She felt like she was laying on soft sand and sleep was coming like the tide to float her away. Her last thoughts were of Elohim. She thought it a good enough name for god, and she decided she wanted Elohim to be her God. If she was to be a slave, better to be Elohim's slave. It was always in Nada's nature to one-up her boss and this would be the best way to remain a slave to E'mat and Leah yet secretly choosing her own master. She smiled sleepily as she asked Elohim if he wouldn't mind being her master because she was afraid of being a slave to E'mat and Leah.

As Nada felt herself floating away on the incoming tide of sleep, her last thought was, *"You are the God who sees me."*

-:--o--:-

The sleepy tide bearing Nada bumped ashore painfully as something slapped her feet. Alertness came slowly which was unusual for her. She had slept more deeply than she could remember, it took another painful slap on her feet before she sat up, fully alert. She saw an older girl with a paddle looking very stern.

"The mistress does not tolerate sleepy heads!" She smacked the soles of her extended feet a third time, this time hard enough to make her eyes water.

Nada stood immediately and followed the others out the door. She had no idea what to do or where to go; apparently everyone else knew so she merged into the flow and did what they did until she learned. Everyone splashed water on their faces from a central basin and washed their hands in what appeared to be some sort of ritual. The girl with the paddle smacked her weapon threateningly into her hand until she copied the others. Dip both hands under-handed in the basin, let the water drip from your elbow – three times – hold your hands up shoulder high and march to the feeding room. It seemed silly, but she learned to do it every morning to avoid the paddle.

There were other rituals at the house that made no sense to Nada. They had to wait with food sitting before them while someone sang a song before they were allowed to eat. Their mistress Leah also expected them to wear freshly washed clothes each day. The slave girls labored mostly at cleaning the daily catch of fish, so it made no sense at all to wash her clothes at the end of the day when they would be completely covered by fish innards, blood and scales the next day anyway! Why wasn't it sufficient to scrape them clean once a week? But Leah insisted their clothes be clean for the morning meal and that meant a cold salt water swim in the sea, then an even colder fresh water rinse in a fountain / bath just inside the patio every day.

Their gunny-sack style tunics were made of a rough flaxen cloth that reached to their ankles. The sleeves were short, above the elbows so not to interfere with their work, tied with a cloth belt. Nada noted enviously that the girl with the paddle had a belt of leather and a loop around her neck also made of leather bearing a small dull stone. She wondered how to achieve that kind of status.

-:--o--:-

Nada caught onto the routine quickly and then was taken completely by surprise on the fourth day. She was the first one awake and waited for the girl with the paddle but instead, Leah came to their room long after the normal time that work should have begun. She clapped her hands together three times to ensure she had everyone's attention.

"Some of you are new, so I want to make sure you understand. Today is the Sabbath Day which is a day of rest. Today we only do the work that is absolutely necessary to cook our food and clean up after ourselves but otherwise we rest today. Our household honors God, the creator of all things. He created the world in six days and rested on the seventh and so we honor our God by honoring his rest. You are not allowed to perform any work today, do you understand?"

Nada was extremely confused. Her family had worked like donkeys every day of their lives and she had learned to work right along with them. To be given a day of rest was a miracle she could not comprehend! She thought of a question and gestured to Leah.

"What is the name of your God who rests?" she asked as respectfully as she could.

Leah smiled at the question, "He has never told us his real name, but he is known to us by many names. We sometimes call him 'El Shaddai' or 'God All Sufficient' or 'El Jireh' 'The God Who Provides' or 'El Roi', 'The God Who Sees Me'". This last name made Nada's heart leap and her eyes showed it. "Ah! I see in your eyes that you are familiar with the God of gods? Have you learned of him from your family perhaps?"

Nada's eyes immediately darted to the floor. "I have no family."

Leah's response was gentle, "You may find that the family of God is larger than you think."

Nada scowled and remembered her request that God be her master, "What does it mean to have a God if I am a slave?"

Leah smiled, "Nada, I have a question for you." Nada looked up expectantly as Leah spoke slowly, "What does it mean to be a slave at rest on God's Sabbath Day?" Nada's mouth automatically opened as if to answer, but closed again in a thoughtful scowl. Leah grinned in triumph as she left the room.

During the morning meal, the experienced girls informed Nada that she was allowed to do as she pleased and go anywhere she liked as long as she stayed within the boundaries of the compound and did not compromise herself by being alone with any male. Nada saw no problem at all with that and hurried off to the rocky beach after cleaning up.

All the other girls used their Sabbath day of rest to sleep. That was fine with Nada; she was used to being alone. As it turned out, that first Sabbath morning was the most amazing and glorious freedom she had ever experienced in her short life. She imagined living a life of idyllic idleness with gulls and terns to watch and stones to throw in the water and crabs to chase as they scurried along the rocks. But by mid-afternoon she was absolutely bored out of her mind and could not understand how old people could sit around fanning themselves so long which is what she saw many of them doing around the household. By evening she could not wait to get back to work skinning fish. She would show everyone she was the best fish skinner they ever saw!

-:--o--:-

Nada had been using knives since she was three years old. She had learned to skin and butcher goats and sheep from her uncle's herds by her sixth year. The daily milking regime and other duties had given her hands both an iron grip and amazing agility, yet fish were outside her experience.

The day after Sabbath found Nada with a fresh outlook. There was an eagerness to fill the deprivation of mental and physical activity. She watched intently as E'mat's fish filet expert demonstrated the procedure to gut, scale and fillet the Rock Cod, Mullet and Bluefin brought in by the boats each day.

The men severed the heads with heavy cleavers and slid the bodies down to where the others could work on the meat with their fillet knives. The men would laugh at each other's weakness when a large fish could not be cleaved with a single chop. Their pride lay in strength, but Nada found a way to compete using her agility rather than sheer muscle. Her deftness with the knife became legendary among the skinner crew within a few weeks of practice. Working with smooth precision and not wasting any motions of her hands or knife, she could soon gut and fillet better than anyone on the dock.

When she grew bored of her tasks, she switched hands and discovered she could perform nearly as well with either. As her work progressed day after day, week after week, she grew bored even with her ambidextrous expertise. She started taking risks such as tossing the knife from one hand to the other without losing pace, then flipping it from hand to hand with a flourish. Everyone was amazed at her skill.

When her day's work was completed, the knives were stored in the sun to temper them. During Sabbath Day, she would invent knife tricks, throwing them into a wooden post from various distances and many other inventive games no one saw. She learned to handle any of the knives but grew accustomed to one in particular. She asked if she could always be the one to use it, to her surprise her request was granted. The other workers at the dock started calling her "Nada the Knife".

Nearly two years passed by and largely due to the hard work and routine, Nada's pain and loneliness seemed to fade. She got along quite well with the other girls and found that one or two would stay awake on Sabbath Day to chat for awhile. She learned of their homelands, places far away and stranger than this land or hers. They were as lost in the world as she.

-:--o--:-

One Sabbath Day, Nada sat on what had become her favorite rock by the shore. The mid-afternoon sun did its best to burn a hole through her back, but a salty, cooling breeze worked to create a peaceful equilibrium of comfort as she sat with her knees drawn to her chin and arms wrapped around her ankles. She stared at the misty horizon in its geometric perfection. Her thoughts wandered aimlessly near the edges of infinity.

"Beautiful." The voice was gentle but it startled Nada as she snapped around to see her mistress Leah approaching. Leah limped painfully and leaned back against Nada's rock with Nada perched nearly shoulder high to Leah.

"Yes, it is beautiful." Nada affirmed as she returned her chin to its resting place on her knees. She had learned that Leah respected Sabbath Day to such an extent that she did not disturb even her animals other than the daily normal milking to relieve their painfully bloated udders.

"I meant you, not the sea." Leah said with a smile. Nada sat up, surprised and a little disturbed. Not one person in her life had called her 'beautiful' before. She hopped down from her perch on the rock and knelt demurely on a patch of sand before her mistress. Leah slumped painfully to the sand at the base of the rock leaning back with the sun in her face.

"I wish we had more time to talk young one, but I am afraid my time is short and besides, many would think it unseemly for me to be seen chatting with a mere slave girl." She said this without offending Nada, it was simple truth. She turned to stare at the horizon, "But I no longer care what anyone thinks." Nada resumed her pensive stare with chin on knees but this time her thoughts of infinity were directed at Leah.

"Do you believe there is a God of gods, Nada?" The question was startling, coming from one who seemed so self-assured and ran her household with efficiency.

Nada tried to answer honestly; she sensed the urgency of Leah's question. "I do not know, mistress Leah. When I am here on this beach, I feel... held... by something I cannot describe. The sea, and every dawn is so beautiful... I sometimes pretend..." she paused and laughed a little girl's dancing laugh, "Mistress Leah, I sometimes pretend it all belongs to me!" She smiled, embarrassed.

Leah returned the smile, "You are wise, for you are correct. The beauty of the earth is the rightful possession of even the lowliest slave. You are very wise indeed. I say there must be a God of gods who created the world to be a beautiful place, but he hides from us. What do you think of that?"

"He hides? Do you say he is a coward?" Nada scowled at this new idea.

Leah's laughter was cut short as the movement induced a spasm of pain. "I think he is not a coward, no. A Creator-God would not be cowardly, that would not make sense. Perhaps he conceals himself out of wisdom and..." She paused to scan the natural beauty of their surroundings, "perhaps he is not as concealed as we think. Perhaps he speaks and writes but we do not understand the language of God?"

Nada's eyes followed Leah's to the sea, "There is a language in beauty, yes?"

Leah's eyes snapped back to lock with Nada's in wonder, "Yes! Nada you are wise indeed! Every woman understands the language of beauty." Then added with an ironic smile, "And a few men." They shared a laugh as Leah struggled painfully to her feet. "I must go."

During the next few months Leah turned up at occasional meals to scold her household about tidiness and any who did not perform the washing rituals to her satisfaction. They hardly ever saw their master E'mat, he traveled on boats to very distant places. Leah began showing up less and less. For an entire month the house was run by the supervisors, no one heard from her at all and talk began that perhaps she had run away with E'mat.

Then the master came to the morning meal the day after Sabbath Day. He was sighing more than usual.

"Leah is dead." A sigh swelled through the room for Leah was both respected and well-liked. He spoke matter-of-factly, but it was obvious he was controlling himself tightly. "I have sold my business, all of you will be sent to the market in Tariq. I am sure a new master or mistress in Tariq will see your fine qualities and you will all find good places to serve." He sighed again.

There was an instant burst of chatter, no one was very excited about leaving this place. Everyone felt safe here, everyone had heard about Tariq – it was an evil place.

E'mat gestured for silence which came about as abruptly as the chatter began. "I have gifts for each of you, something your new masters may let you keep... or not. I want you to know, I thank you for your service and I regret this unfortunate turn of events. Good bye." With those words he left the room without looking back.

Tariq! Fear and dread filled Nada's soul.

Raziel, one of E'mat's supervisors appeared at the door, "This way!"

Too stunned to move, Nada was last out the door. The man passing gifts to the girls paused when he saw her. He motioned for Nada to wait as he handed her a leather neck loop with a bright stone dangling from it.

"This is what I gave you, it will most certainly be stolen, do you understand?" Nada nodded but looked confused. He reached into a fold of his cloak, and held out a piece of plain leather that looked like a knife sheath but square at both ends. Leather straps dangled from each end. "And this is what I did *not* give you."

"Watch!" He quickly unfolded the leather to reveal the glimmer of a gold bar hidden within the folds! Nada gasped as he showed her how to refold the leather so the bar would not spill out.

"It was mistress Leah's intention that you have the means to purchase your freedom. The necklace is valuable, act that way so it will be taken from you. The belt is worthless, act that way so it will *not* be taken from you, understand?" Nada nodded that she understood. "When you are old enough and you have the opportunity, you may purchase your freedom if you have been wise enough to stay in possession of this gift. Now go, and God be with you, young one."

"Thank you, sir. When you see master E'mat, give him my thanks."

"Master E'mat does not know, nor would he approve. Now go child, and may God's hand cover you."

Nada replaced her cloth belt with the leather one and ran to catch up with the others as they crowded onto a donkey cart. She hopped on the back with her feet dangling over the edge. The girl next to her saw Nada's simple necklace, "Is that all you got?" She held out her wrist to display a copper bracelet.

Nada felt the belt snug around the narrowness of her slim waist and cast a wry smile toward the friend she would probably never see again, "Lucky you!" she said.

One of the donkeys complained loudly as the cart rattled its forlorn way back to Edom.

-:--o--:-

3

Redemption

"I know that my redeemer lives
and that in the end he will stand on the earth.
I myself will see him
with my own eyes -- I, and not another.
How my heart yearns within me!"

The Book of Job 19:25;27

-:--o--:-

During their first night on the road, Nada took time to disguise her belt further by rubbing it with grass she found near their camp. After her secretive machinations, she hoped the belt looked to be worthless, fit only for a slave. She wondered if she would know when the right time would come to use its hidden treasure and if that time would ever come. She knew nothing about gold or the ways of trade or the laws of the land. Her mind wandered through endless possibilities that always ended impossibly. Though futile, her imagination continued to explore the dark future ahead as hope lost its way in the distance behind her.

Eventually they approached a city, evidenced by a strong smell of burning garbage and sewage fumes common to all concentrations of humanity. Their hosts for the trip had been a young driver and his older partner, who was supposedly serving as guard. Everyone else thought the older man's actual purpose was entertainment for he seemed to spend his time either sleeping or singing in a drunken stupor -- his singing voice bolstered by frequent libations from a large jug lashed to the cart's sideboard. The driver nudged his partner to semi-somnolence as they approached the city.

"What do you think, Udi? How long since you have enjoyed pleasures at the city of Tariq?"

Udi swayed in the seat as he collected his thoughts as if they were widely scattered pebbles in the road before him. When he spoke, he sounded as if he had not managed to locate all the pebbles. "I know not, my good friend Gera, but good to be back it is, yes. Yes! Good being back." 'Back' was punctuated by a loud belch causing the younger driver to laugh heartily.

The cart jolted over a small stone and Udi leaned so far to the right he nearly fell to the road. Gera held the reins in his left hand, grabbed Udi's sleeve with his right and hauled him erect. Udi's appreciation was overwhelming, "Thank you, thank you, good friend! The hills are indeed steep in this country, no?"

Gera laughed again, "Yes, it is good we are nearly to the city so we can dump these misbegotten creatures off, get our pay and find a tavern, eh?"

Udi agreed, "Yes, yes! I am so dry. I need a drink!" No one on the cart, including Gera or even the two donkeys hauling the load agreed with Udi's self-assessment. On cue, one of the donkeys wailed in complaint.

Udi laughed, "See? See? She is thirsty too! Hurry Udi, we are all... thirsty." His last word trailed off. Gera's rescue services were required again to prevent Udi from becoming a Bronze Age speed bump for the next passerby. Gera had missed catching him last night, but fortunately it was near enough to dusk that he declared it their campsite. The unconscious Udi would have been an impossible reload project.

Gera changed the subject, "Who will buy this trash back here, Udi? Where should we dump them?" Teasing Udi had been Gera's only distraction the entire journey.

Udi tried to turn in his seat to look behind him but was so dizzy he gave up. He began pebble-searching again. "Hmm… I think probably the whorehouse for them. What do you think, Gera? The whorehouse? That is where we usually dump the likes of them."

Gera, unlike Udi, was able to turn around to look at the half-dozen bedraggled and fearful faces packed into the cart behind him. He leered wickedly, "Yes, Udi, I agree… the whorehouse for them!"

The fateful pronouncement was no surprise to most of the young women. Their brief interlude at the house of E'mat the fish merchant had been like a tour of heaven before they returned to their normal hellish lives. Conversely, Nada's life seemed to be slipping downhill fast. She wondered if the laws of Tariq would allow her to purchase her freedom or even if she would be granted the opportunity to redeem herself.

-:--O--:-

As promised, the women were unloaded near the center of Tariq near what Nada guessed was the 'whorehouse' mentioned by Udi and Gera. She had never heard of such a place before today. Her keen intellect was sufficiently capable of extrapolating the various curses and innuendos stored up over the years, however. Her brain's scribes searched among the scrolls in her mental library and ran screaming alarms to her inner sensibility with the conclusion that a 'whorehouse' was a place she did not want to go! Gera and Udi's despicable character, combined with her own deductive reasoning elicited visions of a life of woe that she intended to avoid by any means possible.

Amid the chaos of the city's center, she was shoved into a line of other women to be displayed for sale without quite understanding how it had happened so quickly. She was being herded toward the 'whorehouse' faster then she could have imagined! As the process began, Nada nearly choked in shame as she saw what was happening ahead of her in the line. As each slave woman reached her turn, she was stripped naked, her wrists bound behind her and led out to the hoots and jeers of the crowd. After she was sold, her new master either carried or dragged her away like so much meat. Sometimes the buyer was even a woman! Nada could not figure if these women were being sold to the 'whorehouse' the driver spoke of or if some worse fate awaited them, but she renewed her determination to avoid their fate.

She squeezed her eyes shut at the unfolding scene and silently prayed the first prayer her life, *"God, protect me, go before me and save me from this place."* No one had ever taught Nada to pray, but a prayer also seemed the correct extrapolation from her expanding mental library. The prayer worked to calm her even amid the shouting and clamor of the market.

Somehow, her mind did not shut down or go numb with fear, as had apparently happened to the other women who had accompanied her to the city. Instead, she became hyper-alert, for amid all the other horrible smells of the city, she was aware of something completely at odds with the filthy surroundings —the smell of freshly cut flowers.

She decided her nose must be lying to her, but from her position on the platform, her eyes sought out the source of the delightful fragrance in spite of herself. At last she spied the most beautiful woman she had ever seen floating within the crowd. She was dressed in what appeared to be wisps of blue fog. As the woman moved closer, the fog resolved into flowing silks. A young man dressed in a polished leather tunic, obviously a guard, moved along with her muscling away the crowd.

To Nada's surprise, the woman in blue stopped at the foot of her platform to gaze up directly into her eyes, cocking her head sideways quizzically with a half smile. The woman's bearing reminded Nada of her former mistress Leah but this woman must have a household of a hundred where Leah had a household of a few dozen! Nada's heart ached with loss for her departed mistress Leah. She had been hard and demanding, but fair. Mistress Leah had treated even her slaves with human dignity.

Suddenly, without quite knowing what had prompted her, Nada placed her right foot forward, bent at the waist in formal greeting as Leah had taught all her girls and intoned, "God's blessing upon you and your family, ma'am."

The woman's eyes brightened in surprise. She responded with a barely perceptible nod of her head, "And upon you as well, young one." Then she did something that Nada did not understand at all. She glanced left and right, then directly at Nada, closing one eye firmly only to open it again. Nada did not know how to respond properly, so throwing caution to the wind, she returned the gesture as precisely mimicked as she was able. The woman laughed and walked away chatting with her guard. The guard looked familiar…

Another face in the crowd caught her attention. A strange man was staring intently at her in the place vacated by the woman in blue. He was dressed all in black and his face was a horror of tattoos! Black markings covered half his shaven skull and cheeks. They looked as if the black talons of a bird of prey had gripped his skull. He leered hungrily at Nada, pulled a cowl over his head and strode away.

The auction wore on and soon it would be time for Nada. One of the women behind her noticed her woebegone look. In feigned sympathy she whispered, "Why are you so worried, sweetie? Haven't you ever been with a man?" Nada did not know how to answer. She gestured in the negative.

The women shoved her forward with a contemptuous laugh, "Hey! We have a virgin here! She should fetch a better price, eh!? Get out there, sweet thing, what are you afraid of?! Ha! Ha! Ha!" The other women laughed scornfully as Nada stumbled forward. The auctioneer took a fistful of her tunic to rip it away as she trembled in terror before the hoots of the crowd.

"Let us see the goods!" "Twenty silver!" "There are no virgins in Tariq, but I say thirty for the good story!" The laughter and taunting reached a crescendo, but just then another man from the side strode up to the auctioneer and said something in his ear. Nada felt the auctioneer's hand loosen its grip on her clothing. He bound her wrists as the crowd cursed their complaints.

"Show us the goods!" "What are you waiting for?!"

The auctioneer barked, "Silence! This one gets a private viewing, special purchase!"

Nada scanned the crowd quickly, but saw no sign of the woman in blue. Instead her eyes locked with the man with the tattooed face. He was staring directly at her from beneath his eyebrows. As she watched, his tongue licked his lips from left to right quickly like the flicker of a snake and his lips curled into a smile. Fear numbed all her senses as she was jerked roughly from the stage.

-:--o--:-

Nada was led to a room and knelt facing the door from the far wall. Her leather wrist lashings were tethered to ankle bindings leaving her uncomfortably restrained. She heard the guard say outside the door, "Do you want me to strip those filthy garments off her?" She panicked, but heard no reply and no one entered the room for many minutes. She fully expected to see the man with the horrid tattoos come in to claim his prize. She decided she would fight him until one of them killed the other no matter if she used only her fingernails and teeth!

Eventually, the guard with the polished leather tunic strode in with two rolled up carpets and a pillow. He unrolled the first in the room's center and positioned the pillow at one end, he lay the other carpet in front of Nada and called to the door, "Ready, ma'am."

Batshua Al-Nahdiyah, honored wife of A'dab Ben Hareb the Emir of Edom strode into the room as if borne by a floating cloud of blue silk. She alit on the center carpet gracefully as a butterfly and reclined to an elbow on the pillow, instantly relaxed to gaze upon her captive. Nada nearly wilted in exhausted relief!

She gestured to Nada, "Omar, release her, if you please." Omar unsheathed a small dagger and stripped each of Nada's bonds away with a single slice. Batshua gestured toward Nada and at the carpet, "Sit."

Nada glanced at the carpet. It was so intricate in design, she had not believed a carpet maker had such skill nor had she imagined cloth could contain such beauty. She stared at the grime on her tunic, knees, feet and hands and started nervously wiping the worst of it off.

Batshua noted her efforts at tidiness and was pleased. She mentally checked that off her list of examinations for this prospect. "Child… One of the purposes of a carpet is to collect dirt. I can see my carpet will get an excellent work out with you, now sit." Nada tried to smile but only succeeded in looking sheepish as she crawled from her kneeling position on the dirt floor to a kneeling position on the carpet.

Batshua observed the humility of this young woman (second check mark) but wondered if she would actually follow her instructions. "Do you have a name?"

"I am Nada, ma'am." Nada had heard Omar call her "ma'am" and thought that may be the right title.

"Nada, I do not know where you are from or your culture, but is your current position called 'sitting'? I told you to sit, this may be a long session."

"Thank you, ma'am." Nada unfolded her legs quickly from kneeling into a tailor-sitting position with her hands in her lap, looking more relaxed.

Batshua asked, "Have you eaten today?" Nada suddenly realized she had not eaten since yesterday morning. The men who brought her from Aqaba, Gera and Udi, had been more attentive to their own ale and feeding than to their passengers' comforts.

"No, ma'am."

"Omar."

"Ma,am." Omar hurried from the room, requiring no further instructions.

"Thank you again, ma'am." Nada said, unprompted. Batshua nodded and thought, *"This young one has manners!"*

Batshua began with a brief introduction of herself, giving Nada only need-to-know information. "I am Batshua, a visitor to this city on holiday. I have been doing some 'shopping'. Tariq is an important center for the spice trade and therefore of interest to me and my husband. We are... 'farmers'. But we also have some dealings here. You have demonstrated excellent manners which is rare among the slaves offered for sale in this region. Where did you learn your good graces, from your family perhaps?"

"Thank you, madam Batshua, you honor me with an undeserved compliment." She bowed her head. Batshua returned the gesture, very impressed.

"I have no family." Nada said flatly, without explanation. "Mistress Leah, wife of E'mat bin Jadal, a fish merchant near the Gulf of Aqaba insisted on proper manners for all her household. She is... was... a very kind and fair mistress."

"It was not very kind of her to send you to Tariq." Batshua said, digging for more information.

Nada's eyes swam in a pool of tears. "Mistress Leah died. Her husband seemed... so sad. He sold everything, including all his household slaves."

"Ah. Did madam Leah teach you the greeting that you called down to me from the platform?"

"Yes, ma'am."

"You know of El Shaddai then?"

Nada smiled excitedly, "Yes! Madam Leah said God is known by many names. She said he may also be called 'El Roi', 'The One Who Sees Me'. I like that name best."

Batshua hid her emotions carefully but her eyes began to sting. She had searched for years for a child with the qualities like the one who sat before her now. Apparently God had answered her prayer. She feigned a cough and dabbed at her eye carefully as if to remove a speck of dust. At that moment, Omar returned with a basket of pears.

"I see refreshments have arrived. Help yourself, Nada." Omar lowered the basket and Nada selected the fruit nearest her, not the largest in the basket. Batshua did not miss this and thought "*check*" to herself again. When Omar presented the basket to her, she selected the largest pear and threw it quickly to Nada, "Catch!" Nada was already holding her pear in her mouth with her right hand but casually caught the pear in her left. She acted as if her clever catch was an everyday thing, though Batshua did not know many who could have done it.

"Thank you ma'am." She said as soon as she had chewed sufficiently to swallow.

"Are you left-handed?" she asked. Left-handed people were viewed suspiciously by most cultures. They were often thought to be cursed by the gods. Batshua thought left-handed folk were a mild curiosity and superstition itself was a curse.

"No, ma'am, but I often practice skills with my left hand when I am bored with my right."

"What skills?" Batshua asked with increasing curiosity.

"I served Master E'mat in his fish market. I gained skill with the fillet and skinning knifes, or so his men said. None matched my speed and precision though I could not match their strength."

One of Batshua's eyebrows raised in the universal sign of skepticism. "Omar, lend this girl your knife." Omar turned to Batshua with his face also bearing the universal sign of skepticism, but his boss-lady confirmed her request as a command by scowling. Omar unsheathed his blade, a double-edged, eight inch bronze dagger worn more for decoration than defense. The blade was razor sharp and thin, designed for slicing rather than stabbing. The bronze blade and hilt were so highly polished it could serve as a mirror. Omar flipped it expertly to present it hilt-first to Nada.

She hefted the blade with wide eyes, tossing it back and forth, flipping it several times to get its heft. She performed her knife-flipping hand tricks unselfconsciously. She was not showing off, simply focusing on the tool she was handed, automatically acclimating herself to it as she had done countless times during the last two years. Omar and Batshua were extremely impressed and amazed she had not lost a finger!

"A worthy blade, sir. The handle is a bit heavy, but a fine weapon." Nada's judgment echoed Omar's exactly. This young girl was extraordinary!

"Thank you, miss. I shall speak to the craftsman about his work." Omar said flatly.

"Nada, cut a pear for us, please." Batshua said, challenging Nada to a performance.

Quite comfortable with the balance and feel of the knife, Nada smiled, feeling confident enough to attempt a trick she had performed a few times during breaks at the docks for the worker's entertainment.

She selected a pear from the basket, held the large end up with the tips of her left hand gripping only the small end of the pear. She started with her right arm across her chest the blade level with her left shoulder, paused and breathed deeply once and held it. Fast as a blur, she flashed the knife right, left, right, left, right! She exhaled her breath and nothing happened! The pear remained balanced on the tips of her fingers until she spread her fingers – the fruit fell into her hand severed into six diced pieces.

Batshua and Omar erupted into surprised laughter and applause. Nada smiled her thanks and bowed her head, embarrassed. Remembering her manners, she cleaned the pear juice carefully from the blade by wiping it on her tunic, then handed it back to Omar in the same manner he had given it to her, hilt-first.

Batshua spoke up, "Nada, were you known by any other names?"

Nada smiled sheepishly and ducked her head low. "Yes ma'am. Everyone in Leah's household used to tease me. They called me 'Nada the Knife'."

Batshua thought to herself, "*A strange, unassuming girl with useful talents. It is too soon to tell, but we shall see…I have seen enough to make today's decision. Please God, grant me wisdom! And thank you!*"

"Nada… 'Nada the Knife'." Batshua smiled ruefully, Nada returned the smile self-consciously. "I want to tell you about another name we call God." Nada's eyes displayed keen interest, "He is also known as HaGo'el, 'God Our Redeemer', the One Who Pays the Price. On HaGo'el's behalf, I will be your redeemer this day so that perhaps God will give you the chance to redeem yourself on another day. Do you understand?"

"I think so, ma'am." Nada's heart beat wildly with the possibility that her prayer had been answered, she would escape the fate of the whorehouse! "You wish for me to serve as your slave?"

"No. I do not own slaves." Nada's heart sank like a stone and panic gripped her in its vice.

Batshua continued, "I will redeem you, purchasing your freedom. You must commit to my service as bond-servant until you have paid off the bond-price, usually 4 to 7 years. It is not slavery, you will be paid for your service, but this is a choice you must make and a promise you must keep. Do not make this choice lightly." She smiled craftily, "I am not an easy mistress."

Nada felt like her heart of stone had just learned to swim. "I understand, ma'am. I think…" She returned to kneeling position, hands flat-palmed on her thighs and eyes looking straight into Batshua's, "I will be your faithful and grateful bond-servant, madam Batshua."

Batshua smiled. "Well said. Roll up these carpets and follow me. Omar, tell the others we are heading home and to make ready. Our business in Tariq is completed."

Nada felt some confusion, "Ma'am?" Batshua stopped, "Do you not have to arrange payment with the slave master first?"

Batshua smiled warmly. "Already done, Nada. You have been my bond-servant since Omar first cut your bonds. I have been trying to figure out where to place you in my household. I may have a good idea where you will fit." She winked, which Nada had recently learned is an expression which portends good and unexpected things.

-:--o--:-

4

Safehaven

"Their homes are safe and free from fear;
the rod of God is not on them.
They sing to the music of timbrel and lyre;
they make merry to the sound of the pipe."

The Book of Job 21:9;13

-:--o--:-

Batshua pointed her finger directly into Nada's eyes, "You must follow Omar's instructions to the letter, do you understand?" Nada nodded. Her new mistress disappeared.

Nada and Omar stared awkwardly at each other for a moment. Nada could not get over the feeling that she had seen him before, but she could not place him. She said, "You look very familiar. Have I seen you before?"

Omar's expression was unreadable. He grunted. "Do not be presumptuous. Follow me."

He led Nada through a narrow alley that dead-ended at a walled enclosure where several women had gathered to wash linen in a huge stone-lined basin. One of the women, a very fat, broad-faced one with a cheery, narrow-eyed smile recognized Omar.

"A'llo Omar! What's that you have with you today? She looks like a dead mouse and you the cat who is dragging her to dinner!" Everyone laughed, including Omar. Nada flushed with embarrassment then began to burn with anger.

Omar tossed the fat woman a small piece of silver, "My mistress wants her to be presentable for the trip home. See what you can do."

She caught the metal, examined it and tucked it into a fold of her clothing. She eyed Nada up and down critically. Sighing heavily she complained, "You ask the impossible, but I will make the attempt! Come here, child."

Nada moved hesitantly in her direction. The fat woman glared at Omar, her eyes almost disappearing into the folds of her face, "Omar, go away and return after you have satisfied your thirst for ale and not the sight of a young woman bathing." It was Omar who looked embarrassed now as he scooted away from the women's laughter.

Five sets of strong arms grabbed the diminutive Nada and tossed her like a rag doll into the wash water with their linen. She flayed around, sputtering and spitting water. "Remove your clothing, dear. We shall give you something more decent to wear. Nada obeyed but she clung to her belt, tying it to her naked waist.

The fat woman snapped her fingers, "Hand over that belt, we shall burn it with the rest of your slave's rags. We have much better for you, Omar has paid us well."

Nada panicked, "No!"

"Hand it over I say!" She reached for the belt.

"NO!" she shouted, retreating from the women with a soapy splash. "It is mine! It is a gift, I will not have you dishonor the one who gave it to me."

The woman cocked her head in wonder. She had a history with the bedraggled strays the Emira of Edom had selected from Tariq's rabble over the years. She had never doubted the Emira's wisdom... until now.

She sighed, "Very well, keep it. Only you had best clean it up and keep it hidden. The Emira may not be so tolerant as me. Now come let us get you dry and see what we can do to make you more presentable. Nada secured the precious belt to her upper thigh.

The women dried Nada's raven black hair, combed it and collected it to one side with a tin ring so that it fell over her left shoulder. They gave her a light linen undergarment and pure white dress of a weave so fine it fluttered in the breeze. The dress had a short sleeve for the right arm, but the left shoulder was bare. Nada worried how badly her shoulder would be burned by the sun until a woman handed her a long linen cloth made of the same white material.

She showed her how it wrapped her waist like a sash, looped around her back and over her bare shoulder to be held casually in one arm or tucked in the sash when she needed use of both hands. Nada began to wonder what type of work she could possibly do dressed in this finery. She doubted madam Batshua would ask her to slice and dice fish dressed like this! She felt extremely self-conscious, yet more wonderfully elegant than she had ever dreamed!

Just then Omar reentered the enclosure. He saw Nada standing near the center, framed in the afternoon sunlight. Her desert-darkened skin glowed with unblemished youth in contrast with the whiteness of her new apparel. He opened his mouth to speak, but no words choked out as he gulped soundlessly at the startling beauty standing before him.

"Not bad, eh Omar?" The fat woman spoke Omar's thoughts. "We should have charged you more. The difficult can be paid in silver, but for miracles such as this – you should have paid in gold!"

Nada smiled sheepishly, but impulsively turned around in her new clothes to display them to Omar. He grinned, "Not bad at all, my friends. Madam Batshua will be pleased indeed!"

"To say nothing of your own pleasure?! I see your eyes are bound to this young woman tighter than a camel's howdah!" Now it was Omar's turn to look embarrassed as all the women laughed.

"Nada, we must be going. May God's blessings favor you all, and my thanks." He bowed and left expecting Nada to follow, which she did, turning back toward the women to smile and nod her own thanks as she hurried to catch up with Omar.

-:--o--:-

Omar presented Nada to Batshua who examined her with mock disparagement. "Omar, you deceiver! This cannot be the bedraggled wretch I sent away with you! What have you done with Nada?!" Both young people bowed at her compliment.

"We have a full moon this night, we shall ride until midnight and rest at the oasis of Aqir during the heat of day on the morrow. Nada, you are to ride with me so that I may begin your training. We will arrive at Hareb in a little over three days. Not much time to fill your empty head. Come!"

Nada envisioned sitting in a donkey cart for three days with a grimace. The bruises from her last ride from the port of Aqaba had only just now begun to heal. When she followed Batshua through the Tariq city gates and turned to see what awaited them, she was filled with awe and fear.

Thirty camels and at least a dozen horses were lined up outside the city wall. Two dozen men-at-arms were busily loading the camels with supplies and other packages. Nada wondered if Batshua traveled with her entire household!

One huge man startled Nada greatly for his skin was black as the night sky. She had never before seen or heard of such men and wondered if he was human or demon! He wore silk pantaloons and a broad leather belt that looped around his waist and then diagonally across his bare chest. A large bronze sword dangled from his belt, the kind she had seen the day her family was slaughtered. A dagger was sheathed in the strap across his chest. She shuddered at the unbidden thoughts of her town's slaughter and her mind shrank from the memory.

"All is ready at your word, m'um", the black-skinned man spoke to Batshua with accustomed familiarity and respect. His thick accent pronounced "ma'am" as "mum".

Batshua nodded, "Thank you Negasi. I want you to meet Nada, our newest recruit."

Negasi smiled, "Pleased to make your acquaintance young miss." He thumped his fist to his chest and extended his hand palm out to Nada, "My heart to your heart, my sword to your enemy's heart! Welcome to House Hareb!"

"Nada will ride with me, Negasi. See that my howdah is made ready for two."

"As you wish, m'um." He sped off to his duties without waiting for a response from Nada.

"He is a fierce-looking man, ma'am."

"Not just fierce-*looking*, Nada. You could wish for no better friend, nor fear a worse enemy than Negasi." She said ominously. Nada shuddered at the thought.

"Ma'am… what happened to Negasi's skin? Was he burned in a fire? It looks very painful, ma'am." Nada did not know whether to fear or pity Negasi.

Batshua turned in shock, blinked and then burst out laughing. "Nada, have you never seen an Ethiopian? Negasi is a bond-servant from my father's household in Egypt, which is a very long way from here. There are many people in that land with skin like Negasi's."

Nada looked thoughtful but could only respond weakly, "Oh."

She wanted to ask what a 'howdah' was, but she decided she would find out soon enough. She hoped it was something better than a donkey cart.

-:--O--:-

A howdah turned out to be a platform strapped to a camel's back. There were posts and a canopy that had been removed in order to reduce the weight for Nada. Since they would travel mostly at night, the canopy was unneeded.

One of her servants assisted Batshua to the howdah's pillowed surface while the camel chewed philosophically. Nada's turn came next and when she ascended the beast she was practically thrown into position by the driver's strong hand under her foot. She landed awkwardly but found a spot in the back-center that faced Batshua who sat leisurely at the front facing the camel's right shoulder.

Batshua nodded to a man holding the camel's harness who emitted a long, sing-song cry. The entire line responded with a cry that filled Nada with a primal urge to join them, though she did not know the song's words or purpose. The world began to surge under her as the camel lifted them upward and she clung to the howdah's edges for dear life. With calls of "Hut! Hut!" all the drivers urged their camels forward – the caravan moved toward the north.

Batshua turned to Nada with a surprisingly girlish expression! "I love the start of a journey! Don't you, Nada!? It is so exciting!"

Actually Nada was terrified beyond words, but she managed a thin smile as she clung to the edges of the howdah, "Yes, ma'am."

-:--o--:-

Neither woman spoke for an hour as Tariq shrank in the distant. Each was lost in their own thoughts and did not interrupt or question the thoughts of the other. The setting sun followed the caravan across the sands to the occasional growl of a camel or curse of its driver.

Presently Batshua quit ignoring her servant and turned to her with a sour look, "Nada, the wash-women transformed you into a true beauty but...", she wrinkled her nose, "you still stink of leather. When we reach the oasis, I want you to bathe again and take extra pains. I will not have my servants smelling like a camel's harness."

Nada realized she could not hide her treasure. "Madam Batshua," she almost started to cry, but held herself in check, "I must confess my sin." Batshua looked cautiously curious. Nada reached up under her gown and untied her belt. She handed it silently to Batshua. The belt reeked of old wet leather.

"Ah, this is what I had detected. I had thought perhaps the wash-women had slacked in their duties." She hefted the belt as though detecting something wrong. She laid it out on the platform between them and unfolded it. Nada's hope for the future lay exposed, glowing in the golden glory of the fading sun.

"Nada, where did you get this?!" she turned conspiratorial, "Did you steal it?"

"Oh no, ma'am!" Nada gasped. "It was mistress Leah's parting gift to me. Her doorman said she wished for me to have it that I may buy my freedom one day. He gave it to me in secret the day I left Aqaba for Tariq."

"Do you have any idea what this is worth?" Batshua looked intrigued. Nada gestured negatively. "It would have been worth your life if anyone had discovered it! Nada, you silly girl! This amount of gold is worth a fortune! You could redeem fifty or even a hundred slaves with this, maybe more!"

"Then why did the doorman give it to me with those words? Why would he lie to me?"

"I know not. Maybe he had something else in mind. Maybe he was stealing from his master and once he had gotten the gold out of the house he intended to find you and take it from your dead body, I do not know."

Nada's mouth went dry with the thought of the risks she had unknowingly taken, "What shall I do, ma'am?"

"I do not know. Whatever he said, I think he lied when he said it was a gift from your mistress Leah. Whatever the doorman planned, his plan failed – for now. Perhaps he will hunt for you; this gold is worth many times the wages a doorman could earn in a lifetime." Nada's eyes grew wide in wonder. "You may keep it for now because you will be safe now that you are with me. It is your treasure and your responsibility. But remember that although this is your responsibility, you are pledged to me, so that makes you responsible to me. Showing this to me has pulled me into the doorman's plot. When we reach Hareb, we must find a more suitable hiding place. In the meantime…" Batshua's eyes narrowed threateningly at Nada, "you must learn to trust me, do not keep secrets from me."

"Yes ma'am. I will tell you everything."

The tension on the platform eased a bit. "No child, that also is unwise. Always use your best judgment in what you tell me or do not tell me. I am saying that your best judgment was wrong this time. Use good judgment next time. An important matter such as this could have caused you, me and Omar to be killed when we were without sufficient guards in Tariq."

"I understand ma'am. I am sorry, I will use better judgment."

"Good."

"Ma'am, may ask a question?"

"Of course! You may always ask me questions when we are alone like this."

"Thank you ma'am. How do I become wise to make better judgments?"

Batshua smiled, "Ah! That has a simple answer - by making bad judgments!" They both laughed. Just then the drivers stopped for rest. The camels did not need water, but the horses and people did.

The rest of their journey was uneventful. They rested under palms during the heat of the day, traveling mostly during the cool of the evening and night. Batshua crammed Nada's head full of the House Hareb manners, customs and culture. By the time their journey neared its end, she had grown extremely fond of her new mistress, a feeling her mistress reciprocated.

They had been more or less following a large river northward in order to keep well-supplied with water. After their third full day, they spent the entire night resting and broke camp early that morning heading northeast across hard-scrub country that gently rose in elevation. Batshua seemed to become more and more excited. She roused Nada who had curled up to sleep on the howdah's cradle-like rocking motion.

"Nada! Nada, wake up! I want you to see this!" She waited in anticipation for the moment as their camel crested a long hill, then Nada gasped in wonder. Batshua clapped her hands in girlish glee. "Beautiful isn't it?! We are home!"

Stretched out below them was a huge city with several tall spires capped with turban-like parapets. There were hundreds of white-washed dwellings spaced out in orderly streets spotted with palms and ferns. To their left, the river they had been following turned toward them to cross their way in the valley between them and the city. It then turned again in a northwesterly course, fanned out gently into a large lake and then narrowed to a channel that fell three hundred feet or more to another valley beyond.

Nada was awe-struck. "It is so beautiful! Your household is somewhere in this city then?"

Batshua turned with a sly smile to Nada, not trying to hide the pride in her voice. "Nada, this is not a city, it is Hareb. All that your eyes see in the valley below is the household of A'dab Ben Hareb, the Emir of Edom -- my husband." Nada's jaw dropped in unabashed wonder – her new mistress was wealthy beyond belief!

-:--o--:-

As the caravan plodded its way toward Hareb's main gates, the drivers began a chant. The camels sensed their journey's end ahead as did the horses so they quickened their pace. A cheer could be heard from within the gates as they opened to allow sight of A'dab himself.

He stood in the center of the main thoroughfare to greet the caravan. Batshua could no longer contain herself, she shouted to her driver, "Down! Down!" The driver commanded the camel to kneel. She leaped to the ground and ran to A'dab in a flurry of silks to his embrace and the cheers of the city's people. They walked the thoroughfare as the city welcomed them and disappeared from Nada's sight around a wall of villas.

"You won't have much to do for a few weeks," Omar's voice surprised her as she still sat on the howdah, entranced by the scene. He offered a hand to help her down. "Those two haven't seen each other in a month. We have been away for that long on this trip."

"What am I to do? Did she tell you?" Nada asked, confused at being abandoned so abruptly, but apparently Omar was used to this.

"Not specifically, no, but I know the routine pretty well. I will help you get adjusted. First things first, I'll show you to your quarters. Madam Batshua did say where you are to stay. I can introduce you to some of the other servant girls as well. By the way, you said I looked familiar?"

"Yes, but I am sure I mistook you for someone else."

"I do not think you are mistaken. I think I remember seeing you briefly, two years ago. It was under circumstances not as ah... happy as the homecoming you just witnessed. I did not want to say anything until I was sure. And I did not want madam Batshua to think I was interfering with her plans."

Nada was walking beside Omar, letting him guide her through the township toward wherever Batshua had told him to take her. He stopped beside a gate with a flag hanging outside. He motioned with his chin, "That kind of flag indicates a latrine for women. I will wait here if you need to refresh yourself." Nada had learned one very important lesson from her experiences on the road: 'Never pass up an opportunity to relieve yourself.' She thanked Omar with a polite nod. When she returned she found him whittling on a piece of palm leaf with his dagger.

"Your knife trick with the pear was amazing." He said.

"Thank you, I was lucky." She tried to be humble even though his compliment caused her to be flushed with pride. She studied his face carefully, but no recognition clicked into place. "You were saying we have met before?"

"Yes, I think so." He continued leading her toward their destination in the city. "You had just been captured by Sabean raiders. Our caravan purchased several of the younger captives. We tried to barter for you as well, but another agent had already pre-purchased a set number of women. The raiders had set you apart with them, so we had no opportunity to purchase your group."

Nada wondered at how different her life could have been, but somehow she did not regret her time in Aqaba and felt that if there was a God who created the world, perhaps he had planned this too. She did not voice her thoughts.

"There was a girl from my village who survived the raid with me. We talked a little. I remember her saying that she thought it was my uncle who had killed her uncle Amal. Wait! My uncle married Amal's wife! That would make that girl kin to me, a cousin or something, I think! At least I have a kinsman who survived the raid and I had been thinking I had no family left in the world!" Nada was definitely feeling better about life. "Her name was Frayda. I remember now! You were the young man who came to take her away. Whatever became of Frayda?"

Omar stopped before a gate with a smile, "I thought you would never ask." He shouted past the gate into the courtyard beyond, "Frayda! I have someone here I would like you to meet!"

Though two years had passed, Frayda's recognition of Nada was instant. She ran so fast into Nada's arms she nearly knocked her over. She picked her up in her arms, she had grown large and strong, being nearly a full year older, and squeezed the smaller Nada until her ribs nearly cracked and twirled her in a circle, "Oh Nada! Nada! Nada! I am so glad to see you are safe! I prayed for you every day! I told you we would meet again, I said so didn't I?! Thank you Omar, thank you, thank you, thank you!"

Omar was getting embarrassed by all this girly emotion. He broke in, "Frayda, please show Nada where she is to spend the night, she will need to know the routines. She has no assigned duties for now. Your duties will be to help Nada become adjusted until the Emira assigns her a position. Got it?"

"Of course, Omar. I will! I will, I will, I will, I will! Come Nada, let me introduce you to the others and show you around! I cannot believe this! I said we would meet again, I said so, did I not say so?" Their voices trailed off as Frayda led Nada away.

Omar heaved a sigh, glad to check one duty off his roster. He walked off shaking his head and muttering, "Girls…!"

-:--o--:-

5

Prostitute-Priest

"If the only home I hope for is the grave,
if I spread out my bed in the realm of darkness,
if I say to corruption, 'You are my father,'
and to the worm, 'My mother' or 'My sister,'
where then is my hope—
who can see any hope for me?"

The Book of Job 17:13-15

-:--o--:-

Boshet, the temple prostitute, stretched catlike and luxuriated in the dark confines of her bedchamber. The flicker of hallway torchlight cast diffuse shadows across her supple form as she filled her lungs, inflating her bosom provocatively toward her client. She cast a winsome smile in his direction. All her movements were choreographed to perfection – a dance she had performed countless times over a decade. Her client returned the smile approvingly. Boshet closed her eyes and curved her lips gently upward as if in blissful rest for this was *after.*

But behind the locked doors of her eyelids where no one could see, paced the soul of a trapped tigress ceaselessly probing its cage, yearning for freedom.

Boshet's satisfaction lay only in the application of her skills to manipulate the men she serviced in the worship of Ba'al day after day. Her natural beauty and skill had won her a top position at the temple. It was Boshet who snagged the richest clients. That meant extra tips in clothing, baubles and sometimes rare fragrances, cosmetics or more practical items such as sheep and goats which could be traded for other benefits. Of course the temple took their cut, but because she was among the more desirable and requested women, payment and tips were higher. It all worked out to make Boshet very comfortable in her cage.

And a cage it was for Boshet was a slave. She had been sold to the temple of Ba'al by her father when she turned eight. No man of means, he could ill-afford her dowry. He saw the birth of a daughter as a huge curse and potential financial ruin. Only her mother's protesting screams had stayed her father's hand from killing her outright on the birth bed when he had seen the gender of his child.

On her eighth birthday, two priests from the temple arrived to take Boshet away. They paid her father in silver, enough to live another couple years, perhaps enough to buy a wife who would bear him a son, he thought. As Boshet was led away, she heard her mother's weeping voice call behind her, "Boshet, remember! God's name is Elohim! Ba'al is no god! Elohim is God of gods! He will watch over you!" The last thing she heard of home was her father's meaty hand landing solidly into the side of her mother's jaw to silence her.

At first, little Boshet had worked long hours in the temple's kitchens and warrens cleaning up after the many feasts honoring the various underling gods. Ba'al worship was sensual, his supplicants exhausting themselves in sexual debauchery and gluttony. Though emotionally traumatized at first, by the time Boshet was ten, she had become thoroughly inured to the scenes in the temple courts. Her masters eventually thought her ripe for temple service training.

She was educated in the ways of men and maidens for two years. The temple prostitutes taught her how to drink so that by eleven she was a confirmed alcoholic. They gave her a leaf to chew that made her feel warm and sleepy. By age twelve she was presented to the priests with a dozen other girls for a ritual dedicating them in service to Ba'al as shrine prostitutes.

Only once had she tried to escape with another girl. Her friend had been killed outright. Boshet had been beaten and taken to the washing pool twice a day for a month where her head was held under the water until she passed out. After that, she never attempted escape. She did not hate, or love, or cry or care. All her feelings were drowned away in that pool.

-:--o--:-

Eventually Boshet learned to replace the barrenness in her soul with a lust for power and control. She applied her feminine wiles as weapons against the parade of men flowing through her chambers. They were the only objects in her life she could manipulate. Boshet, the temple prostitute discovered she was very good at something – the tigress in her soul may not be allowed to hunt in the wild, but at least it could toy with its dinner!

That is what she felt today, the satisfaction to know she was the best and that she would get some new trinket or other reward that would cause the other women to burn with jealousy. Her smile became genuine with the only sense of satisfaction possible to her hollow soul. Boshet breathed deeply and purred.

-:--o--:-

The man stirred beside her, interrupting her thoughts. He was very strange, more odd than any of the oddities that had wrinkled her bed linens. His face was marked with a fierce tattoo that looked as if his head were in the grip of a large bird's talons. Besides that, he had apparently used a very sharp knife to scrape off the hair of his chin so he looked more like an adolescent boy than a man. His eyes were very dark, almost black and wide set around a large pointed nose, adding to his hawkish appearance. Boshet found him to be at once frightening and attractive. But he did not look at all attractive when he smiled! His mouth would have fit better on a snake's head.

He was smiling at her now. "You are good." Boshet's slight nod and small curl on one side of her mouth acquiesced to his obvious surrender to the truth.

He continued, "I would like to make you my wife."

Boshet's smile broadened. This was a line she must have heard dozens, perhaps hundreds of times. Her answer was well-rehearsed and purposed to reject her client's offer politely while saving his pride and lightening the mood with a touch of humor. Naturally the proposal was impossible -- temple prostitutes were never sold or given in marriage.

"That could be arranged, I suppose", Boshet's smile broadening to a full grin, "if you happen to be the high-priest's brother-in-law." She waited, expecting a chuckle at her irony so they could get on to the matter of payment. Instead, his expression did not change. What he said next froze her blood and she started to tremble coldly in the stuffy heat.

"In that case, let me introduce myself. I am Ba'al-Hanni, high priest of this temple in Tariq. I am known by many names throughout the land of Canaan and Egypt, for I have wandered far across the earth in service to my lord Ba'al. I have chosen you to accompany me on my next journey." His eyes narrowed ominously at Boshet, "I say again, I want to make you my wife. Do you accept?"

This man was the high priest himself! She had heard terrible rumors of this fearsome man. Boshet swallowed, her mind worked as thickly as her throat! A thrumming sound turned out to be her own heart beating a drum in her ears. She struggled for control and rose slowly to her knees before Ba'al-Hanni. Never before had she felt so vulnerable. She reached for a bed-silk to draw it in front of her. It was not that she felt ashamed of her nudity, she felt *naked, defenseless.*

With the silken sheet gathered tightly against her chest in clenched fists, Boshet asked, "I have a choice?"

"You always have a choice." Somehow his tone conveyed the gentle subtlety of a rockslide while his pronunciation of 'choice' was serpentine. Boshet realized her choice was to comply or be dragged from the room as a corpse. Her years of oppression at the temple had taught her one thing: learn to accept the inevitable... and perhaps the tigress could find a way out its cage!

"I am honored." She bowed her head, let go of her drape and kneeled with her hands flat on her knees before him in utter submission. Both knew her posture was completely disingenuous. She praised herself for surviving the moment, he praised her for the excellent act – she would serve his purposes well.

"Very well. By the power invested in me by me, I declare you to be my wife." A rueful smile, "We shall have our little ceremony duly witnessed later and ah… of course we have already consummated our union." His smile was carnivorous. He stood. "My servants will provide you with new clothing appropriate for our destination."

"Yes, sir. Where are we going? I would like to bring a few of my things." Boshet thought wistfully of a few trinkets she had gathered over the years.

Still smiling, Ba'al-Hanni leaned down to her kneeling form and slapped her face so hard she nearly fell over. His growling voice became ominously heavy as if his teeth were grinding together like boulders in a rockslide. "You came to this place with nothing, you *have* nothing and you will *leave with nothing*. Anything you possess from this moment on will come from my hand. Learn to behave so that what comes from my hand is not pain… or death."

Boshet was so stunned she dared not speak. Her silence apparently satisfied Ba'al-Hanni. He growled as he left, "Wait here, I will send for you." Not only did Boshet wait, she dared not move.

Within a few minutes two young women, apparently twins, arrived to help her dress in fine white and blue silks. Boshet walked from the temple to a waiting camel caravan dressed in sartorial finery beyond anything she had previously acquired through her years at the temple. The elegance and softness of her new clothing did little to soothe the burning hand-shaped pain stinging the side of her face. Ba'al-Hanni was nowhere to be seen which suited her just fine for the moment.

The twins helped her into a curtained howdah atop one of the camels. As the caravan ambled its way out of Tariq, Boshet the temple prostitute made a mental adjustment, "*I am now a priest's prostitute.*" The tigress in her soul paused its pacing, yawned in fatigue and surrendered to its capture – for the moment only. Boshet lay down on the howdah's padding in fetal position, "*Out of one cage and into another*" she thought as sleep carried her away from Tariq and into the wilds.

-:--o--:-

Boshet awoke with no idea how long she had been asleep. It was the sudden stillness of her camel's sitting position that had awakened her. She was also keenly aware of her near bursting bladder. Her camel was kneeling under a palm chewing its cud, the only thing camels ever do when they have nothing else to do.

She hopped down from the howdah and scouted for a private palm. Seeing nothing but busy people everywhere, she dug a hole in the sand between the palm and camel – she was long past modesty at this point in her life and nature overrules modesty in emergencies anyway.

Relieved and thirsty from what she figured had been several hours of sleep in the desert heat, she headed over to a group that looked like they had water. As she approached, everyone stopped chatting and moved away from the water skins to give her plenty of room. She thought it was a very strange way to behave. The man who seemed to be in charge of handing out water acted even more strangely -- he started bowing and apologizing. Men never behaved that way toward her.

"Mistress Boshet! My apologies, I am a fool! I did not see you coming this way, ma'am! My name is Aqil! Please! Please! Let me get you fresh water, do not drink from the same vessels as these dogs, I will fetch you more suitable refreshment!" With that he ran to a camel behind him to fetch a fine pottery jug and cup. He filled the jug at the oasis pool and returned nearly stumbling to serve her. Boshet was completely bewildered; no one had ever treated her with such fearful deference. The man seemed afraid to get near her as if her shadow would poison him.

The drink was satisfying and clean, not like the foul-smelling pond water she was accustomed to at the temple of Tariq. "May I have some more?"

Aqil's hand trembled as it refilled her cup, "Oh ma'am, you may have anything you wish. You are the most honored wife of Master Trader Ba'al-Hanni! If there is anything my humble self can do for you, please honor me with your request."

Boshet wanted to pinch herself to see if she was still asleep and dreaming on the howdah or delirious of sunstroke. Why was this man, these people behaving this way?! "You can tell me where my..." she paused at the word, "husband is."

"Oh, that I cannot tell you for I do not know myself, ma'am. He has gone on business with friends and says he will not return until tomorrow or the next. Master Ba'al-Hanni has given strict instructions to all in the camp that we are to obey your every whim and to teach you, forgive me ma'am, but that is the word he used, to *teach* you the manners of lordship."

"What?! You mean the high pri.., I mean the Master has left me in charge and instructed you to instruct me how to be in charge?"

Aqil smiled in relief, "Yes! Yes! That is it precisely! He said you are a very wise woman and that you would catch on very quickly. Yes! Yes! I am to be at your service, ma'am."

"He did, did he? This seems like a joke to me." Boshet was not in the mood for this.

Aqil's smile vanished. "Oh ma'am, I assure you Master Ba'al-Hanni was not joking. If he is not satisfied with our progress when he returns...", he sliced his own neck with a finger.

"Oh." Boshet did not doubt the literalness of Aqil's warning. Ba'al-Hanni impressed her as a ruthless man. Endowed with a predator's quick mind, Boshet decided she had better adapt or die. "In that case, would you get me something to eat, please?"

Aqil's eyes flared, "No, no, no! Do not ask! You must tell me what you want." He snapped his fingers, "Thusly! I am your servant to command. Try it again."

Boshet saw her error instantly and made several mental adjustments. It was as if the tigress had suddenly discovered her cage door ajar. She began to push it open. This could be very interesting indeed! She snapped her fingers, "I am hungry."

Aqil brightened instantly and clapped his hands twice. The twins who had helped Boshet into her new clothing appeared bowing. "Madam Boshet is ready for her evening meal. Be quick about it." The women bowed and hurried away. "If you follow me, ma'am, I will show you to your tent. Preparations have been made; we hope you find the accommodations suitable."

As Boshet followed Aqil on a path that wound through the palms, she pondered her situation. "*What is this priest's plan? He pulled me from that cesspool temple, plops me down in the middle of nowhere to abandon me with a servant he has told to treat me like the Queen of Sheba! This must be a test of some kind, it has to be!*" Boshet had survived her prior life because of an extraordinary ability to adapt and play the role she found herself to be in. Now she did not fully understand her role, but she did understand that if she did not play it well it would probably mean her life. She decided she would risk it all and throw herself into this new role with everything she had.

She snapped her fingers and spoke disdainfully, "Aqil! The sun is hot! Provide shade! And do not walk so fast, I am enjoying the view."

Aqil snapped around in surprise but grinned approvingly, "Right away ma'am! Very good, ma'am!" He nodded, "Yes! Very, very good."

-:--o--:-

Ba'al-Hanni stayed away two full days, time enough for Boshet to become Queen of the Camp. The twins were tasked with discovering creative ways to complete her wardrobe from various supplies that could be found among the camel packs. She had decked herself out with gold and purple silks. Aqil introduced Boshet to the cook who was ordered to provide her with several interesting entrees. During the two days she was pampered, coddled, indulged and just plain spoiled rotten. But the tigress was getting bored and wanted to go hunting. She had thought of bedding Aqil, but she doubted Ba'al-Hanni would approve of her going quite that far with her independence.

Her 'husband' arrived near dusk on the third day to find Boshet on a mound of pillows getting a scented-oil massage. He observed, "I see you have discovered the benefits of a trader's wife, eh Boshet?"

"Yes, Master Trader. I hope my progress pleases you." Boshet suddenly realized this may be her final examination. Every sense became instantly on edge.

"Not bad, I think you are making excellent progress. Did you learn much from Aqil?" There was a sinister edge to Ba'al-Hanni's tone. Boshet became wary.

"Yes, he is a useful teacher."

"What did he tell you?"

"He said he was to teach me all about being the wife of a Master Trader. I have done my best while you have been away. I had one of the twins whipped for spilling water."

Ba'al-Hanni laughed, "Excellent! That is good. Come! I have something I wish to teach you personally." Boshet began to relax, feeling like she had passed the test.

Boshet snapped her fingers to indicate the massage was over, her attendant helped her dress. "I am eager to learn, Master Ba'al-Hanni."

"This way." He led her over to a sandy area, caught Aqil's attention and motioned that he should join them. "Aqil, stand there, I want to show Boshet something." He moved behind Boshet and stood close to her back with his left arm wrapped around her waist. He drew his sword and placed her right hand on the hilt, wrapping her hand tightly within his on the hilt.

"Boshet, I think you need to get the feel of a sword." He began to swing its three foot length, making swooshing noises. Boshet giggled nervously at this, she had never held a weapon. "Doesn't that feel good?"

Boshet giggled again, "Yes, the sword is heavy, but the strength of your hand on mine makes it light as a reed." She felt it was always safe to compliment a man on his manly features.

Ba'al-Hanni's tone suddenly took on the gravelly tone she had learned to fear and distrust, "Tell me how you think this feels." So saying he drew her arm back with the sword shoulder high and twisted her wrist so the blade was horizontal to the ground. He swung it swiftly in front of her slicing the tip of the blade under Aqil's chin severing his carotid artery and windpipe.

Aqil's eyes flared in panic, but life faded swiftly from them as he crumpled to the ground. Boshet whistled air into her lungs and seemed about to scream before Ba'al-Hanni twisted her around viciously in his arms forcing her to look up in his face. Boshet's scream froze in fear.

"Do not say a word, not one word! He was a fool and now he is a dead fool which is what all fools should be." He squeezed Boshet until she thought she would lose consciousness but released her to stagger at his feet.

Keeping her eyes on Ba'al-Hanni's, not daring a glance to the sword still in his hand, Boshet stared into the coldness of his face not knowing if the blade would find its way to her throat next. Her body twitched violently as he stabbed the blade into the ground next to her feet. "Clean it and bring it to my tent. We will dine together tonight, I expect you to eat well, my love. Tomorrow we leave for Babylon, a long journey. Ponder your lesson." He strode away.

Turning her back on Ba'al-Hanni, Boshet dropped to her knees and vomited violently into the sand. She quickly covered her mess and realized there were tears dripping onto her hands. She could not remember the last time she had cried. It must have been before she was five or six. When she cried then, her father had beaten her until she stopped, she wondered what Ba'al-Hanni would do if he caught her now.

From the far recesses of her soul a distant echo called, *"Dear God. Oh God! Help me!"* Boshet did not know if she was expressing this herself or if this was only a memory of someone else crying for help. Another memory echoed through her mind. She heard her mother calling, *"Boshet, remember! God's name is Elohim! Ba'al is no god! Elohim is God of gods!"* She shook her head to clear it of confusing thoughts and wiped her eyes on her forearms. Her crying shuddered to a stop as her tears dried in the hot desert air.

As she cleaned her captor's sword, the tigress in her soul skulked back to a corner of its cage where there was familiarity and protection from the dangerous wilds. It began to plot against its captor.

Two men came and silently removed Aqil's body.

-:--o--:-

Boshet found Ba'al-Hanni reclining in his tent. With his elbow on a pillow, he cradled his head with one hand and with the other held a chunk of goat leg which he gnawed with predatory gusto. Noticing Boshet, he gestured with the meat, "Put the sword there. Sit." There were bits of flesh stuck to his lips and grease shone wetly on his chin. He shifted to cross-legged position as Boshet sat at the opposite end of the carpet spread with several types of food between them.

With elbows on knees, Ba'al-Hanni continued to munch on his goat leg, "What do you think? The sword is sharp, no? Aqil was certainly impressed with the quality of its edge." He grunted a laugh, ignored Boshet and returned to work at the goat leg.

"Why did you do that?" Boshet's tone was a hoarse whisper.

"Do what? Teach you a few moves with the sword? Bah! It was nothing, I will teach you much more later. Oh, help yourself to the food, no need to starve yourself."

Boshet's stomach was gnawingly hungry in spite of herself. Biology often betrays emotions and morality, the situation was very confusing. "No, I meant why did you kill Aqil?" In spite of herself she tore off a small piece of meat from the pile and began to chew. It tasted good.

"Me? It was your hand on the blade, my dear. Here, try some of this." He held out his gnawed goat leg.

Some deep instinct within Boshet burst into clarity as if she were a tiger prowling a forest that had come upon a patch of oddly colored grass covering a pit: a trap! Do not walk there, skirt around it!

"Thank you, sir, but I am afraid my appetite is weak today." In truth she was ravenous. She spied a small fruit and picked it up, "I shall dine lightly today, by your leave." Her instincts again prompted her to make a solemn vow to herself: I will never accept food or drink from the hand of Ba'al-Hanni, he owns my body but he may not have my soul!

Ba'al-Hanni's eyes turned cold for an instant but then shrugged as he returned to tearing away grotesquely at the goat leg. Watching him, Boshet began to think she was telling the truth about her weak appetite.

"I suppose you are wondering where I have been for the past few days and where we are going next and what my plans for you may be."

"Yes." She said, flatly.

"Then why do you not ask?" Ba'al-Hanni swilled down a long draught of something smelling strongly of the spirits of fermentation. Boshet wished for a little of that herself, it had been more than a day since she had any alcohol. Ba'al-Hanni's eyes began to loll a bit – perhaps he had been drinking before she arrived.

"Alright, where have you been these past few days and where are we going and what are your plans for me?"

He choked, coughed up the wine and laughed heartily. Obviously, he was under the drink's affect. "That's better! Good for you! Oh, help yourself." He gestured to a two-handled vessel which Boshet gratefully grabbed, brought to her lips to slake her thirst and forestall alcohol withdrawal.

He raised both eyebrows high at Boshet's apparent ability to quaff the entire vessel of wine without swallowing. She set down the empty jug with a satisfied sigh. Ba'al-Hanni nodded respectfully.

He began, "Listen carefully." Boshet sat up, alert. She knew she had only a few minutes before the wine dulled her senses. "I am making plans for the ruin of one, A'dab Ben Hareb. To that end we are going to Babylon; it is a three week journey. I have arranged transport with loyal men, camels and supplies. We also have a meeting with a Sabean raider named Harun on the way to Babylon. We meet with Harun day after tomorrow on the full moon. That explains where I have been and where we are going. As for you… are you awake?"

"Yes, I am very much awake, sir." She said with a sigh, trying not to burp.

"I selected you from among many others because you are a most excellent liar." Boshet did not know whether to be complimented or insulted. "You lie with your body, your face, your voice, and your eyes. You are an exquisite liar. You have lied to make your life easy, but from now on, you are going to lie for me and for my purposes." Boshet was all ears. "From this day forward, you are not to think of me as a priest of Ba'al from Tariq. No, instead, I am one of the richest spice traders from the land of Canaan near the sea and you are my beloved, pampered, treacherous and often unfaithful wife. I am like a bird of prey that pecks out my enemies eyes. But you, my 'beloved wife', will be the adder who slithers into a victim's bed with fangs at their necks. Do you understand?"

"Yes. I believe so. But who is A'dab Ben Hareb?"

"That is no concern of yours. When I am done with him, he will want a new name, I am sure! I will wipe his memory from the earth."

Boshet saw possibilities and dangers. The tiger within her soul shook itself awake to stretch its jaws and claws invisibly toward her captor. She thought perhaps Ba'al-Hanni did not know that it was not wise to hold an adder or a tiger by its tail.

She ran her tongue slowly across her upper lip as she leered a reply to her new boss, "I will do my very best for you, sir. Do you think I am lying now?"

Ba'al-Hanni's head tipped back in a long, hideous laugh. "Good. You may go now. We leave on the morrow."

-:--o--:-

6

Handmaiden

"Think how you have instructed many,
how you have strengthened feeble hands.
Your words have supported those who stumbled;
you have strengthened faltering knees."

The Book of Job 4:3-4

-:--o--:-

Nada's eyes fluttered open but she didn't move as sleep slowly evaporated. A dream slipped away leaving an emotional vacuum that thundered shut with the realization that today she must rise to a new responsibility -- that of waking the Emir's wife! Nada, the Emira's new personal handmaiden, had been specifically appointed the task by the great woman the day before. The other servant girls were both relieved and jealous of Nada's honor and obligation. Waking the Emir's wife was looked upon with the same anticipation as one would wake a sleeping lioness.

Three weeks had passed since her camelback ride to Hareb with mistress Batshua. She had been taught the duties of a handmaiden diligently by the Emira herself during the long journey, but that was three weeks ago! Her mind seemed blank and would not work at all now. She cursed her leaking head that seemed to work about as well as that drunken donkey driver Udi's! She felt like she was searching for thoughts like pebbles on a beach this morning and all she could find was mud.

At least she was awake and not dreaming! With semi-alertness, she attempted to rise from her rough straw mat only to discover her movements blocked by the somewhat muddied and rather hairy leg of Omar. His foot was wedged firmly under her stomach. With her other side wedged tightly against the stone pillar adjacent to her mat, she was unable to move.

Omar's toes were wiggling in a most irritating manner and it was in fact Omar's toes that gave her stomach the feeling of butterfly nervousness, not the dream or the anticipation of waking the Emir's wife.

Her eyes followed Omar's leg up the length of his polished leather tunic until it reached the darkness of his face which she could discern only as a glint of laughing eyes sparkling in humor against a sea of stars in the night sky. Nada was not sure if he was smiling or leering, it was hard to tell with Omar. His smile was cleft by one finger held vertically between chin and nose: the universal signal of stealth. She scowled and hissed her thanks as Omar moved quickly and noiselessly away to his duties.   Omar could be creative with his methods to awaken her. She felt conflicted between feelings of grudging gratitude and the faint hope that one day she would find a way to reward his creativity with a bit of creative revenge of her own. All in good adolescent fun of course.

The mere thought of 'fun' struck Nada like a cooling moist breeze that promised rain during the heat of day. It was the first time in her young life that such thoughts had occurred to her. Her impishness was a sign that her new home had already begun some sort of magical healing process upon her… she and Frayda had enjoyed some fun in the past three weeks. Frayda had shown her a place in the river where the women could go swimming! Swimming was such a delicious feeling! She did not come out of the water until her lips were blue, teeth chattering and all her fingertips had wrinkled. Frayda had to pull her out saying she would cut her up for fish stew if she did not! They had laughed themselves hoarse.

She put thoughts of Frayda and Omar firmly aside as she hurried to wash and dress quietly. She made her way through the women's sleeping area soundlessly lest she wake any of the other servant girls which would inspire their just wrath. Her appointed duty for this day was causing enough jealous hostility as it was.

Nada's primary concern was not the other girls, it was her fear of displeasing her new boss, madam Batshua. Frayda had told her that no one knew what happened to the Emira's last handmaiden. There were rumors about what the Emira did to handmaidens that displeased her. None of the rumors were pleasant, hardly any of them were believable, given what she had witnessed of Batshua's character with her own eyes. Still... madam Batshua had said she was not an 'easy mistress.' That thought filled Nada with tremendous apprehension.

Finding Batshua's bedchamber at last, she crept to the circular mound of silk pillows which was partially hidden by a translucent tent of the bed netting. Her trembling fingers sought an opening, pulled the netting aside and her throat suddenly constricted in dryness as she discovered that she could not find Batshua Al-Nahdiyah, Emira of Edom among the bed pillows! Panicking, she felt through the pillows but to her horror, the bed was empty! Without warning, a hand gripped her shoulder! Spinning around, she clutched her chest in panic and fell to her knees with her face buried in the pillows in startled obeisance.

"Now now, dear child! Did I startle you?" Batshua's soft words did nothing to comfort the trembling Nada who had failed in her first official task.

"Forgiffme! Imanunworthydog!" Nada's sobbing pleas were largely muffled as she vainly attempted to speak through the pillows into which she continued to cower.

Batshua smiled but remembered that this girl had yet to prove herself. This could be an act, she had seen many feints at contrition from some who had subsequently betrayed and robbed her. Then there was the matter of a gold bar in Nada's possession. That story had yet to be proven. "Nada! Sit up." The girl did not respond. "Nada! Sit up at once, you are beginning to soil my pillows!"

At this, Nada immediately collected herself and stared horrified at the wet stains on the silk pillow at her knees. She feebly wiped at it with her sash. "Put the pillow down, believe me when I say they are not easily damaged by tears." This revelation caused Nada to relax a little, but she still remained in her kneeling position. She faced Batshua with her eyes unfocused on the tiled floor.

Batshua thought she might scold Nada for sitting there among her bed pillows. She did not yet seem to be aware of her impropriety. She decided to take a different tact.

She said, "Do not be so afraid Nada, what has got into you? You were sent to awaken me, *if I was still asleep*. You have not failed your task. Not yet at least. Do you often react in such fear when you are assigned a task?"

"I have been beaten many times by my uncle and aunt for not performing my work correctly, Mistress… Emira… Ma'am."

Batshua winced and grew angry at the mistreatment of children in general and for this unfortunate girl in particular but held herself in check. Again, she had been conned by those who knew how to play on her pity. She was not about to be conned again. Batshua knew that the instincts of a con-artist were developed by the age of five or so and that those who had tasted of the addictions of manipulation were seldom severed from its affects. However she had a strong feeling that the girl before her was not manipulative.

She may be a liar and a damaged, hurt and bewildered lost child as well, but she sensed something more. She sensed an indefinable quality in Nada that is rare -- there was a solid core of integrity within Nada that was miraculously intact. It was not built there by any circumstance or effort of Nada. It was an inner strength that was clearly a gift from God himself. Batshua doubted that even Nada was aware of it, and she hoped she herself was not a fool for hoping it was there.

Nada was silent and continued staring at the floor as Batshua collected her thoughts. She seemed to be growing more tense. "Nada, first off all I want you to address me simply as Ma'am". Titles, honor and other formalities are demanded by those I am trying to impress. I feel no immediate need to impress you, is that clear?" Nada nodded assent. "Second, take one of those pillows, get off my bed and sit on the floor here in front of me please." At this, Nada's eyes flared in panic once she realized she had been sitting on the Emira's bed the entire time. She bounded like a startled rabbit in her stumbling haste to obey.

As she sat on the pillow as commanded, the air escaped as it accepted her weight, throwing her off balance. She fell over backwards in the same way any gangly fourteen year old would. Embarrassed, she hurriedly attempted to conceal her awkwardness which made the fall only worse.

She appeared to be a newborn calf struggling to its feet with arms and legs unaccustomed to commands from an addled brain. Another decade of practice and she might prove to be a woman of grace but today was not her day. She finally got everything working all at the same time to plunk her bottom on the pillow as instructed. She glanced embarrassed toward her mistress.

Watching the show from her perch on the low bench beside the bed, Batshua erupted into a peal of laughter. Nada's face contorted in tearless pain as she suppressed her agony of conflicted emotions.

With a heart broken by the pitiful scene and shared humanity, Batshua suddenly moved from the bench to kneel before the startled girl. "Nada, come here dear, I think you are alright you know. I am sorry I laughed." As she said this, she took Nada to embrace her but Nada recoiled in horror and visibly stiffened in fear.

Sensing her confusion, Batshua said, "Nada, look at me. Look at me face to face." Nada turned toward Batshua, but her eyes darted about as if she were searching for a place to run. Batshua continued to speak softly, "Nada, I want to give you a hug, the same kind of hug that a mother gives a daughter. I have brought you here today to be my handmaiden. It is a very special assignment and I will have much to teach you if you are willing to learn.

"The first thing you must learn is that you must trust me as a child trusts a mother. Perhaps that is something you have never learned but you must begin to learn that kind of trust today if you are to serve me in the duty I have chosen for you." Batshua paused for a moment to allow Nada to collect herself.

"Nada, will you accept a hug from me? I mean you no harm, I mean only to show you that I will treat you as a servant because that is what you are, but I will also treat you with the respect you deserve as a human being created by the God who has given us both life, because that is also what you are and in that, you are no different than me."

In all her fourteen years of living on planet earth, this was the first time anyone had ever shown motherly affection to Nada. As she felt the Emira's arms wrap around her shoulders and pull her head down to her chest until her cheek rested on the scented silk of her bosom, Nada slowly dared to let her arms find their way around her mistress's waist.

As her eyes closed in dizzy fear and wonder, the cords of something that had been bound very tightly within her began to fray and break loose. Involuntarily Nada's arms began to tremble and squeeze the Emira as her knees also drew up into a fetal position, acting without her conscious thought. A trickle of tears began to squeeze between her eyelids and a high-pitched whine started at the back of her throat. Her mouth convulsed with the effort to withhold her sobs.

Batshua whispered down into her ear, "Child, I think you could use a good cry. My mother told me it is alright once in awhile to just go ahead and cry, no particular reason is necessary." Something like a body-long wave rippled through Nada as she erupted in awkward, hoarse, horrifying cries. Her sobs went on and on as Batshua held her there on the floor until it seemed as if the girl was squeezed empty, dry and bone-thin of tears.

At last Batshua felt Nada's body relax and her breathing become even. Stirring from her rather uncomfortable position on the floor, Batshua spoke in a light-hearted tone, "Nada that was a very good cry. I would rate it as 'superior' in fact, I don't think any of my friends have ever cried quite as well as that." She felt and heard a sniff and a chuckle ripple from Nada within her arms: a good sign.

"Do you think you are ready to begin your training as handmaiden?", Batshua asked as she began to untangle herself from Nada.

"Yes, ma'am." Nada sniffed again, embarrassed by her display of emotion.

Batshua stood. "Good. The first task for you today is to pick out something nice for me to wear this morning. I seem to have spilled water or something all over the front of this." Nada looked at the tear-stained, runny nose-stained front of Batshua's gown with renewed horror and fear. She dropped to her knees with her face to the floor.

"Please forgive me, ma'am. I am a dog to have soiled your clothing!"

Batshua spoke with abruptness. "Nada stand up." She stood with such immediacy one would have thought there were strings attached to her arms and legs, it almost made Batshua laugh but laughter was not called for here. "I am being very patient with you because today is your first day and therefore you have many old habits which I know will take time to break. First, you are not a dog, you are my handmaiden or will be when you are sufficiently trained to the task. Do not refer to yourself as a dog again, do you understand?"

"Yes ma'am" Nada looked confused, she had been called a dog most of her life, except the brief two years in Aqaba.

"Second, your habit of cowering on your knees may have amused your aunt and uncle, but I do not find it amusing. In fact, I find servants who react to me in that kind of fear rather irritating to be around, do you understand?"

Nada paused and hesitantly said, "I am sorry ma'am, I do not understand."

Batshua sighed. "I want you to respect me and obey me out of respect. I do not desire that you fear me as if you were an ignorant animal. You are a human being created by Almighty God and I respect you as one of God's creations. You will honor me and respect me as well. I am the Emir's wife with duties and responsibilities which are not your duties and responsibilities.

You are to be my handmaiden, so you have duties and responsibilities which are not mine. I will remind you of your duties and have authority over you but I also have duties of which I am reminded and I have an authority over me, my husband and my God. Have you understood what I have said so far?"

This was all completely foreign to Nada who had often been treated with less respect than most animals. "I am trying to understand, ma'am. Yes ma'am."

"Well and good. The next time you are tempted to drop to your knees in fear before me, I want you to stop first and recite the names of your fingers."

"Forgive me for being a stupid...", she almost said 'dog' but stammered out, "handmaiden, Ma'am, but what are the names of my fingers?"

Batshua sighed again. "Try counting your fingers, name them with numbers. One, two three… that will give you time to remember that you are not ever to act like a cowardly dog again. Stop and recite the names of your fingers."

"Oh. Yes ma'am, if you wish it to be so ma'am."

"I wish it to be so. Now go fetch a change of clothing for me. I am going to eat with the Emir this morning and you are to accompany me."

Nada's eyes went wide with fear. "We are to meet the Emir himself this day!?"

"Yes, of course. He is my husband, I meet him almost every day. You are to be my handmaiden and as my handmaiden I shall require your services."

Nada's eyes expressed a near caricature of worry, confusion and fear. Batshua halted Nada's run to the wardrobe, "Nada, if you have questions, I want you to ask them." Nada stopped and looked in wonder at her new mistress. "I will instruct you in the proper way to inquire of me when you are unsure of your instructions. Above all, you must maintain respect at all times.

When we are alone like this, maintaining respect is less difficult and correcting any mistakes, such as falling off a pillow", she paused for effect and smiled long enough to catch an embarrassed smile from Nada, "and other ways of making a fool of yourself will be more tolerated. When we are with the Emir or when we are with anyone else, you must use more caution in how you answer and how you ask me for anything, do you understand?"

"Yes ma'am, I understand."

"Good. If fear or anger causes you to be unsure of yourself, recite the names of your fingers. It will clear your mind and also give those around you a sense that you are pondering their words and thereby respecting them, which is very important." Batshua paused; she could see Nada was mentally naming her fingers as they moved slightly, one by one. "Nada, is there something you would like to ask me now?"

"Yes ma'am, but…" She hesitated, the last word was strained as a choked whisper.

Batshua smiled encouragement. "Now is the time to ask, there will be little time later."

Nada's expelled her breath in a sudden heave of courageous resolve. "If we are to meet the Emir today…", she swallowed once, hard, "would you teach me the names of my toes as well?"

Batshua roared with undignified laughter, "Bless my soul, dear child! You are with me but an hour and I'm twice-blessed by your humor! You are gifted by God himself with such wit!" Nada smiled politely at this welcome news but her face displayed a mix of pleasure politely back to her mistress and confusion from not understanding the humor of her own joke. "All will be well, you will find a blue garment in my wardrobe. Please return with that and I shall give you further instructions for the day." Nada ran off, relieved to have an activity that she understood completely.

-:--o--:-

7

Bodyguard

"For you write down bitter things against me
and make me reap the sins of my youth.
You fasten my feet in shackles;
you keep close watch on all my paths
by putting marks on the soles of my feet."

The Book of Job 13:26-27

-:--o--:-

Batshua guided Nada from her chambers into bright early morning light. Nada squinted as the sun caught her full in the face. She failed to stifle a sneeze as she followed at heel to the right and behind her mistress. Batshua turned toward Nada with a raised eyebrow when she heard the curious muffled snorting sound behind her. Ashamed to be caught in the social sin by her mistress, Nada dropped to her knees with her face in the dust. A long moment passed, then an even longer moment. When she was not kicked, beaten, whipped, cursed or even scolded she began to wonder if Batshua had stormed away and to call some guard to kill her insolent servant.

She glanced up and thought she saw her mistress grinning down at her but that could not be! She waited another long moment before she heard Batshua's gentle voice ask with a lilt of humor, "Nada, what are you doing?"

"I am awaiting your punishment, Ma'am."

"For what would I punish you?"

Nada's whole body involuntarily withdrew into itself slightly. Her uncle had often taunted her with questions like that in order to add spice to the pleasure he got out of beating her. It was mostly the same with her aunt. She answered knowing that her response would work only to prolong the interval before the beating began. "I was rude, I am very sorry, ma'am."

"Nada, you have not been rude, but if you continue to lay there in the dust, I am not sure what I shall consider your current behavior to be. Stand up and look me in the eyes, child."

Slowly, with almost rust-creaking hesitation, Nada stood but with her eyes fixed on her mistress's feet.

Batshua sighed in frustration and tried a new tact to pull Nada's mind away from her fear. "Nada, what are names of your fingers?"

At this, Nada actually looked up at Batshua to read her face. She did not understand the face of her mistress because the expression written there was beyond her experience. During most of her life, with the exception of mistress Leah, she had known only faces containing anger, spiteful laughter and disdain. The Emira's face was relaxed and graced with the most beautiful expression she could have imagined if she had the resources to have imagined it. Nada looked into a face full of gentle, uncomplicated *compassion*.

Nada began to murmur softly, held hypnotized momentarily by the strength of Batshua's gentle smile, "One... two..." She did not finish, her voice drifted away into a broad grin that reflected that of her mistress.

Several moments passed until at last the spell was broken by the sudden calling of a bird. Batshua spoke evenly but firmly, "Nada, are you going to grovel on your face like that every time you are stricken by fear?" Nada's mouth and eyes twisted into a silent caricature that expressed "*I hope not*". "Do you not understand that I desire your *respect*, not your fear?" Again, Nada's face communicated plainly that she understood each word but not the meaning the words meant when connected together.

A flash of intuition entered Batshua's mind, the decided to run with it. "Nada, what have the other servant girls told you about me? I want you to answer honestly, I am not trying to get the other servant girls in trouble. What do they say about me and my husband?"

Nada paused, her fingers were twitching slightly as she recited slowly. Batshua smiled approval. "They say you are the richest, most powerful woman in the world and that people live and die by your word. They say the same things of master A'dab, that there is no one in the world richer and more powerful than he."

"Nada, listen carefully to me." Nada gazed into Batshua's eyes expectantly. "Those things the other servants are saying about me and my husband are *compliments*, I appreciate them, but they are *not true*."

"How can it not be true? I have seen the truth of it with my own eyes!"

"You only believe it because you have not been to other places in the world to see other even greater things. The Pharaoh of Egypt makes my husband look like a poor man and a weakling. There are other kingdoms richer than the Pharaoh. There always will be somebody bigger and better."

Nada struggled to conjure up the mental image of a city more magnificent than Hareb, but she could not do it.

"You said you used to cut fish. Put yourself in the place of a fish swimming in the sea." Nada closed her eyes and thought of the swimming she had done last week. "Now as a fish you are trying to imagine life on the land. You can imagine trees because you have seen seaweed, you can imagine mountains because you have seen large rocks. But there is one thing you could not ever imagine in your wildest dreams as a fish – you would never imagine fire!"

Nada opened her eyes wide in surprise and laughed with understanding, "You are right! You are so wise ma'am. I am like a fish trying to think what it is like out of the water!" She laughed again.

"Well, miss fish, hand me your fin and come up to the beach!" She offered her arm, Nada took it confidently and they strode off to see more wonders of Batshua's home.

-:--o--:-

A tall, very muscular man with dark skin stood with his face in shadow outside a circle of purple and white drapes in the garden's center. With his arms crossed and easy stance, he appeared to Nada as if he could have been a tree planted by the entrance. Her pace slowed as she noticed the gleaming bronze sword tucked into his sash. The sword looked familiar, it reminded her of the terrible day of carnage when black-robed men raided her village with swords just like that one. Visions of the flashing swords and echoes of the screams erupted in her mind before she could slam it shut with an effort that jolted her body.

Batshua glanced at Nada curiously, but strode to the 'tree' with a smile, "Naaman, I would like you to meet someone. This is Nada, my new handmaiden."

Naaman stepped out of the shadows to bow from the shoulders up without uncrossing his arms. A broad smile broke across his face like an avalanche of snow. With speech accented by laughter he said, "Good morning madam Batshua. Yes, I caught a glimpse of her as you came near, but now she seems to have disappeared! Is she a genie?" The smile was not the only cleft on his face, there was deep scar running from his right ear to chin.

Nada gasped in fear and hid behind Batshua. Batshua stepped to one side in consternation and scolded her handmaiden, "Nada, it is proper to return a greeting once you have been introduced."

Nada pointed at 'Naaman', "He is not 'Naaman'! I know him! He is A'jin! A murdering Sabean!", 'Sabean' was spit as a curse with such force that Nada nearly sprayed spittle over her mistress, "He murdered my family, destroyed my village and sold me into slavery! What is he doing here?!"

Naaman took this accusation without losing his smile, but his eyes looked pained.

Batshua raised her eyes and prompted Naaman, "Apparently the two of you have met. What do you have to say, Naaman?"

Naaman lost his smile and turned to Nada. "I am very pleased to see you again young one, if you ask me for a drink, I promise not to pour it on your head this time." Nada continued to glare. Batshua's look said she was waiting to hear the rest. Naaman tried to put his smile back on, "And I must say, you look much better without a leather collar around your neck."

Batshua interrupted, "Naaman! Your sense of humor is renowned! But Nada and I are waiting to hear the truth. I thought you had told me the whole truth but apparently not, if what Nada says is true."

Naaman continued, "Everything I told you is true ma'am." He then looked directly at Nada. "And everything this child says is also true, but not in the way she believes it to be true. It is true that I was part of the raid on her village that day, but I killed no one, I only made the others believe I killed her people. I picked up the dead ones and cut off their heads or hacked off their arms. It was a terrible thing, but I was looking for a way to escape from them and so I had to go along until I found my chance to get away. You see, I am a soldier of Sheba, the honorable defenders of our homeland."

Batshua prompted, "I know some of this story. I think Nada should hear the rest. Tell her how you fell into a band of raiders."

"I.. was drunk one night and fought a man. He fell over and struck his head – he died. It was an accident but his brother has now sworn to be his avenger of blood. I ran until those men found me. I did not know who they were or what they did, so I made them believe I was one of them until that night at the oasis when I met the young man Omar sent by A'dab Ben Hareb. He said A'dab would give me sanctuary and so I escaped."

Nada was not buying this story. "You drew your sword to kill me that day."

"No young one, I only frightened you with it. I knew the boss-man, Harun would not want me to kill the slaves. He is greedy."

Batshua concluded, "Thank you Naaman. I am satisfied. Nada?"

Nada was noncommittal, "As you wish, ma'am. May I ask some questions?"

"Of course."

"Does Frayda know he is here?" she asked Batshua.

Naaman answered, "Yes, I have explained all this to Frayda with Omar listening."

"Why hasn't Frayda told me about him?" she asked Batshua, pointedly ignoring Naaman.

"I do not know, perhaps she did not think it a worthy subject. I understand she has been very pleased to see you again." Naaman continued to address Nada politely, but his eyes were deeply pained.

"Why is he called 'Naaman' now?" She directed her question to Batshua as if Naaman did not exist.

Naaman spoke up, "May I answer that, ma'am?" Batshua nodded, "When I came to this place, my name meant 'Gold', but that name does not suit me. I offered my sword in service to A'dab Ben Hareb vowing to change my life if he would give me a chance. He agreed and said 'Be pleasant'. And that is what Naaman means."

Batshua was an astute observer of humanity. As she looked toward Nada, she smiled at what must be happening inside her head. An imaginative vision materialized before her eyes. She imagined

Nada's head as a library full of scribes furiously writing scrolls, all arguing with each other, tearing up each other's scrolls and rewriting them until the scrolls would fit properly in the library. She hoped Nada's scribes reached a consensus soon. She prided herself for having taken the chance on this tragic child and silently prayed thanksgiving to God for his obvious hand at work in bringing them together.

Nada let Naaman off the hook just a little, "Thank you for your honesty, Naaman. I will ponder this."

Naaman's smile returned in full dazzling splendor. He turned businesslike to Batshua, "The master returned from his morning prayers some time ago. I am certain he is eager to see you ma'am." He bowed low to the floor as he drew aside the drape with a practiced courtly flourish.

Batshua smiled thanks and turned to Nada with an impish grin, "Well, shall we see what the old boy's been up to?"

Nada did not look at Naaman and gave him a wide berth as she scooted past.

-:--o--:-

Following her mistress past Naaman, Nada encountered a scene of sensual wonders unlike anything in her experience. With a hand motion, Batshua indicated to Nada that they were to remove their footgear which consisted of simple linen slippers for Nada and silk slippers with inner linings for Batshua. She instinctively knelt to assist Batshua with her footwear as her mistress sat regally on a low marble dais obviously provided for guests.

As Batshua's inner socks were removed, Nada stifled a gasp and desperately attempted to hide pity for her mistress's sickly-looking feet. Her toenails were horribly reddened as if they were badly bruised or diseased. She nearly swooned in sympathetic pain to think of the courage her poor mistress must endure to walk with such grace having her feet in such horrible condition!

Batshua noticed her handmaiden's sudden discomfort. "Something wrong, Nada?"

"No ma'am... it's just that... no, ma'am."

"Nada, I want to you speak your mind to me. I intend to have a handmaiden who is well educated in all matters and that pertains especially to matters of my personal care. Now please tell me what is on your mind."

"Well, ma'am, I... I am very sorry to see you in such pain with your feet. You have the courage of the gods to be walking with such grace on feet as diseased as these."

The two women had tacitly agreed to a whispered conversation once they had entered the enclosure. There was an aura that made the surroundings so peaceful that normal conversation seemed almost irreligious though there was nothing that appeared to be sacred other than an extreme sense of beauty everywhere. But at Nada's whispered lament concerning her mistress's painted toenails, Batshua burst forth with a musical laugh that echoed across the tiled floor.

At the center of the circular enclosure, the floor surrounded a small pool of about ten feet in circumference. Spaced about the pool were palms, ferns and various flowering plants. Prior to Batshua's outburst, the only other discernible sounds within the hundred foot enclosure were the gentle trickle of water and a few songbirds.

In answer to Batshua's irreverent laughter, a deep male voice called from somewhere on the other side of the pond with a hint of his own laughter, "Batshua! Is that you?!"

Batshua settled herself to a chuckle and answered, "Yes, I'm here with my new handmaiden. We'll be a few moments if you can busy yourself with something..."

"Oh. Yes, well certainly. I was just... well... tell Naaman to call the girls to serve food when you are ready, no hurry really."

"Yes dear. I will only be a moment more. I am about to ask my new handmaiden to cure my feet."

"What?! What is wrong with your feet?" He asked, suddenly alarmed.

"There is nothing wrong with my feet."

"Good, then your handmaiden should have no trouble curing you. Please hurry, I am quite hungry."

"Yes dear."

Nada whispered in surprise, "There is nothing wrong with your feet? But…"

"Nada, you have never seen a woman with painted toenails before? We use dye from the Henna plant, it is how all the finer women adorn themselves. Do you really think the color makes my feet look sick?"

Nada looked down at her mistresses feet quizzically with her head cocked to one side in thought, saying nothing. Watching her kneel there looking for all the world like the dog-like creature she so wished Nada not to emulate, Batshua did not know if she should laugh or grab her in a hug for being too wonderfully real. She decided upon both, took her by the hands and stood up with her.

"If you think my feet look sick, I shall be plain-toed for you."

"No, no, no… I…"

"Yes, yes, yes… To tell you the truth, my husband thinks my painted toes are a silly indulgence too. He has often spoken of it. I think your candor may be a good for me. For us…"

"Candor?"

"Your characteristic of speaking your mind forthrightly and with respect."

"Hmmm… I have lived only fourteen years, but I have learned that this 'candor' of which you speak is not appreciated by many of the other people I have known."

"That at least, is candid." They both laughed.

Nada thought that it felt very good to laugh with Batshua. The tension between them began to ease. Laughing seemed to be good medicine. Something was happening inside her and it felt very, very good. It was like oil poured on a dried and cracked wound inside her.

"Nada, go tell Naaman that we are ready to eat. Normally you would assist me by washing my feet and then wash your own. I will take care of my own feet this time while you are speaking with Naaman, then you may wash your own feet. I would then enjoy giving you a quick tour of my watchtower before we sit with him for lunch."

As Nada hurried off to Naaman, Batshua sighed gently. The stillness of her husband's enclosure seemed to wrap itself around her in a moment of complete peace and a sense of utter rightness with the world. She had experienced rare moments like this before and treasured them. Using the linen towel and water basin beside the dais, she scrubbed the Henna dye from her toes, it took quite awhile. Batshua noticed that Nada was a long time returning from her simple errand with Naaman.

-:--o--:-

Nada returned to find her mistress posed on the marble dais as if she had been sculpted there by the finest craftsman in the land. The statue came alive with a smile, "Ready for a tour? We have time before we meet with A'dab." That her mistress appeared to be asking her what she wanted to do next, to be giving her a choice was very unsettling. Other than her lonely Sabbath Day vigils on the Aqaba beach, choices had been completely outside her experience until meeting this woman. Batshua's question both delighted and disturbed her. She pushed away the disturbing feelings to ponder them later.

"Yes.", she responded quickly, "Naaman said he will call the servants. May I ask a question?"

"Yes, I thought you might have something on your mind. You were with Naaman a long time."

"He bowed to me. I do not know what that means." Nada's eyes were furtive.

"He bowed to both of us on the way here. It is a courtesy."

"This was... different."

"Explain."

"When I told him to summon the servants I was... well... I was very rude. But he was not rude in return."

"That is like Naaman, he is an honorable man."

"I do not understand men. I do not even look on him as a man, actually. I see him only as a murdering Sabean." Again she could not help spitting when she said 'Sabean'. "Yet, even after I was rude and I turned to go, he called to me and asked if there was a way to make peace between us. He said that if I am to be the handmaiden of his master's wife, we would be seeing a lot of each other and we should make amends. I said I did not see how there could be peace unless he could bring back my family. He could vanish into flames and black smoke, I did not care. There would be no peace! I turned away again, but again he called me back, but this time with his sword drawn! I was very frightened, but that is when he bowed. He held his sword toward me with both hands while he kneeled on one knee. His head was bowed low. He said, 'My life, for the life of your family.'"

"Good God!" Batshua did not speak profanely, her outburst was religiously accurate. "What did you say?!"

"I was frightened, but my heart was very moved. I did not know what to say. Something urged me with words that came to my lips before I could think about them. I said 'Perhaps my family is larger than I thought, my brother. Let there be peace between us.' He stood, put away his sword and said, 'Peace, my sister.'

"What happened between us? What does it mean? I am still frightened, but I am no longer frightened of Naaman."

Batshua's tone became urgent, "Nada, you must speak of this to no one, do you understand? No one!"

"Alright, but…"

"Naaman has pledged a life-debt to you according to his Sabean ways, yet he is my husband's bodyguard. We cannot have divided loyalties in this house, yet I am not sure Naaman's loyalty is actually divided. My husband may not see it that way. Speak of this to no one, do you understand? I see the hand of God in this, but not his purpose. I already can see that God is using you to cause much chaos in every life you touch!" She smiled at Nada's confused look. "Hold Naaman's pledge in your heart and ponder it long and well, child. Do not take this lightly."

"Yes ma'am."

"Come, I have something I want you to see. It is my very favorite place to go when I have something I need to ponder."

-:--o--:-

8

Meet the Master

"The lowly he sets on high
and those who mourn are lifted to safety."

The Book of Job 5:11

-:--o--:-

The two walked slowly around the perimeter of the enclosure to allow Nada time to absorb its tranquil beauty. A structure soon came into view that seemed very strange to Nada's eyes. It appeared to her as if a huge ship's mast poked through the roof with shelves encircling it in an upward spiral. She could not deduce the purpose of such a structure for the shelves were apparently unused -- nothing stored on them. Nada gestured curiously toward it and asked, "Ma'am, what is the purpose of this!?"

Batshua said, "Ah! That is a stairway to my watchtower. My husband had it built for me that I may sit at its height to watch for his return when he is away on his business journeys. We have time, would you like to see?"

Nada looked confused, "A stairway?"

"Yes, a pathway of steps to the sky. Have you never seen stairs?"

"I have seen steps that lead to the roof of a house, but nothing as magnificent as this!" She peered up into gloomy loftiness that seemed to stretch up into an imaginary heaven.

"Come! The effort will put a sharp edge on our appetites!" Batshua stepped with an excited liveliness that eased Nada's fears. Her mistress seemed very much at ease, in fact she seemed to anticipate the climb with childlike enthusiasm. Nada could not help but share in her mistress's girlish camaraderie as she attempted to keep pace.

The steps were of strong cedar boards at least two inches thick and extremely sturdy but the airy spiral structure allowed the climbers to clearly see the floor growing further and further away. Nada slowed down as vertigo dampened her enthusiasm. Batshua laughed down at her teasingly, "Come Nada! Hurry! I thought Naaman had said you were a genie! Aren't genies supposed to be able to fly?"

Nada grimaced ruefully at the taunt and swallowed her anxiety with renewed determination. "How many steps are there?" she asked, somewhat out of breath. Batshua did a quick calculation in her head, knowing Nada probably did not have any mathematical training, "A ten of tens." Nada tried, but she could not conceive of so many. Batshua laughed again, "C'mon Nada, I will race you to the top! I am not as old as you think!" Laughing, she leaped forward with her handmaiden in close pursuit; fear forgotten in competition.

The stairs ended at a dark wooden circle, brilliant light leaking around the edges. Batshua stopped to catch her breath, pleased that she had won the race against her younger competitor. When Nada caught up, Batshua allowed time for her breathing to become normal and then said conspiratorially, "Nada, let's play a game. This is best if you close your eyes, so give me your sash." Nada appeared confused but had no choice but to obey her mistress, who seemed to have reverted to a child for the moment. She tied the sash around Nada's eyes, opened the door and led her out, stumbling onto a platform into warm mid-morning heat with a gentle cooling breeze. Nada felt queasy as she sensed the platform moving slightly beneath her feet with the wind.

Batshua said, "Now keep your eyes closed until I say to open them. There is a handrail in front of you, grab onto it." Nada did and its polished wooden strength gave her comfort and bearing. Batshua removed the sash and said, "Open your eyes!"

The scene before her caused Nada to inhale once with such sharp intensity there was an audible whimpering sound. Her eyes reflexively snapped shut and her hands clamped tight onto the railing in a death grip. The vista of terrifying beauty hovered like a dream behind her eyelids as her breathing became ragged with the onset of vertigo-induced panic. Batshua slid her arm around Nada's waist while gripping her shoulder gently with the other. She spoke softly, "You are fine, just take it in a little at a time. Few have stood where you now stand to see what your eyes now see. Enjoy this moment, Nada."

Tears squeezed out from under Nada eyelids as she willed them open. Her heart danced wildly in joy and fear. She would have swooned were it not for her tight grip on the rail and her mistress's steady, firm support.

They were perched atop a circular minaret capped by a pillared dome about eight feet in circumference nearly seventy feet high. The tower stood on the eastern side of a three hundred foot canyon that stretched away to the west. The tower's own shadow draped across the canyon's wall and into a river in the valley's floor. The sense of height was almost mind-numbing to Nada's amazed eyes. The sight was so sensually intense, every part of her body was tingling and trembling. She knew if she lived a thousand years she would never tire of the scenes below her.

To the north were herds of sheep and goats with shepherds leading them by the hundreds out to a still-water river that gently flowed westward to where it cascaded over the cliff to mate with the valley's river. She looked to the east and could make out a camel caravan of perhaps fifty traders meandering slowly toward the village on the eastern foot of the tower. Directly below were shops and tradesmen all busy with their day's business. She could make out a fruit market, a meat shop, linen and silk merchants. Beginning to feel more confident on the platform, she turned excitedly to the south side to see a huge cluster of green palms and ferns where the river had flowed from the south and made a large, lazy turn west. The shepherds were grazing their flocks at a spreading pond before the river narrowed its course into a misty cascade to the valley. Interspersed between the palms further out were whitewashed adobe homes which she thought must belong to the shepherds, workers and tradesmen.

Nada turned to her mistress in rapturous awe, her eyes bright with wonder, "My lady, I do not know how to say what is in my heart! I have never imagined anything so wonderful, so full of life and beauty! You are the most blessed woman on earth!"

Batshua smiled her acknowledgement broadly, "Yes, I am blessed Nada. I am blessed to be wife of A'dab Ben Hareb, Emir of Edom. Look well, child. For all you see in any direction are the lands of my beloved husband!"

A voice startled both women as it echoed up from the trap door which they had left open, "Ah, my darling Batshua, are you trying to corrupt the young lady with your bragging or is it my own head you trying to fill so full it will burst?"

Nada and Batshua turned to see the face of kindly middle-aged and heavily-beard man that seemed to be floating toward them out of the trapdoor's gloom. He joined them at the railing and laughed heartily with his hands clasped behind his back. His angular face was finely chiseled with large eagle-eyes, a rudder-like nose that seemed to steer him when he walked. His chaotic eyebrows contrasted his neatly trimmed beard that hung at least eight inches from his chin. Over all, his face would have been most imposing and austere except for the soft gentleness of his mouth that always appeared about to laugh. The wrinkles in the corners of his eyes indicated he laughed often, which indeed he was doing again now.

"I am sorry, I did not mean to startle you so. What you said my dear, is the truth but it is not the entire truth. God owns all of this land, and I, or rather we, are privileged to be its stewards. The only thing I truly 'own' are my thoughts which I keep surrendered in daily discipline to God so I am not quite certain that I own even my thoughts. What do you think?" He cocked one eyebrow at his wife.

Batshua smiled at this philosophical nonsense, and brushed it aside with a rejoinder of her own, "Dabby, how dare sneak up on me like this?! I wanted to introduce Nada to you properly down at the pool and now you've gone and spoiled everything as usual." Her tone was an exaggerated pout intended to tease, her words contained no heat.

A'dab sniffed and screwed his face up in exaggerated thought. "Well then, I see no clear way to rectify the situation unless I close my eyes, stumble back down the stairs and whap my head on the tiles with sufficient force to remove all memory of this presumptuous peek. Since I am already here enjoying the view and, dare I say, the company of my beloved, and furthermore since I have no desire to beat my head senseless today, may I suggest our lunch be served here and you make your introductions now? After all I did forewarn Naaman of my plans to mount the minaret, so our food should be along presently."

Batshua sighed and bowed to the inevitable which seemed always to be the only course of action when it came to her husband's frustratingly irrefutable logic. "Very well. Dabby, I would like you to meet Nada. She has been with us for three weeks. Today is her first day of training as my handmaiden." She turned to Nada, "Nada, this is A'dab Ben Hareb the Emir of Edom and my beloved, surprise-spoiling husband."

Nada stood rooted in place. She was absolutely, unequivocally terrified. Here she was standing at the pinnacle of power with two of the wealthiest and most influential people she had ever known. Yet they were acting like adolescents! Even so, A'dab seemed to treat his wife with deference and respect. She had never observed a man treating a woman this way before. Then here she was being introduced to the master even though she was a mere servant. To be given this honor was more confusing than she could comprehend. She stood blinking without knowing what to do or say.

A'dab broke the awkward silence with a gesture toward Nada. "'Shua, I have observed behavior such like what is now being demonstrated for us by Nada during many of my hunting expeditions. When the young feel threatened by the unknown, they freeze in place even though a more suitable course of action might be to face the unknown bravely or run away. It is as if God the Creator has instilled within all creatures the idea that if we remain very, very still we shall become invisible. Of course this would only be possible if Nada here was a genie of some sort. Is she a genie? Hmmmm?" A'dab smiled beatifically at Nada as he rocked back and forth on his feet. He had yet to unclasp his hands from behind his back.

Batshua scowled at her merciless tease of a husband, rolled her eyes once in Nada's direction then poked her bare foot out from beneath her robe, sans Henna dye. "Well, genie or not, she did cure my feet!"

At this revelation, A'dab threw back his head and laughed long and loud. He brought his hands together and applauded in an exaggerated style, "Well done! Well done, Nada, the genie who cures feet! Now there is a feat that causes me to bow to you, my dear." And Nada's eyes grew and grew as A'dab Ben Hareb the Emir of Edom, the most powerful man she had ever seen or even heard of bowed deeply with a broad, sincere smile.

Nada finally found her voice and hoarsely whispered to Batshua without taking her eyes off A'dab, "Ma'am, I do not know what to say." Batshua rolled her eyes at her husband in mocking admiration. "Oh, don't be taken in by his charms. He is quite harmless you know. The most polite thing you can say is something like 'Thank you sir, but Batshua's feet are in God's hands'. I think that will satisfy the moment."

Nada gulped and said, "Thank you sir, my mistress's feet are in God's hands."

A'dab nodded reply, "Well said young lady. You are wise to give God credit for his work, yet I believe praise is also due to a servant of God when one is a willing instrument. Do you agree?"

Nada turned once again in a whispered aside to her mistress, "What do I say now?" Batshua replied as if her husband could not hear either of them, which of course he could. It was all a fun game to everyone. "You can say something like 'You are too kind.'"

Nada bowed with her best flourish, mimicking Naaman as closely as possible, "You are too kind, sir."

The bow both surprised and delighted Nada's hosts. They laughed their approval.

'Dabby, I am hungry! Didn't you say Naaman would send the girls right along with food?"

Right on cue, they heard giggling voices struggling up the stairs with a clatter of pottery.

-:--o--:-

The servant girls spread fruit, boiled eggs and covered dishes steaming with rice onto a carpet near the edge of the platform. A curious bird landed on the railing and began to chirp enviously at the feast. A'dab shooed the feathered bandit away with a laugh, "Bah! Even here we are not safe from thieves!"

The two girls had kneeled to one side in case their services were required, but A'dab dismissed them "My thanks, you may go." Their eyes begged questions because he was breaking custom, but they bowed repeatedly as they backed away down the stairs. Their diminishing whispers echoed quietly during their descent.

A'dab turned to Batshua as he munched noisily on a pear, the juice running down his gray-streaked beard, "Beloved, have you discussed privacy protocols with your handmaiden?"

Batshua was sipping tea from a thinly turned cup that looked to Nada as if it would break in any hand less delicate than that of her mistress, "Er... only somewhat my dear. We have had a very busy morning."

"Shall I then? I intend no disrespect to you by instructing your handmaiden. I merely assume you are fatigued and hungry and may wish to give more attention to your meal for the moment."

One side of Batshua's mouth curled up in a half-smile as she bit into a piece of spiced, oiled flat bread she had rolled into a cigar shape. Her eyes danced with humor at her husband. Sparring with him was always fun and doubly so when she had a scorekeeper like Nada as audience. She mumbled assent as clearly as she could with her mouth full of bread and choked down more tea. A'dab turned to Nada.

"Nada, please come closer." She had been kneeling behind and to the side of her mistress in the proper position of a servant. The servants had brought pillows for A'dab and Batshua so they were reclining comfortably. A'dab took one of them and placed it before the spread of food between Batshua and himself. Nada hesitated, her eyes darted a question at her mistress who nodded affirmation. Nada managed to sit in tailor fashion on the pillow without falling off, a feat noted by Batshua with some amusement.

A'dab continued to speak to Nada as he ate fruit slowly and with less noise. "Nada, my beloved has chosen you to become her handmaiden, but I must ask you if you are willing to accept this role." Nada's eyes blinked confusion – she thought her choice had been made back in Tariq. He spoke again as if he could read her mind, "Batshua may have been somewhat presumptuous with you," he eyed his wife significantly, "but until this moment, you have been her handmaiden *candidate*. You now have a decision to make and a short time to reconsider. If you say that you do not wish to be my beloved's handmaiden, I will send you down the stairs to Naaman who will find a home for you among the shepherds or tradesmen in the village. I am sure there are many families among us who are in need a fine young lady such as you to look after their sheep or perhaps their children." This prospect did not sound appealing to Nada at all, not after the wonders she had seen today.

Continuing to read her mind without her permission, A'dab continued, "That prospect may not seem very appealing to you from your perch on this platform. But consider this: the role of a handmaiden has both privilege and responsibilities. The most important responsibility is that you must be completely and utterly reliable in matters of privacy regarding what you see or hear from your mistress and me. I do not mean that we think you would be a gossip or spy to spread rumors. I mean that as her handmaiden, you must be extraordinarily *cautious* in everything you say so that you do not even *accidentally* reveal private matters. The penalty for any breach of confidence is a day's journey into the desert where you will be left alone to God's mercy. To my knowledge, God has no history of being merciful to those so abandoned. Do you understand and do you still accept? Think it through."

Nada's face went limp. She realized that the past three weeks were a preparation for this moment. She now understood that the hardships of her life had all served as a foundation upon which she could rely to make this life-changing decision -- her first real choice. Clarity left her no true alternative -- she would never, could never go back to the life she had once endured. She would move forward!

Her face resolved into relaxed confidence as she looked at her mistress, then into the expectant eyes of A'dab Ben Hareb. "I accept."

There had been an unconscious tension between the three on the platform that tensed their bodies, much like trying to sleep in a tent with a mosquito. With Nada's two words, the tension was swatted away and all three visibly relaxed their postures. A'dab glanced at his wife, "You have chosen well." Batshua's eyes sparkled in gratitude and pride.

Then A'dab Ben Hareb did a thing that made Nada feel very strange. He selected a piece of bread, tore off a chunk and *passed the bread to her.* Sensing the significance of this act but not fully understanding it, Nada accepted A'dab's gesture and started to chew it in synchrony with his own morsel. He then handed her a cup which she held while he gestured with a pot of water. As she held the cup with both hands to steady her trembling fingers, he filled it, but to her astonishment he kept pouring past the brim until it overflowed running down her hands into her lap.

Nada wondered at this until she glanced at Batshua who had tears streaming down her face. She asked, "Nada, do you understand the honor my husband has just bestowed on you?" Nada slowly gestured in the negative. "This is an ancient shepherd's ritual. By sharing his bread, he means that you are under our household protection -- we will guard you with our lives and fortune. Then he filled your cup to overflowing. You must understand this. A host fills a guest's cup while the guest is welcome and stops refilling the cup when it is time for the guest to leave. But when the host fills the cup to overflowing, it is an honor that signifies you are always welcome and you may stay as long as you wish." Batshua's voice nearly broke with emotion, "You have been highly honored young maiden, is there anything you wish to say?"

The import of what A'dab had done was only just beginning to break through into the hidden dungeons of her soul. Fearful and dreadful spirits full of hatred for all the wrongs done to her were rattled loose, chased away and the empty dungeon cells splashed clean with the water of honor and respect dripping from her hands. She sat transfixed as the Spirit of Life and power filled her with the potential for a new life of respect and honor. She vowed deep within her soul that she would never, ever betray this moment or these two people who had conferred upon her this knowledge of herself that somehow she knew could only be sourced from the God they dare not name. She longed to know more! She yearned to seek A'dab's wisdom and the way of respect and honor that brought about people of integrity such as these two who sat with her now. All this passed through her mind in a near instant before she spoke.

She searched her memory for appropriate words, something worthy of the moment. At last a few words floated to the surface from her early childhood when she was with her aunt at the joining of a man and woman to be married. She spoke with near child-like hesitation, "From my... heart of hearts... sir. I will... honor thee. I... pledge my... faith... to thee."

A'dab nodded acceptance of this and turned to Batshua, "Intelligent child. I believe she will serve you well. Do you find her acceptable?"

"Oh Yes. Yes, indeed." Batshua's answer was flatly emphatic. "I told you she was a 'diamond in the rough'."

"Hmmm, we shall see soon enough." He reached into a fold of his robe and pulled out a gold ear-loop. It would just fit inside a circle made by his thumb and forefinger, the looped metal about one half the diameter of his pinky finger. He showed it to Nada, then handed it to Batshua who tucked it away, "Batshua will fasten it to your ear later. It is a symbol of your status as handmaiden. You are to wear it always, do not ever remove it, do you understand?"

"I understand." Nada tried very hard not to leap from her seat and dance for joy! She was to be given jewelry! Even though it was a symbol of bondage, it was jewelry and not a slave's manacles! Her heart raced with adolescent anticipation.

A'dab stood but continued to speak, "One more thing Nada," She looked up at the tall man and wondered if she should stand as well. "The house of Ben Hareb does not own slaves, at least, it is my policy that we do not own them for long." Nada's eyes blinked confusion. "My wife has purchased your freedom and you have just made a free choice to become her handmaiden which is a position known as bond-servant. I believe she may have already explained that to you. The earring is the symbol of your commitment which shall be for seven years or the Year of Jubilee which so happens to be six years from now when all bond-servants are released from their obligations. You will be assigned living quarters conveniently close to your mistress and receive normal servant's wages for my household plus a small bonus suitable for your status as handmaiden."

Nada's head was spinning with this news. "*I am to receive wages?!*" she thought.

A'dab turned to leave, "My business here is completed, unless you have anything further you require of me, my beloved?"

Batshua chuckled and with a casual wave of her hand, dismissed her husband. "No my dear, I think you have charmed, bemused and confused my young lady sufficiently well for one day, thank you."

Neither spoke until after A'dab was well out of earshot. "Well Nada, what did you think of my Dabby?"

"He is a most amazing man."

"Yes, isn't he?" Batshua's thoughts were difficult to read. "He is wise beyond my understanding. At times I believe there is no one else on earth who is wiser than him and at other times he can frustrate me so greatly that I want to call down the very hosts of heaven to curse him!"

Nada's breath caught in her throat and her hand cover her mouth in horror. Batshua laughed, "No my dear, I am speaking nonsense and remember that I have your word no other will hear my nonsense, correct?" Her eyes grew dark and foreboding and Nada's stomach turned to ice. "Do you have any questions? You must have many."

"Er... it has been a long morning, ma'am. I wonder where I am expected to... well... I mean I have had much to eat and ah... much to drink."

"Oh! My goodness of course! There is a vessel for that purpose over there near the door. I will enjoy the view of the valley below and then we shall have much to talk about once we are both comfortable. This place is my favorite for making plans and I have more plans to make today."

-:--O--:-

9

Confessions

"Teach me, and I will be quiet;
show me where I have been wrong.
How painful are honest words! "

The Book of Job 6:24-25

-:--o--:-

Both women lingered long at the railing, each wrapped in their private euphoria. Batshua swept the entire panoramic splendor of her lands into her eyes in one exaltation of beauty. Her whole being felt a oneness with her husband in the garden below, her God above, the people and their work in the distance around... she breathed deeply and exhaled a slow sigh of utter peace.

Nada's eyes were closed and her lips lifted into a dreamy curve. Her mind held almost no thought, but swirled with the most wondrous mixture of emotions she had ever known: safety, freedom, confidence, destiny, hope and youthful, burning anticipation of tomorrow! Her heart beat rapidly in its attempt to contain her passions, she began to grip the rail fiercely as tears streamed unashamed down her cheeks to cascade across her now widely smiling lips to splash in salty exuberance on her tongue. *"What is happening to me?"* She thought as she thrilled to her own irrational joy.

Sensed, but unseen, another presence stood with Batshua and Nada. The loving hand of God, Elohim, Creator of All, softly caressed the minds of his beloved children for only a moment longer, then withdrew. The only physical evidence of his passing – a sudden breeze that shook the platform beneath the women, breaking their reverie.

A light laugh bubbled from Batshua, "Did you feel that?"

Nada was almost dizzy, "Yes, a strong wind. I felt the tower move."

"No, I mean before that. Did you feel what I felt?"

Nada turned to Batshua with her face radiant and streaked with tears. Nada could only nod ascent. Her eyes questioned, but she suddenly looked sure, "I have felt this before, but not so intense."

"Truly? Explain." Batshua had never met another besides her husband with a sensitivity such as Nada's.

"During the years I spent as a slave in Aqaba, I spent many days alone on the beach during Sabbath rest. I have seen that you observe Sabbath Day here, but in Aqaba, Sabbath Day was different. I was alone for most of them. It seemed to me that... well..."

"Go on, Nada, please continue." Batshua encouraged.

"I felt as if El Roi himself would visit with me on the beach. I could not see him, but I felt like he could see me there and I could feel him and know him to be watching me, watching over me."

Batshua moved to Nada to take both hands in her own. "You are an amazing young woman. So much has happened to you, yet you seem to have turned toward God instead of anger and bitterness. God has blessed me with you."

Nada blushed and wished desperately she could be worthy of Batshua's words. Her face looked pained. "There is something you should know." She could not look her mistress in the eyes.

"Nada, you have pledged your confidence to me, I pledge the same to you."

"I... I am full of evil!" And she began to weep helplessly. Batshua had felt God's presence before. She knew the caress of God's hand was a significant event and its purpose would be more complex than she could discern. For the moment she could see that something in Nada and herself had been unsealed. She felt confident to follow the path of her instincts to affirm Nada's place and her rightness, not her false sense of evil.

"Nada, my dear child, I am a better judge of character than that. In fact, so is A'dab and for that matter I have learned to trust Naaman's judgment. I do not believe you would be able to hide your evil from us if that were true." She gestured to the pillows, "Tell me what you mean."

She began her story indirectly. "It is not for nothing that I am called 'Nada the Knife'." Batshua raised an eyebrow at this, but withheld comment and judgment. Nada continued her story. "I spent many Sabbath days alone on the Aqaba beach. I used the time to ponder my life and... to practice with my fish-cutting knives. We left the knives in the sun to harden them, so I practiced near the cutting tables. I discovered many tricks for throwing and stabbing and tossing hand to hand. That is how I learned the trick with the pear." Batshua nodded understanding but her eyes questioned, there must be more to this story.

"One day, one of master E'mat's fishermen found me down by the cutting tables. He did not notice what I was doing, that I had a small knife in my hand, so I quickly hid it in a few turns of my sash. He yelled at me and grabbed my arm, he seemed to be full of wine and mischief. I was very, very frightened!"

"I can imagine you were very frightened indeed! How old were you? Twelve? Thirteen?"

"I do not know the day of my birth with certainty, but I think I was thirteen, almost fourteen. This happened not long before the end of my time in Aqaba."

"What happened next?" Batshua had a very good idea what happened next.

"He intended to harm me, he intended to violate me. There was no one around to hear my cry for help. He threw me to the sand under the cutting tables and fell on top of me. But as he busied himself with his tunic, I unfolded the knife from my sash and almost with a will of its own, the knife found its way across his throat." Nada's face held the stone-cold look of a dam about to burst.

Batshua stared thoughtfully at her handmaiden. She did not doubt that this young woman was a gift from God, but as she had discovered, most of Elohim's gifts came wrapped in multi-layered packages. Surprisingly layered packages. What could she say about this?! She must think it through carefully.

Nada's story could not have ended there. Killing a man, even in self-defense is a capital crime. For a man to be killed at the hand of a mere maiden would have brought so much shame on that man's family… how had Nada gotten away with this?

Batshua said with some incredulity, "Nada, I cannot believe you just walked back to your master's house with blood splattered all over yourself."

"No. I sat there for a long time not knowing what to do. I could not think, I could not even feel, I felt empty and lost. I felt as if I were in a bad dream from which I could not awaken. It was then that I heard my mistress Leah calling. She sometimes joined me on the beach to talk. I believe mistress Leah also knew of the God, El Roi, but she called him by another name. She said her favorite name for him was 'El Jireh', the 'God Who Provides'. I began to cry and she ran to me."

"She found you there with the dead fisherman?"

"Yes. She did not seem surprised that the fisherman had attacked me. She said he was a drunkard and a violent man and that her husband never cared for him."

"What did she do? This is an unbelievable story, Nada." Batshua wished she could have known mistress Leah.

"She told me to put the knife back and to wash my clothes carefully in the sea while she waited. She said that my clothes had many old stains of fish blood from work at the tables, a few more stains would not be noticed. I did as she asked, scrubbing my clothes with sand. After that she and I went back to the beach to a rock where we sometimes liked to talk. She comforted me there while my clothes dried. She warned me never to tell anyone and neither would she would tell anyone. All that night we acted as if nothing happened. By morning the fisherman's body had washed away on the tide, other men found it many miles down the shore and reported it to master E'mat. Everyone assumed he had met with robbers."

"So I am evil, for I have killed a man and lied about it with my silence. Am I not evil?" Nada seemed somehow relieved to have finally unburdened herself of this secret.

Nada's face looked expectantly at her mistress. She no longer had the look of a dam about to burst, she reminded Batshua of a dog that had been caught chewing its master's sandals and would now guiltily bear any punishment meted out. She had bared her soul and presumed fair and honest judgment would surely flow as a logical consequence of her trust in Batshua's wisdom. Ah… misguided youth, thought Batshua.

Batshua was thinking more in terms of problem transfer. Nada had a problem, her relief lay in the fact that she had transferred it to her mistress for judgment, a responsibility clearly belonging to God alone. That thought inspired her with wisdom above her own expectations! Perhaps God had a plan in all of this.

Batshua began carefully, "Nada, before I answer you, let me suggest that perhaps God himself may have already provided an answer."

"I do not understand."

"I know that we both just experienced that moment of utter, blissful peace soon after my husband left us alone here. I know you felt it too, you seemed very moved." Batshua's tone searched Nada for affirmation.

Nada's face returned to the pleasant serenity of the recent experience re-flooded her heart. "Yes. Yes, I did."

"I have rarely experienced such moments, but I have come to know such moments as 'the caress of God's hand'. During those moments of serenity, I know I am held in the very hand of God my Creator, that all is well, that I am loved and at peace. I treasure those moments, they fill me with courage and hope! It is as if God is holding me, his child, very close to himself and saying, 'I delight in you!' That is why I think God has given you an answer already. He is saying that he delights in you. Your past was washed away with the tide, Nada."

"Yes, I see." She smiled, somewhat hopefully. "That is how I wish to feel. But tell me, why does God not hold us in his hand like that always? I experience such moments of dread, fear and doubt that almost make me despair! My heart yearns to be held by God's hand forever! I wish for those moments to last all of my lifetime!"

"Ah! I have wished for that as well. But if God always held us so, would we not be but his pets? We are his children, not his pets. God desires that we grow and behave as human beings whom he loves and wants to see mature and grow. We are not God's mere playthings, we are not his pets."

Illumination dawned on Nada's face like the morning sun, "Oh! I see it! So God will inspire us now and then so we do not despair, but if he always held us in his hand, we would not be free, we would no longer be human because to be human is to be free!"

Batshua eyed Nada suspiciously, "Have you been receiving private philosophy lessons from A'dab without my being aware? You sound just like him!" They both laughed.

Then Batshua turned serious, "Nada I do not have a complete answer for you. But I can tell you that I do not think you are evil, nor do I believe God thinks you are evil. If you had killed that fisherman without feeling any regret, fear, loss or remorse, perhaps I would judge you differently, but I see that you have a heart that is honest and true."

Batshua paused for thought, then continued, "Let me say this however, I do believe that the 'caress of God's hand' portends difficult days ahead for us, because in my experience, God always braces me before a storm. I have an uneasy feeling about the days ahead, it is a nameless fear. We must be wary and strong."

This new thought filled Nada with a strange resolve. "I will be as strong as God enables, mistress Batshua. After all, I am 'Nada the Knife'!" They laughed again, the guilt of Nada's confession tempered slightly by the most common of all human defenses: humor.

"Nada, just how skilled are you with knives? I have seen some evidence, the trick with the pear, and the amazing way Omar's blade came alive in your hands that day in Tariq. You are very impressive. Tell me more, you may have a skill that is useful."

"Honestly, ma'am, I do not know for I always practiced alone. The other workers at the fish-cutting tables marveled at the speed and quality of my work, none were better though many were stronger. As far as other skills with a knife, am I wise to say that against an opponent who does not know I am armed, I am extremely skillful."

That, thought Batshua, was a frighteningly wise deduction from one so young! "I want you to keep your skills secret and I will provide time and opportunity for you to practice. Perhaps some time with Omar will be in order. He is the only other one in the household who has witnessed your skill."

At the mention of Omar, Nada blushed, to Batshua's delight. She had plans for those two.

"And now, since you have shared a secret with me, I believe it is appropriate that I share something with you, my young handmaiden." Nada sat up straighter to show her mistress she respected the importance of the moment.

Batshua stared long and hard into Nada's eyes, she seemed to be making up her mind. "My husband A'dab has ten children, seven wonderful sons and three beautiful daughters... I... have none."

Nada stared, blinking without comprehension.

"God has kept my womb closed. I am barren. A'dab's first wife bore him six fine children, then died of childbed fever after the seventh. Three others were born to concubines who have since been provided lands of their own. A'dab never sees them, they live quiet, comfortable lives in distant parts of Edom."

Nada asked, "What was master A'dab's first wife like?"

"I never met her, but I understand she was a wonderful woman, A'dab still grieves for her." Batshua paused, lost in thought. She seemed at a loss how to proceed with her story.

"How did you meet master A'dab?" prompted Nada.

"It was during one of his business trips, after the year of customary mourning for his wife. That is to say, we met *formally* after that year at my homeland in Egypt. I had reached the age of majority, fifteen, and my father knew A'dab through his father. The families seized the opportunity and arranged our marriage, but God had more of a hand in that than our families." Batshua smiled broadly. "A'dab and I had met several times during the prior year on his trips and by then we were deeply in love." Batshua's smile looked like an impish young girl's. It made Nada laugh.

Batshua turned serious and continued her story, "I became pregnant shortly after we wed, but I could not carry the child full term. Since then, God has not favored me with another child. I fear that my marriage to A'dab is not complete unless I am blessed by a child of my own."

"But... but master A'dab loves you! It is obvious to anyone who sees him!" Nada was astonished.

"Yes, Nada. And I do so love him, but God's will is God's will. I have not known the joy of bearing a child to my husband's knee. I have not been so blessed these twenty years, though A'dab and I pray daily for God's will."

Now it was Nada's turn to hold her mistress's hands in her own. "I am so sorry, mistress Batshua. How can it be that this is not known to all in the household?"

"It is known to all. That is not the secret. My secret is my bitterness. It is like a live thing growing within me. The yearning for a child is so strong that I fear it will break my spirit in two! I fear that this bitterness will consume my soul and turn me against my husband and my God! I am fighting this battle within my soul but I fear I am losing the fight. I gather children around me whom I love in hope that my bitterness of soul will be mended by love for others. Indeed, my joy in discovering you has been a very healing balm, but the darkness in my heart is still creeping in. I feel judged by God and rejected by my husband even though I know that neither is true. My head and my heart are at war with my soul! This inner war is going to destroy me!" Now it was Batshua's face that looked to be a dam about to burst.

Nada threw her arms around her mistress and allowed her to weep. Her instincts were correct. Crying cured nothing, but it did provide a temporary decompression of emotion. Batshua cried for a long time.

Finally, when her weeping ebbed, Nada spoke softly, "I am only a foolish child, but my former mistress Leah seemed to be a wise woman. She taught me another name for God that maybe you have not heard."

"Oh?" Internally, Batshua felt slightly foolish, and awkward, using her young handmaiden as she did now — she should be confessing all this to a priest, not a child. Nevertheless, Nada seemed able to bear this burden. Batshua promised herself she would not lean on Nada like this again.

"She was very sick of a disease that caused her bones to become brittle and break. I know it caused her a great deal of pain even to walk, but she walked down to the beach that day the fisherman attacked me and even ran to me when she heard my call. I asked her how she could do all that with her body in such pain. She said it was because her God gave her the strength, he is 'El Shaddai', 'God all Sufficient'."

Batshua pulled a wisp of hair out of her handmaiden's face and smiled. "Nada, you are indeed a gift to me."

Nada raised one eyebrow at her mistress and grinned impishly, "A gift?! I thought master A'dab said I was to be paid!"

Batshua sat back on her heels in stunned surprise, then both women erupted in laughter and hugs.

-:--o--:-

Batshua stood in sudden decision. "Nada, stand up." She withdrew the earring her husband had given to her earlier. The loop looked strong and stiff but Batshua bent one end apart easily to reveal an inner pin.

"I see that your ear was pierced at one time, the opening is still there."

"Yes, mistress Leah pierced the ears of all her slaves and made us keep a piece of wood in the opening until it healed. I never understood why. She died before I ever found out what she intended."

"No matter now. This is for you, it is the symbol of your fealty to me." She pressed the ring snuggly into place. "Is that too tight?"

Nada wiggled her head, the ring dangled on her ear lobe. It was a delightful feeling for her, the loop felt strangely heavy, but comfortable. She felt very elegant. "It is fine. What does 'fealty' mean?"

"It means you have sworn an oath to be loyal to me as a bond-servant."

"In that case, the ring fits very well indeed!" Nada smiled.

"Good. Do you have the gold bar with you, the one you showed me on the caravan ride to Hareb?"

"Yes…" Nada sounded hesitant.

"Come with me, I have an idea I want to explain." Batshua led the way down the circular stairs.

As they descended the stairs, Batshua outlined her plans to her handmaiden and confidant. "We will be leaving on a long journey in a few weeks. Omar will accompany us, Negasi will lead the caravan as usual." Batshua could almost feel a warm glow emitting from Nada when she mentioned Omar. *"Batshua, you jaded old match-maker!"* she thought smugly to herself.

"Will master A'dab be coming?"

"Not this time. He has business down south, we are heading north on a tour of our herds. A'dab is stopping by our eldest son's home. His son is inviting all his brothers and sisters to his birthday celebration."

They were nearing the bottom of the stairs, much to Nada's relief. Her fear of heights had given her great angst near the top. "Both you and master A'dab will be joining your son at his birthday celebration, yes?"

Nada felt Batshua tense, "No. The children enjoy their celebrations best without their parents' company." Nada was only fourteen, nearly fifteen, but her imagination needed no nudging.

Batshua led Nada from the base of the stairs around to the opposite side of the massive wooden tower. She moved a small settee aside to reveal what appeared to be the stump of an old branch that had once grown from the gigantic tree used to construct the tower. Casually glancing around to be sure they were alone, she instructed Nada to help her pull on the stump. It pulled out revealing a small compartment within.

"The craftsman who built the tower showed this secret to me. He is dead, so only you, A'dab and I know of it. Give me your gold bar, it will be safer here."

Nada reluctantly removed the leather strap from its snug place around her thigh. She had grown so accustomed to its presence she rarely noticed it. Batshua placed the bar and its leather container elbow-deep in the secret chamber. When she withdrew her hand, it contained something else which she held out to Nada.

"What do you think of this? You may find it more useful than gold… for now." Batshua wore a sly smile.

Nada's eyes flared wide. Her mistress held a small, double-edged dagger of such fine craftsmanship it must be worth a king's ransom! She accepted it with her right hand, the hilt seemed to slide into her fingers as if its maker had measured it specifically for her. The six-inch blade blended into the hilt smoothly, making the blade and hilt the same thickness with no protruding edges. The hilt had only small scalloping to give fingers a grip but otherwise from end to end, the knife was thin, smooth and strong. This dagger was perfectly balanced for throwing, extremely strong and tapered for stabbing and double-edged for slashing. It was also designed to be incredibly easy to conceal – an assassin's weapon!

Automatically, she tossed it hand to hand and flipped it somersault fashion once, twice in each hand to her mistress's amazement. The blade and hilt danced a sparkling fire in the garden's soft light.

"Madam Batshua, this is a wondrous blade, I have never beheld its like! What metal is this? And what fashions the handle? It is a thing of rare beauty and so perfectly balanced! It fits my hand as if each was made for the other!" Nada's enthusiasm was unrestrained.

"The metal is called 'iron'. The secret of its making is known to but a few and none in these lands. The handle is from the tooth of beast you have never seen, an elephant's tusk. An Egyptian noble presented it to my husband and he gave it to me. I have no skill in its use as a weapon nor am I so inclined to merely adorn myself with such a deadly bauble. Here…" She reached into the hidden chamber again to bring out a wide leather belt inlaid with finely tooled designs. The belt was tapered to be easily wrapped about the waist, but had broad ends three inches wide.

"Look!" She took the dagger from Nada to insert it into a hidden slot behind one of the broad ends of the belt. She wrapped the belt around herself as a sash, the wide part holding the dagger dangling loosely at her thigh.

"If you wear the belt thusly, the dagger is completely hidden. The design is very clever. The weight and width of the leather completely conceals it because the other end of the belt is counterweighted. I would like you to have this, so that no one else may know that there is a young woman with me who is armed and skilled with a blade. I shall let Omar and only Omar know of our secret. I want you to teach your skills to him, and he has skills that you may learn as well."

Batshua had not taken her eyes off her handmaiden as she spoke. Nada looked very serious, her eyes distant, lost in thought. "Nada, I know I am asking much of you. Do you accept this responsibility? I am asking something more of you than just handmaiden. Omar is my bodyguard, but you will become my secret guard. Do you think you can do it?"

Nada's eyes refocused into her mistress's. "Yes."

"You seem very sure. Tell me what you are thinking."

Nada took a deep breath, "When I killed the fisherman, blood splattered from his throat onto mine. The touch of his blood affected me horribly. I thought I would choke and die before I could crawl away and breathe again. My hands were also stained with his blood. I washed them again and again for many months. I did not think my hands would ever feel clean.

"Mistress Leah saw me washing at the beach, she said she knew a cure. She gave me a plant, she called 'hyssop'. She said that if I prayed and asked God to clean my hands with the hyssop, he would.

She asked God to clean my hands once and for all, then she brushed my hands with the branch. It was like a miracle!"

"Your mistress Leah was a wise woman."

"Many of the other girls complained about her, but I did not. The work was hard, but I was not mistreated by mistress Leah."

"So Nada, you can hold this dagger with clean hands?"

"That is what I was pondering, madam Batshua. I do not know what actions would make me feel unclean. When I held your knife, my hands felt alive and acted once again as if they had a mind of their own! I liked that feeling but it frightened me because that is how my hand moved against the fisherman."

"I understand that. So what is your conclusion?"

"I think…" Nada paused to frame her words carefully, "I think that if I am attacked again, perhaps my hand may hesitate." Then Nada looked straight into Batshua's eyes with an assurance that made Batshua's skin ripple with emotion. "But if you are attacked, the dagger in my hand would fly to your aid with a life of its own. Of this I am sure."

Batshua handed the belt to Nada but held the weapon between them. Nada looked into her mistress's face to find an expression of utter fierceness and determination. She could not believe it possible that Batshua's beautiful eyes could suddenly become that of a warrior's. She spoke evenly, but her words bore deep into Nada's soul, "Protect me as I protect my husband and all of House Hareb. Swear it."

"I swear it. With all my heart and my very soul, God as my witness." Nada spoke without blinking.

Batshua's visage relaxed, she released the belt and knife to her handmaiden who donned it in resolute silence. Batshua returned the secret door to its place, the pair left the enclosure to find Omar.

-:--O--:-

10

Conspiracy

"There are those who rebel against the light,
who do not know its ways
or stay in its paths.
For all of them, midnight is their morning;
they make friends with the terrors of darkness."

The Book of Job 24:13;17

-:--o--:-

Harun looked to Almaqah, the moon-god of his people and wondered if his god gazed down with favor upon this night's gathering. Almaqah's full brightness made it more likely that Harun could see assassins hiding in the shadows -- he felt sure there would be more than one.

He knew that he cared less for his god than his distant moon-god cared for him. Yet he prayed for his god's indulgence anyway and cursed himself a fool for praying. Harun did not truly believe the moon was a god, but he knew of no other and at least this was a god he could see.

For Harun to consider the bidding of some god-forsaken foreign priest and the whore he called 'wife', flared his instincts with a primal fear he could not name. Suspicion clenched his teeth and soured his stomach as he urged his mount closer toward a darkened mound of stone where the silhouetted figures of a man and woman stood motionless in the moonlight. The silvery glow of Almaqah drew strange shadows this night; darkness crept at the edge of his visage as if demons stalked his path. Even as he clutched his sword's hilt, he felt as if its metallic strength would melt away by the cold sweat of his own hand.

Harun had smelled the stench of fear in men before battle, but this was not a battle! How could it be that the air around this rock stank of fear and death?! If he could sense the fear of his brothers-at-arms, could they also be alerted to his own? He would show no weakness! Harun swallowed drily and handed his horse's reins to an armor-bearer. As agreed, he walked the final few dozen feet to their meeting place on legs growing weaker with every step. At last he stood before the priest and his woman. He nodded a greeting, theirs but a shadow's flicker in reply.

"Welcome, friend. Be at ease." The priest's predatory smile denied his words. Moonlight glinted on wide set eyes buried within his cowl.

Harun spoke abruptly, "Let me see your face, priest. I am here to listen to your words, but I will not hear lies. A man's face speaks the truth even when his mouth lies."

"Ah, truth. Truth is elusive." He tossed his head arrogantly, the cowl slipped away to reveal an intensely lurid expression framed in a horror of facial tattoos that wrenched Harun's gut. The priest's face made Harun wish he had not asked for the cowl to be removed.

"I am Harun Al-Rashad." He gestured toward his men below. "I have forty men with me, if any are with you, they are well hidden for you seem completely unguarded." He looked casually around the small hillock with casual contempt and smiled evilly at the priest's foolish vulnerability. His fear abated as he assured himself he was in a strong bartering position with an obviously naïve opponent.

"I am Ba'al-Hanni." He lowered his head and stared at Harun through his eyebrows. "Why do you believe I am unguarded?"

Harun cocked his head to one side and thought of the riches he could extract from this deal. The priest had hinted at a job that required his band of thieves and he would be paid well for his services. This fool would be a push-over, he would demand a high price!

"Is that your bodyguard, master Ba'al-Hanni?" He gestured at the woman with his chin. Insulting the priest would teach him who was the master here -- it was Harun!

"That is a fine horse you have, master Harun." Ba'al-Hanni stared directly at Harun, ignoring his insult.

"Yes. One of the best in Edom." Harun was a bit wary at this sudden change of subject.

"From here, he looks unhealthy to me. I believe you shall have to borrow another mount from one of your men, unless you desire to walk back to your camp." Ba'al-Hanni had not removed his deadly glare from Harun, nor had he even blinked.

Suddenly a horse screamed from below and there was a great commotion and shouting from among Harun's men.

Ba'al-Hanni growled a warning at Harun, "Do not move!" Harun's air of superiority vanished, he began to sweat.

"A'jal! What is going on down there!" He yelled at his armor-bearer without taking his eyes off Ba'al-Hanni.

The horse stopped its screaming, but snorted wildly. Harun heard its panicked attempts to breathe. The commotion quieted, but Harun distinctly heard a muffled thump as his horse collapsed to the ground.

"A'jal! Speak!"

The reply sounded incredulous, "Your horse, sire! It was bitten by a snake, an adder I think. I am sorry sire, your horse is dead."

Ba'al-Hanni abruptly sat and smiled warmly at Harun. "Please be seated my good friend, your concerns about my safety are very touching. As you can see, I am well guarded." He gestured at Harun,

"Truly, sit down before you fall down. We have business to conclude, we shall not be long."

Harun sat so hard he nearly bruised his buttocks. His legs no longer had the strength to hold him. Who was this man and what powers did he command?!

"Harun!" A'jal's voice called from below, "Harun! What shall we do?"

Ba'al-Hanni gestured with his open hand, giving Harun permission to speak. Harun's did not take his eyes off Ba'al-Hanni, his voice sounded somewhat hoarse, "You are a fool, A'jal! I am busy, do not interrupt me again!" Ba'al-Hanni smiled wickedly in approval.

"I shall be brief, Harun. I require the services of you and your men for a simple task of robbery. It should not be too difficult for you, but it may require that you hire a few more than your current rag-tag crew of forty thieves. You are to steal the oxen and donkey herds of A'dab Ben Hareb, the Emir of Edom. I would suggest that you acquire sufficient herdsman to handle the cattle after you have captured them. I suspect your men are rather good thieves but they are probably inept cattlemen. Be certain to hire sufficient herdsmen to do the job." Ba'al-Hanni began to pick at his fingernail casually as if he had asked Harun to fetch a loaf of bread.

"Are you mad?!" Harun exploded. "I have heard of this man! He has a thousand oxen and hundreds of donkeys, they are guarded by nearly a hundred men, well-trained in the arts of war. I could not steal them with four hundred men! Even if I could pull it off, why would I!? There would be no profit to split among so large a raid."

Ba'al-Hanni's tone turned sweetly venomous, "I will warn you once." He looked significantly at Harun, "My sanity is not in question and these lands are full of thieves. Speak more respectfully to me or I shall find new robbers to do my bidding. You are about to become rich beyond your wildest dreams."

Ba'al-Hanni paused and looked deep into Harun's eyes with a look so cold and sinister, it made Harun's skin crawl. Harun actually

suppressed a shudder. He asked Harun, "Would you rather be rich...
or dead? I am growing impatient with your indecision." Ba'al-Hanni
looked down casually at his hands and continued to pick at something
under his fingernail.

Harun was sweating again. He dared not take his eyes off
Ba'al-Hanni, but he was certain there were snake-like movements in the
moonlit shadows just out of sight to his left and right. What was this
man's power?! He decided he had best play along, "How shall I
accomplish this thievery, master Ba'al-Hanni?"

"Better. I like your attitude." Ba'al-Hanni was smiling warmly
again. "When you attack, A'dab's herds will be unguarded. You will
have to deal only with the tenders and herdsman. Leave none alive. Do
as you wish with the cattle, they are not my concern. You are to strike
during the second full moon of summer, is that clear?"

"I will do as you say. Second full moon of summer." Harun
wanted to get away from this man, he was insane! They both stood to
strike hands, sealing the deal.

Ba'al-Hanni tossed Harun a small leather bag. He trapped it
against his belly with one hand. Harun noticed the bag's heft – perhaps
a full pound. "That is your down payment. If your raid is successful,
your final payment will be more gold than you can carry in both arms.
We shall meet in at the temple of Ba'al in Tariq on the autumnal
equinox. Do not be late."

Harun repeated the directions, "The temple of Ba'al, autumnal
equinox, yes."

"One thing more Harun," Ba'al-Hanni was staring at Harun
from under his eyebrows again. "If you think you can agree to this now
only to back out later, you are gravely mistaken. I have eyes and ears
throughout this land. If you do not keep your word, I will find you.
Your fate will be worse than that of your horse. You should watch
where you step, my friend, there may be an adder at your feet."

Harun automatically looked down around his feet, to find
nothing. Fooled! When he looked up, Ba'al-Hanni was gone! How?!

His woman was left standing there shrugging in a way that communicated almost comically, *"I do not know how he does that."*

She sidled over to Harun sensuously to stroke his face and smile suggestively. "My name is Boshet and I am the snake at your feet my husband warned you about." She purred and let her hand slip slowly from Harun's face as she slithered away into the darkness.

-:--O--:-

"That went well, I think." Boshet mused to Ba'al-Hanni when they met at the next day's camp. She was munching on a fruit, he gnawed on a chunk of meat as usual.

"Yes, I think so too. What did you say to him after I left?"

"I told him I was the adder at his feet you meant to warn him about. I do not think he was amused, but I saw in his eyes that he desires me."

"Excellent! That may be useful. In your opinion, do you think he will follow through?"

"Hmmm…" Boshet found Ba'al-Hanni's question curiously respectful. She had not considered that he would request anything information from her; hitherto his attitude had been one of abrupt command. "You offended his pride and I believe you frightened him spitless. I could smell his fear. It is possible he pissed himself at one point. In my opinion he will follow through to salvage his pride and prove to himself and to his men that he is not afraid of you or of the task."

Ba'al-Hanni glanced up at Boshet. His eyes beheld her with a look of surprised respect. "Well spoken."

"How did you manage that trick with his horse and those snakes?" She asked nonchalantly, but she was more than a little curious. The dead horse and shadows of shakes crawling around their hillock had frightened her nearly as much as Harun.

Ba'al-Hanni tossed the tattered bone contemptuously into the pile of others. "It was not a trick." He looked askance at Boshet to note her reaction. She looked sidelong at him and her body involuntarily leaned away from him.

"Do not ask how deep the well unless you intend to drink it dry." He quipped ominously and began to chew into another roasted goat leg.

Boshet scowled in thought, "*I guess that means I should mind my own business.*"

"Where to next?" she asked.

"Many days ride from here. Enjoy today's rest for the road ahead is long, hot and dry." He threw down the other bone, burped loudly and stomped off to his tent.

To her surprise and relief, Ba'al-Hanni did not want her for sex. She guessed that Ba'al-Hanni was a manipulator and knew Boshet to be cut from similar cloth. Insulating himself from her primary avenue of manipulation prevented her from misappropriating skills he intended to be used against his enemies. Manipulators knew how to not to be manipulated.

Ba'al-Hanni had also tightly controlled her alcohol. Her few days of withdrawal had been torture! At first she found all this to be a relief because she was finally sober and alone with her thoughts for the first time in ten years. The bad part about being sober and alone with her thoughts was that Boshet did not like her thoughts.

She longed for a jug of wine or an anonymous man that she could use to numb her mind again. Instead, she kept thinking about escape and about what an evil man with whom she had become entangled.

He was a player who could not be played, but surely he must have a weakness she could exploit. The tiger in her soul hungered to be free, hunting on its own in the wilds. But it was as if the tiger in her soul wore a collar, bound to a new master's beck and call – performing on cue without the wit to act on its own. Boshet detested her life with Ba'al-Hanni. For now she swallowed her anger and waited in hateful sullenness, searching for a chance to spring upon her captor in vengeance.

-:--o--:-

Three weeks later, Boshet was ready to kill herself from boredom. Her howdah had become a prison. It rocked her into a semi-stupor during the day as her stupid camel plodded its thirty mile daily grind through the desert heat. There was no relief at night because the cramped and stuffy daytime howdah turned into her claustrophobic nighttime tent. The howdah was too small, the cushions too stiff, it stank of her own dried sweat and camel spittle.

Listless days blended into sleepless nights as they alternated traveling days and nights, balancing speed and weather conditions. She slept while the howdah-oven desiccated her body all day and stared unblinking all through the starry nights with no one to talk to and unable to sleep. She became so time-confused she could not tell if a week had passed or a month. There was nothing to eat but dried meat, nothing to drink but tepid water. She wanted to scream!

Just before Boshet decided she would voluntarily surrender to the insanity crawling its way into her mind like sand sifting and grinding into the roots of her hair and begin to call down curses upon Ba'al-Hanni and her camel for ignoring her, the desert and sky for their endless boring featurelessness and the briny water that failed to slake her thirst and all the stringy dried meat stuck between her teeth which she could not remove no matter how she picked at it --- they reached Babylon and the Great Kingdom of Mari, Green Jewel of the Euphrates.

The caravan had just reached the summit of a long dune, the wind whipping yet more sand off its crest into her eyes when Boshet beheld a sight in the valley beyond that was far more beautiful than any of her dreams.

The valley contained a wide brown river running a meandering course from west to east, each bank lined in verdant greenery. A huge city circled by thirty-foot walls lay nestled in the center of groomed fields that splayed out into the fertile valley. An inner wall bounded dozens of tall white spires surrounded by hundreds of lesser structures, each glaringly white against the green palms and ferns growing along the busy streets. And grass! There was grass waving in the gentle breeze. Moist zephyrs carried the exotic scents to her nostrils and she inhaled, deeply refreshed.

Boshet sat up straight on her platform, pulled back the curtain of her howdah and stared awestruck at the panorama. In the line of camels ahead, Ba'al-Hanni pulled aside and waited until Boshet caught up. He rode beside her and watched proudly as Boshet admired the city.

"My second home. What do you think?" he asked, sounding almost human.

Her discomforts forgotten, in fact, her hatred for Ba'al-Hanni temporarily abandoned in the wash of excitement flowing through her, Boshet was exuberant, "It is so beautiful! Words fail me. What is this place?"

Ba'al-Hanni face broke into an uncomplicated smile. Boshet was taken aback. He seemed to have lost some of his demonic appearance despite his facial tattoos. "I grew up here." He sounded almost whimsical. "The region is Babylon, the home of the Chaldeans. This is the Kingdom of Mari. It is a most impressive place, yes?"

"Yes indeed, most impressive. You grew up here?" she asked. It was difficult to think of Ba'al-Hanni as a boy or as having been someone that a mother once loved.

"Yes, from the time I was a youth of around ten until I had acquired my second wife on my twenty-first birthday. But my memory may have faded in the sun." He spoke as if Boshet had asked him what he had for dinner yesterday and was casually declining to recall something so inconsequential. Boshet noted the complete lack of emotion. She decided to risk a slightly more probing question.

"Will I have the opportunity to meet your wives?"

Ba'al-Hanni turned to stare at her but the focus of his eyes went past and through her to some place on the horizon behind her. It spooked her thoroughly.

"No." He replied tonelessly. His tattoos seemed to converge and darken again on his face. The demon-look had returned as he stared at and through her. Boshet wondered if there was any humanity actually left in him.

The camels had picked up their pace, sensing the water ahead and perhaps anticipating the prolonged rest. Dogs from the city began to bark in the distance, breaking Ba'al-Hanni's reverie.

His smile was back, Boshet decided it must be an extremely rehearsed one for she could not tell the difference from this one and the smile she thought had been genuine. Somehow she knew he was disingenuous now.

"We will have two days to refresh ourselves before my business in Mari commences. Our time here will put your lying skills to a worthy test. You may find Mari to be an interesting place. It is a city run mostly by women and... clay tablets." He laughed and waited until he was sure he had her full attention.

He continued, "I have more influence than power in this city, which you will see for yourself in the next few weeks. Words are binding here, so the fewer words you speak, the longer you may live. The people of Mari are not fools. They have a nasty habit of beheading liars and thieves." Boshet nodded understanding, but internally she was confused and terrified.

"What is our business here?" asked Boshet, searching for some clue to her role.

"Thievery and deception." He said with a jackal-like grin.

Dropping that bit of information like a rock in her wine cup, he clucked his tongue to urge his camel back toward the front.

-:--o--:-

During the two days of promised recuperation from the long journey, Boshet discovered a few of her advantages and several deficits as she compared herself to the Chaldean women. One thing became clear: Ba'al-Hanni intended her mostly for display purposes. He had meant it when he said to speak as little as possible. The women of Mari were intelligent and educated, they could actually read and write!

But Boshet soon realized she was intended to be an object of jealousy. Compared to even the fairest of Mari's jaded and aged aristocracy, Boshet was a stunningly beautiful creature and in the glowing prime of youth. As she followed Ba'al-Hanni to his business meetings, she exuded natural feminine grace. Her allure dripped from her like sweet, slippery honey all around her husband so that no one could conduct business in his presence without being distracted by his beautiful, seductive wife.

Ba'al-Hanni was very pleased, for all he wanted from Boshet was distraction while he bartered and traded with his adversaries. She latched onto her role with instinctive enthusiasm.

Her boss's words were hardly analyzed for nuances of deception. Boshet merely moved in a provocative yawn or shifted her thighs beside him to watch in amusement as his opponent's eyes shifted from business analysis to sexual fantasy. The tactic worked even if Ba'al-Hanni's negotiator was one of the city's female administrators. Feminine disgust and jealousy are as distracting as masculine fantasies. Boshet enjoyed playing each one without adding a word to the conversation.

Two weeks of this and Boshet was growing bored. She had barely listened to anything Ba'al-Hanni had been saying – something about camels in El'Hajar, but he finally concluded. "You are good." he said at last, "You are very good. Our business here is complete."

"We are leaving then?" Boshet was disappointed, this place was extremely comfortable. She did not realize how backward and rough her homeland had been. The Babylonians were so advanced and civilized; the people of Tariq seemed primitive by comparison. She had seen wonders…

"Yes, the final pieces are nearly in place. We must talk." He led her into a garden between the two walls of the city. They had often passed by it on their way to the inner residences during the past two weeks. Boshet had noted its groomed beauty with longing.

"You like this place, yes?" Ba'al-Hanni walked beside her slowly, his hands clasped behind his back. It occurred to Boshet that this was the first time they had ever been alone together. Even on that first day in the temple, they had been within mere yards of other prostitutes in the adjoining chambers. The garden was a place of peace and solitude, it seemed to wrap her in serenity.

"Mari? It is the most wonderful city I could imagine! I would never tire of its beauty."

"I mean this garden, what do you think of it?"

"Oh, the garden is like a piece of heaven. Does the city's king maintain it for the people?"

Ba'al-Hanni smiled. "No. It is a private garden. It belongs to I'sin al-Ur a former resident of the city who departed his homeland shortly after his wives and children were murdered during King Hammurabi's attack upon it some years ago. There are few left who remember this man. I hear he became a wandering priest, and now travels the land to and fro, seeking revenge for his misfortunes."

Boshet stopped dead in her tracks to stare at Ba'al-Hanni. "This is your garden. You are I'sin al-Ur."

"You are good. You are very good." He continued to walk, eyes unfocused on the horizon.

"What is the manner of your revenge? King Hammurabi is dead and so are most of his sons, is that not so? I have heard the women of the city speak of this." Boshet had learned much with her ears open and mouth shut these past two weeks.

"I seek to destroy the one named A'dab Ben Hareb, the Emir of Edom! I shall make him suffer as no man has ever suffered and you are going to help me!" Ba'al-Hanni's voice began to take on the gravelly, rock-slide tone that Boshet feared. He saw the panic in her eyes and immediately regained control.

"As payment, I will give you this garden. It will be your land to do with as you wish. I have no further need of it." Boshet was so stunned she could not breathe, but... how could she trust this volatile and treacherous man?! She needed more information.

"You are most generous, master Ba'al-Hanni," she hoped he did not see through her duplicitous effort to calm his temper with sycophantic over-politeness, "I will do as I must. But tell me again, who is A'dab Ben Hareb? Why do you wish to destroy him and how will it be done? I may need to know about my role if I am to assist you."

"Bah!" Ba'al-Hanni turned back to his slow stroll, but his hands were now clenched tightly behind his back and his chin jutted angrily forward.

"A'dab Ben Hareb is my cousin. My father, his father were brothers. Half-brothers, actually. A'dab inherited his vast lands in Edom. My father bequeathed a pittance to me here in Babylon. Through toil, conquest and blood, I built an empire only to have it all stolen from me by Hammurabi's sons. When I requested aid from A'dab, my request fell on deaf ears. For that he will suffer as no man has ever suffered."

"Oh." Some instinct triggered a memory deep within Boshet. She risked a question, knowing anything she asked could bring the tip of Ba'al-Hanni's sword to her throat as easily as it had come to the waterman Aqil that first day in camp.

"Have you considered contacting your brother A'dab? Perhaps he will share…"

Ba'al-Hanni turned and spit viciously into Boshet's face. "Fool!" He seemed to grow bigger as he loomed over her cowering figure. The claw tattoo on his face darkened ominously as he shouted her down. "His father and my father may be brothers, but his god and my god are NOT brothers!" He slapped her face. She fell to her knees as he continued to shout.

"He claims his god to be lord of the heavens. Hah! My god is lord of the sky, earth, beast and pestilence! He believes his god protects him, but I shall prove that he is false! We shall see whose god is god!" As Ba'al-Hanni yelled down, Boshet felt the very ground beneath her begin to tremble. His shadow blotted out the sun making her feel a sudden chill.

Ba'al-Hanni whipped his robe aside in a quick turn to stomp away toward the city. "Follow me!" he shouted as he strode away.

Boshet wiped the spittle from her face onto the grass with her hands, then ran almost tripping to catch up. A thought raced through her mind, "*Run away!*" But she stifled it, where could she run?!

He slowed, allowing her to catch up. He placed his arm gently around her shoulder. Boshet trembled against his side, not knowing what violence could be coming next. Instead, his smile was back as if they had just enjoyed a pleasant walk through the Mari City botanic terraces. He used a corner of his robe to wipe the remaining spittle and tears from her eyes and cheeks.

"I am sorry I frightened you, I get carried away sometimes." He sounded as if he was apologizing to a dog he had overly chastised for some small offense. "Come with me, we have one more piece of business to handle in the city, then I shall give you instructions for the next part of your journey. We are about to part company, news that I am sure will not displease you." He smiled gently and led her to a scribe's dwelling Boshet recognized.

-:--o--:-

"...to be deeded in perpetuity to the bearer of this ring, duly witnessed..." As the scribed intoned the markings he had just completed, Ba'al-Hanni removed an ornate signet ring from his hand and pressed its design into the scribe's mud pallet next to the scribe's cuneiform inscriptions. He handed the ring to Boshet along with a golden chain so it could be worn around her neck.

"The land is deeded to the ring, don't lose the ring or you lose the land, understood?" Boshet nodded in bewilderment. This had been a very strange morning.

"Scribe! One more thing to witness, if you please." He turned formally to Boshet and grasped both of her shoulders in his hands.

"Boshet of Tariq, wife of Ba'al-Hanni, servant of almighty Ba'al: I divorce thee, I divorce thee, I divorce thee." Then he made a spitting motion into her face but nothing came out but air. "I already spit in your face once today, I think we can dispense with that part." He smiled. Turning to the scribe, "Scribe, please add a note that the holder of the deed is a free woman of Tariq." Boshet's could not believe what he had just done. She did not know what to feel. She wanted to shout for joy, but any emotion in front of Ba'al-Hanni was dangerous. She restrained herself, but she felt like dancing for joy -- she was free at last!

Ba'al-Hanni, in his typically brutal fashion, spoiled the moment. He put the chain around Boshet's neck and held it with the ring in his hand under her chin, "Be sure to do everything I require of you, my beauty, lest this gold chain become a choker." He let it fall against her chest with a laugh.

After preparations for the caravan were completed, Boshet fell into an emotionally exhausted sleep on her howdah until they stopped several hours outside the city. To her surprise, Ba'al-Hanni had split the caravan, assigning drivers and the twin servant women to her. He filled her with instructions, made her repeat them several times, then took off to the west while she angled southwest toward their rendezvous in Ba'al-Bek on her own.

On her own! Boshet thrilled to the thought! The tiger in her soul was out of its cage at last.

Or so she thought.

11

Premonitions

"When I think my bed will comfort me
and my couch will ease my complaint,
even then you frighten me with dreams
and terrify me with visions."

The Book of Job 7:13-14

-:--o--:-

Nada moved from the general servant's quarters into a large, comfortable room just outside her mistress's suites. Upon hearing this news, her friend and kinsman Frayda smothered her with effusive praise. For weeks, Nada was the subject of every conversation among the servant girls. Her elevated status was very much envied. Everyone picked at Frayda for any bit of information possible. As kin to the mistress's handmaiden, Frayda discovered an elevated status that she played to full advantage.

Nada's new room was twelve foot square with a narrow window. The curtained door emptied to a short hallway leading directly to Batshua's room in one direction and the general servant's courtyard where she had quartered with Frayda some distance in the other.

Nada found she no longer needed Omar or the night watchman to awaken her because an annoying bird would chirp obnoxiously from her windowsill each morning. But this morning something else startled her into alertness – her mistress was struggling to breathe! She grabbed a lantern and ran to her aid.

Batshua was having a bad dream. She writhed in her sleep, legs twitching as if running from some horror. Nada whispered loudly, "Mistress! Are you alright?"

Batshua sat upright, unseeing and uncomprehending in her semi-sleeping state. She stared in stark terror at Nada's lantern before wilting into tears. Nada set down her lamp and ran to comfort her.

"I am alright, it was just a dream." Batshua was still panting heavily.

"When I was a small child, my aunt told me that if you spoke the dream, you denied it's power…"

Batshua recovered quickly. "No, I'm fine. Really, it's alright now."

Nada would not be put off so easily. She was beginning to understand her mistress and had learned where a few of the secret doors of her soul where hidden. She withdrew a step. "Ah, you are wise not to speak of your fears. We do not need this…" and blew out her lamp, leaving them in near total darkness. Waning moonlight seeped through a narrow window to bounce off the far wall. Bedroom windows were very narrow to frustrate intruders.

Batshua inhaled sharply, "Don't!" She realized her nightmare fears were still with her as she struggled to control her panic. Then they saw a light coming toward them in the hall and realized it was Omar.

"Omar?!" She called, her voice tremulous.

"It is I, yes. I heard voices. Are you alright ma'am?" Omar was all business.

"Yes, of course. Nada and I are having a little chat. Light her lamp, since you are here, and do not wake the rest of the house." Omar obeyed then quietly withdrew to ponder the silliness of women who chatted in darkened rooms during the third watch.

Once Omar was out of earshot, Batshua scolded her handmaiden, "Alright Nada, you have made your point. I do not enjoy

being shown to be the fool I am. Even though I am the fool I am."
Neither of them laughed out loud at Batshua's convoluted self-
assessment, but their stomach muscles constricted just a little so that a
whisper of laughter escaped their nostrils. It was the only stress relief
they allowed themselves under the circumstances.

Nada had set the lamp on the carpet between them. The flame
had steadied and so had Batshua's resolve.

"My dream was terrible. I stood atop my watchtower and saw
a black cloud coming from the north only it was not a cloud –
hundreds of black birds with enormous talons were converging to
attack our lands. They destroyed everything and began to come after
me in the tower, ripping at my face and head. I ran down the steps as
the tower swayed back and forth, it fell with a crash just as I reached
the floor. My life was spared but all the beauty of my garden and home
was destroyed."

"That is a terrible dream. No wonder you were so frightened."

"I believe that sometimes dreams can be warnings from God.
Do you believe that, Nada?"

"I do not know. I do not like to think that our God would
frighten us with bad dreams."

"But what if something very bad was about to happen and
God used a dream to prepare us, to get us thinking correctly about
ourselves and life. We would be better prepared for the bad thing
when it happens. The bad dream would be a gift in that case, don't you
think?"

"That is wise, ma'am, yes." Nada looked very troubled and
introspective.

"You look very disturbed, Nada. You should not worry. I do
not think my dreams predict the future, so do not let my dark visions
cast a shadow in your mind."

Nada's mouth drew back into a grim line. "It is not your dream alone that concerns me, mistress. I thought I could be brave to comfort you as you have done to me many times. But when you described your vision… I have also had dreams of dark birds clawing at my head. I did not wish to trouble you with my fears."

The women stared at each other for a long time. Batshua reached a conclusion, "Perhaps this is indeed a warning from God then. We must not fear. But neither should we sit idly while disaster overtakes us!"

"But what can we do?!" Nada was nearly fully grown but her people tended to be small. As she sat before her mistress in the candlelight, she looked delicate and childlike. There was nothing in her demeanor that seemed like 'Nada the Knife' who had pledged to defend her mistress a few weeks earlier.

But the candle's flame had ignited resoluteness in Batshua's eyes. The red light of pre-dawn cast its diffuse glow across the room, spreading the promise of morning and spring. She stood and offered her hand to Nada to stand with her, leading her to the window that overlooked the valley and river below.

"A'dab has traveled west on business, he will be away until mid-summer at least. We will go forward with my plans to do a bit of traveling ourselves." She pondered her decision as she stared into the valley. Finally, she nodded to herself – the mental picture of her plans completely formed in her mind. She turned from the window and looked Nada up and down.

"Nada, what progress have you made in your practice sessions with Omar?" She eyed the dagger-belt dangling from Nada's night silks. Since giving her the belt a few weeks prior, she had never seen her without that belt. She apparently slept with it! Batshua grinned to herself in approval.

Nada did not wonder about this quick change of subject, she was getting used to her boss's swift decision-making. Once Batshua made up her mind, Nada usually had to keep running mentally and physically to keep apace. "Omar is very strong but... clumsy. Clumsy compared to me, that is." She corrected her assessment of Omar quickly. "I am weak compared to him of course, but we are working on each other's weaknesses with our weapon practices. I believe his handling of blades has grown more graceful compared to other men and I have increased my strength compared to other women."

"Has anyone seen you practicing?"

"No, we have been careful to keep our skills secret."

"Excellent. A thief may get past the guards of a dining room but be stopped by a mere butter knife if the thief does not know the butter knife has been sharpened, yes?!" They laughed.

"Nada, tell Omar we will leave on our journey to inspect our lands. He is to let Negasi know that he will be granted his wish to join the camel races. I also wish to pass by the shepherd's areas. I am always thrilled to see them at lambing season. I believe we will bypass my son's birthday preparations. Clear so far?"

"Yes, ma'am. This sounds very exciting!" Nada was jumping up and down on the inside.

"We shall see." Actually, Batshua was jumping up and down on the inside too. There was nothing better to cure fear than *action*! Her peripatetic lifestyle was probably a symptom of her gnawing fears.

"One more thing, Nada. For this trip, I believe you should have a companion other than your jaded old mistress. Besides, if you have someone attending to your own daily needs, you will be more able to attend to mine. I want you to select a girl from among the servants. Do you have someone in mind?" Batshua's eyes glinted in delight for she already suspected Nada's choice.

"Oh! I would bring Frayda, my kinsman. Would you approve of Frayda?" If Nada's shadow had been free to act in accordance with what was going on inside her mind, the shadow would have been turning somersaults and pumping its arms hooting, Yes! Yes! Yes!

"The girl you choose will be your *servant*. As your kinsman, will Frayda be willing to submit herself to you as *servant*?"

Nada's shadow stopped hooting and became quite serious.

"I see." Many thoughts flashed through Nada's mind instantly. "I will explain the situation to Frayda to see if she will accept. I wish to honor her as you have honored me, to lift her up as you have lifted me up. But I do not know Frayda very well. Perhaps she will not respect the honor given to her. She may try to take advantage of her new position. That would be disrespectful and a disappointment. We will face hardships on the journey. If she remains a true servant in spite of the hardships, perhaps she will prove her mettle and we will become trusted friends."

"Or not." Batshua finished for Nada. She marveled at her handmaiden's wisdom. "But well said. I will leave the decision with you. If Frayda becomes a problem on this trip, she will be your responsibility. I will advise, but any decision regarding her will rest with you." Nada nodded solemnly.

"We leave in three days. What are we waiting for?! Let us begin our preparations!"

-:--o--:-

Hareb became abuzz with activity, once news spread of the Emira's excursion. Negasi looked almost clownish as he worked with a constant, ivory-toothed grin throughout the preparation days. He bragged ebulliently of his prior camel races and spoke so eloquently of the superior qualities of his dark-haired racing camel that Nada scowled in bewilderment when she finally saw the ugly thing. Its hide was matted with great tuffs of hair from the spring molt. She indulged Negasi by affirming the beast's beauty, but inwardly she cringed. He seemed infatuated with the horrid, stinking mass of slobbering lips and knobby knees. Men! She thought, only men could care for such a foul-looking animal.

Frayda accepted the invitation without listening fully to all the conditions. Nada found herself swept up into the older and larger girl's arms in a most undignified manner to be spun around while Frayda cried, "Thank you! Thank you! Thank you! I will be so happy to accompany the Emira on her journey! Thank you! Thank you! Thank you! Oh Nada, you are such a wonderful friend!"

Nada pondered this reaction and worried that perhaps something would have to be done soon to curb Frayda's enthusiasm and to let her know that she was accompanying the Emira's *handmaiden*, not the Emira. Time enough for that in the days ahead. For now, she was very glad to have a girl her own age along. She had spent so much time alone or in the company of older women. Nada had not lived a normal child's life. Frayda's girlishness seemed as foreign to her as Negasi's camel.

As it turned out, Frayda's immaturity caused her to stumble headlong into the hornet's nest of Batshua's ire, giving the Emira a perfect opportunity to set Frayda in her place. The day of their departure had arrived. Most of the town had turned out to wish them well on their journey, lining up along the main thoroughfare toward the city gates. Over forty camels, about half loaded with supplies, lined the road. Many of the men were also leading horses. Goats were tethered in the train as well. Their route would take them along well-watered springs and rivers toward the northeast. Spirits soared with high adventure and it was in this spirit that Frayda spied Batshua. She broke rank and ran to her, stopping before her feet to bow low.

"Emira Batshua! May I say I am so very grateful to accompany you on your journey! It is an extremely great honor!" She craned her neck upward from her bowed posture with great expectation of a blessing from the Emira.

To Frayda's surprise, Batshua looked down her nose at this grand gesture, ignoring Frayda entirely. "Nada!" She called out sharply.

Nada came running quickly, "Yes ma'am?"

"Who is this?" Gesturing imperiously at the bowing and confused-looking Frayda.

"Ma'am, this Frayda. She is… my servant… and a surviving kinsman from my homeland." Nada was being extremely formal, she recognized her mistress's tone.

"Inform your servant that she is accompanying *you* on this journey and that she is here due to *your* good graces, not mine. I expect you to keep better track of your servants in the future, is that clear?"

"Yes ma'am. My apologies ma'am, I am sure Frayda meant no disrespect."

"No need to apologize for the ignorance of your servants. But it is your duty to instruct them in proper manners. See to it." Nada glanced down and saw either sweat or tears, perhaps both, dripping into the dust from Frayda's bowed face.

"I will, ma'am. Thank you. Come, Frayda." Nada spoke gently. They turned back toward their place in the caravan line.

Batshua called softly, "Nada…" Nada looked back over her shoulder to catch her boss's sly wink and smile. She smiled and nodded thanks, then continued to her place in line. She felt assured she would have a more teachable servant, who could perhaps learn to become a loyal friend.

-:--o--:-

A ram's horn sounded. The commotion died away suddenly as if the horn absorbed all conversation in a spreading circle throughout the crowded thoroughfare. Only the animals held no regard for the stillness of the mid-morning. The horn sounded again, but this time in the baleful rhythm of a monotone song. As the last notes of the horn echoed its lonely melody from the distant hills, a voice Nada recognized as Negasi began to sing. His singing carried the words clearly but they were in a language Nada did not recognize. Still, the exotic melody moved her with its strange emotional quality. It filled her heart with yearning and yet a sense of place and rightness with the world. She found her heart filled with a nameless longing.

At last the song ended. The entire company mounted, camels and horses alike complaining or snorting in their eagerness to be away. Leather creaked and gravel crunched beneath hooves, the morning air vibrant with the sounds of humans and animals preparing to leave the safety of hearth and home.

Batshua sat aloft in a beautifully draped howdah. She had provided a smaller version for her handmaiden's camel behind her. Frayda received an umbrella-like shade which was far better than many of the other servants in the group. Once the line stood ready, Negasi shouted a command and they peeled away in grand procession.

Unbidden, the silence of the crowd broke like a wave on the beach, crashing into a noisy cheer. Everyone smiled and waved as they passed, wishing them safe journey and God's blessing.

Batshua's body rippled effortlessly with the sauntering rhythm of her camel. Her regal head rested lightly and relaxed, she looked as if she was born to ride. The Emira of Edom knew how to travel in style.

-:--o--:-

The same could not be said of Frayda. She and camels were not meant for each other. She had ridden into Hareb on a donkey cart, the ride out of Hareb was her first on a camel. Camels do not stride like horses with their right front leg moving in unison with their left rear leg, then alternating. Instead they step with both right legs, then both left legs. This causes the camel to sway much like the deck of a ship in heavy seas. If that is not bad enough on the stomach, camels froth at the mouth and swing their long necks around to deploy their spittle in the direction of an unwary rider. If the rider happens to be a young teenage girl with a sensitive inner ear and delicate constitution, the environment atop a camel is not conducive to one's appetite or to holding down one's lunch.

A half hour into the trip, Frayda vomited wildly all over the wide expanse of her camel's left side. It complained bitterly, much to the amusement of its handler whose raucous laughter declared his lack of empathy toward the frailty of women. The only assistance he offered: aim her next load of puke on the other side for balance. Funny, very funny, thought Frayda as she considered several vile assassination plots against her camel handler and wished her arms were long enough to choke the foul beast beneath her.

Caravans do not stop for vomiting servant girls. Frayda's desperate heaves erupted every fifteen or twenty minutes for the next three hours until she finally fell forward into an exhausted sleep. They stopped mid-afternoon near a small stream. Frayda collapsed into unconsciousness under a palm, her handler took the camel downstream to wash the filth from it.

"What can I do for Frayda? She is miserable." Nada was serving fruit to Batshua. She felt very concerned for her friend.

"No one ever died from such a sickness, although she can die from lack of water. Make sure she has plenty to drink. Force it on her. Today will be hard, tomorrow should be better, you will see. She will adapt, most do." Batshua seemed heartless, but somehow Nada thought her tone carried enough information to convey concern. She ached for her friend, but she could do little for her.

As they mounted for the next leg of the journey, Nada observed Frayda's handler whisper something in her ear. He handed her a water bag too. Frayda kept sipping the water and sat very erect, her head held in a relaxed sway much like Batshua's. She vomited only once before they made camp for the night. Evidently the handler gave her a riding tip that worked.

"How are you doing, Frayda? Ready to eat something?" Nada thought she looked a little less green.

"I think so, thanks. Let me serve you first." She stood on wobbly legs, sat abruptly and vainly tried to stand again.

Nada smiled. "You are going to stay put for now. I will be right back." She returned with two plates heaped with fruit and dried meat along with a pot steaming with tea. "You may be in better shape for your duties tomorrow."

Frayda began to cry. "I am such a failure. I have failed you twice today."

Nada felt she needed to keep the upper hand, yet still encourage her servant-friend. "Frayda, today is not quite over. If you eat your food and do not throw it up, I will count today as a success." Frayda looked up surprised with her mouth full of meat.

"Blethew!" She poked the meat into her mouth with her finger causing both of them to laugh. "I am sorry! I mean, 'Bless you!'"

Frayda felt much better with a full stomach. She cleaned up after their meal then knelt in front of Nada. "I have a serious question for you."

Nada was using a sprig of dried grass to clean away meat wedged between her teeth. "Ask anything."

"What do I call you? I mean, I feel so ashamed for the way I behaved with mistress Batshua. She really put me in my place. I have thought much about it and I want to understand my place... my role as your servant. I do not know how I should address you."

Nada smiled, she remembered having the same conversation with Batshua not long ago. "You are right, it is an important question. I am the Emira's handmaiden. If you dishonor me, you dishonor her. To show respect to me also shows respect to her. But at the same time, you are my friend and kinsman, Frayda. I have not forgotten that, nor will I ever forget that."

"I am older than you, and... well, larger than you. But since you have arrived in Hareb, you seem much older than me and there is something about you that does not seem small. You have strength that I do not. I am glad to be called your friend." She bowed her head. "And I am proud to be called your servant as well."

Nada smiled, very much relieved. "We agree that our situation is complex. It is complex, but not bad, yes?"

Frayda smiled and looked around. "Truly. It is not bad, not bad at all."

"I shall ask the advice of the Emira regarding what is the best title for me. That way, we will both know."

After the meal, Frayda assisted Nada with her bedding, saw to her own and slept better than she had slept in a very long time.

-:--o--:-

At breakfast, Batshua told Nada she could expect the other household servants to refer to her as 'my lady'. This new appellation made Nada feel very strange. She expressed her misgivings as Batshua planned for their arrival at the camel races day after tomorrow.

"Nada, you must learn to accept the title without taking it personally."

"'Not take it personally?' I do not understand."

"Well, have you ever been cursed or called a bad name?"

Nada laughed. "Of course! I have been called by the names of most all the vile creatures that creep on the earth and cursed by all the gods in the heavens above and hells below." Batshua joined Nada in her laughter. It caused her to spill tea into her lap which only amplified their fun. Nada was such a refreshing joy, thought Batshua, she had a way with words.

"Did you take those curses personally?"

"Hmmm…" Nada considered her response thoughtfully. "It hurt for a long time, I thought maybe the words were true, that I was a vile thing and under a curse of the gods. But one Sabbath morning on the beach in Aqaba, the water was very, very still. I saw my own reflection in the water with crystal sand sparkling in the sunlight all around it. It was a very beautiful thing. It seemed that I heard a voice whispering to me, 'This is how I see you.' I knew then that I am created by God and part of God's creation. I felt honored to be part of the world that God created all around me. So from that day on, I brushed all the curses away."

Batshua smiled warmly at her handmaiden. "That is very wise, my lady." Nada blushed at her mistress's use of her title, "Allow me to add to your wisdom." Nada shifted to signal she was paying attention. "As the handmaiden of the Emira of Edom, you will receive blessings and titles such as 'my lady'. They will feel good, unlike the curses. But just like the curses, you will be tempted to take the blessings personally, just as you were tempted to accept the curses personally. Do not succumb to that temptation Nada, for the blessings of men will corrupt your soul as surely as their curses. Remember that you are still Nada, a woman created by God and part of his creation. That is sufficient for your soul. Do not let your soul feed on either blessings or curses. Rather, allow your soul to feed on the certainty that you are blessed by God."

Nada pondered Batshua's words with awed expression. She realized her mouth had gone slack so she closed it with a quick swallow.

"Thank you, madam Batshua. I praise God that he has brought me to you."

Batshua's smile broadened. "Well said, Nada. That is exactly the right response. Praise belongs to God, but I certainly don't mind receiving some gratitude for sharing some of his wisdom. We will both need his wisdom as we navigate the temptations of the crowds gathering at El'Hajar two days hence." Batshua's warning sounded ominous.

Just then Omar arrived with a platter containing something sizzling. Batshua looked delighted. "Ah! Thank you Omar! Nada, would you care to share an egg? Omar there is plenty for you as well, why not stay to join us?"

Nada exclaimed, "I am so hungry from the journey, I think I could eat a dozen eggs!" Batshua and Omar shared a secretive glance as he set the platter down.

"Are you sure, Nada? Perhaps you want to share just this one egg between the three of us." Batshua gestured to the platter. It contained an enormous fried egg spilling over its edges. The plate was deliciously garnished with spices, rice and fruit.

Nada's eyes flared in stunned surprise. Batshua and Omar burst into laughter. Withdrawing humor from the bank of Nada's inexperience was a source of much entertainment for them and, they thought, academically fruitful for her. Nada sighed at them in frustration – teaching! Batshua was always teaching and her instruction took a bite out of Nada's pride every time. Ah well, an education is expensive no matter how you get it.

"You are playing a trick on me!" she protested. "I know you! No fowl on earth has an egg of this size! The cook has created a trick for your amusement!" She tore off a piece and stuffed it into her mouth haughtily.

Batshua's smile was pure evil delight. "Eat your egg, my lady. The day after tomorrow, we shall see if you eat your words with as much gusto." She shared a laugh with Omar again, but Nada's looked told them she was far too knowledgeable of the world to be fooled by the likes of them!

The following night, two small, darkly clad 'thieves' crept into the sleeping area of Batshua and Omar. They carried oblong shapes they had obtained in secret from the camp's cook. Unnoticed, the pair placed their prizes into the foot of their enemies' bedding and stole away into the darkness.

As the tired camp repaired to bed, Batshua felt the cool hard mass against her feet and yelped! She felt around for it and discovered: an ostrich egg! *"That little imp!"* She thought, but smiled wickedly as she considered, *"Game on!"* The giant egg spent the night resting securely next to her lamp.

Omar was not so fortunate. He sat down at the foot of his bed to remove his sandals. Both his bedding and language required extensive cleanup. He spent an uncomfortable night under the stars, sans bedding, thinking dark thoughts of revenge against a diminutive, mischievous servant girl. He could not decide if he wanted strangle or hug her. *"Nada,"* he thought, *"If you ever become my wife, I shall have you cooking eggs for the rest of your life!"* The thought pleased him greatly as he drifted off to sleep under a shooting star.

-:--o--:-

12

Enemies

"The caravans of Tema look for water,
the traveling merchants of Sheba look in hope.
They are distressed, because they had been confident;
they arrive there, only to be disappointed.
Now you too have proved to be of no help;
you see something dreadful and are afraid."

The Book of Job 6:19-21

-:--o--:-

Omar woke the girls early. He held one hand innocently behind his back, but he made no attempt to hide the smirk on his face.

"Good morning, milady." He intoned, bowing with grandiose formality to Nada. She eyed him suspiciously, well-aware that revenge would be forthcoming due to their clandestine escapades the prior evening. "I bring a gift from madam Batshua along with instructions for the day. You are to dress in your finest sartorial splendor as we ride into El'Hajar later this morning. Madam Batshua wants to afford her people a grand entrance." Omar turned to go.

Nada prompted, "Omar, aren't you forgetting something?"

"Hmmm? Oh! The gift! Of course, my mistake, milady." He unfurled a giant ostrich plume and presented it to Nada with a flourish.

Nada had no idea what it was. To her eyes, it looked like the strangest fern she had ever seen. Its leaves were so soft and elegant...

Omar held it so close that a breeze caused it to tickle her nose. Indeed, the plume tickled all her senses delightfully. "What is it?"

"Why... it is a feather... from a giant bird that does not exist." He paused and eyed Nada significantly, "But according to legend, it lays its eggs in the bedrolls of unwary travelers." He squinted his eyes sarcastically and strode away. Nada's attempt to feign innocence failed artlessly. She feared (rightly) that she and Frayda had begun a war against an exceedingly superior opponent.

"*This will be an interesting day!*" she thought. She used the feather to tickle Frayda who was still lazily asleep. "C'mon, you! I am hungry and you were supposed to be serving me breakfast by now!" Frayda leaped to obey. She halted abruptly at the strange thing in her lady's hand. She explained, "It is a gift and a message: they know." Both girls giggled with conspiracy as they considered their next move.

-:--o--:-

The corners of Batshua's howdah were decorated with ostrich plumes this morning. Nada likewise fastened the feather to her howdah. Fortunately, Frayda's camel-sickness had abated during their second day on the road. Both girls were dressed in silky flowing pants that gathered at the ankles. They also wore long linen tunics that ended high on their thighs. The tunics provided modesty yet freedom of movement and coolness in the late spring warmth.

When Omar saw them, he said they looked like a couple of genies and asked if they knew any magic. Nada did not answer, but her look was sufficiently glaring to let Omar know that if she had known any spells, she would have used one to make him disappear in a puff of black smoke. He laughed and trotted away on a glistening black stallion. Nada realized that her intense dislike of Omar was turning out to be a great deal of fun. Her emotions churned in strange ways as she watched the handsome mounted man cantor gracefully away.

-:--o--:-

Batshua dropped out of line parallel to Nada. The path had become grassy and strewn with shrubs and other vegetation. They were obviously climbing into a mountainous region. The sun was very warm, but the air contained occasional breezes with a surprising chill. The caravan plodded upward into the foothills.

Isn't this is a beautiful country?!" Batshua called across the eight to ten feet separating their mounts.

"Yes, very beautiful. What is the name of this land?"

"The people of this region call it, Ba'al-Bek. They named it after their pagan god, Ba'al. It means 'river of god', for the city of our destination overlooks a river in the Bekaa Valley. My husband installed a local governor and renamed the city to El'Hajar which means 'God's Stone'. Some of the people here do not care much for the new name, others are learning to accept it as they discover the ways of Elohim are wiser than the ways of Ba'al."

"If master A'dab is ruler of this city, why does he not command that all the city bow to Elohim? Why does he allow those who believe in other gods to live in his city?"

Batshua smiled. "Nada, what color is the sky." Nada winced. She had not meant to elicit another philosophy lesson so early in the morning.

"The sky is blue. Everyone knows this."

"The sky is often red at nightfall and early dawn, is it not? And is not the sky black at night?"

"Yes, but…"

"The sky is blue because the light of the Creator makes it blue, is that not correct?"

"I have learned that to be so, yes. When there are clouds hiding the light of the sun, the sky is no longer blue. And when the light of the sun disappears behind the edge of the earth, the sky is no longer blue. It is the light of the sun that turns the sky blue, yes."

"The followers of Ba'al are like a people who say the sky is not blue, Nada. They say the sky is black. They deny the Creator, they deny that God created all things. Instead, they worship power and seek power by worshipping created things instead of the Creator. So, in a way, they say the sky is black, because they oppose the light that comes from God the Creator."

"I think I see…"

"Nada, if I commanded you to believe that the sky is black, would you start believing that the sky is black?"

"I would pretend to believe it, because you are my mistress. But I could not believe it in my heart, because I know the sky is blue."

"It is the same with the followers of Ba'al. Unless they come to understand the light of God for themselves, they will continue to believe the sky is black no matter who tells them the sky is blue."

Nada began to understand what her mistress was trying to say. "That is sad."

"Yes. And it is also dangerous which is what I came back here to talk to you about."

Nada turned sideways on her platform. She knew her boss was about to say something very important.

"You and Frayda will be on your own much of the time in the city. I will ask Omar to keep an eye on you of course. But this place is not the same as the town around our household. You must be very cautious. There are people here who would do you harm."

"I will be cautious, ma'am." Nada promised.

Batshua's face was grim, but then it softened. "I do not mean to fill you with dread. There may be enemies lurking in El'Hajar, but we have many friends there too. We shall go about our business with caution, but our caution will not prevent us from having a bit of fun as well." She cocked an eyebrow at Nada impishly and signaled her camel's handler to return to its place in line. An hour later, after a climbing through a steep mountain pass, the city came into view across the breadth of a sloping plateau.

-:--o--:-

Nada pulled back her howdah's curtains to get a better view. After they had passed beyond a gated log palisade, dogs and children ran out along the road to meet them. A scrawny brown dog barked along, nipping at her mount's heels. Her camel barely noticed, or so she thought. It continued chewing its cud methodically, but surely it must eventually run out of patience with the annoying mutt. As she wondered about this, she saw her camel turn its long neck around to bend low and spit a large wad of thick juice directly into the dog's face. It ran off to the city shaking its head, much to the amusement of the handler.

A young boy of five or six ran along the train holding up two apples. He yelled "Hungry? Hungry? Buy for a pittance!" He was extremely dirty and dressed in rags. When he approached Nada's camel handler, he shoved the boy hard into the ditch where he sat crying in a most woebegone manner. Nada felt he looked to be the most pitiful of all creatures on earth.

She caught his eye and held out her hand. He brightened instantly and threw an apple to her, she caught it deftly. The boy looked up with a strange gesture, reaching toward her and rubbing his thumb across his fingers. Oh! He wanted payment. Thinking desperately, she found a small silk hanky about six inches square in a corner of her howdah platform. She balled it up and tossed it. The boy unfurled it with wide eyes and ran off to the city without a backward glance.

Nada bit into her apple and spit it out onto the road abruptly, throwing the rest into the bushes. It was full of worms, that treacherous little troll! She looked up when she heard laughter coming from the line ahead. Batshua had watched the entire transaction. Grrrr... sometimes she felt like such a fool in front of her boss.

Batshua called over to her with laughter in her voice, "Welcome to El'Hajar, my lady! The people here have a saying: 'Trust in God, but tie up your camel!' They have been traders for over a thousand years! You just paid that boy a month's wages for a rotten apple. I think he is now your best friend!" She clapped her hands and laughed with glee while Nada pouted, arms crossed. Yes, she had much to learn.

-:--o--:-

The caravan rounded a curve that allowed a panoramic view of the Bekaa Valley to their left. Nada beheld the site in awe. Dotting the green valley were hundreds, no, thousands of camels! Interspersed among them, mostly along the narrow river were perhaps two dozen camps. Each camp displayed a banner of bright colors in differing patterns flowing in the afternoon breeze. A huge pavilion stood on their side of the river. It was nearly hidden from view because of the precipitous steepness of the hillside upon which they now rode. Hundreds of men meandered through the valley performing incomprehensible tasks.

The lane having widened, Batshua moved along side her handmaiden once again. "The men below are preparing for the camel races which commence in a few days. Do not venture there unattended, they are a rough lot."

"I did not think there were so many camels in all the world! Do they all race?"

Batshua laughed, "No, only a few are the racing kind. This is the breeding grounds of my husband's herds. The majority of what you see belong to him."

Nada could not comprehend the wealth of her master and mistress. "The governor of this land cares for all these camels for your husband then?"

Batshua laughed again. "Nada, we are still in the province of Hareb. This land belongs to my husband, so you might say the governor of this land 'belongs' to my husband. We will not be setting foot outside our own lands while on this journey."

Try as she might, Nada could not believe what her mistress had just spoken. To travel nearly four days within one's own backyard! How awesome is that?!

They arrived at a series of wide stone steps leading up to a pillared porch. Nada thought it must be a temple of some sort.

"Ah! Our summer home! We will refresh ourselves and rest this evening. Tomorrow I have a surprise for you and your servant. I think the two of you and perhaps Omar may as well enjoy a bit of racing fun before the real races begin." Nada's eyes begged questions but her mistress would say no more.

-:--o--:-

After breakfast, Nada and Frayda found out where ostrich eggs came from. The actual beast looked much sillier than the grand bird of Nada's imagination. If this was one of God's creations, she felt God must have a sense of humor. It was a very odd thought, to think that God had created such a strange-looking bird! Observing the long neck and knobby legs, she wondered if perhaps God had made it with leftover camel parts. Nothing about the pitiful beast had any virtue worthy of her admiration, save the plume decorating her howdah. She silently apologized to God for her critical thoughts as she inspected his handiwork.

The ostrich farmer was a big-bellied man who could not speak without shouting and laughing. Nada wondered if he ever drank water. She had heard that ale diminished a man's hearing while simultaneously strengthening his vocal chords. This man was the first clear evidence to support that theory.

"Ride, ride! Oh, you must ride my fine birds! For the Emira herself, I charge you nothing, nothing! Ha! Ha! You are my most honored guests! No charge to servants of the Emira! Ride my pets, young ones! Ha! Ha!" If he yelled any louder, the entire town would come running, which in fact they were. His impromptu races were obviously a source of great community entertainment.

Batshua's expression was unreadable except Nada understood her fate to be sealed. This was to be her punishment for the eggs-in-the-bedroll stunt. She bowed to the inevitable and surrendered to bird-justice with resignation.

The farmer selected two ostriches from the corral. He covered their heads in small sacks and brought them to the girls. Nada looked grim, Frayda was in near panic. With the farmer giving boisterous instructions the girls were planted atop the birds with their feet braced around the birds' massive, muscular thighs. They were told to hold tightly onto the leading edges of the bird's wings with both hands. Then they were led to a fenced corridor several hundred feet long. Much to their chagrin, it appeared as though the entire town had spontaneously gathered to watch as two young maidens were sacrificed to the bird-gods.

Batshua and Omar did not help matters. They positioned themselves fifty feet down the course from the starting line and began betting each other in overly loud voices ensuring that Nada and Frayda would hear.

> Omar: "What are their chances, ma'am?"
> Batshua: "Slim to none. You have to stay on the bird to win. I say both will fall before they reach our position."
> Omar: "Are you betting on Nada?"
> Batshua: "No way! I'm betting on the bird."
> Omar: "Frayda's bird looks hungry, don't you think?"
> Batshua: "Yes, now that you mention it, and Frayda looks delicious."
> Omar: "These birds are meat-eaters then, right?"
> Batshua: "We shall see, we shall see."

Nada was not the least bit fooled by their teasing. Her eyes were narrowed, she clenched her legs around the bird firmly. She had no intention of falling off. She could see that the grounds were splattered with bird dung. She gripped her bird's wings with all her strength! Jaw set and jutting forward, she was the perfect image of a bird jockey awaiting the starting call.

Frayda, on the other hand, had gone into a state of primordial, unthinking, fear-induced monomania. *Hold on! Hold on! Hold on! Hold on!* Her ears blocked out any sound, her heart beat so rapidly it fluttered painfully in her chest. She felt herself sliding into unconsciousness when...

"Go!" The farmer pulled the bags off the ostrich heads simultaneously. Both birds jerked forward. Nada's bird pulled out ahead immediately and the crowd began to roar, but then something very strange happened. The sudden movement of Frayda's bird beneath her buttocks jolted her mind free of its stupefaction. Her lungs deflated into a blood-curdling, high-pitched scream.

Unfortunately for poor Frayda, her bird took this as a cue to double its speed. The bird's frenzied running induced a wild state of hysteria within Frayda – she screamed with every breath! This further panicked her bird to even more super-avian velocity. Frayda passed Nada as if her bird was in slow-motion! Frayda's screaming made an odd sound effect on the crowd as the high-pitched girlish scream increased in pitch as she approached, then suddenly lowered in pitch as she and her hyper-kinetic bird swept past. The crowd cheered wildly for this was the best entertainment they had witnessed in months!

Two assistants caught Frayda's bird at the finish line to help her dismount. Frayda did not stop her screaming until both her feet landed solidly in the dust. The sudden stillness was replaced by roaring of the ebullient onlookers. Nada crossed the finish line a full five seconds later.

When Batshua, Omar and the ostrich farmer caught up with them, the farmer was ecstatic.

"Aha! Ha! Ha! Never have I seen my bird run so swiftly! You win because you are a coward! The brave young lady loses because of her bravery! Ha! Ha! You teach old Haran something new! The brave do not always win! Ha! Ha! Here is your prize, young one!" He handed her a brightly colored ostrich plume.

Frayda was an emotional wreck but she accepted the plume tenuously with a trembling hand. She had fear-tears in her eyes, making tracks down her dusty cheeks. The plume had been dyed in blues and reds. It was much bigger than the one Omar had given Nada. Frayda turned to her boss, "My lady?" Nada nodded her approval with a grin. Batshua watched the two with interest. The interaction proved to her that both of them may have just grown an inch.

The crowd dispersed. Many mused aloud that they may copy the young maiden's racing tactic when next they raced on Haran's birds. Screaming like a girl may bring them luck, perhaps a prize. "Don't be foolish Nasir..." one was heard saying, "You will never get your voice that high." "Yes, I can! I will wear a tight belt!" Their conversations drifted away toward town.

"Nada, a word with you..." Batshua gestured with her chin and walked away from the others. Nada followed. "I have business with some people here in El'Hajar. You and your servant need to go to the market to purchase supplies for yourselves. Our next destination is cooler, you may need a blanket and warmer clothing. Shop freely, but do not purchase more than you weigh."

"But madam Batshua! How do I... I mean I have nothing with which to buy..." Nada stammered.

"All the shopkeepers know me. Tell them who you are and that they are to deliver the goods to the household of madam Batshua. They will receive a fair payment. If you see an item that you believe I may not approve, ask them to set it aside for you until we can look at it together. You are to approve or disapprove of Frayda's purchases, I will hold you accountable for whatever she buys in your name."

Nada was very excited but, "This is a great deal of responsibility ma'am. I don't know..."

"Neither do I know, Nada." She smiled at Nada's surprised look. "No one knows if shoulders are ready for responsibility until their shoulders have borne it. I believe you will carry this responsibility well or I would not place it upon you. Now go find Omar. Be certain that the three of you remain in eyesight of each other at all times, understood?"

"Understood, ma'am." Batshua left without another word.

-:--o--:-

Nada found Omar with Frayda. She had stuck her ostrich plume down the back of her tunic and secured it with her sash. It fanned out over her head like a small parasol.

"What do you think?" She twirled around to make the plume flutter. Wearing her feather, the taller girl now looked as if she were the leader of the three. They joked about it in good fun.

Nada laughed, "It's you, Frayda. It's definitely you. Madam Batshua has given us leave to do some shopping. She has pledged Omar as our bodyguard." She cocked an eyebrow playfully at Omar, "I am looking forward to having two servants today."

Omar gave Nada a narrow look, "I can assure you, my lady, that I shall watch over you with the same diligence that I give to our mistress's donkeys." He smiled, *your turn.*

"Donkeys, hmmm?" she turned to Frayda. "Come Frayda, let us see of this donkey-chaser can beat us to the first shop!" she turned and ran pell-mell up the hill toward town, Frayda on her heels leaving Omar trying to catch up. Dressed as he was in leather armor, a sword dangling at his side, sprinting was not an option.

-:--o--:-

The girls didn't intend to outpace Omar. Nada thought he would catch up with them at their first shop, so she browsed their wares. It was leather goods. She had never beheld such fine craftsmanship! There were belts and satchels and leather footgear. Footgear! Didn't madam Batshua say they were heading for colder climes? Nada looked at her bare feet and wondered if she would need warm footwear. She had gone barefoot her entire life. The idea seemed so foreign, but then everything about her new life was foreign.

She picked up a pair of moccasin-like slippers. The shopkeeper leaped to her with effusive praise of their qualities. He held out a pair of pants and a jacket. He urged Nada to try the outfit on over her current silken garments. The items fit perfectly, but Nada felt silly. She felt no need to be dressed so warmly. She decided to set the items aside to ask her boss about it later. The shopkeeper agreed and said he would hold an outfit ready for Frayda as well. They turned the corner outside the confines of the shop nearly running into a very angry Omar.

"Do that again and I shall have your heads!" He was fuming.

"Oh Omar, we did not mean any harm, we're just having a little fun." Nada could not take Omar seriously, he was always teasing her.

"Madam Batshua has warned me to keep you in my eye at all times. Did she not say the same to you?"

"Yes, of course, but…"

"Then that is what we will do, because we respect madam Batshua, correct?"

Nada could not refute Omar, he made a good point. "Yes Omar, I am sorry."

"Alright. No harm done." He seemed mollified. There is a shop ahead that sells woolen wear. You may find clothing there more to your liking.

Nada brightened, "Thank you, lead the way."

They climbed a long stairway and rounded a corner into a courtyard paved with flat stones ringed with upright blocks that looked like granite. The courtyard was perhaps thirty feet in diameter and rimmed with tall hedges blocking all views except a portion of the city and the Hekaa Valley below. It was a beautifully secluded place, Nada wondered idly what the city looked like at night from here. She could imagine campfires and torchlight scattered throughout the valley.

Omar looked sheepish, "I must excuse myself. Do you mind waiting here? I must... relieve myself."

Nada blushed, "Not at all, take your time, this place is lovely." Omar slipped away.

Frayda and Nada stood pondering the sights below when they heard footsteps hustling up the stairs. They thought it must be Omar until they heard female voices.

"Hurry! They are alone!"

Panic flared in Nada, but it was too late. Two women flashed past her, they looked exactly the same, twins!? They ran past her and subdued Frayda who wilted in fright onto her knees. One of the women bent Frayda's arms around viciously behind her back and covered her mouth with her hand to prevent her from calling out. The second, seeing that Frayda was well in hand, started toward Nada.

The world slowed down and time seemed to crawl before Nada's eyes. All her senses flew into hyper-alertness. Instead of fear-induced tunnel vision, her view expanded to take in the whole scene. One attacker was busy with Frayda, the second was coming toward her from about eight feet away. Neither woman appeared to be armed.

She had practiced fighting week after week with Omar. During their exercises, he had often pretended to attack her in exactly the way this woman was approaching her now. Nada's reactions came almost without thought.

Her hand flew to her leather belt and slipped it off in a smooth motion. Instead of running away as the woman expected, Nada surged forward, swinging the belt at her attacker's neck. The belt's heavy end looped around the larger woman's throat. Nada grabbed the free end with her other hand, crossed it around her attacker's head so the belt was looped twice around her neck. She jumped up and past the woman, swinging her legs up and around in a wide arc. Nada's light body swung against the woman's neck bringing her toppling to the stone tiles with Nada landing on her back. She heard the woman's breath escape her lungs in a huffing sound with the force of the impact.

Still holding the two ends of the belt, Nada pressed her advantage with a knee into the woman's spine, pulling up with all her might on the belt and wrapping the two ends around her own left arm. With her right arm, she grabbed a fistful of the now helpless woman's hair, pulled it up hard to face her partner while twisting the belt tight against her throat with her left hand. Her victim began making gurgling noises and tried vainly to reach back at Nada.

"Let her go!" She growled at the woman holding Frayda.

Seeing no response from Frayda's captor, Nada twisted the belt in her left hand harder. Her captive's eyes began to bulge, the gurgling halted as no air was able to get through her windpipe.

Nada did not see Omar arrive at the top of the stairs, but Frayda's captor did and also saw him silently unsheathe his sword. She released Frayda who fell whimpering to the ground. "Come, Frayda." Nada called her friend. Frayda obeyed, staggering. Nada twisted her grip on the belt until she felt the woman's body grow limp, then she released her. She unraveled her belt and slung it around her waist as casually as if she were dressing for dinner. She had not taken her eyes off the other women.

"She will live," pointing her chin at the woman near her feet. "Follow us and you will not." She turned to leave and was shocked to see Omar standing there. His expression was unreadable.

"Take us home, Omar. We are done shopping for today."

-:--O--:-

"Fools!" Boshet was incensed. "I send you to *talk* to the Emira's servants and you *attack* them! Am I surrounded by *IDIOTS?!*" She paced back and forth, trying to think. She did not know how to remedy this situation, but she had to find a way. Arghhh! How could anyone be so *stupid?!*

"I am sorry, mistress." B'jin spoke up. "It was B'jal who thought it best to capture them, to take them somewhere we could, you know, convince them to tell us what we wanted to know."

"Stupid! Stupid, stupid, STUPID!" Boshet was approaching apoplexy. "Is this true, B'jal?! Did you really think you could kidnap the Emira's handmaiden?"

"Well, I..." Whatever she might have said was cut off by Boshet's vicious slap to her face. B'jal dropped to her knees, blood streaming from her mouth and nose.

"SAY NO MORE!" Boshet clearly had reached her limit with these two morons. She considered turning B'jal over for the sport of her guards. She had solved a discipline problem with another of her servants that way. The girl's screams lasted nearly the whole night. No, Boshet still had use for B'jal and B'jin. She was not ready to throw fresh meat to the guards just yet.

"How did two young women defend themselves against you?" She had noticed the bruises on B'jal's neck and face.

"Their guards intervened, we thought they were unguarded." B'jin lied.

"I'm surprised you were not killed outright then. You were supposed to be watching, keeping your eyes open. Have you noticed anything else? Any means by which we can gain an audience with the Emira? Although you and B'jal are twins, you seem to have more intelligence that she."

"I observed something that may be useful. But..."

"Speak of it, I will decide whether or not it is useful." Boshet was very tired of her servant's lack of imagination. Or of their exceedingly stupid imagination!

"As the Emira's caravan came into the city, her handmaiden purchased fruit from a boy beggar. She overpaid by giving him a silk item. He still has it I think. Perhaps you could talk him into a rare case of trader's conscience?"

Boshet smiled. "Very good. Yes. I shall say the boy was in our employ and I cannot sit idly by while servants of the Emira are defrauded. Very good indeed. Fetch the boy at once. And make doubly sure that you are not seen again by anyone in the Emira's household."

"Yes ma'am…" B'jin left.

B'jal looked up at her mistress and grimaced as Boshet removed a camel whip from a hook on the wall. It would be many days before B'jal's face and back healed sufficiently to be seen in public.

-:--o--:-

Batshua was outraged when she heard of the attack. She was intensely curious how Nada was able to defend herself. Omar explained the rigorous routines they had practiced prior to the journey. He praised Nada's natural agility and surprising instincts. Frayda said she had never seen anyone move with such quickness. For her own part, Nada did not remember much of it, she said she only remembered feeling extremely angry that anyone was about to hurt her friend Frayda.

Everyone promised to be more careful.

The camel races were due in two days. Negasi had his entry well-groomed. He felt confident of some prize. Entries from as far away as southern Chaldea had come to compete in the yearly event. A'dab's vast herds were the talk of every campfire.

The day before races officially began, madam Batshua held court in a vast chamber of her home. Nada had been told that her earlier assessment had been correct. The home had been a temple prior to her master and mistress taking it over as a residence. Her mistress was seated at the far end of a large hall, her handmaiden sitting next to her on the dais on a chair slightly smaller than her mistress's. Her handmaiden's servant sat on a pillow at her lady's feet. The scene might have been cut from the wall of an Egyptian pharaoh's tomb, which was precisely the effect Batshua hoped to project.

The city folk approached one at a time, presenting their various grievances or concerns regarding land allocations, water rights and on and on. This was usually A'dab's job, but since he was way out west, the responsibility fell to the Emira. Batshua dreaded this work, but she dispensed justice with equity and grace as God gave her wisdom.

Nada was very bored. She spent the hours counting cracks in the tiled floor. With Batshua's teaching, she had learned to count to twenty, she had names for all her fingers and toes now. She smiled inwardly at the thought. She attempted to listen to each of the supplicants bowing before her boss, but they all sound alike after awhile. How did Batshua listen to each one as if she cared? Nada admired her grace and patience.

She had nearly fallen asleep twice, but Frayda nudged her awake. Thank goodness for Frayda! Her curiosity was different from her own, this whole affair seemed to fascinate her endlessly.

A woman and small boy approached. Nada sat up with sudden interest. The boy looked familiar and something about the woman was very different. She was the most beautiful specimen of female beauty Nada had ever seen! Nada was proud of her own mistress's comeliness, but this woman was beautiful in a way quite different than Batshua. Her beauty dripped off her body like a flowing stream, leaving a trail of dazed attention from everyone behind her. Her body rippled in rhythms of sensuality that were dazzlingly provocative. Nada thought she must drive men wild with desire.

The dirty child beside her was a glaring contrast, he looked terrified.

The woman bowed low. Batshua gestured, granting permission to speak her case.

"I am Boshet. In our tongue, my name means 'shameful thing', but I am afraid it is little Jabal here who has done a shameful thing.

Haven't you, Jabal?" She looked down at the boy, expectantly. He nodded slowly in the affirmative. Nada noticed that the woman's voice seemed to drip honey but she felt it carried a poisonous undertone. She could not help but think in terms of how similarly beautiful and lithe were the appearance and movements of a poisonous snake.

"Jabal works in my household picking fruit. I understand that he met your caravan on the way in and attempted to sell fruit to you." Nada remembered her anger at the little urchin, but anger was replaced by pity for the scared little boy standing in front of her today.

"He should not have been selling fruit for one thing and he received overpayment for the second thing. Didn't you, Jabal." Again the boy nodded affirmatively. He looked about to disintegrate into tears any second.

"Is there anything you would like to say, Jabal?" Boshet prompted.

Jabal dug the silk hanky out of a pocket in his raggedy tunic and held it out toward Nada. "Here." He could not look up, his eyes stared blankly on the floor in front of his feet.

Batshua and Nada exchanged looks. "Nada, I think you should make the call on this one." Nada nodded.

She left her chair to kneel before the trembling child. "We made a fair trade. You may keep it."

"No!" Boshet interjected sharply, the sound echoing in the hall. Her abruptness startled everyone, including the boy who could contain his tears no longer. "I mean... I am sorry, I did not mean to speak so sharply. It is just that, well. What would he do with a silk hanky?"

Batshua was scowling at Boshet, bewildered at her reaction. Nada lifted the boy's chin, forcing him to look into the kindness of her eyes. She gathered the hanky into his dirty hands and held it there. "This is yours. Do with is as you wish." The barest of nods moved his face, then he grinned and disappeared out of the temple.

"Well," Boshet declared, "I suppose you have the privilege to spoil my servants... I am only trying to do the right thing."

"Indeed." Batshua felt like saying more but kept it to herself. "Our business here is completed today. Boshet, won't you join us for afternoon tea in say, half an hour? I am in need of fruit supplies for the next part of my journey. We'll meet on the north patio. Ask for Omar, he will guide you."

Boshet seemed surprised and delighted. She bowed and left, or as Nada noted, she *glided* away.

Batshua turned to Nada. "Opinion?"

"I do not trust her. I do not think that boy was her servant. I have never met one, but I think Boshet is a servant of Ba'al."

"Frayda, what is your opinion?" Frayda was taken by surprise, Batshua never spoke directly to her.

"She is very pretty." Nada had observed that Frayda's judgments were accurate and shallow.

"Yes. Yes she is. But I think we have just met our enemy." Batshua stared thoughtfully at the space vacated by Boshet.

"If you think she is the enemy, why did you invite her for tea?" Nada was very confused.

Batshua did not move her head, but her eyes turned into small slits as she cast a beady glance toward Nada. "When the enemy is close enough to shoot you with an arrow, the best tactic is to draw them closer so you can stick'm with a dagger." The proverb shocked Nada and Frayda into scandalized silence. Then they saw Batshua's expression and everyone burst into laughter.

-:--o--:-

Tea time was tense. Boshet was no fruit trader, that much was obvious. Batshua went through the motions and contracted with her to supply several hundred pounds of dried apples for their journey to the pasture lands. Batshua rightly figured that a conniving witch like Boshet would have no trouble securing the shipment within the week before their departure. Boshet was setting up something and Batshua did not have to wait long for her to tip her hand.

"I bring ill tidings, madam Batshua." She looked significantly at the others reclining around the patio, "Ill tidings that should be for your ears only."

"One moment." Batshua whispered to Omar who stood and motioned at Frayda. They left, but Boshet looked curiously at Nada.

Batshua said, "You may continue, my lady Boshet. Nada *is* my eyes and ears."

Boshet clearly did not approve of this scenario, but she continued despite her unspoken objections. "There is a plot afoot against your camel herds here in Ba'al-Bek. I have knowledge that the Chaldeans are planning a large raid on these lands later this summer."

Batshua's expression changed from impatience to disdain. "Interesting. That would require a bit of planning. Chaldea is nearly a three week journey. Why would they bother to come so far for camels?"

"Hammurabi's remaining sons", Boshet said carefully, "require mounts for their wars of conquest. The Kingdom of Mari and its surrounding lands are in chaos."

Batshua asked, "I know of Hammurabi and his rule of Babylon a generation ago. But just why should I believe anything you tell me, Boshet? What evidence do you have that would convince me of your claims?"

"Very little evidence, really. I feel like a traitor, for it is my ex-husband Ba'al-Hanni, a high priest of Ba'al who has conspired with the Chaldeans to carry off the raid. He is the one who has knowledge of your lands and has passed this knowledge on to the Chaldeans."

"That name is unfamiliar to me. You say he is your *ex*-husband?"

"Yes. It shames, me to reveal that I did not please him. I was surprised that he did not have me killed, he is a ruthless man. He abandoned me in the Kingdom of Mari of the Chaldeans. He did not leave me without resources, I have a small company of servants and sufficient silver to buy supplies to reach my home in Tariq. I wonder if my mother is still alive there. I... do not wish to see my father ever again."

Boshet's technique for mixing truth with fiction had served her well in the past. She seemed to be making headway with her current target. "I think you have already figured out that I am acting only as an agent for the fruit seller and not a very good one. Trading fruit is not my primary occupation."

Batshua's smile was difficult to interpret, "And just what is your primary occupation?"

Boshet feigned embarrassment. She was very good at it, she had done many performances like this for her temple clients. She found it excited them. For her current purposes, she hoped her performance would elicit sympathy. "I was shrine prostitute at the temple of Ba'al in Tariq. It was my father's doing. Ba'al-Hanni secured my release, he is a man of great influence." She hung her head as if she expected Batshua to strike it.

"I wondered. The temple of Ba'al is like a festering sore within the city of Tariq, which is itself a broken bone." Batshua said matter-of-factly. She stared at Boshet in thought, closed her eyes, breathed slowly in and then exhaled even more slowly. When she focused on Boshet again, her eyes were full of resolve. For the first time, Boshet lost her look of arrogant confidence.

"I wish you Godspeed on your journey to Tariq. If I may prevail upon you to visit the household of A'dab Ben Hareb within a month's to six week's time, I am sure my husband will want to hear your story firsthand. If you have the means to prove your story, bring proof to Hareb. My husband is a generous man and will reward anyone who warns him of treachery. Be sure of this, Boshet – he is also a just man and deals with treachery swiftly."

"You are most gracious, madam Batshua. I accept your kind invitation and will make every effort pay you a visit." Batshua's warning did not faze her in the least.

Batshua nodded, dismissing Boshet.

"Opinion?" Batshua asked Nada who seemed ready to burst with questions and commentary.

"She is a skillful liar. She mixes truth with lies and stirs it all together." Nada was trying to help.

"Yes. Well said. I do not think even she knows the truth. My instincts tell me that A'dab needs to see her for himself. Perhaps he will unravel the truth from her lies. Perhaps even Boshet herself will come to understand the truth."

"Do you mean that Boshet may come to realize that the sky is blue?"

"You are a very bright young lady." Both laughed, well aware there were enemies amassing outside their gates. And now she had invited an agent of the enemy into House Hareb.

Privately, Batshua dispatched two messengers who would carry news of the Chaldean raid to A'dab with all due haste.

-:--o--:-

"Well done. You are ready for your last task." Ba'al-Hanni seemed pleased with Boshet, but his tone was flat and difficult to interpret. He and Boshet were standing together on the small secluded patio where her twin servants had accosted Batshua's servants. Nearly midnight, the town was asleep. Light from the half-moon lit the patio dimly.

"I do not believe madam Batshua believed a word I said. She is... quite astute. And also a just and noble woman. I have never met anyone like her."

"Bah! She is weak, watch her. She will abandon her husband and bring him to grief. I am going to enjoy watching the pain she will inflict upon him." Ba'al-Hanni seemed very confident of his prediction. For some reason, Boshet found herself hoping he was wrong.

Ba'al-Hanni handed her a sealed leather pouch. "Here. Be extremely careful with this." Even Ba'al-Hanni handled it very gingerly.

"What is it?" Boshet did not want to touch something that even the priest feared.

"It is pain. Pain for A'dab Ben Hareb. Do not worry, it is not deadly. It is a rare poison from the cold lands many months travel northward. If I wanted him dead, I would not be going to half this trouble. I want him to *suffer*."

"What is your plan then?" Boshet was in too deep to back out now, but if there had been a back door, she would have fled long ago.

"Our friend A'dab will be hearing very bad news this year, soon after your visit to him. Your warning of the raid on his camel herds is only intended as a taunt, a tease to make him believe he has a chance to avoid the disaster that is about to befall him. He does not, his doom is already sealed." Ba'al-Hanni could not help himself. He stopped to laugh hideously. Boshet found him completely repugnant.

"What of this?" She held up the leather pouch.

Ba'al-Hanni's eyes flared, "Hold that down, you fool!" He grabbed her arm to force her hand away from their faces. "Do not breathe the dust from the bag or let it touch your skin or you will rue the day you were born!" Now Boshet began to panic.

He continued. Keep this inside another bag which I shall give you. After A'dab receives his bad news, he will mourn his losses. When you find an opportunity, drop its contents into the waters he uses for ritual cleansing. It will be difficult for you to accomplish without being detected. I will leave that to your creativity. Frankly, I do not care if you are caught so long as A'dab uses the waters at least once. Once you have completed this final task, I do not care to see you again. If you do not complete the task, I will know it and you will wish that you had never been born!" Ba'al-Hanni was growling now, "You will beg for me to end your life before I am done with you, do you understand?!"

"Yes. Yes, I understand master Ba'al-Hanni. I will do as you say."

Ba'al-Hanni disappeared into the darkness, leaving Boshet alone on the patio holding the bag of pain.

-:--o--:-

13

Peace

"You will laugh at destruction and famine,
and need not fear the wild animals.
For you will have a covenant with the stones of the field,
and the wild animals will be at peace with you.
You will know that your tent is secure;
you will take stock of your property
and find nothing missing."

The Book of Job 5:22-24

-:--o--:-

The camel races were a huge letdown to Nada. She watched them with her face resting in the palm of her hand. Her cheek pushed into her hand so hard it distorted the corner of her mouth into a clownish caricature of adolescent boredom. She thought camels were boring to ride and even more boring to watch. Nada found Frayda's effervescent enthusiasm for the whole affair mildly irritating.

She did feel bad for Negasi. He won his first heat, but was eliminated in the finals. His prize racing camel was found to be pregnant which disqualified it. Negasi's displeasure with his camel's infidelity was a great source of humor for everyone but himself. He and his love-struck beast would be the butt of some very rough humor for many months to come.

Frayda and Nada were able to complete their shopping without further incident. They each made sure the necessities of nature were completed prior to venturing into the market. Omar turned out to be good company once he decided to stop teasing the girls.

He complimented Nada on her reaction to the attack by the twin women. He said he doubted he would have been so swift. Nada demurred. She said it was Omar's training that had saved them. During one of their colloquies of co-congratulatory conversations, Frayda -- feeling a bit left out -- had asked if she could be trained to defend herself. Both turned instantly with a simultaneous, "No!" It was a funny moment, but their humor was lost on poor Frayda who pouted the rest of the day.

Negasi began packing for the next leg of their journey to El-Gabal, a cooler, hilly country two days ride north. He added another supply camel and found a scruffy-looking mount for himself. He reluctantly decided to leave his pregnant racing camel behind.

-:--O--:-

For many weeks now, Nada and Omar had secreted away from the townships or camps to practice their fighting skills. Now they had Frayda as audience and chaperone. Since Frayda had witnessed Nada's defensive maneuver and had become her servant, Batshua thought it best that she accompany them.

Frayda marveled at Nada as she leaped at Omar, using the weight of her body against his height to topple him. The various moves they invented against each other astonished and delighted her. Frayda thought Nada was too wiry and slender to be beautiful in the same elegant way as madam Batshua or lady Boshet. But still, she admired Nada in much the same way she enjoyed watching a summer storm.

Nada seemed like a force of nature -- she moved with the speed of wind and yet had the grace of a bird landing on a windblown branch. No matter how Omar tossed her about, Nada could roll to her feet prepared for defense! After their hour of practice, the two warriors glistened with sweat and a glow that Frayda recognized as maturing love. She felt no jealousy, only affirmation and the hope that one day she might be so blessed.

-:--O--:-

Batshua had dispatched two riders with an urgent message for her husband. They were to carry word of Boshet's news to A'dab and return to her with his decision regarding redeployment of their guardian forces. Unencumbered by the heavy packs of a normal caravan, the riders would reach House Hareb in half the time it had taken the group to reach El'Hajar. She trusted the riders and she trusted her husband's wisdom, but dark visions in the night continued to rob her of sleep.

Three days after the conclusion of the races, Batshua's caravan left El'Hajar without fanfare and angled toward the northeast.

Batshua's departure from El'Hajar did not go unnoticed.

A cruel smile distorted Ba'al-Hanni's black talon tattoos into a tightening grip of his dark eyes as they watched the dust of Batshua's riders disappear into the hills. All was going according to plan.

-:--O--:-

The group wound its way through the hills. On the morning of the third day, they began climbing slowly through rocky terrain. Nada noticed that an odd sort of quiet settled among them. She was told they would reach the high pasturelands within just a few hours after breaking camp. This information was related in a nearly reverent whisper. The normal clamor seemed to have been dampened by this chilly, dew-sparkled day. Everyone went about their business with a relaxed sense of purpose, speaking minimally.

Two hours later, the camels strained up a narrow pass. Nada felt her camel slipping in its effort, she nearly panicked at the thought of toppling off her platform. She grabbed the howdah's edges as her mount made a few last determined lunges past the crest of the mountain pass.

When she looked up, she had no words for the scene spread in the vast valley below. If beauty can break your heart, then Nada's heart lay in a thousand scattered pieces.

For all her life, Nada's world had been colored in shades of brown -- sand, dirt, muddy rivers and dried grass. Even the bowl of sky above her head always seemed to be muddied with a dusting of desert silt.

The vastness of the pasturelands met her eyes with a crystalline beauty of pure verdant fields back-dropped by white-capped mountains. A huge lake spread in the valley's floor like a giant mirror. Thousands upon thousands of wooly sheep grazed all along the valley with their tiny lambs prancing about in the grass. Batshua turned to her handmaiden with a smile of pure joy.

"This valley is good for the soul. It is full of the blessings of life!" she called. As more of their group crested the rise, they spread themselves along the sloping lea side by side. Nada found herself resisting a wild urge to dismount and run pell-mell through the grass with her arms open wide, she could think of no other way to express her joy. *Sear this vision into my memory, O God, Creator of all good things!* She discovered herself praising the Creator for a job well done. *"You must truly love your children to provide such places for them to dwell."* she thought.

To Nada's surprise, her mistress called to her camel tender, asking to dismount. Nada's tender followed suit as did those of Frayda and Omar. She saw Batshua unlacing her slippers.

"C'mon, Nada! Take off your slippers, let's go barefoot!" Nada complied, scowling with curiosity. What is so special about going barefoot? She walked out to where Batshua was standing. Her bare feet thrilled to the feeling softness of the loamy soil and moist grass laced between her toes! She knew: the pasturelands were pure heaven!

As soon as Nada joined her mistress with Omar and Frayda, she bolted away like a rabbit, "Race you to Serenity Rock!" She called out behind her. She had a lead of at least sixty feet before anyone could react. They gave chase, laughing curses at their mistress's deceptive ways.

Back with the camels, Nada's handler said, "I'll wager tonight's share of ale that lady Nada wins. She is as swift as a wild falcon."

Batshua's handler, a ten year veteran of House Hareb smiled greedily, "No way! My mistress cheats! You watch." They spat in their hands and sealed the deal by slapping the spittle between their palms.

Nada easily caught Batshua and passed her within fifty feet of their goal – a large rock formation high in the valley overlooking the distant lake below. As they neared the rocks, Nada could see a large, flat ledge overshadowed by a natural granite roof.

Batshua suddenly fell to the grass with a stifled cry and began to writhe in pain holding her ankle; "Oh! Oh! My foot, oh! Oh! Oh!" Nada did an immediate about-face, Omar and Frayda also stopped to assist their mistress.

Their sympathy was their undoing. Mistress Batshua leaped to her feet to sprint the few yards to the rock. She stood in triumph as her crew walked slowly toward her, eyes ablaze with scandalous betrayal.

"Now, now, children! All is fair in love and war… and this is a war that I love!"

Nada raised an eyebrow, hands on hips. "You cheated."

Batshua, still a little out of breath, pointed a finger at Nada, "I improvised!"

Omar spoke up, "You should know better than to try beating the mistress at games she invents, Nada. If she can't win with the first set of rules, she invents more suitable ones. It is her game after all."

Nada relaxed. "I see that you are right Omar." She looked askance at her miscreant mistress. "I shall endeavor to invent a game of my own then."

Batshua responded with mock horror, "Ho! Ho! I shall be very careful when I slide my feet into my bedroll tonight."

Nada did her very best to feign the Falsely Accused Innocent, "I can't imagine what you mean! Come, Frayda, let us prepare lunch for our victorious mistress." She held her nose regally nigh as she stomped back toward the supply camel. It is not easy for a featherweight girl to stomp barefooted in high grass and soft loam, but the effort paid off – Batshua's laughter pealed across the valley. She was delighted with her handmaiden's daring sense of humor.

-:--o--:-

The rest of the caravan arrived and everyone ate whatever did not require cooking. Batshua explained the reason she called this place "Serenity Rock". She and her husband A'dab enjoyed camping out here as young lovers early in their marriage. They had given the rock its name after enduring a stormy night huddled within the small protection provided by its jutting stone. When the storm ended that next morning, the valley and they had survived to witness a glorious rainbow, the first Batshua had ever seen. The two of them still occasionally returned to enjoy the peacefulness of the valley.

"A rainbow? What is that?" asked Nada. It was outside her experience.

"It must be seen to be believed. It is as if God has painted the sky. A rainbow represents God's promise that he will not utterly destroy mankind. It means that he has planted his archer's bow in the ground as an everlasting pledge of peace, just as the warriors of old would place their bows in the ground in their oaths to end battle." Batshua explained.

"It sounds beautiful..." Nada said, trying to visualize it, but completely unable. "Does it rain here very much?"

"The rainy season is about over now, the rain will pick up again toward the end of summer. This valley is very fertile, as you can see. House Hareb has around seven thousand sheep and even so, there is no danger of overgrazing."

Try as she might, Nada could not get her mind around a number as big as "seven thousand." Batshua might just as well have said she owned all the sheep on earth.

"Enjoy this land, we will be leaving in three days." Batshua said with some sadness. The peace of Serenity Rock descended on the entire group. Everyone enjoyed their light meal with a sense of relaxed, unhurried stillness.

-:--o--:-

The camp made ready for the final leg of their journey. The shepherd's pens were a three hour ride at the north end of the valley. Batshua pulled Nada away from the group.

"I would share some thoughts with you privately, my young lady." Batshua seemed to be in a strange mood. The earlier lightheartedness of the race to Serenity Rock was gone. She seemed worried.

"What is troubling you, ma'am?" Nada feared that she had stepped over some boundary with her humor and was about to be disciplined. Her stomach tightened in stress for the tongue-lashing she would soon receive.

"I do not know, child. I am experiencing a nameless dread. I suddenly feel as if the mountains around us will soon collapse to crush and suffocate me."

Nada was relieved to know she was not in trouble, but now her tension shifted. She felt her mistress's distress. "What is the source of your fear?"

"I believe lady Boshet's warning has something to do with it. Her lies have some threads of truth, but I cannot discern her plot. I fear that no matter what I do, a great disaster will befall House Hareb. It is a very intense feeling, I feel overwhelmed by it, even in this place of peace." Batshua's eyes had the look of a hunted animal.

"We should return immediately to Hareb then. Master A'dab needs to be warned and you should be with him during a time like this." Nada searched for the right words, she felt that her words were trivial and meaningless.

Batshua stared past Nada, "I love my husband. I honor him above all others. He is my very life."

Something about the way Batshua said the words made Nada believe she was repeating her wedding vows in order to make herself believe them again. She again felt the deeply rooted fear within her boss – a dread that her husband's love was not complete because of his wife's barren womb. Batshua punished herself and would not trust her husband's love, nor God's love. Her ever-growing bitterness was self-perpetuating and self-defeating.

Nada wondered if Batshua even trusted God's wisdom and that thought suddenly reflected into her own life! How could it be that she, Nada, had come to be so trusting of a God who had allowed her to live such a painful childhood? The panic of distrust seized her as it was seizing Batshua until she grabbed hold of herself and thought, *"No! I met God in Aqaba! Or rather, he met me. He is a God who sees me and he can be trusted!"* The memory flooded the void in her faith. She suddenly felt as if Serenity Rock had become a living thing, a cupped hand that was holding her firmly in place.

"Madam Batshua…" Nada broke her mistress's reverie. She looked up, startled.

"Perhaps Serenity Rock is all we need to see of this place. Maybe we should go home now."

Batshua was obviously taken aback by her handmaiden's bold proposal. The Emira was not one to act quite so precipitously. Yet… She stared in thought for a long time.

"You are right!" she said. Her mood lightened as if a sack of wheat had been removed from her shoulders. "We will camp here tonight and return straightway to Hareb on the morrow! Omar!" She instructed him regarding the change of plans. Omar looked surprised, but obeyed. Batshua beamed at Nada.

"This is for the best! I feel it, don't you?" Batshua's resolve to leave for home was firming up.

Nada was not sure why, but she also felt a heavy burden had been lifted from her spirit. "Yes!"

"We will stay the night together on Serenity Rock. Use a few extra blankets for padding. Besides…" she winked at Nada, "I want to keep an eye on you, Omar and Frayda. No mysterious visitations tonight!" Nada managed an innocent look before her boss laughed and sped away to instruct the crew about their return trip.

-:--o--:-

That night, there was light shower at the north end of the valley that did not approach their camp. Nada awoke to see her first rainbow. She and Batshua took it as God's seal on their changed plans.

As Batshua and her entourage began its return passage down the mountain pass, a pair of eyes on a distant ridge closed tightly in cursing disgust. He had hoped to time this event to include the Emira's death or injury with the shepherds. How ironic it would have been to kill or wound A'dab's beloved in this place! He would just have to find another way.

Ba'al-Hanni began his demonic incantations. He raised his arms and wind whipped his robes into an ecstasy of power! He could feel his god filling him with the strength of earth, sky and fire. Demon-power flowed through him. Thinking he controlled the demons swirling around him, he directed them on their way. They laughed in derision, for it was Ba'al-Hanni, The Deluded One who was under their control, the fool! Soon now, the demons would turn the tables and have their own way with their host.

Within just a few days, this valley would be seared to ash in a satanic rage of fire. Spittle flew from Ba'al-Hanni's mouth as he spoke words of homage to his demon-god. His dark eyes flared in hatred, his facial tattoos seemed to come alive to flay his skin raw. Power! This was power!! He reveled in it as his hoarse laughter echoed across the valley.

He began to sing.

As Ba'al-Hanni recited his grotesque song, dark clouds began to form in the northern end of Akkar Valley, portending the doom of all within.

14

Ruin

"Why is life given to a man
whose way is hidden,
whom God has hedged in?
For sighing has become my daily food;
my groans pour out like water.
What I feared has come upon me;
what I dreaded has happened to me."

The Book of Job 3:23-25

-:--o--:-

The trek home for Batshua's caravan was an uneventful grind.
The heat of early summer made daytime travel difficult. However a full
moon lit their path until the third night watch, so travel was somewhat
slower as they picked their way along in the dimmed light, but cooler
air.

The company bedded down by lamplight and slept most of the
daylight hours in the shade of palms growing by the river they were
following. They camped at El'Hajar for a few days to resupply. Negasi
decided he would rather have his racing camel deliver her misbegotten
calf in Hareb so she was tethered to the end of the line with the goats.
She complained bitterly at this indignation.

Eight days and nights later, Hareb came into view. Batshua's
mood changed. She did not look forward to discussing Boshet's news
with her husband. A potential raid on El'Hajar presented a difficult
decision. Given limited guards to watch their resources, where should

they be deployed? Most were busy chasing Sabeans thieves who were constantly chewing away at their herds. Batshua was filled with foreboding.

As it turned out, House Hareb was filled with guests.

A'dab Ben Hareb had returned from his business trip to the west with a caravan-full of his relatives. Brothers and sisters had returned with him to celebrate some sort of family event. A'dab had neglected to inform his wife. Their grandchildren, nearly forty of them were running around creating all sorts of mischief. Apparently their parents had volunteered the Hareb Household as guardians of the grandchildren while they celebrated their eldest sibling's birthday at his villa a day's ride north.

A'dab's son was so self-centered! To Batshua, that young man was constant sand in her eyes. If he only knew what his father went through, praying and offering sacrifices to God on his children's behalf! Batshua prayed for patience, but she did not have the patience of her husband. A'dab seemed to believe that his children would sow their wild oats and grow out of their foolishness. His tolerance for their indulgences frustrated her to no end! And now they dumped all the grandchildren on them just when she needed A'dab's attention on security matters. She growled to herself in frustration.

Batshua's caravan did not re-enter her beloved city in grand procession, it was simply absorbed into the swirling chaos. So much for a happy homecoming.

-:--o--:-

Nada observed the stress growing within her mistress. Madam Batshua was fond of children, yet she appeared to be impatient and short-tempered with her own. Her grandchildren seemed to irritate her and she avoided their presence. In Nada's opinion, most of the children were mild-mannered and curious. One or two needed watching, but her mistress behaved as if all of them had just come from playing in the sewers. Her cold attitude toward them was so unlike her.

All A'dab's grandchildren were between three and ten years of age. House Hareb was never quiet, day or night. Nada, Frayda and Omar were often sent on errands to discover the whereabouts of two or three of the more adventurous ones.

Frayda turned out to be an intuitively precocious detective. Her capacity to foil the secret culinary experiments of one four year old boy who had nearly managed to poison an evening meal with pepper sauce, became legendary within the first week. A'dab had laughed himself silly when the flagitious little miscreant's nefarious plot was exposed. "Boys will be boys" said he. Batshua was less amused.

Nada found she was not only sent searching for children during the next few weeks. She also spent more and more time trying to find her boss. Batshua seemed to be making herself scarce. Nada noticed something else – the Emira was also making herself thin. Apparently the stress of her household had affected her appetite.

Into this swirling, laughing, crying, complaining, doting, stressed-out Household of A'dab Ben Hareb strode the provocatively lithe, presumptively smiling and sexually inviting form of Boshet, temple prostitute and servant of Ba'al. When Batshua saw her, the first thought that ran through her tortured mind was, *"Dear God, not now!"* In her current emotional state, she could not tell if she was praying or cursing. She ran to the top of her watchtower and wept alone. No one saw her for an entire day, save Nada when she finally found her.

-:--O--:-

"I thought you might be here." Nada spoke softly. Batshua was at the railing, looking westward across the deepness of the valley. The night sky was aglow with a full moon, the second of summer. A gentle breeze fluttered her mistress's blue robes that seemed colored a deep indigo in the dim moonlight. She did not answer her handmaiden but a slight movement of her position indicated she was aware of her presence. Nada moved up beside her. They stood quietly for a few minutes.

"There is a storm coming." Batshua broke the silence at last. The remark confused Nada. She had grown up in the desert and was very attuned to changes in the feel of the air. She could sense weather variations as well as any desert creature.

"I do not feel it, perhaps you know better than me." Nada prompted.

"I do not mean the weather. There is a storm coming to House Hareb. I know it." Batshua pronounced this with the finality of prophecy.

"I have lost the battle. I do not know what to do next. I promised myself that I would not lean on you again the way I did up here before. It is not fair to me or you." She turned to Nada but her eyes were empty. She was looking... elsewhere. "I am sorry, Nada."

Again, Nada had no appropriate words, nor did she feel that silence was the right response. She moved to her mistress's side and tenuously wrapped an arm around her waist to comfort and support her mentor and friend. Batshua burst like a soap bubble to Nada's touch. She fell into her handmaiden's arms, sobbing like a child.

Nada held on awkwardly with Batshua kneeling to her handmaiden's shorter stature. Then the Emira of Edom lost all semblance of strength and pride. She fell to the floor, pulling Nada with her. Nada sat with her arms wrapped around her mistress, bracing her back against the railing. Batshua curled into a ball, her head against Nada's chest, sobbing hoarsely.

Nada had no idea what to do. Mistress Batshua had always been the one central point in her life that was strong and wise. She counted on her wisdom and grace. She viewed her as somehow more than just a woman, she was the Emira! This was a very strange thing. Now she held just another human being in her arms. A human being who could be as weak as anyone else in moments when strength and grace was needed. Nada became frightened and felt very much alone.

Suddenly Nada realized her mistress must also be feeling frightened and very much alone! But what could a young teenage girl do that could help? She squeezed her eyes shut and prayed to El Shaddai, God All Sufficient -- *Help me to help her!*

An idea floated into Nada's thoughts. During that wonderful moment before their caravan had left Hareb, Negasi had sung a song of departing. She did not know the words, but its haunting melody had lingered in her heart. She began to hum it softly...

When Nada finished the song, there was a long moment of utter peace. Batshua had stopped crying. She sat up and wiped her eyes with a heavy sigh.

"Oh! I'm such a mess! Sorry about that! I don't know what came over me." She tried to smile, Nada smiled back.

"I didn't know you could sing." She said. Nada just grinned. "Do you know the meaning of the words to that song?"

"No... but I love the melody."

"It is an ancient song of departing from Negasi's homeland. I asked him what it meant. He just smiled and said it did not translate very well. He did say that it is a promise to return home no matter how long the journey or how many the hardships."

"It is a beautiful song."

"Yes. And it reminds me that I have a home here and I am not behaving as a very decent wife and host. Thank you for finding me, Nada. You are good for me."

Nada felt that her efforts had been worthwhile but somehow there was a core of bitterness within her boss that had not been healed. She still seemed like a volcano that had leaked a bit of lava, but could still blow its top at any moment. The realization gave Nada a very uneasy feeling.

"We'd better get some sleep, tomorrow is likely to be a big day." Without another word, Batshua left Nada alone on the platform and walked down the stairs into the darkness of her private chambers.

Exhausted from the search for her mistress, the late night and the emotional expenditure from dealing with a sobbing woman, Nada curled up on a pillow and fell asleep on the platform. Her last thought before sleep overtook her was of the last night she slept on the roof of her house. A'jin had awakened her to destruction, death and slavery the next morning.

-:--o--:-

Nada awoke to déjà vu. Her eyes fluttered open to see the sandaled feet of Naaman, known in a former life as A'jin the cutthroat Sabean who had raided her village a lifetime ago. She looked up at his scarred face. Sleep still confused her mind, she did not remember where she was and could not figure what Naaman was doing in her bedroom.

She suddenly sat up in the bright sunlight.

The expression on Naaman's face froze her. He looked very serious. "I am sorry to awaken you, my lady. Your presence is requested in the garden below within the hour. You have time to refresh yourself."

"Thank you, Naaman. What... what has happened?" Nada swallowed hard. She remembered Batshua's prophetic pronouncement during the night.

"Bad news, I am afraid. Very, very bad news. Master A'dab will hold court in the garden. Mistress Batshua will be with him and desires that you be present as well."

"Can you tell me anything?" Nada wanted to be prepared with something, somehow.

"I cannot tell you much because I do not know much. But this I know. Somehow, Master A'dab has been betrayed. Sabeans..." Naaman hung his head at the reference of his former countrymen, "During the night, outlaw Sabean raiders have attacked the master's herds of oxen and donkeys in the west. That is all I can say for now.

Please come, make yourself ready. We must be strong for our friends."
He nodded formally, his way of saluting his lady, and left.

Nada had only just turned fifteen. By the grace of God she had
defeated a rapist in Aqaba and in the heat of the moment had nearly
choked an attacker to death in El'Hajar. But the forces swirling around
House Hareb seemed immense and unstoppable compared to mere
human beings. As she hurried down the stairs her movements caused
her belt with its hidden dagger to slap against her thigh. She thought
ruefully that it was a puny weapon against the forces arrayed against her
friends.

-:--o--:-

Within twenty minutes Nada had managed to find something
to eat, splash water on her face and don fresh apparel. She hurried back
to the garden enclosure, stopping to tell Frayda of the impending
meeting. Frayda would be late, she overslept a lot. When Nada arrived
at the garden, Omar was already standing with Naaman at the entrance
so she walked past. Everyone look very grim.

She was surprised to find the enclosure empty. Not knowing
what to do or where to sit, she walked to the watchtower stairs and sat
down on the first step, elbows on knees, her chin resting in her hands.
There was such an eerie stillness in the garden! Her sense of foreboding
abated momentarily as she basked in the natural beauty of the place. A
small bird landed on a bush within arm's length of her. It seemed to
look directly at her, unafraid. Nada sat up, but her movement did not
frighten the bird away. It began to preen itself casually.

"You don't seem to care much about anything that's going on
here, do you!" She whispered to the bird. It stopped preening to look
at her, cocking its head to the left and right. It chirped an answer,
appearing curious. Nada laughed. "God's creatures don't have a care in
the world do they!" The bird fluttered its wings and puffed out its
feathers. Nada smiled. "I think I know what you're trying to say." The
bird just chirped and hopped to a lower branch. "I think you're trying
to say that no matter what happens, God watches over us right?!" The
bird chirped in reply then fluttered its wings again and flew away at the

noise of people coming through the entrance. Nada sighed and went to see what fate awaited Household Hareb.

-:--o--:-

Master A'dab led mistress Batshua to a marble dais near the small pond at the garden's center. She looked awful, like she had not slept all night. Master A'dab did not look much better. They were followed by all his brothers and sisters. Apparently someone else in the household had taken charge of the children.

A'dab and Batshua sat on the dais, Batshua caught Nada's eye and motioned for her to take her place. She moved to the floor beside her mistress, resting her arm on the dais. Frayda arrived with cushions so the two girls made themselves comfortable on the floor beside their respective mistress's.

A commotion at the entrance turned everyone's head. Nada was shocked to see Omar leading Boshet into the enclosure. Her hands were bound behind her back. Omar held her arm firmly, he did not look pleased. A'dab's relatives began to talk among themselves. He brought her forward to stand before the master of the house.

"Speak!" A'dab's voice punched through the babble and silenced it.

"Whatever do you mean, sir?" Boshet's tone was impudent, bantering.

His eyes narrowed, clearly he was enraged. "You know exactly whereof I speak! You come into my house, share my bread and water, and partake in the safety of my home. You bring news of raiders from Chaldea who will attack my camel herds in the north only to divert my guards so that Sabean dogs may attack from the south!" A'dab was beginning to shout.

"I speak the truth sir. The plot against your camel herds is true. I was there when my ex-husband conspired with the Chaldeans..." Boshet hung her head. She was on trial for her life and she knew it. Her heart beat wildly, but she controlled herself, calling on all her skills.

"I was a fool to believe such a fantasy, the Chaldeans are too far away to pull off such a raid. I..." A commotion outside the entrance interrupted whatever he was about to say. Two men were arguing in the hallway.

"I must speak with master A'dab immediately!" yelled the first.

"No, I must speak with him first! He must hear me first, I tell you! Let me in, I say!" the second man hollered past Naaman into the enclosure, "Master A'dab, master A'dab, I must speak with you! Please sir! Emergency sir!"

"Naaman, let them come!" A'dab was having trouble coping with the situation which was quickly getting out of control. Batshua had gone numb. She was holding onto Nada's hand, gripping it so hard she was nearly causing her pain.

The man who had insisted on speaking first ran to A'dab and fell kneeling at his feet. He looked awful. His clothes where tattered and had burn marks. He was covered with scrapes and bruises. He was trying to speak, but only sobs could be heard from his tightly crouched position at the feet of his master. A'dab leaned down and gently lifted him up, holding his face in his hands.

"Tell me your news, son. God will help us bear the burdens we cannot bear alone."

He took a shuddering breath and began. "I am Zahur, from the pasturelands. I..." He began to fumble for words, but when he looked into his master's eyes, he regained a bit of his composure. "I am your servant, sir. A shepherd of your flocks north of El-Gabal. I have been honored to see the increase of your flocks for lo, these past ten years."

A'dab leaned back, "Bring Zahur water!"

"Thank you, sir." He drank and it seemed to calm him.

"What news from the shepherds? Were you attacked on the way here?" A'dab prompted.

"No sir." He started to lose composure again, his mouth began to tremble in fear. "The pasturelands are no more!"

"What?!" Batshua spoke up sharply. A'dab moved a hand to calm her. "I was there not three weeks ago!"

"I saw your caravan, mistress. I was not far from your camp near the rock, perhaps a three hour hike away. I had been searching for strays in the highlands." Batshua sat back, waiting to hear the rest. "I saw you leave the next morning. Had you stayed, you would have witnessed the disaster that befell us. Perhaps it is only the hand of God himself that saved you, for no one else but me was spared."

"Spared from what, Zahur?" A'dab needed to hear the whole story.

"A storm, sir. The likes of which I have never seen! It fell upon us from the north. Lightning and rain so hard that I could barely see to walk. I made it to the rocks where the mistress had camped, else I would have been killed for it was then that the hail came. Stones from the sky as big as my fist. I waited under the shelter of the rocks for two days while the storm raged. When the rains stopped, the sun turned hot but lightning came and set the fields afire. Sir, I made my way between fires to the shepherds camp, but none where alive. I saw no sheep alive either. All had been killed in the hail and fire. I am sorry, my good master. I should have died with them," his emotions began to break his voice, "but it has taken me all these weeks to walk this distance to report to you." Zahur broke down into unashamed sobs.

"Bless you, Zahur. You shall be rewarded for your diligence. You are a faithful servant." A'dab spoke woodenly, but as graciously as he could. He seemed distant as if in shock.

Batshua spoke up sarcastically as Zahur was led out, "Rewarded? How? With what?!" A'dab turned to her with a pained look.

"Naaman! Is there another messenger?" A'dab remained calm, but his control was breaking.

The next man limped in with Naaman's help. He had been wounded in the arm and leg on his right side. A'dab recognized him. "You are Tahir, a camel trainer from El'Hajar, are you not?"

"Yes, my master, I..." Tahir swallowed and looked down at his feet. He could not bring himself to say what he had come to say.

"I fear you have bad news for me. I will guess that it is has something to do with Chaldeans raiding my camels. Is that not so?" A'dab was staring at Boshet.

Tahir looked up in shock. "Aye, sir! How could you know?!"

A'dab spoke to Omar as he nodded to Boshet, "Release her! She has spoken the truth." Omar cut loose her bonds. A'dab bent low with his hands on his knees to rub his eyes with both palms. He did not look up, but spoke with resignation, both his hands covering his face. "Tahir, tell me your story." Batshua rested one hand gently on her husband's shoulder.

"There were three large raiding parties, master A'dab. They rode into the city on swift horses from the north and south while a third attacked the few trainers and herdsman who were tending the camels. None survived, the city was torched."

"Where were you? How did you make it out alive?"

At this, Tahir lowered his head. "I am a coward, sir. When I saw the riders coming, I ran to my racing mount and we outpaced the horses. I got away from them, but my camel took a bad step and broke its leg, I was forced to destroy it, else I would have arrived here sooner. They were not so concerned with me anyway, they had three thousand camels as spoils to divide. I am sorry, sir. I should have fought them."

"No Tahir, fighting was the duty of my guards. Why were my guards not able to defend the herd?"

"What guards?" Tahir asked, "I saw only the few household guards at your summer home. All were slain."

"What?! I dispatched nearly one hundred guards to you two weeks ago! They never made it?"

"Sir, the raid happened two weeks ago, right after mistress Batshua returned through El'Hajar on her way home. Your guards must have been in route when the Chaldeans hit us, for they were nowhere to be found."

A'dab was suddenly very tired. He rubbed his forehead in an effort to conjure thought from it.

He was still leaning forward with his elbows on his knees, he appeared to be praying, saying something under his breath. Batshua rubbed his shoulder absentmindedly. No one in the room knew what to do or say. A reverent silence had descended.

Tahir finally spoke, "Sir I…"

A'dab waved him off. "You have done well, son. Omar, see that Tahir is cared for, would you?" Omar nudged Tahir and led him quietly from the room. The air was thick with the impact of disaster. No one had an inkling of the financial losses these attacks would mean. Two were by men and one seemed to be from the hand of God. For nature itself to attack and kill the shepherds and sheep! It seemed to be a betrayal of A'dab by God himself! These thoughts weighed heavily in the silent room.

The silence did not last long. A voice cried in frustration from the hallway, "I tell you he must hear me! I have traveled all night! I bring news he must hear! Do not delay me!"

"Ah!" A'dab looked up with a smile, "That will be my physician telling me I have head lice! The final straw to break the camel's back!" Everyone, even Batshua burst out laughing. Good ol' A'dab! What a noble man to be offering up a jest to help relieve the heavy burden of others when he was so burdened himself! Batshua smiled and patted his back in reassurance. No matter what happened next, with good humor and grace, they would muddle through, they always had!

When the last messenger stood swaying before them, everyone sobered instantly. He was an absolute wreck! Blood was oozing from his right ear and one of his eyes was swollen shut. His left arm was bound painfully against his chest, apparently broken. His face looked wracked in pain.

He tried to bow, but nearly collapsed in the attempt. Omar quickly brought a high wooden stool that he could use to support himself as he gave his report.

"I am Nadim, a friend of your eldest son. I am afraid I bear ill tidings." Nadim's eyes were wild with fear.

"Speak, Nadim. We shall bear your news with what grace God may grant us.."

Nadim cast a pained look at Batshua, then stared into the eyes of master A'dab. He seemed to be framing the right words. He took a long breath through his nose with his eyes closed, then began. "I attended your son's birthday celebrations this past week. Many of my brothers and sisters, cousins and friends were also in attendance." He seemed to choke up when he mentioned his family. He controlled himself, took another long breath and continued. "As we partied yesterday, a strange storm swept in from the desert, a whirlwind the likes of which I have never seen. It blew sand in through the windows so hard that all the food was spoiled immediately. The wind was so strong, everyone huddled down on the floor to get away from the stinging sand. It seemed like the wind would tear the very roof from the house."

"Did you hide on the floor with the others?" Batshua prompted.

"I am a very curious man, ma'am. I had never seen or heard of a storm so strong. I went outside to have a look at it. No sooner had I stepped out of the door when I heard a terrible crash! The foundation of the house had given way! The walls collapsed and the roof fell in!"

A'dab stood in panic. "What of my sons? My three daughters?! Are they alright? Please, tell me my children are alright!"

Nadim swallowed and shook his head. "I am so sorry, sir." He looked at Batshua. "Ma,am. No one survived. My family is gone as well." Tears streamed from his one good eye.

A hoarse scream filled the shocked room. At first everyone's eyes locked on Batshua for they thought it was her. But then the screamer took another breath and screamed even louder. It was A'dab! He grabbed at his cloak near his throat and pulled with all his might. The fabric tore to his waist exposing his bare chest as hoarse screams were torn from his throat again and again.

He yelled "Noooooo! Not my children! Take me instead!" He turned his agonized face toward the heavens, exposing his bare chest as if he expected God to plunge a dagger into his heart. He roared out his pain again and again, then collapsed to the floor in a paroxysm of agony, sobbing and beating his fist on the tiles in futile denial. "No, no, no, no…"

Batshua let him lay there as she stared straight ahead in shock. A'dab convulsed as if he would vomit. He drew his knees into his chest, wrapped his arms around his legs and rocked in endless sobs.

One by one, then in a flood, A'dab's relatives left the enclosure. Boshet was dragged along in the human flood that drained the room. Only Batshua, Omar, Nada, and Frayda remained vigilant over the crushed and broken form of Edom's Emir. Batshua motioned to Omar who quietly walked to his mistress. She took Nada's hand and placed it in his with a squeeze, then motioned to the door. They walked out with a weeping Frayda following. Nada turned back toward her mistress, who gave Nada a reassuring nod. As she watched, Batshua knelt to comfort her husband.

It was going to be a long, lonely night in House Hareb.

-:--o--:-

15

Abandonment

"My relatives have gone away;
my closest friends have forgotten me.
My guests and my female servants count me a foreigner;
they look on me as on a stranger.
I summon my servant, but he does not answer,
though I beg him with my own mouth.
My breath is offensive to my wife."

The Book of Job 19:14-17a

-:--o--:-

A'dab and Batshua stirred awake to the scent of flowers late that next morning. A bird sang sweetly just a few feet from where their heads lay on pillows some anonymous servant had provided during the night.

"I had a very bad dream, my love." A'dab smiled into his wife's face. The answering pain in her face told him: it had not been a dream. His eyes closed around encrusted tear residue. He sat up, surprised to find he was not in his bedchamber, disappointed that he still lived.

Alone in the garden, he and Batshua had been intimate during the night. He could remember losing himself in their mutual love. She had provided the only solace to him she could give.

The terrible news that had been delivered in surrealistic, rapid succession was more than his mind could process. The messages

appeared like Egyptian hieroglyphs painted on the walls of his soul --
intended for some other man who must have dwelt there, not himself.

His thoughts turned to the woman beside him. She was a good
and wise woman, a wondrous mixture of bold and cold, intimate yet
aloof, brash and rash, calculating but impetuous. His woman sparkled
with all the complexities of a masterfully cut gem and how he loved
her! He had always felt like the two of them were the perfect alloy of
tin and copper, a perfect bronze marriage. She represented the
suppleness and golden beauty of copper, he the strength and resilience
of tin — complementing each other's strengths and weaknesses. He
thanked God daily for his Batshua!

He stood and splashed his face with water from the pond.
Batshua straightened her clothing just in time to hear Naaman call from
the entrance, "Your pardon, madam Batshua, master A'dab. Lady Nada
is here with someone who wishes to speak with you. Are you prepared
to receive them?"

A'dab looked a question at Batshua who looked a little
perturbed by the early intrusion, but nodded her ascent.

"Let them come, Naaman." A'dab called. The two lords of the
household readied themselves on the stone dais in front of the pond.
To their surprise, Nada came in leading Boshet.

Batshua noticed that Boshet no longer carried herself with the
slinking movements of a prostitute. She walked gracefully, but it was
just a walk this morning. There was nothing in her carriage that was
provocative in any way. Something had changed.

Nada spoke, "Madam Batshua, master A'dab. Lady Boshet
came to me after the gathering last night. We have talked at length
about a great many things. A great many things… Lady Boshet wishes
to repeat to you what she said to me last night. And," Nada was having
trouble finding words, "And she has a request to ask of you. A request
with which I do not agree!" The last statement was stated with a glare
at Boshet.

Boshet looked at Nada sorrowfully, then her eyes begged permission to speak. A'dab's hand opened in a palm up gesture, madam Batshua looked very impatient, as if she would rather have eaten breakfast first.

Boshet knelt. "First, my request is that you grant me a quick and painless death, for after today, my life is forfeit at the hand of Ba'al-Hanni. Death by his hand will be neither painless nor quick. I believe your method of execution would be merciful."

Batshua merely raised an eyebrow, A'dab looked pensive. Too many other thoughts were running through the master's mind. He did not know if his broken heart could bear another blow, he braced himself and prayed for wisdom and grace.

Boshet continued, "This was to be the final blow to you, sir." She held up a thick leather satchel. "I do not know what kind of poison it contains, but Ba'al-Hanni warned me that it is extremely dangerous to touch or breathe. He wanted me to poison your bath with it." She placed the satchel on the floor in front of her. Everyone involuntarily moved away from it.

"I have been a very skillful liar since my youth, so I know you have no reason to believe me now." When Batshua heard this, she drew her mouth into a thin line that seemed to say, *You aren't telling us anything we don't know, sweet-lips!* "I want to set my life in order before I die, it seems only right." With that said, she removed the gold chain from her neck and handed it to A'dab.

"This is the reward Ba'al-Hanni promised to me if I performed his bidding. That is his signet ring. It is deeded to land in the Kingdom of Mari of the Chaldeans. I will not need the land, for I will be dead. You may keep it for yourself or do whatever you please with it."

A'dab turned the ring over in his hand. When he saw the crest, he clenched the ring in his fist. Tears streamed down his cheeks. "Boshet, did Ba'al-Hanni tell you where he got this ring?"

Boshet did not want to say this part. She hesitated. A'dab looked up at her, demanding an answer.

"Sir, he said his name was once I'sin al-Ur and that he is your cousin."

"No, Boshet. He lied to you. All my brothers and sisters are here with me at Hareb. I know all my cousins very well. I'sin al-Ur was my father. He was killed by Hammurabi's men during the battle for the city of Mari. I was a young man then, but I was there to see my father die. All that he had in Chaldea was taken, including this ring. Ba'al-Hanni is an exquisite liar. I wonder who he really is."

"Then the ring belongs to you. It is only right that you have it once again. I shall die in peace."

A'dab sighed a heavy sigh, squeezing the ring tightly. "I shall ponder the meaning of this. Are you ready, Boshet?"

"I am to die now?!" She hung her head and began to weep softly.

"In a manner of speaking, yes." A'dab stood and walked to a few feet into the garden while Batshua and Nada watched curiously. Nada especially, she could not imagine master A'dab doing any harm to Boshet.

He snapped a twig from a small bush, dipped it the pond and returned to bow before Boshet on one knee. He cupped her chin in one hand and gently lifted her face. Boshet held her eyes shut, tears streaming down her cheeks.

A'dab intoned, "Cleanse me with hyssop and I shall be clean; wash me and I shall be whiter than snow." He sprinkled the water from the hyssop branch onto her face. The droplets mingled with her tears. Her chest shuddered with sudden relief – she would not die! For the first time in her life, Boshet felt clean and new! This was death of a different kind, for she felt as if it was her old life that had just died.

"A new name might be in order. 'Boshet' no longer seems appropriate, for your shame has been taken away." A'dab smiled through his pain, it was an old habit that he could not break.

Boshet opened her eyes. They sparkled impossibly bright with a joy she could not express. "I do not know what to say! How is your goodness possible? You... I mean... with all you are facing! How can you show mercy to me when God himself appears to be withholding his mercy from you?"

A'dab scowled. "Now, Boshet! Who are you to judge God? Hmmmm? God's mercy or lack of mercy is not for you to judge, nor am I in the place to judge God. I came into this world with nothing, and I shall most assuredly leave this world with nothing. The Lord has given and the Lord has taken away. I shall ever praise the Lord!"

Nada and Boshet marveled at A'dab's amazing declaration of faith in God. Batshua's face appeared to be carved of stone.

Batshua finally broke the reverent silence, "Is anyone else besides me hungry? I feel like I could eat an ostrich egg all by myself!"

A'dab stood, helping Boshet to her feet with a chuckle, "Batshua, you are always the practical one!" Everyone else joined in the laugh. "Naaman! Can you get the girls to serve us some food before we all faint?"

"Right away, sir!"

Nada moved to Boshet and gave her a huge hug. Batshua squeezed her husband's hand. "We'll get through this day and see what happens tomorrow." She whispered. He whispered back, "That's the way! That's my 'Shua!"

After breakfast, A'dab repaired to his private chambers. As customary for a father in grief, he ritually shaved his head and beard. Batshua did not recognize him at their next meal and she withdrew from his touch, finding his appearance suddenly foreign. She could not help herself, she felt guilty, but he did not look like her husband anymore.

-:--O--:-

During the following month, Batshua and A'dab became more and more like a poorly forged sword. Her tin and his copper were no longer alloyed as one. A coldness grew between them so that with every blow of the blacksmith's hammer, new cracks emerged in the sword, splintering their relationship.

News of the disaster spread like a wildfire throughout Edom and beyond. House Hareb became a hub of frenetic activity as the financial empire of A'dab Ben Hareb slowly crumbled to ruin.

The grandchildren were of primary concern. The older children were in shock and mourning. Their uncles and aunts bickered over inheritance rights, fighting over the scraps of wealth that remained. Messengers arrived from all directions to call in debts that could not be paid. Spice deliveries promised in the fall would be forfeited and contracted with a competitor. Other produce of the lands such as wheat, olive oil and wine would go undelivered because without their camels and donkeys, House Hareb no longer had the means to deliver them. The list of grievances went on and on.

A'dab and Batshua held court every day, attempting to administer their business with fairness and equity. They divided the remains of the wealth among their debtors as best they were able. Often their business associates were sympathetic and merciful, more often they faced a growing consensus that House Hareb had fallen under the judgment of God and deserved the misfortune that had befallen it.

The absolute unfairness with which all their friends and relatives delivered their uncharitable judgments began to show its effects on the Hareb household. One by one, A'dab's brothers and sisters left, dividing up the grandchildren among themselves. Some, the youngest brother for one, left one evening without so much as a farewell or a thank you for a month of hospitality. His eldest sister said her farewells coldly and formally. She hinted, rather pointedly, that the presence of a prostitute of Ba'al in A'dab's household may be the reason for evidence of God's displeasure. Her cutting remarks worked as a wedge between A'dab and Batshua even though Batshua had never before suspected her husband of any impropriety. A'dab took his sister's hollow accusation in silence and bid her Godspeed on her journey. She left in a huff.

-:--o--:-

Not knowing quite what to do with the poison Boshet had presented to him, A'dab decided that the best course of action would be to burn it. He noticed that the smoke had a very unusual odor...

Three days after burning the poison, he started scratching his arms absentmindedly as he listened to the daily complainers and whiners lined up before him and his beloved wife at court. The day after that, during the sixth week of their ordeal, blisters began to appear on A'dab's arms. When he woke the next morning, he was covered with terrible, itching blisters and in agony.

-:--o--:-

Batshua came to her husband's chamber carrying a tray of tea. When she saw A'dab, she dropped the tray in horror. The tea pot shattered on the floor at his feet. Hoarsely, he said, "Do not come near, it may be contagious." Batshua ran from the room and did not return for many days.

A'dab picked up a piece of the broken tea pot and sat on the floor. He began to scratch at the blisters with the sharp edge of a broken shard. He noticed that when the blister tore, the fluid that leaked onto his skin irritated and reddened it. The next day, new blisters formed where the fluid had leaked. Experimentally, he began to scrape around the blisters to relieve the terrible itching and burning pain, being careful not to break the blisters. Painfully, he collected washing powders and soap from his bedchamber and limped to his garden enclosure, carrying a pillow.

He parked himself by the pond and began to scrape his skin again. Whenever a blister broke, he washed the area carefully in the pond with soap, even though the pain was intense. He observed that the blister reformed within a day but it was smaller. However no new blisters formed on the nearby skin from the leaking fluid. He felt like

God had perhaps shown him a way to survive this new torture. He set himself toward the task of enduring it.

Naaman was not afraid of catching anything from his master. Even if he was contagious, Naaman's loyalty did not permit him to leave his master's side. He figured that if he could stand between his master and an assassin's spear, a minor itch or two would be no big deal. One way of dying was as good or bad as the other to a Sabean warrior. He served A'dab all his meals and kept him supplied with soap.

After a week of Naaman's constant care and no apparent effects on him, the rest of the household concluded that A'dab's affliction was not contagious. Batshua came for a visit, her demeanor was cold.

Sensing his wife's mood, A'dab opened the conversation carefully. "It's good to see you." A'dab tried to smile, but his facial skin was too tightened by painful blisters and his tongue was slightly swollen, slurring his speech.

"You've looked better." She said with a slight attempt at humor. A'dab grunted a laugh in response. "I want to know something." she said more seriously.

"Ask. I will keep nothing from you." He turned his eyes toward her, he hoped she saw his love.

"How can you be so stubborn?" she demanded.

"Stubborn? I am not sure what you mean." This was a question he had not expected.

"I suppose you think you call it 'faithfulness' or 'integrity'. I believe you are just being stubborn. You know that God is punishing you for some secret sin and you are stubbornly hiding it. I think this is a direct result of your relationship with that lying whore, Boshet and she has managed to poison you somehow!"

A'dab looked pained, "My beloved, Boshet has turned to God and he has forgiven her. Perhaps you should forgive her too."

Batshua snorted in derision.

A'dab continued, "As for the poison, I am grateful that she did not use it. I thought long on its disposal. I finally decided upon burning it several days ago. I thought it the most symbolic means of getting rid of it."

"So you are still stubbornly holding onto your so-called integrity?" Batshua was nearing the end of her patience.

"My dear..." A'dab wanted to say more, but there was a disturbance at the entrance. He stopped and smiled as Naaman escorted in Nada and Omar. Naaman remained.

Batshua did not let her husband finish, she plunged forward with her own agenda. "I asked Nada and Omar to come. I want you to witness this, A'dab. Nada, come here, child." Nada obeyed, looking confused. Batshua reached to her right ear and unfastened the ring that had dangled there for nearly a year now.

"Here, take this." Nada obeyed, but looked very pained, she was not sure if she was being punished. Batshua continued, "I hereby release you, Nada and you, Omar, from your obligations as bond-servants to the Emira of Edom. I declare you to be emancipated adults. I shall find a way to compensate you fully from my personal treasury as if you had served out your required years."

She turned toward A'dab who looked very downcast. "As for you, A'dab Ben Hareb, since you are obviously cursed by God, I suggest that you return the favor! Admit your sin. Curse God and die!" To the gasps of her former servants, she turned on her heel and strode angrily from the garden without looking back.

A'dab called after her, "Batshua, no! Don't be foolish! This is not right! You are playing the fool!" It was no use, she was gone.

-:--O--:-

Naaman spoke up, "Shall I go restrain her, sir?"

"No. No, of course not. But thank you, Naaman. You are a good man, but Batshua must choose her own path. I believe she has chosen the wrong path. A dangerous one." A'dab was in extreme physical pain, but each of his friends could feel his heart aching for his wife.

"What will she do? Where will she go?" Nada worried.

"If I know Batshua, she will probably return to her father." A'dab had tried to remain standing, but he was too weak. He sat on his pillow and resumed his methodical scraping of his blisters.

"Her father lives a very long way from here. Batshua is Hebrew. Her father lives in Goshen, a fertile land east of the Nile delta in Egypt. It is a three week journey... and difficult."

Naaman spoke up, "I know this place. It is not so far from my homeland of Sheba."

"If she goes near Sabean territory, then it is indeed a dangerous journey." Omar interjected. "We should accompany madam, Batshua, she needs protection." Omar did not like the idea of her mistress riding out into danger. He was still thinking in terms of being her guard as he had been serving for the past three years.

"I do not think my 'shua desires company just now." A'dab knew his wife well.

"Pardon my impertinence, sir. But what did madam Batshua mean when she declared lady Nada and me to be 'emancipated adults'?" Omar raised an eyebrow at his Emir.

A'dab tried to grin, but it hurt his lips. "Good thinking, young man. It means that you are as free to make any decision that you wish as long as you have the resources to carry it out. You and Nada are as free as me in fact. Perhaps more so, because you are more able to carry out your own choices than a broken down and very sick man such as you see before you now."

"I see…" Omar said. He stretched to his full height and turned formally to Nada. Taking both of her hands in his, he looked down and said, "In that case, my lady Nada, I would like to ask you to be my wife. Do you have someone whom I should ask permission to marry you?"

Nada was completely flummoxed. She blushed and stammered. Naaman and A'dab looked on with smiles, waiting for her answer. "I… well, uh… Yes! Of course I want to be your wife, Omar! But… I am twice an orphan. There is no one…" her voice trailed off as her eyes turned to the Emir of Edom who had been more than a father figure to her this past year.

"Nada, I give my blessing upon you both! I had a strong feeling about the two of you." A'dab's smiles were very lop-sided now because of his blisters. But even through his pain, his eyes shown with love and pride.

"Thank you sir. I do not mean to rush along, but…" Omar did not seem impatient but he was certainly driving at something.

"Yes, if I deduce your logic correctly young man, you wish to accompany my renegade wife on her flight as a married couple, is that correct?" Master A'dab and Omar seemed to be cut from the same cloth.

"That may be the wisest course, yes."

A'dab turned to Nada, "Nada, are you willing?"

Nada considered her options rapidly. She could deduce Omar's plan. By setting them free, Batshua had inadvertently given her and Omar the ability to become essentially their former boss's peers. "I am willing."

"Alright then, I can perform the ritual now. We have Naaman as witness, but the law requires two witnesses. We will need one other." A'dab was winking at someone over Naaman's shoulder.

"I will be a witness." Boshet walked into the garden. She had been listening to most of the conversation from the entrance.

"Naaman, you have slacked in your duties as guardian of the entrance! I shall overlook your deficiency this once." A glimpse of A'dab's old sense of humor bubbled back for a moment.

"A thousand pardons!" Naaman said, his grin stretching his facial scar comically.

"I will be a witness on one condition: I must be allowed to accompany the newlyweds on this journey. I may be invaluable in dealing with certain... types of people... they will encounter."

Nada preempted her husband-to-be, "We shall be honored to have your company, lady Boshet." Omar smiled his approval.

A'dab performed a simple, priestly ceremony. He was very careful not to touch them. Usually, the priest would have joined the wedded couples' hands in his own, he instructed them to hold hands with their seconds and spoke of how all were held in God's hand.

-:--o--:-

At the end of the short ceremony, Omar was anxious to get started in pursuit of Batshua. A'dab and Nada had other thoughts that were less impetuous, more practical. Naaman looked very troubled by something.

"There is the matter of a dowry, since I seem to be acting in the role of father to Nada..." A'dab pulled out the gold chain bearing his father's ring that Boshet had turned over to him several weeks ago. "I will keep this safe until your return. Nada and Omar, you are now landowners. Boshet, I think your sentiments are in tune with this idea?" She nodded warmly. He turned his attention fully to Boshet, "God will not forget you, Boshet. And neither will I. Remain true to God and God will provide for you." She accepted his pronouncement with grace.

"As for your resources for the journey, I am afraid I am at a loss. These past two months have drained my treasury, so I can provide very little. My beloved spoke of her personal treasury, but unfortunately, she departed without imparting any of it, yes? You have made a decision to go after her, but you have no resources to execute your decision. Welcome to the world of an emancipated adult." He smiled with lopsided irony.

Nada's eyes lit up with a thought. "Wait here, I will be right back!" She ran around to the back side of the watchtower pillar and withdrew her leather pouch from the hidden chamber. She placed the pouch in A'dab's lap where he unwrapped it to his vast surprise.

"Nada! Where did you get this?!"

"Does that matter? It was a gift and it is mine to do with as I choose. Will it be enough to finance our trip?"

"More than enough, young lady. I am in your debt! It will take me some time, a few days to purchase the necessary camels and supplies. I think you should make good use of the time to prepare." He winked at Omar.

Omar hesitated, but decided to say what was on his mind. "Master A'dab, I am young. With no offense to my new wife, so is she. If she agrees, and if you agree, I believe it would be wiser of me and her to commit ourselves as servants to you, to House Hareb and transfer our original service commitment from madam Batshua to you rather than remain completely independent. Do you see the wisdom of this?"

A'dab considered this for a moment. "Yes, a most wise decision, young man. Nada, do you agree?" She nodded ascent. "Then I accept you both into my service. Not as bond-servants, but has hirelings with full staff privileges and authority. How is that? Be careful, for you act and speak for House Hareb as its agents."

Omar and Nada bowed formally.

Naaman stepped forward. "Sir, a moment. I have a confession to make."

"Today seems to be a day for surprises. Go ahead, Naaman." A'dab looked up expectantly at his trusted bodyguard.

"As you may know, I was in the raiding party that destroyed young Nada's village years ago. Although I did not participate in the carnage, I was still part of the raid and I treated the young Nada roughly. As a result of that raid, she was sold into slavery in Aqaba. To make amends with my lady, I pledged my life to protect her. Perhaps I did this in haste, having already pledged myself to your service. Now I am torn between two pledges. I feel that to satisfy my honor, I must accompany lady Nada on her journey with her husband Omar. If you will release me from my bond, I will fulfill my vow to lady Nada."

"Well said, Naaman. But I do not release you." The tension in the room rose dramatically. "Instead, I request that you honor your service to me by protecting the lady Nada and all in her party as you would protect me. Thus by honoring your vow to her, you also honor me. In the mean time, my three closest friends will soon be here and I shall be comforted by their wise counsel and protected by their company. Thus, there is no conflict to your honor or your service. Will that suffice?"

Naaman's grin was back, "Yes sir! Yes indeed! You are a wise man. Thank you."

"Good, these matters are settled. Batshua will have quite a head start, but you may catch up with her, as God wills. One thing more for you all to bear in mind..." They all turned their attention to him, sensing he would say something very important, "These tragic events have inspired me to change my name. Be sure to let Batshua know when you find her." A sparkle of hope twinkled in his eyes at those words. "From this day forth, I am to be known as 'Job', for I am greatly oppressed."

Naaman, Omar, Nada and Boshet all bowed. They all said, "God be merciful to you, master Job."

"God be with you as you prepare for the days ahead. Please return to me in three days. And now, I must rest if I can." He lay down painfully and closed his eyes.

-:--o--:-

16

Pursuit

"Why do you hide your face
and consider me your enemy?
Will you torment a windblown leaf?
Will you chase after dry chaff?"

The Book of Job 13:24-25

-:--o--:-

Naaman, Boshet, Nada and Omar left Job alone in his garden.

Frayda met them in the outer hall with news of the Emira's departure. The grapevine in House Hareb evidently worked very quickly indeed.

"We saw madam Batshua leaving with Negasi through the west gate. She was dressed like a kitchen servant, but everyone knew it was her. What has happened?!" Frayda was very perplexed.

Nada did not explain any more than Frayda needed to know. "Much has happened. I must ask you, no, I must *command* you to silence. You will accompany me on a long journey. You will tell no one of the purpose of our journey or where we are going or who you are with. Be ready to leave in three days. Can you do this, my friend and kinsman?"

Frayda looked very frightened at Nada's tone of command. "Yes, my lady. But what shall I say when others ask me about my preparations?"

Nada scowled "You may tell them that your lady Nada and her new husband Omar are taking a holiday. Say nothing more." At this, Frayda was about to grab Nada and twirl her around, but caught herself. Nada held out her hand. Frayda kneeled kissed it, then they hugged.

"God's blessings upon you both! I am so happy for you!" She looked up at her friend and boss, then smiled warmly at Omar. She turned and hurried off.

"Do you think she will be a problem?" Omar wondered.

"Give her a chance." Nada was learning to trust her friend as well as her own instincts.

Boshet spoke up. "I have been thinking about my own usefulness on this venture. I want to help. I know a few languages that I picked up during my time at the temple. Perhaps I can help serve as interpreter."

Omar stopped. "I have a better idea, but it will put you in danger. You do not have to agree."

"Speak of it, Omar. I wish to be useful."

"I do not want to offend you, but apparently, your most useful talent has been your ability to lie." Boshet looked pained, but she said nothing. "A skillful liar may serve us well as it may protect madam Batshua."

"What are you getting at, Omar? You are not making any sense!" Nada was getting angry because he seemed to be insulting Boshet.

"Well, it occurred to me that lady Boshet and madam Batshua are approximately the same size. If she were to wear madam Batshua's clothing and ride in her howdah and if you were to act as if you were her handmaiden…"

"A decoy! Yes! Anyone who may wish madam Batshua harm would believe madam Batshua to be with us, not with Negasi! That is a splendid plan!" Boshet was enthusiastic. The others gained a new level of respect for Boshet. Her courage was as evident as her selflessness.

Naaman said, "I am commanded by A'dab... master Job I mean, to protect you. I have friends among the camel tenders. Some are good fighters, I could convince a few to come along if you do not object to having a few of Sheba's warriors by your side."

Omar said, "Find as many as you can Naaman. The road will be long and dangerous, so choose men who have allegiance to the Creator, not Almaqah."

Naaman said, "Done, sir!" He left grinning at the prospect.

Nada said, "I will find proper clothing for you from among madam Batshua's things, Boshet. We will meet in the morning to assemble supplies and work out a final plan to present to master Job."

-:--o--:-

Boshet left, leaving Nada and Omar alone in the hallway outside the servant's quarters. The sun was just beginning to dip below the horizon, glowing in a swirl of subdued hues. Omar moved to Nada's side and wrapped an arm around his new bride's slender waist.

"I did not mean to rush you into a decision like this, asking you to be my wife in front of everyone I mean. I was unfair, but our times are difficult, I acted on instinct." Omar spoke gently, he and Nada had shared many intimate conversations during their daily fighting practices. They knew each other's moods well by now.

"How long had you thought about it, Omar? Tell me the truth."

She felt his stomach muscles ripple with a suppressed chuckle. "I believe God himself hatched the idea the night I sat on that ostrich egg! I knew then you were meant for me." They both laughed. Nada wrapped her arms around her husband and squeezed him tightly, her head against his polished leather tunic.

They walked along, arm in arm past the servant's quarters where Omar shared a barracks with the other guards. House Hareb was quiet this evening. The past two months had seen an exodus of many staff as the lords of the house had to let them go; they no longer had the means to pay them. Some had remained unpaid because they loved the masters of Hareb.

Omar and Nada kept walking, quietly enjoying their first moments alone.

"Nada, I have no home or dwelling place of my own, no place to bring my wife. I.." He trailed off, at a loss for words.

"Omar...!" She responded in a teasing tone. "We are standing conveniently just down the hall from my own ample quarters!" He pulled his hand toward her room with a smile. Omar had dutifully awakened her in this very room on his rounds on many mornings. It was a beautifully appointed space.

He noticed a peculiar attribute – Nada seemed to have a penchant for collecting pillows. She and Batshua shared a joke concerning their first day together when she had fallen off a pillow to her mistress's great amusement. Ever since, Batshua rewarded her with a pillow for any little favor so her sleeping area had a veritable mountain of them.

Nada led Omar into the room, pulling the thick curtain shut. A cool desert breeze fanned the thin veil hanging over the window. Bright moonlight streamed through the translucence of the wispy silk fluttering over the narrow opening. They quietly undressed in the near darkness.

"I have something I should tell you, my love." Nada spoke hesitantly.

"Oh?" Omar braced himself for a heartbreak. He half-expected this, knowing some of Nada's history.

"Yes," she continued quietly, "you have not asked, but given my past as a slave and all, I think you should know. God has protected my honor. I think he intended me as a gift to you. I am a virgin." Her voice whispered softly on the evening breeze.

Omar breathed a heavy sigh of relief from his end of the heavily pillowed bed. "I suppose that complicates things a little."

"It does?" Nada was surprised.

"Yes. I am honored and pleased to hear that God has preserved you. You are a miracle. A gift from God himself. But you see, I am also a virgin."

"Then how does that complicate things?" Nada was confused and not a little delighted to hear this news.

"Well, I was sort of hoping that at least one of us would know what to do!"

Nada's voice took on an impish lilt, "Hmmm... I see your point. We will just have to figure something out. But... you will have to find me first!" With that she dove under the mountain of pillows!

"Hey!" He started tossing pillows in his search and their laughter echoed down the hall.

-:--o--:-

Boshet lay awake trying to sort out the exciting new thoughts floating around in her head. She heard the faint laughter from Omar and Nada. A peaceful smile curved her lips. She knew the place in her heart where such innocent intimacy should be located had long ago been burned and scarred beyond recognition. Yet it felt good and warm to know her new friends could experience it.

Boshet's hope lay along a different road than the young lovers down the hall. The onset of sleep began to quiet her fretful mind, her scarred soul lay still. She felt safe and protected and even loved and respected in this house. She had never experienced these feelings before. Genuine love and respect – a balm to her wounded spirit.

Although Boshet had been raised in a temple, she began to whisper the first real prayer of her life, "God, grant me peace. Allow me to find a place of serenity. Somewhere, some place, may I find solitude and peace, away from those who use me so that I may learn to be useful. Show me that I can give freely, so that others will stop taking from me." Boshet's soul was badly burned, but all souls can be healed by the one who created the human heart. Thoughts of her mother's voice echoed distantly in her mind, *"Boshet, remember! God's name is Elohim! Ba'al is no god! Elohim is God of gods! He will watch over you!"* She smiled dreamily and knew her mother was right. God began working on an answer to her prayer. She fell into deep sleep.

-:--o--:-

Naaman discovered a creative way to select which of the camel tenders and drivers he would trust. He 'borrowed' a small idol of Almaqah from one of the tenders he intended to banish from House Hareb the next day anyway. Then he lined up the men outside a tent and sat behind a table inside. There were openings behind him on the left and right with loyal guards stationed at each opening. He sat on the right side with one sword laid on the table before him, an identical sword in front of the Almaqah idol.

As the men came in, one at a time, he said, "Choose your weapon." Those who asked about the sword in front of him were told, "That is the sword of Elohim, the God of House Hareb, the other is the sword of Almaqah." He would say nothing more.

The men who selected Almaqah's sword were directed to his left where they were paid their wages and released. The sword was confiscated. Naaman was pleased to find thirty good candidates with his test.

From the thirty candidates who selected Elohim's sword, he hand-picked eight whom he felt knew which end of the sword to actually stick into the enemy.

-:--o--:-

Omar and Nada woke late that morning in a tangle of legs, arms and pillows. They heard a rattle of pottery outside the curtained doorway. Nada felt extremely vulnerable given her lack of clothing as did Omar, they stared at each other shamefaced. Nada clutched two pillows to her chest.

"You missed breakfast!" "We brought you something, compliments of lady Boshet." It was the same servant girls who had served food that morning at the top of madam Batshua's watchtower eons ago. They spoke in tandem. "We will not disturb you!" "Happy wedding morn!" "Blessings upon you!" "Enjoy your breakfast." They giggled musically as they padded down the hallway.

Both young people dressed hurriedly to get to the food. Nada was first, she was ravenous. She spied down the hallway with just her head poking out through the curtain. She felt so silly, but it was the awkwardness of their new status not fully settled into their psyche. Both felt stealthy for some strange reason, like they should hide what they were doing and what they had done the night before. Did everyone feel this way? Nada pulled the tray into the room and they pounced on the food. No food in their memory ever tasted so sweet!

"Nada," Omar spoke as he crunched on fresh fruit, the juice spraying out the sides of his mouth, "have you given thought to what you will say to madam Batshua when and if we find her?"

She had eaten like a starved jackal. She reclined on a stack of pillows sipping tea but sat up to a tailor position at her husband's question. "I do not know. I can only hope that my presence, our presence, reminds her of home, that she is loved -- loved by us and her husband. There is little I can say, only God can change a heart."

"You are wise." He said. "How did you become so wise so young?"

"Hmmm… my stomach is full of food and now you are trying to stuff my head full of nonsense. That is not wise!" She smiled her thanks at his compliment all the same.

Nada finished her tea with a gulp. "We should be going, don't you think? Today we must finalize our plans for the journey to Goshen."

-:--o--:-

On the third day, Omar, Nada and Naaman approached Job's garden. He was seated among three other men who sat around him silently. Their head and beards were also shaved, they had stripped themselves bare to the chest. To Nada's eyes, their faces appeared dirty...

When Job saw the three approaching he stood painfully and motioned for them to be quiet and to remain where they were. He hobbled over to them and led them into the outer chamber.

"What is going on, master Job?" Nada inquired.

Job sat on a low bench outside the entrance to his enclosure, he kept his voice low. "My three dearest friends have arrived, Eliphaz, Bildad and Zophar. They have traveled a great distance when they heard of my distress. Each has taken a vow of silence which they will not break for seven days. They meditate with me, covering their faces with ashes. Thus they do to pay homage to my brokenness." Job began to weep. "They are good men. Good men sent from God himself to comfort me in my hour of need. I am highly honored by their presence."

This was almost too much for Nada to bear. To see this man who was so strong and respected brought so low, covered with ugly sores and in such pain! She wanted to run to him and throw her arms around him in comfort, but she knew that such a gesture would cause him even more pain. He was beyond the reach of her love. Her eyes filled with tears, searching for some answer, some way to console the tortured, dying man before her.

"Master Job, you once told me that God is the God of possibilities, is that not so?" She asked.

He turned toward Nada and his eyes burned bright with strength and wisdom. "Yes, young one. There is nothing impossible to the Maker of all things. Whether this," he lifted his hands to indicate his destroyed body, "or this," gesturing around him to indicate his ruined lands, "is from the hand of God himself, I know not. But this I do know – though he slay me, yet will I hope in him. There is always hope, child. Do not despair."

The group felt as if a breeze had passed through them, filling them with purpose and resolve. Nada wondered if this was a brief touch of the 'caress of God's hand' she and her mistress had experienced together on the watchtower. Whatever it was, she felt refreshed and confident.

"I must return to my friends soon. I am sure that eventually, they will have many words of wisdom to share with me." He smiled with his painful half-smile.

Job continued, "I have managed to secure sufficient camels, horses and supplies for your journey. Nada's gold will supply the remains of House Hareb for many months. In fact..." He paused and looked very thoughtful, "this will enable me to continue paying my household guards that have returned from their failed mission to El'Hajar. I am certain many would have remained loyal without pay, but a warrior deserves his wages and House Hareb will need good defenses in the days ahead. It appears that I am truly in your debt, my lady." He attempted to bow but the effort was too painful.

"There are no debts between friends, master Job." The master smiled at Nada's grace.

Naaman spoke up. "We had better get moving if we desire to make our first camp by dark. There is no moon tonight."

Job said, "I will not delay you further. Blessings on your journey. I trust your efforts will be fruitful." He limped painfully back to his place among his friends.

-:--O--:-

Boshet joined them once she could not be seen by Job. The group had agreed it would be best for all concerned if Job did not see her dressed in Batshua's robes. With a silky veil draped across the lower part of her face, Boshet was indistinguishable from the Emira attired in her blue and white finery.

The caravan lined up on the main thoroughfare of Hareb was only a bit smaller than the one Nada remembered from just a few months prior that spring. Her thoughts raced back to her mistress's premonitions of disaster and tortured dreams. What she feared had come to pass.

Despite her secret confession to Nada, Batshua had succumbed to the bitterness in her soul that she had fought so long. Nada could not understand the complex enigma that was her mistress Batshua. How could she turn against her beloved husband at a time when he needed her most? The temptation to despair was strong within Nada, but she felt duty-bound to this woman who had lifted her out of slavery, redeemed her and rescued her from a life that the woman who now impersonated Batshua knew only too well.

She shuddered at the memory of how close she had come to Boshet's fate at the slave market. Then she looked at her handsome husband riding his black stallion beside her. Her heart swelled to near bursting with pride and love. No, it was not duty that motivated Nada to seek her fleeing, irrational mistress, it was gratitude.

Her thoughts were interrupted by a blast from a ram's horn. Silence descended on the small crowd gathered at their send-off as the veiled Boshet-Batshua stepped aboard her elegantly decorated howdah near the front of the line. Whispers rippled through the gathering, *"I thought the Emira left days ago!" "Where is she going now?!" "I had not known she had returned, did you?"*

The disguise was working. If her own people, were fooled, then if there were any treacherous souls among the household, they would also believe the Emira to be with Nada and Omar. Nada had no reason to believe anyone in House Hareb would betray the Emira, but she was beginning to understand a wise proverb her mistress had passed along, "Granted I am paranoid, but am I paranoid *enough*?"

The ram's horn sounded again, this time with the monotone song Nada remembered from the spring. It resonated in her heart achingly. So much had changed, so much destruction and loss between the two melodies!

Naaman sang! Who knew he could sing!? The thought of music coming out of that scarred face seemed so incongruous, but the melody was clear and the words were, well… scandalous! Something about a fair maiden's virtue not spared by a returning warrior. Nada and Frayda looked at each other with their hands covering their mouths, embarrassed. Mercifully the song ended quickly, the crowd shuffled their feet and applauded the Sabean's well-intended effort politely. Nada made a mental note to speak with Naaman about his repertoire, but at least he made an effort to observe the formalities.

All the necessities of customs filled more or less adequately, the caravan peeled away out of town and headed south to the less than boisterous sounds of subdued townspeople.

-:--o--:-

From a hill across the valley from Hareb, a pair of hate-filled eyes watched the caravan depart the safety of the city's gates. The muscles of his jaws rippled the skin of his cheeks, making his dark tattoos appear to be clawing at his face.

Ba'al-Hanni's spy in House Hareb had informed him that the Emir's wife had departed three days ago disguised as a servant. Ba'al-Hanni was no fool! He enjoyed feeding his lying informant's remains to the jackals that surrounded his fire at night. It was entertaining to watch them fight over the pieces he threw to them.

Now he had seen with his own eyes! The Emira was even now leaving with her faithful little vixen and entourage. Obviously they were heading south. The faithless woman wanted to go home to Papa! Ba'al-Hanni laughed to himself with nefarious glee. He would ensure she got home, but only after she knew the shame and brokenness of a ravished body! His plans for the ruin of A'dab Ben Hareb included the complete shame and degradation of the proud Emira! He nearly drooled at the prospect.

Unknown to Ba'al-Hanni, the hand of God covered Nada and Omar's caravan securely. God's hand was also upon Ba'al-Hanni as he followed along, shadowing their caravan. But God's hand was slowly closing into a fist around the evil priest of Ba'al.

-:--o--:-

Nada and Omar decided their first major rest stop would be Rosh-Ramen city, otherwise known as El-Elyon, the City of God. Their pace had been grueling with everyone mounted. They were able to nearly double their daily distance, but it cost them greatly in fatigue and nearly lamed their mounts. They were able to reach the city in only two and a half days but they would require at least a full day's rest. Even with the rest, they would be a full two days ahead of their normal pace.

Nada and Omar found a small inn just off the center of town that had an adjoining room available for Boshet. Frayda would sleep in a hammock outside the door as befit her station. The doorway was shaded by a light reed veranda. The rest of the crew made beds for themselves in the stables with the animals which were down a short path from the inn.

A few hours later, an extremely exhausted horse carried Ba'al-Hanni to the edge of Rosh-Ramen. The stallion's sides were heaving desperately as it tossed its head side to side wild-eyed, froth dripping from its mouth. He dismounted and handed the reins to the innkeeper.

"In the name of all that is holy, sire! What have you done to this precious creature?" The innkeeper was clearly outraged by the condition of the poor animal.

Ba'al-Hanni's look might have killed the innkeeper had his attention not been totally focused on the horse. As it was, he barely heard Ba'al-Hanni mutter, "Shut-up!" as he staggered off to a room without another thought for the animal he had whipped and beaten beyond the limits of its endurance.

To remain hidden from the caravan, its pursuer had been forced to follow a longer route. His cruel pace had been incredibly difficult to maintain. As he entered the inn, his horse's rear legs quivered and buckled from its effort. Finally, its knees locked together as dehydration and shock took its toll on the creature's fevered brain. It fell over with a final convulsion and died.

-:--o--:-

Dark clouds roiled over the horizon just after the sun reached its noon zenith. Thunder rumbled in the distant hills. The rainy season of fall was upon them, but an unusually intense storm was building. Rain started pelting in huge drops so big they made small craters in the dusty streets. The early splatters actually raised a cloud of choking dust before the sky itself burst to loosen a torrent that pounded everything to mud.

Nada and Omar pulled Frayda into their room to prevent her from drowning. She looked extremely bedraggled and grateful. The rain made such a racket, they almost did not hear Boshet's muffled scream from the adjoining room. A heavy curtain hung in the doorway. When Boshet called, Nada did not hesitate, she rushed through the curtain just as Omar shouted, "Wait!".

Omar heard his wife's startled gasp and cry. He ran to her aid and nearly impaled himself on Ba'al-Hanni's sword. He held Nada like a sack of grain with one arm wrapped firmly around her chest, clamping her arms immobile against his own. Nada flailed, kicked, and tried to bite her captor, but she was small and Ba'al-Hanni's strength was demon-strong. He felt nothing, nor did he flinch at her struggles. His eyes were on Omar. Omar's eyes were on the point of the sword a few inches from his throat.

"Call the other." Ba'al-Hanni commanded Omar.

"Frayda, come." Omar called without taking his eyes of Ba'al-Hanni. Frayda appeared behind Omar in the doorway.

"You!" Ba'al-Hanni spoke to Frayda without taking his eyes of Omar. "Sit in the corner beside your mistress." Frayda was frightened beyond conscious thought. She could not figure out what Ba'al-Hanni meant. He was holding her 'mistress' in his arm! The other woman this intruder had tied hand and foot at the far end of the room was Boshet, not her mistress. She stood rooted in place, frozen in indecision.

"MOVE!" Ba'al-Hanni shouted in a voice of command that only caused Frayda to lurch one step forward toward Nada.

"FRAYDA!" Omar took over, "Go sit in the corner beside madam Batshua!"

Frayda protested weakly, "But she's not…"

"SHUT UP, FRAYDA AND DO AS YOU ARE TOLD!" Omar's desperate instructions got through Frayda's fear-dimmed thought processes. She ran to the corner of the wall where Boshet was propped up against a pillow, curled herself into a ball and hid her face between her knees.

Ba'al-Hanni had had just about enough of Nada's struggles. He turned his attention to her, squeezing her until face turned red. She could no longer breathe.

"Stop at once or your boyfriend dies." There was no bluff in Ba'al-Hanni's tone.

"Nada, please." Omar caught her eyes. He shook his head in the barest signal and his expression spoke volumes: *"Wait, my love. We will get our chance!"*

Nada went limp. Ba'al-Hanni dropped her at his feet where she lay panting, but unresisting. He turned back to Omar, "Strip!"

"Great!" he thought, *"If I live through this, I will never live it down."*

He started with his weapons, which he assumed was Ba'al-Hanni's main concern. He dropped everything carefully behind him. When he stood naked, Ba'al-Hanni knew he had the room in his control. He grabbed a fistful of Nada's hair and ordered Omar to follow, "Come!"

He threw Nada to the right side wall where she landed in a heap. He used his sword to slice through the bonds holding Boshet's feet together. He had tied her hands behind her back tightly enough to make her cry out in pain, which was what had alerted Nada. Fortunately, her veil was still in place. He grabbed Boshet's feet and dragged her flat onto her back, her hands now uncomfortably bent underneath her. She groaned in renewed agony.

"You!" He turned to Omar. Tie up your little vixen! I do not wish to be bitten again.

"With what?!" Omar questioned sarcastically, he was getting fed up with this.

"Use her belt, you fool!" Nada always wore her long leather belt. It had a secret. Omar used Nada's belt to tie her hands to her feet. As he did, he slipped the hidden dagger out of its sheath and palmed the hilt in his hand with the blade hidden up his forearm. He moved to the wall opposite Nada and sat dejectedly to watch his captor's sport with his mistress.

Ba'al-Hanni's plan could not be more glorious. He exalted in its culmination! His demonic power, garnered carefully through a lifetime of dedication to Ba'al, the true power of the earth, the Prince of the Air, god of storm and pestilence, had finally brought him to this! The ruin of A'dab Ben Hareb's empire, the desecration of his enemy's body, wracked with sores and pain. And now! His enemy's wife lay helpless beneath his knees! Her trembling body would soon be ravished; the humiliation of House Hareb would be complete!

He leaned forward in a near ecstasy of anticipation to peer into the eyes of his tortured victim. He lay down his sword to hold her throat and viciously slapped her face. Her veil fell to the side and... ?!

The fist of God squeezed shut.

The face was Boshet! How?! He had been betrayed! The room heaved in a violent shudder as thunder crashed and demons flew screaming from the room! Ba'al-Hanni, the mere man leaned back in confused shock! What was this treachery!?

Boshet smiled, blood streaming from her nose. "What is wrong, my love? Are you not happy to see your beloved wife again?"

Ba'al-Hanni felt a terrible pain and pressure at the base of his skull. Boshet squinted as he spit on her and stuck out his tongue. But then she saw it was only a brief illusion. His 'tongue' was not at tongue at all, but a dagger! And it was dripping blood.

In the moment Ba'al-Hanni sat back, Omar had leaped with the speed of a striking snake, driving Nada's knife through the back of his head and out his mouth, severing spirit from body instantaneously. Ba'al-Hanni fell over in twitching death.

Unashamed of his nakedness, he untied his wife then donned his armor. Boshet was weeping, not in sorrow but relief. Frayda moved to her and released her bonds. Everyone noticed the silence – the rain had stopped.

Light streamed in from the window and framed Frayda in a warm glow. She looked different somehow. Older.

Someone needed to say something. Frayda decided it would be her. "I believe this means that God has once again placed his Hand of Protection on House Hareb." The others looked at Frayda with something approaching respect.

Omar walked over to the corpse of Ba'al-Hanni and jerked the knife free of his body. He wiped it clean on his victim's robe.

"I agree." He said, as he handed the knife back to his wife grimly.

-:--o--:-

Naaman appeared in the doorway with a smile that vanished in the instant he took in the scene. Frayda left Boshet and clung to him with both arms wrapped tightly around his waist. Nada noted this surprising move and thought, "*Interesting…*".

"What has happened here? Who is this?" Naaman's arms automatically moved to hold Frayda but his shocked attention was on the lifeless man with blood pooling around his head.

Boshet stood and began to wipe herself clean of the filth that had splattered her face. "Truly, Naaman, we do not know. He said he was a relative of master Job, but apparently that was a lie. He was a priest of Ba'al and he held me captive as his slave-wife for a time. Whoever he was, he is dead and that is what matters now." Boshet's pronouncement broke a tension in the room. There was a finality in her manner that everyone sensed. Intuitively, everyone realized that Ba'al-Hanni had come alone, acting in the hubris of his own power.

Naaman had a few practical matters in mind. He picked up Ba'al-Hanni's sword and examined it critically. He rolled the body over to detach the sword's sheath.

"This is a fine blade! I know not its equal. Master Omar, may I assume the death blow was dealt by your hand?" Omar nodded. Naaman cut the air a few times and sheathed the blade with a snap. He presented it to Omar formally, holding it underhanded with his head bowed.

"May the sword of the vanquished be mighty in the hand of the victor. Thus we honor you, master Omar, noble warrior and defender of House Hareb."

Omar accepted the blade with both his hands. For a moment, the two men held it between them firmly with their eyes locked, warrior to warrior. Naaman released his hold and backed off a step, arms at his side, smiling at his friend in respect. Omar fastened the sword to his waist, it looked just fine there.

"Naaman, I shall ask you a favor." Omar said.

"Anything, sir."

"I shall need training in the use of such a fine weapon." Omar eyed Naaman, one man to another.

"Ah! That will be a great honor!" Naaman beamed at Omar's compliment. Proud of his swordsmanship, Omar's submission to his guidance affirmed his skill. "And sir, you may return the favor to me by adding to my skills with the dagger. I am most impressed with your efficiency." He pointed to the corpse with his chin. Most dagger kills in Naaman's experience had been butchery. To kill a man with a single stroke...

"Thank you, Naaman. But I shall have to refer you to my master trainer instead." Naaman looked bewildered. Omar gestured toward Nada who was sitting cross-legged near Boshet. "May I present, Nada the Knife."

When she saw the sparkle of admiration in her husband's eyes, Nada could not resist showing off just a little. She withdrew her blade, flipped it quickly hand to hand, hit the hilt with the back of her hand mid-flip spinning the blade upward and then caught it by the hilt with her left and to slide it back into its sheath so swiftly Naaman was not certain what he had just seen!

"By the gods! I mean... your pardon! Never have I... my lady!" Naaman blinking in disbelief as were Boshet and Frayda.

"Yes!" Omar continued. "By the gods indeed. Actually, by God's great goodness, I believe. My lady is exceptionally skilled. Madam Batshua thought it best we keep her skill a secret, but since we may face other enemies, it may be best that you know. This knowledge should not leave this room, agreed?" Everyone murmured ascent.

The late afternoon heat began to make the room uncomfortably warm. Boshet stood.

"I think it's time we consider what we do about cleaning up this mess. As for me, I do not wish to spend the night in this room. No offense to my lady and master's gracious hospitality."

As if in answer, the innkeeper appeared at the door with two armed men. The situation became very complex again, perhaps they had remained talking too long!

"There he is, the murdering swine! I see you have already saved me the trouble of bringing him before the magistrate. What did he do, try to rob you?"

"In a manner speaking, yes." Omar did not want to reveal too much.

The innkeeper was no fool, nor was he blind. He could see a beautiful woman with a bleeding nose, and a bruised face. Her robe was torn in several places. "I see." He said with an understanding nod.

"Do you know this man?" Omar asked.

"No. He rode to me on a horse he had beaten beyond endurance. It died, for he gave it no mercy. My sister lives just outside town. She and her husband heard the horse's labored breathing, so he ran to offer aid. This evil swine did not stop whipping his horse and when my brother-in-law tried to stop him, he was killed for his efforts. My sister ran to me and recognized the horse at my inn. We have been searching for him ever since. Thank you again for killing him, you have avenged my sister. I will take him off your hands now. I have other rooms for you, with my compliments!" The innkeeper was out of breath.

Naaman stooped to search Ba'al-Hanni's body and clothes. There was nothing else of value but a large ring on the index finger of his right hand. He pulled it off. "Master Omar?"

Omar considered. "Lady Boshet? A souvenir for you?"

She looked like she was about to say no, but then reconsidered. "Yes. Yes, I believe I will take that. Thank you." Naaman tossed it to her. The men with the innkeeper dragged the body out, they all followed. Omar and Nada turned to look back.

Nada said, "It's strange, but I never felt like we were in any danger, not once during all of that. I felt strangely protected with the strength of rage even after you told me to be quiet." She smiled up at Omar.

"I felt the same way. It was a controlled rage, an almost reckless feeling. I knew that no matter what that man tried, he would fail and we would win. As you say, it was very strange." Omar said.

Nada mused, "Madam Batshua and I experienced something not unlike this once. She called it 'the caress of God's hand', but this was different. I think what we experienced might be 'the strength of God's hand', do you think so?"

"We will have to ask master Job when we get home." Omar said. Until he said the word 'home' he had not truly considered that their trip would end in success -- that they would return home alive. It gave him a thrill. They turned away and left the bare room with all of Satan's plans drying in the dust behind them. House Hareb was on the mend.

-:--o--:-

There was a minor stir that night among the grave diggers of Rosh-Ramen. The body of Ba'al-Hanni could not be found. A trail of blood led toward the north out of the city, but suddenly ended.

-:--o--:-

17

My Father's House

"How I long for the months gone by,
for the days when God watched over me,
when his lamp shone on my head
and by his light I walked through darkness!"

The Book of Job 29:2-3

-:--o--:-

Batshua Al-Nahdiyah stood outside the gate that marked the boundary of her father's holdings. There was no guard, these lands were secure and the gate only symbolic. To Batshua's travel-weary eyes, it represented an exit as much as an entrance. If she opened the gate and stepped into her father's domain, she knew it meant surrendering to her father's will and that she had truly abandoned her husband.

Wild thoughts of turning back to Hareb or living a life in hiding flickered through her mind like flashes of lightning. Images of A'dab's blistered, oozing skin, his labored breathing, his swollen tongue and fetid breath made her shudder with guilty revulsion. There was no way home. If she ran, she could foresee herself standing in a line of women at a slave market with her own face replacing that of the terrified young Nada that day in Tariq. She shook her head and the visions disappeared as if a rock had dashed the surface of a pond.

Looking up, she saw her father's house in the distance. A young boy detached himself from a small flock of sheep between the house and the gate. He began running pell-mell toward the gate. She had been seen! She sighed, too late to back out now. After all, her path had been decided the day she had secreted her way through the west gate of Hareb. She decided to wait until the boy arrived. He looked to be about ten years old.

-:--o--:-

The bright-eyed youth opened the gate with a sly grin. "Well-met, my lady. I am Ruben, keeper of sheep and watcher of the gate. If your camels are thirsty, there is a well not far along this path. I will guide you there and gladly draw water for them." Batshua returned Ruben's grin, he was obviously very proud of his role.

"Thank you, Ruben. You are unusually kind to strangers. Tell me, young sir, is it your habit to offer water so freely to travelers such as me and my companion?" This sort of behavior was not common among the people of Edom. Strangers were usually held at arm's length or even the point of a sword until certain rituals of introduction or fealty had been observed.

"Oh yes, ma'am! My father has often warned that I should never be rude to strangers for they may be angels in disguise. Certainly you are beautiful enough to be an angel, though I have never met one personally." He looked somewhat disappointed at this thought. "And as for your companion, I have never heard of an angel with skin of his color, but I shall not withhold water merely because of my ignorance in these matters. My ears would burn for a month or more from the lectures of my father, should I fail to honor his guests!"

Batshua laughed at the boy's precocious candor. "Who is your father? He sounds like a priest or a teacher of some kind."

The boy's eyes went wide in wonder and pride. "Oh, he is both of those and more, ma'am. If you have traveled these lands, you must know of Asher Ben Hadad the master of this house. He is known throughout Goshen as the wisest of the wise. I aspire to be as wise as him one day, but as his youngest son, I am fit only to watch sheep and open gates for any angels who wish to visit our humble dwelling."

Batshua found his smile completely irresistible. And somewhere within the stream of words, she realized this intelligent, endearing little fellow was none other than her baby brother! Her emotions crystallized, shattered, melted, dripped into puddles, pooled together again and then vainly attempted to reassemble into anything resembling what she should feel. Oh well, time enough for that later. First things first.

"Ruben, may I introduce my faithful attendant, Negasi." Ruben and Negasi nodded politely to each other. Batshua took a deep breath. "And I am Batshua Al-Nahdiyah, eldest daughter of Asher Ben Hadad. I am very pleased to meet you... brother Ruben." She bowed formally.

Ruben's eyes went huge, his jaw went slack. He recovered quickly though, young genius boys usually do. "My father is going to kill me three times for not being prepared for your arrival, my sister! I beg your forgiveness! I was unaware..."

Batshua held up her hand to stop his self-flagellation. "My arrival is unexpected, Ruben. There is no offense." She stopped to think for a moment. "Is my father well? Is he at home?"

"Yes! Yes! He is not far!" Impetuously, he turned to run.

"Wait!" She laughed. "Negasi, is there room for this young man with you?"

"Of course, m'um. Ruben, why run when you can ride, yes?!" He laughed with a great expanse of teeth.

Ruben was ecstatic. "Oh! May I? I have never ridden on a camel! Do they bite? May I steer it? What is its name? Is that one a male or female? Why are their necks so long and their tails so short?" Batshua liked the boy, but wondered if his brain or mouth ever slowed down. They mounted and began the final slow walk toward home. Fortunately, Ruben was far too excited about the ride to become camel-sick.

-:--O--:-

Batshua's reception by the rest of her family was mixed. She met some younger sisters who had been born during the twenty years since her marriage to A'dab. They had returned to her home only once a mere five years into their union. Other sisters had matured beyond familiarity. Her birth-mother had died from childbed fever after her oldest brother was born. Batshua had a nanny but never really bonded with her.

Batshua's fondest memories of home were seven precious years spent in near daily conversations with her father. From her eighth year until she wed A'dab, she and her father rarely missed their walks and talks. Because she was his firstborn and daughter of his beloved first wife, Asher held his daughter close to his heart. She was a connection to the memory of a woman whom he deeply loved. He found in his daughter a charming image of her mother that helped him prolong memories he cherished.

Asher taught his daughter to read and write, which was almost unheard of for girls in Goshen. Under her father's tutelage, Batshua memorized Hebrew history, tradition, culture and even learned some mathematics. She had a head stuffed full of the tools of independence, but she had neglected, or perhaps had not had the opportunity, to acquire the necessary tools of relational interdependence because she had never seen it modeled between her mother and father.

-:--o--:-

Asher Ben Hadad rose early on the second morning after his daughter's arrival. As usual, he and little Ruben walked together from the sheep enclosure out to the small pasture midway to the gate where Ruben would serve his double duty. Asher's joy these days was chatting with his youngest, a boy so full of wit and curiosity! He laughed to himself. Of his eight sons and five daughters, this young boy burned with a brightness matched only by the flame of Batshua herself. *Ah, Batshua! Why have you brought distress upon my house in the autumn of my life?* He sighed.

"Is there something wrong, father?" Ruben was very attuned to his father's moods.

"No, my son. Well, perhaps. My thoughts have turned upon your oldest sister, Batshua this morning." He walked slowly with a staff. About two dozen sheep ambled along behind them.

Ruben looked up with a grin. "I like her. I have never met a queen, but I think she is what a queen must be like." Ruben was kicking stones along the path as they talked. Occasionally a stone would get lodged between his toes and sandals. He would hop along on one foot while he pulled out the stone, still talking, able to concentrate on every word his father said and not realize his antics were providing great entertainment.

"Your sister is in great pain." Asher spoke solemnly.

"Is she sick? She does not seem sick to me." He screwed up his face in concentration.

"No, not that kind of pain. She feels the pain of guilt and loss. Can you imagine how you would feel if you turned around and all your sheep were laying dead in the field?"

"Oh! That would hurt, yes." Ruben's eyes reflected upon this. He wanted to understand his sister.

"This pain has caused your sister to forget who she is."

"She told me who she is, father. Her name is Batshua Al-Nahdiyah! How can you say she has forgotten who she is?"

"Ha! Ha! You examine everything as if you are looking at the surface of a pond and do not think there could any fish swimming beneath!" Asher scolded his son with a nudge to his shoulder to let him know he spoke in jest. "Come now, you must go fishing for deeper thoughts."

"Okay. Do you mean she has forgotten that she is a wife to her husband, a ruler in the land of Edom and most of all that she is a beloved child of God?" Ruben looked up out of the corner of his eye, hoping he was close to the right answer.

"Very good, Ruben. She is all that and more. Batshua is my daughter, your sister and a friend to many who love her. In her pain, she has abandoned them. This is not a good thing she has done, yet I am glad she is here. With God's help, I hope to remind her of who she is." They walked a few moments while Ruben absorbed this. Asher continued. "And whose she is. By the way, my son, she has spoken at length of the friends she left behind. They do not seem to be the kind of people who would accept their abandonment lightly. I believe we will have visitors soon."

Ruben looked up in surprise. "More visitors from Edom?" He seemed excited at the prospect.

"Yes, I believe so. If they arrive in the next day or two, I want you to welcome them, and ask them for a few days indulgence. By that, I mean for you to ask them to be patient. Take them to the guest house that they may refresh themselves and rest from their journey, but do not tell anyone but me that they have arrived. Can you do this?"

"Yes sir, that will be fun!" Ruben loved intrigue.

Asher cocked an eyebrow at his mischievous offspring. "Enjoy yourself then. I may be wrong, but I have a feeling we will have visitors soon." He kissed his son on both cheeks and walked the half hour back to his house praying for wisdom. His daughter needed healing in her soul that only God could provide. Asher hoped only that he could keep Batshua's attention focused on the right things long enough for God to work a miracle in her spirit.

-:--o--:-

During the afternoon of the next day, a road-weary band of Edomites met a ten year old gatekeeper who somehow had clairvoyantly foreseen their arrival. He also stubbornly refused entry to his domain.

"Yes! As I have been trying to say, master Asher Ben Hadad has requested that you refresh yourselves in the guest house for two days. Is this such a burden to bear? It is a most exquisite guest house. It is fit for a king, should a king ever come this way." Ruben was being very polite, but unequivocal. He assured them he would let the master know of their arrival, but they were not to see Batshua until master Asher gave his permission.

They talked it over. Nada said, "I don't like it. We came all this way. This is no way to be treated! The least he could do is come out himself, not send a hireling boy to shuffle us off to who knows where! This treatment is an offense." The Emira's handmaiden was very put out.

Ruben grinned at that. "If you want, I could fetch the master's son. Would a visit by master Asher's son ease your mind? I am sure he would come talk with you and clarify everything."

"Yes. That would be much better." Nada looked down her nose at the boy.

"Okay then, if you insist." Ruben took a step backward, raised an arm high over his head, lifted a leg and twirled in a full circle. Nada and company stared at him as if he had lost his mind. Ruben gestured wildly with his arms and spoke in an over-loud, over-formal voice, "Presenting Ruben Ben Asher, Lord of the Sheep, Defender of the Gate, beloved brother of Batshua Al-Nahdiyah!" He bowed deeply, pressing his hand to forehead, heart and a then a final flourish. He looked up expecting applause.

Nada stared, mouth agape. The rest of the group looked as if they were chewing onions. When Nada found her voice she took a step toward Ruben and bowed. "Young master Ruben, I am ashamed of my behavior. We will gratefully accept the hospitality of your guest house and await word from your father. Please accept my humble apology."

Ruben waved her off. "No apology needed. I should have introduced myself right away, the fault is mine. I like you. I can see that my sister has chosen good friends. Perhaps I will have good friends like you one day." Everyone looked a little more relaxed and sensed that Ruben was acting under his father's instructions.

Ruben continued. "Now, a favor. Could I ride one of your camels to the guest house? I think I like camels! I think I like you, too!

Will you consider becoming my friends? Please promise that you will not tell father that I tricked you into believing I was only a hireling! I need to memorize your names! You speak with a funny accent! Do you think I speak with an accent? That would be very funny indeed, for my father says I speak most eloquently! Are any of you angels? I have always wanted to meet a real live angel! Do you know Negasi? I do not think angels come with skin of his color, but then I do not know everything."

Everyone laughed at Ruben's rapid verbal antics. He was obviously over-endowed with intellect causing his brain to burst with thoughts that spilled out his mouth in a constant torrent.

They found the guest house more than adequate accommodations for the next two days. Ruben turned out to be the live entertainment who kept them constantly amused. The time passed quickly.

-:--o--:-

"Come walk with me, my daughter." Asher's gentle old eyes gazed down on his beloved child as she sat alone the morning of the third day. He had just returned from his daily trek with Ruben. The lad had filled his father's ears with tidings of Batshua's friends. Asher's heart was lifted by his son's assessment regarding the high quality of his daughter's companions. He had learned to trust Ruben's sense for character. The boy seemed to have a second sight that peered past the duplicitous or shallow. Her friends would be a balm to Batshua's soul if they allowed God time to prepare a way in her for them.

Batshua looked up from her reverie. Her father offered his arm. She stood and accepted his closeness. This was the moment she had longed for and now that it had finally arrived, she was disturbed to find herself filled with uncertainty. Would her father scold and condemn? She condemned herself on many levels, she felt herself a failure and a coward. To her own eyes, she was no more than a scared girl running home to Papa's arms. It was not an image of herself she admired.

No longer dressed in her fine silks, she had borrowed a dress from a sister. Broad rust-colored stripes ran shoulder to ankle with a cloth sash that she used to dab a tear away from her eye. Her father saw the emotion but said nothing. After a few minutes of silent trekking, their way rose gently to a small knoll where the path divided. Asher stopped at a small wooden bench at the crossroad and sat. They had been walking for just under an hour. He handed his daughter a piece of raisin cake he pulled from a small satchel dangling from his side. They munched on it thoughtfully. Batshua had forgotten the taste, her mind flooded with childhood memories.

"I call this the Mercy Seat. There is room for two. Come... sit." He patted the bench beside him. Batshua sat and slid her arm into his, leaning her cheek against his shoulder. She was instantly intoxicated by the manly smell of her father and overwhelmed with longing for the peace and security she once felt as his child. She knew it was a foolish thought, but for the moment she was transported back in time to those wonderful years with him. For a short span of time, just for now, there was not a thing wrong in the whole world.

The moment passed, but... she would long remember its healing balm. "*Thank you, God, thank you for whatever mercies I may receive, though I deserve them not.*" She prayed silently with a long, slow exhalation.

"Why do you call this the Mercy Seat?" Batshua asked curiously.

"An interesting question." Asher closed his eyes in thought. "I have often lingered at this divide in the path to rest on this bench. I have sat here with a heavy heart pondering decisions, contemplating my life. I have often prayed here and I have often argued with God here." He paused and smiled down at his daughter.

She decided to take the bait. Looking up with a grin, she quipped, "You have argued with God? Did you win?"

He smiled broadly. "Just once. God let me win an argument once."

"Really?! What did you win?" Batshua was intrigued.

"Justice. I argued with God for justice. I learned to regret it." Asher was serious now, the smile was gone.

"Why is that, Papa? I think justice would be a good thing to ask of God." Batshua was also serious. Many things were running through her mind now, numerous were the injustices mounting on the list of complaints she would bring before the Maker if given the chance!

"Ah, my dear. I thought so too. But justice is the business of God granting everyone what they deserve. That sword has two edges. I learned that to my great loss. Fortunately, I lived through it because apparently God has a sense of humor as well." They both laughed.

After a thoughtful pause, Asher continued, "After that affair, I named this bench the Mercy Seat. It sits between two paths that represents two choices for me. One is mercy, the other is justice. Ever have I prayed for mercy since that day God showed my lack of wisdom in demanding justice. I leave justice to him and him alone."

Batshua stood. She felt like crying, but she refused. Her teeth bit down angrily on the words that were fighting to come out of her embittered heart. The forces at work in her spirit threatened to rip her in two.

"I know what you are saying!" she spoke sternly at her father, but also past him. She was speaking to God as well. "You want me to surrender! You want me to abandon my claim to justice!" She faced the two paths as her father sat on the bench between them. How could he know this was exactly her struggle?

Her stubbornness had its grip on her soul. She stood with her arms rigid at her sides with her fists clenched and growled up at the sky. "Arggghhhh!!!!!! Do you not know what has been done to me?! To A'dab?! To us?! We have lost everything! We are nothing! The life we knew is gone! It has been stolen from us by evil enemies and the mindless wrath of nature itself! God's own creation has turned against us. We have no future! No hope! We are lost! God has abandoned us!!!"

As soon as she said those final words, she knew they were not true, her heart told her so. She had just lied to herself. Now why would she do that? Tears streamed down her face and she felt ashamed to lose control of her emotions in front of her father. She was an adult now, no longer a weak child.

Asher watched. Before long, Batshua's used both her palms to press the tears from her eyes. She turned her gaze once again to her father, in control and ready to listen.

"Batshua" he pronounced it again in the ancient dialect, "Bath'Shawa, Daughter of Prosperity, *who are you?*"

She looked at him with a great heave of sadness. "Alright. Alright, I will not give up my *hope* for justice, but I will not tell God how to deliver it. I will leave that to his wisdom. I guess who I am, is a woman in need of God's mercy, Papa."

Asher smiled and patted the seat next to him. Batshua returned to the bench, but she kneeled at her place and laid her head on the bench instead. Her father placed a hand on her head and breathed a short prayer, "El-Rophe, the God who Heals, grant us mercy."

-:--o--:-

Batshua didn't want to move. This moment was transcendent. The war she had been fighting inside herself felt like it was over. She was finally at peace and utterly relaxed. But biology seemed to trump even the most deeply spiritual moments. Her leg was getting cramped and the raisin cake churned strangely in her stomach. Her stomach had been bothering her all morning, in fact.

She decided she should get moving again. She thought God had played a trick on human beings to make them able to be so attuned to his spirit on the one hand, yet so prosaically attuned to his creation and the necessities of nature on the other. She groaned a little as she stood to smile at her father.

"Thank you, Papa. I shall remember this day!" She figured he would probably want to head back to the house.

"We have one more stop. Are you willing?" He looked eager.

"Sure!" Batshua sounded more enthusiastic than she felt. Something was grumblingly wrong with her stomach today and she was a little light-headed. She did not want to let on to her father.

Asher offered his arm and they trundled down the left path that led down into a small valley into the village. Fortunately, the way did not seem long. There also appeared to be a latrine just outside the fence surrounding the town, which was a good thing! Batshua ran behind the fence and threw up the raisin cake.

They walked to the center and turned past a fruit seller where Asher found his destination – a pottery shop. An old man sat at a spinning wheel, his hands caked with mud. A heavy stone, resembling a millstone rotated at the foot of the table. A young boy squatted at the base stone and kept the whole mechanism turning at a fairly even speed. A wooden axel, well greased by animal fat, pivoted from a position under the flywheel up through the table to the disc where the old man worked the mud. The boy slapped at the flywheel to keep it going. The old man could have worked the flywheel with his feet, but it would have made his work more difficult.

Batshua watched with interest, she had never observed pottery in the making.

To her amazement a beautiful jar began to form in the potter's hands. The curves were graceful, the vessel grew tall and slender. But then as she watched, the potter changed his mind. He smashed the vessel down into a pile of mud again with his fist! Batshua was shocked and disappointed. She felt her father's hand on her forearm. "Keep watching." He said.

The wheel kept turning, the potter sprinkled a little water onto the mess and began to work it again. He grabbed a large handful of mud from a pot next to his table and threw it with a slap into the ugly pile on his spinning disc. It looked hideous! But the hands kept working, the disc kept turning. Before long, a large serving bowl began to take shape. It was huge! The potter's hands were very skillful. Before long he had worked a design into the sides and added a graceful lip.

An air-pocket appeared in the side of the bowl, a defect that would mar its beauty. The potter simply took some more mud from his tub next to the table and skillfully worked it into the defect until the new mud blended perfectly. As she watched, there was soon no defect at all! Batshua was very impressed.

The potter finished his creation, removed it from the disc and set it on a shelf to dry. It would be fired in his kiln some days later. Asher bent down and took some of the mud that had fallen to the floor earlier in the day. It was hard and cracked. He asked the potter if he could make something from it. He said, no, the mud must stay moist. Once the mud has fallen from the wheel, it lost its ability to be molded. "Ah!" replied Asher with a thoughtful nod.

They looked around the shop. Batshua spied a teapot that looked very much like the one she had dropped the morning she had seen A'dab covered with boils. Her father noticed her interest and purchased it for her. They thanked the potter for his skillful demonstration and left.

-:--o--:-

"Thank you for the teapot. I… recently broke one just like it." Her father nodded acknowledgement of her gratitude. "I suppose it's philosophy lesson time, right?" Batshua knew her father well. He smiled and raised one eyebrow at her.

"You do not think I brought you all this way to buy you a souvenir from the land of Goshen did you?" Batshua thought maybe he should have wiped the sarcasm that was dripping from the corners of his mouth. She laughed. Her father was so lovable in moments like this.

"I believe I saw what you wanted me to see. Shall I expound, extrapolate and elucidate?"

He smiling condescendingly, "You always were my star pupil, my dear. However, you should know there is one who I believe exceeds you mental proficiency. Young Ruben is a becoming quite a remarkable philosopher. When he is not torturing toads, that is." They shared a laugh. Batshua thought the only person she had ever met who was bright enough to match wits with her father was her own husband A'dab. That thought gave her a pang of regret that she set aside for now.

"So tell me, what did you see?" Her father interrupted her thoughts before they wandered too far off track.

"There was much symbolism in the potter's work. Let us presume that the potter represents God and you and I are the mud. Well... presume I am the mud. Let us keep this simple. The first vessel grew beautiful and tall, but for some reason we do not know, the potter decided to remake the vessel."

"Did he discard the mud?"

"No..."

"The mud was still mud, while it was formed into the beautiful jar or smashed down into the messy pile? Was the mud a vessel which then became mud again or was the mud always mud?"

"Stop it! You're making my head hurt." She rubbed her forehead in thought, Asher smiled with exaggerated innocence at the sky, clouds, birds and all the beautiful things he saw that his daughter could not. Ah... life was good. He was enjoying himself.

"Please continue, Batshua. You're doing well." He prompted.

She cast a look at her father that would have burnt a lesser man to ashes, but he continued stubbornly to dwell at peace with the universe, unperturbed by the burning rays shooting out of her eye sockets in his direction.

"The mud was always whatever form the potter wished the mud to be. It is the nature of mud to be formed by the potter's hands.

Mud… symbolic of me…" she sighed, "must stay surrendered to the potter by staying on the potter's wheel in order to be properly formed."

"I see. What happened then?" Asher responded in a tone that meant he had already figured this all out and was merely waiting for his daughter to catch up.

"He made a different vessel, a large serving bowl."

"Wait, are you getting ahead of yourself? You may be forgetting something very important."

"I was going to come back to that!" Actually, she had no idea what she was forgetting, she was merely stalling for time so she could think.

"Oh. Excuse me. Keep going. I wish I had shown this to you when you were younger. That would have been interesting." They were halfway back to the crossroads.

"Ah, yes! The potter brought more mud in the mix. Thanks for the hint." Catching his reference to youth and growing older while they talked about the extra mud.

"You're welcome. Not that you needed it." Asher chuckled.

"The extra mud represents new experiences, friends, relationships, family… These are things the potter brings to reform us, me, to create a new, larger vessel – a larger life. A vessel more suited for service, a serving bowl. How am I doing? Did I get everything?"

"There may be a few cracks in your theory. That is another hint." He said in his most professorial tone.

"Oh! The defect. We are human and we have human frailty and faults, but the potter can bring in more mud. That represents other people, experiences, and relationships that cover or fill our defects. It is as if we act together as a complete vessel. Acting more in unity or family, like that."

"You are very good. Has anything fallen by the wayside? Hint, hint?"

She thought hard, they were nearly at the Mercy Seat, she was looking forward to a rest, both physically and from her father's prodding. "Oh yes! The mud that fell off the potter's wheel. Once it was away from the potter's hands, it became hard and unworkable." She stopped, suddenly filled with an incredible feeling of guilt.

Asher turned and looked at her gently, but significantly. "You learned the lesson of the potter's hand very well, my daughter. Very well indeed."

She sat at the bench. Her head was spinning and it wasn't all just her conversation with her father. She was suddenly nauseous and threw up again, this time she could not hide it. She felt very embarrassed to be sick in front of her father, but he took it in stride. The nausea left quickly, it was very strange because she did not feel feverish or ill in any other way. Her father had a leather pouch of water, he gave her a few sips and she felt much better.

"There's life in you, my daughter." He smiled.

She chuckled and shook her head to clear it. "Thanks for the assurance, Papa. I know I am still young, I don't think I am ready to keel over just yet."

"That is not what I meant my dear. There is life in you. You are with child." She turned to stare at him in shock!

"How do you...?" She started to protest, but he smiled warmly.

"You do not know?" He asked incredulously.

"I have missed my time, but I thought it was from the stress of all that has happened as well as the exertion of my recent travel. I... this is impossible!" Yet she felt within herself that his assertion was true.

"It is not impossible. It is a gift from God, the God who makes all things possible." He nodded sagely at her.

Batshua was trying to get a grip on reality. Too many things were happening. If she was on a potter's wheel, it was spinning far too fast!

"My daughter, I am not a prophet. But when I first saw you, something warmed my spirit. Something within me knew you bore my grandchild, I cannot tell how I knew. But now we know. I think it may be best if A'dab knew that he will have an heir after all."

Her heart tore open anew for her husband. "A'dab is dying." No tears would come, she had already shed enough tears for A'dab that would have filled a river from here back to Edom.

Asher took his daughter's shoulders in his hands and forced her to look in his eyes. "If your husband is ill, then you belong with him. You cannot know when God brings death, just as you cannot know when God brings life." He eyed her abdomen to make his point.

"Oh Papa! I could not bear to watch him die! I could not!" Batshua squeezed her eyes shut. "That is why I ran away! His pain tore at my soul!" Images of A'dab scraping his festering, oozing skin burned in her mind. She was on the edge of becoming hysterical. Asher's hands held his daughter firmly.

"Batshua!!" Her eyes flew open at his shouted command. "This may sound harsh, but it is the truth -- A'dab must bear his own pain, just as you must bear yours. You are not wrong to run away from his pain. But you are wrong to run away from your own."

She unwound from her panic. "You are right. Running away does work anyway. My pain travels with me, but..." she looked straight into his eyes, "I am ready to face whatever I must face." They held their gaze for a moment. Asher saw the beginnings of her renewed faith. He nodded.

"Do you know who you are, my daughter?"

"Yes." She said with confidence. "I am the Emir's wife."

"Good. I have lost my daughter to a better man. Again." He laughed and Batshua joined him.

"Tell me, Bath'Shawa, Daughter of Prosperity, do you know *whose you are?*"

She knew exactly what her father meant. She paused and framed her words carefully. "Yes, my father, Asher Ben Hadad, priest of Goshen, I know to whom I belong. I am dedicated to my husband A'dab and he to me, but my heart, soul, mind and strength belong to God. I know A'dab would say the same. We both belong to God."

"So A'dab's life or death... your responsibility? A'dab's pain... your responsibility?" Asher was not making this easy.

"I see what you mean. I am not in the place of God. I care for my husband, I love him. But he is ultimately in God's care. I should not have run away. I did not need to run away. I guess I fell off the potter's wheel, did I not?" She looked at her father somewhat sheepishly.

"Yes, but unlike the potter we saw in town, God is able to set things right. Perhaps your visit here will be brief? If so, I will not be offended." He smiled.

"Sending me away so quickly?" Answering his question with smile of her own, but she also sensed that he was right. "I would like to spend a few more days getting to know Ruben if you do not mind. He is a wonderful boy."

"I am glad he has had the chance to meet his eldest sister." They left the bench and began to stroll back toward the house.

When they had nearly reached home, Asher stopped to open the door to let Batshua enter first. As she passed the threshold, he said in an off-handed, impish tone, "So Batshua, Emira of Edom, I would hear you tell me something of a certain young woman called Nada the

Knife who arrived at my guest house yesterday. She and her husband Omar have been teaching Ruben the most amazing things!"

Batshua whirled around to face him and the look on her face was an absolutely priceless treasure! He grabbed her arm to prevent her from stumbling backward through the doorway. Keeping his daughter off-balance had been one of his favorite pastimes during her youth. Today had been a very good day.

-:--o--:-

18

Secrets

"A word was secretly brought to me,
my ears caught a whisper of it.
Amid disquieting dreams in the night,
when deep sleep falls on people,
fear and trembling seized me
and made all my bones shake."

The Book of Job 4:12-14

-:--o--:-

The evening meal was an amazing celebration. Asher started with a solemn prayer of thanksgiving for everyone's safe arrival. He thanked his daughter's friends for their faithfulness.

Batshua stood and gazed at the faces reclining around the huge feast her father's servants had spread on the low banquet table. So much had changed in the few weeks since her departure! That Nada and Omar had married so hastily was surprising, but welcome news. The story of Ba'al-Hanni's death and how Boshet had risked her own life as decoy moved her deeply. She did not feel worthy of their friendship. She struggled for words.

She looked at her father, then into the eyes of each of her friends. Negasi, who had remained loyal to her even though she knew the personal cost it meant to him. She had pulled him away from all he loved at Hareb. Naaman, the Sabean warrior and her husband's bodyguard. Now he guarded Nada and Omar. Her actions had torn at his loyalties too.

Then Nada and Omar! Oh, how she had hurt them… practically adopting them as her own children, then abandoning them in anger. She winced at the thought. She turned to sweet Frayda who looked so much older now. She had passed her over when choosing a handmaiden in favor of Nada. Yet Frayda had strengths she had not seen.

Last of all her eyes fell on Boshet, perhaps the most complex person in the room. Boshet looked the least relaxed of anyone at dinner. Batshua sensed she had something to say that no one would want to hear. She wanted to trust Boshet and wanted to be trusted by her, but the path to reconciliation might take a while longer.

Batshua's friends returned her long look with respectful silence. At last she began to speak, "My tone with you all was somewhat more lordly when I believed I had the authority of wealth and power. I know better now. I am not speaking to servants, or handmaidens or guards. I am sharing my heart with my friends. I am humbled by your faithfulness in coming to find me here. Thank you." She paused and looked at each of her friends again. She repeated her gracious thank-you individually, naming each of her friends and receiving a nod in response.

Batshua continued, "I will return with you to my husband A'dab and beg his forgiveness. I know him to be a wise man. When I left, he said I was talking like one of the foolish women, and he was right. But that will be between him and me and God. Again, thank you all and blessings on you and on my father's house."

It wasn't the greatest speech anyone had ever heard, but the right words had been said that would get Batshua and A'dab back together and that was all that mattered. Nada and Omar nodded at each other as if to say, "Mission accomplished." The mood was getting much lighter around the feast, everyone started bantering about the trip home and complimenting the food and so on.

Boshet gestured to master Asher, "May I speak?" He nodded approval. The room quieted down as Boshet rose to her knees rather than to her feet.

"Madam Batshua, my former husband Ba'al-Hanni is not the only enemy of House Hareb." The room was suddenly very still. "Ba'al-Hanni contracted with the Sabean outlaw Harun Al-Rashad to rob you of your cattle and slaughter their keepers." At the mention of Harun, Naaman, Frayda and Nada all clenched their jaws. They glanced at each other and spoke volumes with their eyes. It was Harun who had ransacked Nada's village and killed her aunt and uncle. Frayda's whole family had been slaughtered by him and his cutthroats. Naaman had run with Harun briefly, he knew of the man's treachery.

Boshet elaborated, "Harun may not know of Ba'al-Hanni's death, but eventually the news of that day in Rosh-Ramen will spread. Harun will learn that the Emira of Edom and her servant killed his benefactor, denying him payment. What do you suppose he will do then?"

The room erupted in fearful chatter. The homeward journey did not look so filled with anticipation of a joyful reunion. No one knew if even now there were roving bands of Harun's raiders lying in wait for them along the roads. Batshua looked pale.

Omar's voice cut through the fear with authority. "Silence!" He stood. Batshua had not realized how tall he had grown in this last year. He was nearly eighteen years old and had put on a lot muscle this summer. Omar had become a man.

He bowed to Asher, "I beg your indulgence, master Asher. I meant no offense to you or your household. I meant only to still this babble of fear."

Asher smiled. "Continue, young man. If your words have the ring of truth, it will be evident to all."

Omar turned to the group, "House Hareb may lie in ruins and master A'dab," he paused and corrected himself with downcast eyes, "master Job, sits at its center in pain." He spread his arms wide. "But are we not House Hareb? Are we in ruins? I say we are not. I say *we* are the riches of House Hareb! We are not in ruins for we are full of the strength of God." His strong arms seemed to embrace them all and as he turned his hands into fists.

"Boshet!" she seemed startled as her attention pulled away from the wonderful moment of unity and focused on Omar. "How did you come to know of Harun's plot with Ba'al-Hanni?"

"I was at Ba'al-Hanni's side when he and Harun hatched their plot." She said.

"What else do you know?" Omar asked politely. He had learned to trust Boshet and saw her as an ally.

Boshet thought about it. "Harun was to meet Ba'al-Hanni and me at the temple of Ba'al in Tariq at midnight of the autumnal equinox. Harun would be paid in gold. A lot of gold."

Omar did some mental calculations, "That is a five weeks from now."

Boshet stared at Omar, "What are you thinking, you foolish young man?!"

He fingered Ba'al-Hanni's finely crafted sword hanging from his hip. Doing his best to imitate the evil man's leering tone he said, "A little face paint and a change of clothing... what do you say, Boshet? Shall we keep the appointment?"

-:--O--:-

Everyone, including Asher tried to find fault with Omar's plan. No one relished the idea of Omar walking into Ba'al's temple masquerading as a high priest during one of the most loathsome festivals to their demon god. Boshet had her own nightmares to overcome. Reprising her role as the temple's most notorious vehicles of worship filled her with nausea. But as the group talked over their plan, they could see no flaw in it. If God went before them, they would succeed. If God was not in this plan, no effort of theirs would matter.

Batshua, Nada and Frayda were to be brought to the temple by Ba'al-Hanni and Boshet as captives, displayed to Harun in gloating victory over House Hareb. Naaman would certainly be recognized by Harun. They would play that as if A'jin had been recruited by Ba'al-Hanni for his own evil purposes. The plan would be to draw Harun away from the temple with as few men as possible where they would spring their trap. All hoped that an unsuspecting enemy's soul would splash into Sheol's lake of fire before their first drop of blood hit the floor.

Batshua secretly dispatched Negasi to Hareb with a message for A'dab containing details of their plans. She told the others she had set Negasi free to go in peace to his homeland south of Egypt. In truth, she had freed him, for he had served her well and true. The man had become a true friend of House Hareb. Once her message was delivered, Negasi would be released from his bond-servant obligation.

Omar's plan looked good, but Batshua wanted a back-up plan. The Emira had learned one very important lesson from her father, "Never venture into the desert with only one skin of water."

-:--o--:-

An odd mood settled over the Edomites as they prepared for their treacherous journey homeward. Frayda spent more time chatting quietly with Naaman whose spirit had grown tender in ways that amused Nada. She could not imagine the man who had threatened her life that day in her village as anything but a ruffian or brute. Frayda's gentleness seemed a balm to some wounded part of Naaman's soul and he imparted something of an oaken strength to her former willowy obsequiousness. The two opposites seemed to complement each other in unexpected ways.

Boshet found an unlikely friend in Ruben and his small flock of sheep. They understood each other. Ruben's mind worked rapidly, but try as he might, he could not compete with the incredibly changeable and multi-hued personality of a former charmer of men. Ruben was absolutely smitten by her beauty and wit. For her part, Boshet was fascinated to interact with the first superbly intelligent male in her life who felt absolutely no sexual tension in her presence. She could relax with Ruben and found him extremely enjoyable company.

Omar and Asher spent a lot of time finalizing details for their journey which left Batshua and Nada a few long afternoons to become reacquainted. Their relationship certainly needed some catching up.

They found themselves alone, walking along the path toward the Mercy Seat.

Batshua spoke into the awkward silence. "I no longer know what to call you." Nada turned quizzically at her former mistress. "You are not my handmaiden. You are not even a servant of House Hareb. Now that I think of it, as a married woman who owns land, you should be addressed as 'mistress'. That has a nice sound. The world changes and we change with it."

"Madam Batshua, I..." Nada began, but could not think of anything to say.

She held up her hand. "Batshua only, please."

Nada grinned. "That solves our problem, Batshua. No titles are necessary between friends." She took her friend's hand. They walked all the way to the bench in silence.

Batshua said, "Sit for a moment, Nada. I am weary." She continued to hold Nada's hand. The smaller woman's hand was calloused and strong. "Nada, I know you can keep a secret. I have something I want you to keep in your heart until I can tell A'dab myself."

Nada anticipated her friend's secret. "Job. A'dab has asked that we call him Job now. And I will tell no one that you are with child."

Batshua snapped her face toward Nada, "My father told you?! I will have words with that man!"

Nada frowned, "No. I knew your secret soon after I first saw you. I have always had this gift." She tapped her nose. "I can always tell. When I was a child, no woman in my village could keep her condition secret from me. Some accused me of being a witch, but it is only a very good sense of eyes and nose." She laughed and her friend relaxed.

"I am frightened by our plan to reenter Tariq. When I traveled there as the Emira of Edom, my power and status protected me. Now I will enter as a prisoner. My heart shrivels within me."

Nada looked directly into her friend's eyes. "Believe me when I say, I know just how you feel." Batshua suddenly felt ashamed of her fear. She realized that Nada had faced the exact scenario she had described when she was only twelve. "You rescued me then. This time, we go into the lion's den with purpose and a plan. God will protect us and fight for us."

-:--o--:-

Asher sat with Omar and Naaman on their final night in Goshen. He said, "Your faith in the God of our fathers is strong, young man. But be sure your faith is in God, not in your sword or in your plan. God laughs at the plans of men."

"My prayer is that God is laughing at the plans of our enemies." Omar quipped. The others laughed, but the underlying mood was somber. He grew serious. "Truly sir, if what Boshet says is true, and she has given me no reason to doubt her, we must strike down this man Harun ere he comes to us in Hareb when we are weak and without defenses. If God does not go before us into Tariq, then his will concerning us is deeper than I can fathom."

Omar stared pensively into the flame of a small lamp flickering dimly between the three men. The tiny points of light reflecting in his eyes seemed to intensify how focused he had become on the incredibly dangerous task ahead.

"Omar." Naaman interrupted the tense silence. "We Sabeans have a proverb. I do not know how well it translates, but… it says, 'Trust in the Moon god, but remember, the sun also rises.' Perhaps your God, excuse me, our God," he smiled self-consciously, "would find no sin in your heart to discover we had an emergency escape plan, should we discover God does not honor our first plan."

Omar reached over and clapped Naaman on his shoulder. "Ah Naaman, you are a practical man! Our people have a similar proverb: 'Trust in the providence of God, but carry two water bags into the desert!' Do not worry, my friend. We shall keep our mounts refreshed and ready to flee like a dog with its tail between its legs should our plan fail. 'A live dog is better than a dead lion', no?" They laughed heartily with much more confidence than any of them felt.

-:--o--:-

19

Retribution

"The lamp of a wicked man is snuffed out;
the flame of his fire stops burning.
The light in his tent becomes dark;
the lamp beside him goes out.
The vigor of his step is weakened;
his own schemes throw him down."

The Book of Job 18:5-7

-:--o--:-

Tariq was crowded with revelers and it stank more than usual.

The smell of Tariq brought Nada back to her first bumpy ride
in the back of a donkey cart. She had been so frightened of the
unknown that day. Today, she faced the known with a different kind of
fear. With her husband and friends beside her, the caravan edged its
way into the seething mass of debauchery with a faith that triumphed
over trepidation.

Nada held no fear of Harun or his men. She had not possessed
her life long enough to consider its loss of huge consequence.
Circumstances and powers beyond her control had shaped her chaotic
life -- she had never made plans beyond tomorrow. Nada the Knife
was a young woman living in the moment, her physical prowess and
skills honed to near perfection. As she surveyed Tariq from atop the
gently swaying camel, her instincts were alert, not dulled by undue
emotion or over-confidence.

Human beings such as Nada were extraordinarily dangerous to an arrogant enemy like Harun.

-:--o--:-

Boshet had coached Omar on Ba'al-Hanni's personality during the long hours of their journey. Omar was a passable actor, but he sometimes failed to take his role seriously. He kept falling out of character to crack a joke. This habit frustrated Boshet because any failure of their ruse could mean their lives.

Boshet would play the lead role much of the time because she knew the temple routines. Omar would feign illness or fatigue, wave off conversation disdainfully and allow Boshet to be his mouthpiece as much as possible. It was in this mode that the party arrived at the temple gate.

Two guards waved for them to halt. "No weapons within the courtyard during the Feast of Almaqah!"

Omar, dressed in a black silk robe with a broad cowl, lowered his hood. He and Boshet had spent two days searching among the craftsmen in Rosh-Ramen. They had finally discovered a supplier of dyes that would suffice for Ba'al-Hanni's tattoos. The black dye did not run when Omar sweated, but with a bit of scrubbing could be removed. With his head and face shaved, Omar had become a temporary Ba'al-Hanni look-alike.

Both guards snapped rigidly erect. "Master Ba'al-Hanni! I did not realize it was you, sir! Of course you are exempt. The others in your party may leave their weapons with…"

Before the guard could finish, Omar signaled his stallion to rear up. It was a stunt he had enjoyed showing off to Nada many times. He gathered the reins in his hands and tugged a fistful of the horse's mane. As his horse screamed and reared, Omar pulled his sword. He twisted his wrist and when his mount came down alongside the guard he struck the side of his head with the broad side of his sword – a devastating blow that knocked the guard unconscious with a bloody ear. He whirled the horse around and aimed the tip of his sword at the next guard's throat.

The metallic sound of a dozen swords being pulled from sheaths could be heard along the wall to their left. The guard under threat of Omar's sword made a small motion with his hand and gestured to the other guards with his eyes, not daring to move his head.

"Let them pass!" he shouted. "It is the high priest and his company!" He looked back up the length of the sword, "I beg your forgiveness, master. I was not expecting you." Omar just grunted with contempt and sheathed his sword.

Boshet spoke up, "My husband is weary. Summon servants to assist us to our quarters immediately."

"Are you not, Boshet?" the guard looked at her curiously.

"*Madam Boshet*, if you please." She spat.

"Madam Boshet then." He eyed Ba'al-Hanni nervously. Omar had replaced his cowl. He stared at the guard and fingered the hilt of his sword. The guard decided he had best comply. "As you wish." He called instructions to a man inside the gate. The party dismounted and moved into the temple courts. Omar and Boshet's mounts were led by an old man in ochre robes.

Omar leaned in close to Boshet and turned his face back to where Batshua and Nada were still mounted. They had been bound atop their horses as prisoners with Naaman leading them. He winked at Nada and whispered to Boshet with a half grin, "Well, that went rather well I think. Maybe I'll join the priesthood when we return to Hareb!"

"Shut up you fool! If you do not get us killed here, your vows to the priesthood will be the only thing preventing me from choking you to death!" she hissed back as she rolled her eyes and prayed for patience!

Batshua, Nada and Frayda had no trouble at all pretending to weep and tremble in their captivity. But they were hiding their tears of laughter at the antics of the two bad actors in front of them.

-:--o--:-

They approached a pair of very tall double doors. The old man seemed to be slowing down the closer they came. Finally he stopped about twenty feet away, apparently unwilling to proceed. He turned to his high priest and spoke in a rather sinister, conspiratorial tone.

"I am very sorry, sir. You must know your arrival here was unexpected at this time." He looked as if he were baiting Ba'al-Hanni, setting some sort of trap for him.

Omar did his best impression of an impatient Ba'al-Hanni, "What is the meaning of this?! Open these doors at once!"

"But, your gardens are occupied, sir. We honor Ba'al, sir. It is a celebration..." Somehow, the old man managed to pronounce 'sir' like the hiss of a snake.

Omar got the idea, but he knew their group needed a safe haven within the temple. This was a do-or-die moment. He decided to go for broke and motioned for Naaman to join him.

"Ba'al can be worshipped, but not at the expense of my comforts!" He strode past the old man, nearly knocking him over. He reached the doors and shoved them open with a loud SLAM! He glanced around at what appeared to be a circular garden built around a central pool. There were three rooms off to the left side with steps leading to each. The garden was completely circled with a high stone wall. The pool was filled with cavorting, naked human beings.

"OUT!" he shouted, "GET OUT NOW!" Sword in hand, he moved menacingly toward the pool which began to over-boil with scrambling humanity. Men and women flew past him toward the door in startled terror. One or two made a half-hearted attempt to grab a robe, but they were quickly discouraged with another burst of shouts, "BEGONE I SAY! MOVE!"

The rest of the party dismounted as other guards gathered at the doors when then heard the disturbance. Omar quickly restored his cowl lest he be recognized as an impostor and conferred with Boshet.

"Tell them your master is weary. Tell them whatever you want. Get everyone inside these doors so we can think clearly and talk privately." Boshet nodded.

Boshet leaned close to Omar and whispered, "Good job." Omar sighed his thanks and turned to search the premises.

-:--O--:-

The doors snapped shut with the entire party inside, including Naaman and all eight of his men.

Omar opened with a stream of questions, "Who was the old man, Boshet? Should we worry he might recognize me? Are there any other exits out of here? We're safe for now, but I don't know how long I can keep this up! If any of those naked people got a good look at me, we are dead!" Omar was pacing back and forth, the stress of the last few hours had obviously been more of a burden than he had let on.

The women were untied now that the group was away from the prying eyes of the temple's residents. Nada moved to her man and gently took his arm. She pressed her cheek to his shoulder and whispered something to him. It seemed to calm him considerably. He stopped pacing and began to relax, his head bowed low as he struggled to control himself. Everyone waited in silence.

"I am sorry, all. My beloved wife just reminded me that my fretting adds little to the success of our plans." He tried to smile and got halfway there.

Boshet spoke evenly, "The old man's name is Lamech. I remember him well. He used to serve the girls food and... he had other disciplinary tasks. He does not remember me, I was very young. At another time, I would have killed him without a second thought, but madam Batshua's God has apparently instilled a conscience within my heart. Believe me when I say that I find this new character trait most inconvenient in the presence of man such as Lamech."

Batshua interjected, "I have often found a conscience to be both a blessing and a curse. But Boshet..." she paused and looked significantly at her new friend, "I have learned to regret setting aside my conscience for convenience... or revenge." Boshet nodded her understanding. Batshua continued, "Should you get the opportunity, I would hear the story of you and Lamech. Perhaps I may help you bear the burden of your conscience."

That concept had never occurred to Boshet. She had never considered telling anyone of the man who had drowned a young girl sixty times.

Boshet turned to Omar, "I have never been in this part of the temple. We should search these rooms. As far as anyone recognizing you, it seems unlikely that the common worshippers or those such as the temple guards would be close to Ba'al-Hanni. He had the nasty habit of killing anyone who got close to him. He seemed to enjoy it. I do not know why he spared me unless I had not completed some part of his plan. I am sure he would have killed me sooner or later."

"There are two women who will know right away that you are an impostor, Omar." Boshet continued, "They are the twins who attacked Nada and you at Ba'al-Bek, B'jin and B'jal. I punished them severely for their harm to you. Before I came to you in Hareb, I sent them back to Ba'al-Hanni. Now that he is dead, I do not know where they may be or what they know. They are like loose ropes dangling from an overloaded donkey cart. They may trip us up."

Just then Naaman, who had not been interested in any of this conversation but had been looking over the residence, called out, "Look here!" Everyone except his men, who were only interested in finding a place to sleep for the night, migrated to the sound of Naaman's voice.

They found Naaman looking out a wide window onto a market area about fifteen feet below. "This may serve as an emergency escape."

"How so? Do you expect us to fly to the street?" Omar was always sarcastic with Naaman, the two were good buddies.

"No, Omar. My plan is that your wife flies to the street, then I throw you down so she can catch you." Naaman's toothy grin failed to elicit the desired response from his friend so he shrugged. "Look straight down."

Apparently someone at the market liked things tidy. The dirt and sand accumulating in the pathways of the market had been swept up and piled against the wall under the window for years. The pile reached halfway to the window. The pile of sand would make a very soft landing for anyone wishing to leave the room rapidly. The market shops were a maze of ramshackle huts stretching for a half mile. It would make an escapee difficult to follow.

"Excellent, Naaman. Is this the only other way out?" Omar felt a little better but his surroundings still made him claustrophobic.

"Yes. Three rooms and a courtyard. This room has the only exit, other than the door we entered." Naaman was thorough.

Boshet said, "I believe Harun will come here tomorrow night. Doubtless he will refuse to surrender his weapons, just as we did. If we are lucky, he will bring only a few of his men or perhaps the temple guards will disarm them for us. I suggest only Ba'al-Hanni and Boshet meet him, that is who met with him when the plan was hatched in the spring."

Omar agreed with Boshet's assessment. "We need a signal. Something to indicate when the trap should be sprung. We also need a signal for retreat in case something goes wrong."

Batshua moved close to Nada and whispered, "What could possibly go wrong?"

-:--O--:-

Everyone spent an uneventful night. Boshet used her prior knowledge of the temple's logistics to get food delivered to their quarters. They were not disturbed for most of the following day. Evening light cast long beams of light through the dust-laden air of the garden when three booming raps on the door startled everyone into sudden action.

Naaman and his guards moved swiftly to the one room that had their emergency exit. Batshua, Nada and Frayda sat beneath a palm tree in the garden where Omar hastily tied their hands back to back. He moved to a throne-like chair on the far end of the pool, cowl covering his face. In less than a minute the room appeared to be occupied only by the high priest, his consort and captives. Boshet moved to answer the door.

Lamech stood there with Harun, a half dozen of his men, and to Boshet's horror, B'jin and B'jal! The three women glared at each other in contempt. Harun spat in the dirt at Boshet's feet.

Lamech's eyes were outlined in black face-paint, giving him a hideously evil look. "I see that I do not need to make lengthy introductions as you seem to already be acquainted." He laughed as if he thought himself a funny man. "If master Ba'al-Hanni is ready to perform the sacrifice, bring the captives. I have prepared the altar."

Boshet was thoroughly confused but she dared not let on. She had to play this out to the end, they all did, for their lives depended on it. "Excuse me, did you say, 'the sacrifice'?" Boshet tried to act casually curious rather than shocked.

"Yes of course. Is this not why master Ba'al-Hanni has surprised us by bringing the captive mother and her children? Every year at this time a child is sacrificed to Ba'al-Hammon with the child's mother forced to watch. It is the high-point of the harvest ritual and a most sacred offering to our god. Surely you know this." Lamech was very condescending, his eyes mocked her.

Boshet stood her ground. "Master Ba'al-Hanni does not share all his plans with me, especially those regarding his priestly functions. He is deep in meditation. I dare not disturb him while he is in communion with his god. When he rouses from his contemplations, I shall inform him that you will be prepared at the altar. I am sure he will be ready soon." Boshet was making this up as she went along.

"And master Harun," she said as the turned toward the Sabean, "you will of course attend the ceremony. I am sure you will find it most... instructive. Master Ba'al-Hanni and I will conclude our business with you immediately afterward."

Harun spoke harshly, "See that I am not delayed further."

Boshet thought it best to call Harun's bluff. She remembered his sweating fear at their last encounter. "I counsel you to patience, my dear Harun, else you may find yourself begging for another mount from your men."

Suddenly Harun did not look so confident. "I will... enjoy the ceremony. You may tell master Ba'al-Hanni that I will be waiting... *patiently.*"

"*Oh, that must have hurt him to say that!*" thought Boshet as she presented Harun her best evil leer.

Lamech had aspirations to replace Ba'al-Hanni as high priest. He longed for a single misstep that would allow him to dispatch the younger man. Treachery was a way of life and death at the Temple of Ba'al. He nodded his assent with a sinister smile at Boshet's excuse for Ba'al-Hanni. If he showed up late for the ritual, perhaps Lamech could have him executed for sacrilege. He bowed and led Harun and his small group away.

Boshet closed her eyes in a sigh of relief and snapped the door shut.

-:--O--:-

"What?!" Omar shouted as he tried to concentrate. They had just made their first contact with the enemy and his plan had already failed before it had even begun.

Batshua called, "Release us, Omar. We must think of something else. Perhaps God will show us a way through this." Omar cut their bindings and helped Nada to her feet. To his surprise, Nada did not seem the least worried.

"My husband," she whispered to Omar, "Look at madam Batshua's face. I have seen that look only once before, when I swore fealty to her as she gave me the belt with the hidden weapon. I believe we are in the presence of a true lord of House Hareb once again."

It was true. Power seemed to gather around the Emira of Edom as she stood among them, fists on hips.

Batshua spoke once again with the authority of House Hareb, "None but the unrighteous will die tonight. Naaman, assemble your men! Our plans have changed, we must adapt." Naaman obeyed. Everyone surrounded Batshua.

"Alright, they are expecting a sacrifice. We shall give them a sacrifice they do not expect!" Her commanding presence left no doubt in anyone's mind.

Boshet interrupted, "Madam Batshua, there are many among the worshippers who are unwilling servants of the temple. They do not deserve death…"

Batshua raised her hand to silence her. "I know. And God knows this as well." She looked at each of the men and women in the circle. With the singular exception of Nada, she saw fear written on their faces. Her heart broke for them, because she knew that their fear broke the very heart of God. What could she say that would dispel their fear? What was the confidence within her and Nada that gave them such inner peace and assurance? Suddenly she knew…

"I must make you understand what we are risking our lives for tonight." She waited until she had their full attention. "I bear in my body, the heir of House Hareb." Realization of this amazing miracle flooded their awareness. Shock, wonder, awe, joy…

"Yes. God's own plan for the future of Edom is unfolding here in this room. He has planted the seed of renewal – God's gift of life is present even in this temple of death. Do you believe God intends for his enemies to prevail against his plan? I say the enemy will not prevail this night! So say you all?"

Again she looked at each pair of eyes around the circle. Where there had been fear, there was now its opposite: she saw love! Love of life, love of God and love of all for which they had striven these long weeks. This was victory. Victory already theirs! A thousand soldiers could have burst through the doors and slain them now, but they would still have won, for they had beaten back their fear, they had united in purpose – they were once again a House, the righteous people of House Hareb.

"Alright then." Batshua sighed in relief. "Here is what we will do. First of all, Omar – go wash your face. I am sure you want to start being Omar once again…" Omar moved to the pool, wearing a warriors fierce grin.

Batshua turned to Frayda, "Naaman, bind Frayda securely. She will be our sacrifice."

Frayda shrank back, but then straightened with an eager grin. "Yes ma'am! This is something I can do well!" She held out her hands to be bound.

Naaman grinned broadly at the new love of his life as he approached with a rope in his hand, "Do not worry, young one, I believe I know what madam Batshua has in mind."

Frayda responded, "I am not worried. But I am going to ACT very worried because that is the way a sacrifice should act. I will be a good *distraction*, I know I can do that very well. Just do not be so distracted that you forget you are supposed to *rescue* me, right?!" Naaman laughed warmly at the courage of the delicate young woman in his hands.

-:--o--:-

Naaman led a solemn procession out through the double doors of Ba'al-Hanni's garden. Frayda's hands were bound at her wrists. She was herded along, surrounded by seven of Naaman's guards. They sneered and laughed as she struggled along. She made a spectacle of herself crying and cursing at them as they shoved her stumbling into the dirt. Behind the guards, her 'mother' and 'sister', Batshua and Nada wept bitterly and fatalistically at the thought of the poor child's imminent death. Boshet prodded Batshua along at the point of a dagger with the hooded Ba'al-Hanni himself bring up the rear with head down and hands in a prayer position in front of his face. His robe's deep cowl and the position of his hands completely obscured his face.

Boshet moved close to Omar and whispered in panic, "I count seven guards! Where is Naaman's eighth guard?! Have we been betrayed?"

Omar hissed back, "Shut up you fool! Are you trying to get us killed? Now it will be my turn to choke you!" Omar turned toward Boshet, she could just make out his face deep within the shadow of the hood. He was grinning like a thief. He kept his hands in his prayer position, bowed to her and continued to the altar.

Batshua had dispatched the eighth guard out the window on a secret mission of her own. She had told Omar, but there had been no time to inform the others.

Lamech and Harun had apparently busied themselves in the outer courtyard by drinking heavily. Lamech noticed the procession coming their way and signaled to a group around the corner. A young man with a drum started beating a slow rhythm while girls danced around the group throwing spices and dried leaves onto Frayda.

The drummer's tempo increased slowly as they approached a stone altar. The dancers writhed with desperate enthusiasm, sweating profusely in their passion to please both their god and the priests of the temple. Naaman reached the stone altar, an inverted cone with a flat top. He turned and stared dispassionately as his guards placed Frayda on the altar. Her hands were stretched over her head and tied to a pole at one end of the stone, her feet tied with a length of rope stretching to a pole at the other.

Batshua and Nada were forced to kneel in front of the altar, about six feet away from it. Naaman and his guards positioned themselves on the left behind Batshua, Harun and his men were to the right behind Nada. Lamech stood next at the backside of the altar with Omar with Boshet kneeling at Omar's feet. When all had reached positions, Omar raised his left hand high.

The frenzied chanting and drums that filled the room suddenly shattered into a stillness that almost hurt the ear with its abruptness. The dancers froze into sweating statues. The only sound in the vast hall – a flame fluttering in the mild breeze.

Slowly, Ba'al-Hanni, high priest of Ba'al drew his sword from its sheath. The grating metallic sound of its wicked blade singing a prolonged tune of death as the hand drew the full length from its sheath and held it high in the firelight. For a long torturous moment, the blade remained aloft, suspended between life and death.

Then a voice immense with power ripped out of Omar's throat. "In the name...", the crowd's anticipation of blood intensified, "In the name of El Shaddai, the God of House Hareb, I set you free!" The blade descended on Frayda's bonds and then whirled a second later to remove the startled head of Lamech, aspiring priest of Ba'al. The dull sound of skull bone dropping to stone preceded the softer thump of Lamech's body slumping lifeless beside it.

In the shocked silence, Omar threw back his hood to reveal the noble face of a young warrior of Hareb. He jumped onto the altar and shouted, "Who is on the LORD's side? Run to me and live! Fight for your freedom! Ba'al is no god! We fight for the mighty God of all the earth, El Gibbor! El Gibbor!"

Harun wanted to shout curses in reply and thought of several but he could not make his voice work. He reached toward the awful pain in his throat with both hands then looked at the blood gushing from the three wounds sliced across his neck. His last conscious thought was, "Who...?" but his killer, Nada the Knife was already dispatching his second guard. Numbed by the suddenness of their attackers and too much wine in preparation for a human sacrifice, Harun's two guards fell quickly to Nada's dagger and Naaman's flashing sword. B'jal and B'jin fled panicked into the crowd.

Frayda huddled with Batshua beneath the shelter of the altar. Nada, Naaman and his guards encircled them in a ring of fel blades. None of the temple's supplicants seemed inclined to approach the armed group on the stone platform. The shrine's guards were another matter. They recovered from their shock quickly and began to close in, swords drawn.

Omar repeated his offer, "All who wish to live, come to the altar! We fight for the Lord God of all creation, El Shaddai, the God of Abraham, Isaac and Jacob, the God of A'dab Ben Hareb, the great Emir of Edom! You have a choice! Life or death! Choose life!"

"The Emir is dead! His house is in ruins!" someone taunted from the crowd.

Batshua shouted in reply, "House Hareb stands in victory before you now! Do we look as if we are dead or in ruins?"

"Yes! As a matter of fact, you look very much like a ruined house to me." A voice sounding like rocks grinding together echoed up from the crowd. Ba'al-Hanni hobbled toward them with B'jin and B'jal on each arm. His speech was slurred and he limped badly. One side of his face sagged and the arm on that side was limp, but the man walking toward was indeed the high priest of Ba'al returned from the grave!

"You should have removed my head, you fool. It takes more than a little knife wound to kill the high priest of Ba'al!" He struggled toward them with demonic hatred flaming in his eyes.

He broke free of the crowd and stood before them with about thirty temple guards at his back. In arrogance, he laughed hoarsely, knowing his enemy would soon be sacrificed to his god on the very altar they now desecrated.

A knife flashed through the dozen feet separating Ba'al-Hanni from the Edomites. Spinning in practiced perfection, it struck under his left breast piercing his aorta and deflating his lung. His laugh choked off in huffing cough.

"He is right, Omar. Remove his head." Nada the Knife said flatly.

The twins dashed away to either side as Omar leaped to the opportunity. With a flash of Omar's sword, Ba'al-Hanni's head made a sickening thud as it landed on the stone flooring. He would not be so quick to heal from this wound! Omar dashed back to the altar and stood at the ready before the guards behind Ba'al-Hanni realized they had lost their leader once again.

The guards started to shuffle forward in confusion, duty-bound to defend their temple, but confused without its leader. The defenders of House Hareb made ready to take as many of them down before they were overrun by superior numbers.

But then the sound of a ram's horn drew everyone's attention to the temple gates. Over seventy five mounted warriors galloped into the courtyard, surrounding the entire crowd, guards and Omar's last stand at the altar of Ba'al.

Batshua pulled Frayda to her feet. The Emira raised her hand in greeting, "Well met, Negasi, faithful friend of House Hareb and honorable servant of God Most High." Naaman's eighth guard had been successful in alerting Negasi's men who been hold up outside the north gate of Tariq. Negasi must have made an absolutely inhuman effort to muster that many men and get here by the appointed night of the full moon.

She turned to the guards and the crowd, "I will repeat master Omar's offer one more time. We set before you a choice between life and death. Choose to be servants of Ba'al and die or surrender to the

God of House Hareb and live. I implore you, by all that is holy, good and true, in the name of El Gibbor, our Mighty God – choose life."

A great reverent silence descended in the hallway. To some, it was a terrified silence, to others, a blessed relief from a life of bondage, to still others it was a frustration of just one more oppressive burden placed upon their confused lives that they did not understand. Yet the silence lasted only seconds before being shattered by the sound of dozens of weapons clattering to the floor in surrender.

A great cheer rose from the mounted warriors which was enjoined by those in the crowd when they realized their lives of slavery to the temple had ended. Two of the dancers moved to kneel at Batshua's feet to weep their gratitude.

Batshua raised her hand for silence. "This temple, its lands and all within it are hereby claimed as a possession by conquest for House Hareb. All slaves will be cared for and are under the protection of House Hareb, but we do not keep slaves. We will hire you, should you decide to stay, but you are free to go if you wish." That brought a murmur throughout the crowd, she raised her hand again for silence.

"The honorable master Negasi," she gestured to him, he bowed from his mounted position in response, "is hereby appointed regent of these temple lands. Your first task, master Negasi," she directed her gaze at him, "will be to break down this altar, pull down the Asherah poles and burn all that remains of anything resembling service to Ba'al. From this day forward, the penalty for worship of Ba'al on these lands, is death. This hall will be cleansed, by fire if necessary. I want to see this place of ignorance and superstition turned into a place of education and service to God the Creator. Where children were once sacrificed, I want to see children taught to read and write, both boys and girls." That definitely brought murmurs from the crowd. No one had heard of such a thing!

Batshua could go on, but she was getting weary and so were the people. "Go to your homes, leave your weapons behind." She spied two twin women trying to blend in with the crowd. She whispered to Omar who ran and caught up with them.

"Going someplace special, my ladies?" He grabbed their arms none too gently and led them away to the former priest's quarters.

Negasi lost his smile as he realized he and his warriors were stuck with one bloody mess of a cleanup. "*Ah well,*" he thought to himself, "*I will be a janitor for tonight, and I will be a king starting tomorrow!*" His smile returned, broad as ever!

-:--o--:-

20

Judgment

"Do you know the laws of the heavens?
Can you set up God's dominion over the earth?
Can you raise your voice to the clouds
and cover yourself with a flood of water?"

The Book of Job 38:33-34

-:--o--:-

Negasi held court the following day, starting about mid-morning. His soldiers had taken the few hours after daybreak to break down Ba'al's altar. There was a pile of stone rubble and dust in its place. Regal-looking chairs were procured from various rooms within the temple and placed on the wide dais where the altar once stood. The largest chair became Negasi's judgment seat, the others were his advisors – Batshua, Nada, Omar, Naaman, Frayda and Boshet. Court was now in session.

Everyone had tried to talk Negasi into dressing formally for the occasion, but he would have none of it. He would wear what he always wore: silk pantaloons, leather sandals and his wide leather belt strapped across his bare chest. He had added a larger dagger holder to the diagonal chest strap. The hilt was within easy grasp of his left hand, the blade was gleaming warning to his enemies that they should inspire no motivation for its use.

Negasi was a most imposing figure. His well-muscled chest and arms terminated in a thickly corded neck topped by a smoothly shaved head. To the superstitious denizens of Tariq, it must have appeared that a black-skinned demon had overthrown their temple! But Batshua had picked Negasi because she knew he was an instinctive leader with a just and honest heart.

-:--o--:-

The first case concerned the temple guards. That was settled fairly easily as they were monetarily affiliated with the temple rather than religiously devout. He offered their captain a month's severance pay in gold if they would vacate the temple never to show their faces again upon pain of death. Negasi fully expected such a windfall profit to cause half the guards to kill the other half in tavern brawls and then the survivors would drink themselves into oblivion. The small investment in gold would be worth the entertainment to the people of Tariq and may help the local economy.

Gold was no problem for Batshua and Negasi once they had convinced B'jin and B'jal to reveal the location of Ba'al-Hanni's stash. They had dragged the twins into their quarters last night and had been treated to a fearsome display of intimidation by Boshet. Negasi guessed that the twin's last encounter with her was still fresh in their minds because when Boshet reached for a camel whip, B'jin immediately wilted and pointed to the center of Ba'al-Hanni's garden pond. A bit of swimming turned up two bronze chests with several hundred pounds of gold and precious gems. House Hareb was back in business!

Two priests with their hands bound behind them came before the judgment seat next. They complained bitterly about justifiably prosaic matters such as how did the new rulers expect to feed the residents of the temple?! A large part of Tariq's economy depended on the wealth that flowed through the temple because of its services. Not just prostitution, but meat and grain offerings to Ba'al represented the main food source and wealth of its priests and prostitutes. What would replace it?

Batshua's promise of turning the temple into a house of learning would take time. For today, these people needed to eat. Negasi leaned thoughtfully toward the two priests, elbows resting on knees and hands clasped. "How many priests among you?" he asked.

They turned to each other deciding which would answer. The elder spoke, "There were twenty of us, four have escaped into the desert where I expect they will die. Two others were found dead this morning – by their own hand."

"Fourteen then. And how many others live in this place and on the grounds?" Negasi bowed his head further and moved a hand to stroke his forehead. He was concerned. The priest's answer did not ease his stress.

"There are twenty eight women and four men in service to Ba'al among the bed chambers. A little over forty children serve in various temple duties, kitchen, gardening, laundry. Another two dozen slaves, but you need not concern yourselves with them! They are the city's garbage. Turn them back out into the streets to fend for themselves." The priest spat the last with contempt. Batshua cocked an eye in his direction. The younger priest glanced at his embittered old mentor and hung his head shamefully. Negasi watched the dynamic between them carefully.

"You there!" Negasi spoke to the younger priest. "Who are you and what was your position here in temple?"

The older man interrupted, "He is my student! You deal with me!"

Negasi lowered a cold stare at the older priest. He spoke slowly and darkly, "If you speak again without my permission, the consequences will be most unpleasant for you." The priest returned Negasi's stare but said nothing.

He repeated his question to the younger man, "Who are you?"

The younger man stammered slightly but found his voice, "I am Wajib. It is as Jamal said, I am a student-priest of Ba'al. I have been at the temple three months now."

Negasi relaxed back in his chair, "Wajib, what do you think of madam Batshua's idea, that of turning this temple into a great library and a center of learning for the city of Tariq?"

Wajib's eyes virtually exploded with wonder! "Oh! That would be a marvel! Why... some of the children here are very bright indeed! Before I was I forced into temple service by my father I was..."

"Shut up, you fool!" Jamal shouted down the younger man, "Do not speak blasphemy to these foreigners! By Ba'al most high I curse thee! May thine intestines blacken so you vomit them out of your detestable maggot-ridden mouth!" The rest of Jamal's curses grew incomprehensibly arcane and vile.

Negasi stood, shaking his head with a wry smile. He had a thick goat-hair sack in his hand. He walked slowly to Jamal and slid it down over his head. By this time, Jamal had started to foam at the mouth. Negasi motioned with his chin to one of his guards who came with a partner and hauled Jamal away kicking and screaming curses.

Negasi walked back to his chair and heaved a sigh, he looked a question at Wajib.

"Where are you taking him?" Wajib was horrified. He knew the reputation of priestly curses. He expected to die at any moment.

"We are arranging a quick meeting between Jamal and his god. I believe Jamal is in for a vast surprise. Oh, do not worry, Wajib. Ba'al has no power here. This place is under the protection of El Gibbor, the Mighty God, creator of all. That man's curses have all the power of a braying donkey." Negasi laughed heartily, his expanse of white teeth a gleaming contrast against his black face. Wajib tried to laugh, but he was still too nervous.

"Can you read and write, Wajib?" Negasi asked.

In the distance, they heard a dull thud and Jamal's faint curses suddenly desisted. Wajib swallowed hard. Negasi's expression did not change, he was waiting for Wajib's answer.

"Can I read and write? Yes. As I was about to tell you, I was a scribe in my father's business before our misfortune forced him to sell out. I had no choice but to enter into employment in the temple as bond-servant and acolyte to Jamal who is... was... the high priest's record keeper."

Batshua spoke up, "Wajib, what was your father's business and what misfortune occurred?"

He negotiated a trade, mostly in cattle. He had many contacts with Phoenicians along the coast and even some Egyptians within the Nile Delta. He had negotiated a trade between a Phoenician named Ashtzaph and a Sabean named Harun Al-Rashad. The deal was for delivery of many hundreds of oxen and donkeys. My father received gold in payment from the Phoenicians, but before he could deliver it to Harun, his caravan became trapped in a freakish storm that bogged down their camels and carts in deep mud. They were attacked by bandits that came out of the storm. My father was terribly wounded but survived to tell the tale. Harun did not believe him and so he slew my father."

Wajib, with his hands still bound behind his back, was the picture of a thoroughly beaten man.

Batshua conferred with Negasi. After a moment, Negasi nodded affirmatively, then he addressed Wajib.

Negasi asked, "Wajib, how much gold was your father to be paid for his part of the transaction?"

"He was an honorable man sir." Wajib was visibly trying to control his emotions. "He would have received a pound of gold, though that was less than one part in a hundred for the work he had done."

"I see. And you have records to prove this?" Negasi asked.

"Yes sir. I kept meticulous records for all my father's dealings. They are stored safely in my father's house." Wajib was proud of his heritage, that much was certain.

Negasi had reached a decision. He stood and pulled his dagger from its sheath on his chest. Wajib's eyes flared in panic. But Negasi reached around Wajib and sliced his bonds free. He walked back to the chair and slid the dagger into its sheath with a solid click.

"First," Negasi held out an index finger toward Wajib, "show me proof that your father was to receive the payment in gold from Harun and I shall pay you double." Wajib's eyebrows shot up with surprise. "Second," Negasi's second finger came out toward Wajib, "You may be interested to know that Harun's body is among those burning in the pyre outside. By now, Jamal's body is also there."

A slow smile broadened Wajib's face. "That is good." His whole body seemed to relax as he stood easily an inch taller. Perhaps this black-skinned man spoke the truth – Jamal's curses no longer had any power.

"Yes, it is very good. Third," another finger, "If you are willing, madam Batshua and I would like to appoint you as first professor and record-keeper of the new Library of Tariq."

Wajib blinked in disbelief. A few moments ago he was under the thumb of one of the most oppressive and hateful men he had ever known. He himself thought these people were about to execute him. Now they were going to settle accounts for the dishonor to his father and both his enemies were ashes and gases floating skyward outside while he was to be appointed to a position he could never have aspired to even if he had lived to be a hundred!

Instantly, he sank to one knee. "I humbly accept with my thanks. I will serve the Library of Tariq to the best of my ability."

Negasi smiled, "Excellent! Is anyone else hungry? I am starving! Making decisions such as this whets the appetite. Let us break for an hour to eat lest my judgment is impaired by my growling stomach!" He clapped his hands to the servant girls. "Bring food and drink! Professor Wajib, care to join us?"

-:--o--:-

Wajib was an excellent conversationalist. He seemed to be a good man who had fallen among scoundrels, time would tell. Once their meal was finished, Negasi and the rest returned to their judgment duties, Wajib left to retrieve evidence of his father's Phoenician agreement.

No one was looking forward to the next encounter. B'jin and B'jal were led to the dais. They stood unfettered before Negasi with the low pile of the altar's rubble separating them from their judge. They may have been twins physically, but their demeanor was markedly different. B'jal stood defiant while B'jin stared at the pile of stones dejectedly. It was B'jin who had broken into tears the night before and revealed the location of Ba'al-Hanni's gold against the cursing protests of B'jal.

Negasi eyed the two women speculatively. He turned to Boshet, they whispered in conference briefly. Boshet turned to Batshua who had listened. The Emira nodded her assent to Boshet.

Negasi turned to the twins. "The lady Boshet has an offer for you which, quite frankly, is against my better judgment. Since she has the longer history with you, I will defer to her discernment in matters concerning you." B'jin looked up at Boshet with hope written on her face, B'jal's lips curled in contempt.

"If you will swear personal allegiance to lady Boshet, you will be released into her custody as lifetime bond-servants."

"And what is the alternative?" B'jal spoke to prevent her from accepting the deal. B'jal always took the lead.

Negasi scowled. "The Anvil."

B'jal sneered. "The Anvil?"

"Southeast of Tariq, the desert flattens into a barren waste we call 'The Anvil'. The sun beats down upon it so hard some say it will melt the sword within a warrior's scabbard. You will be taken there bereft of food and water to find the mercy of God. None have ever discovered God's mercy upon the Anvil, perhaps you will be the first. I encourage you to accept lady Boshet's gracious offer."

B'jin looked at Boshet's compassionate eyes, "Lady Boshet, I humbly…"

B'jal shouted her sister down, "Lady Boshet can go to hell! I would rather die than spend my life serving that traitorous, murdering whore!"

"No, my sister! You cannot be so proud! Do not throw your life away!" B'jin begged her sister to be reasonable.

"Pfft!" B'jal spat. "You are no better than them. Such a trusting fool! Go with them! I will die alone."

"No, B'jal. I will die with you." B'jin spoke softly, but firmly.

Boshet spoke down softly from the dais, "B'jin, listen to your own advice. Do not throw your life away."

B'jin shook her head and said flatly, "She is my sister. Take us to the desert. Perhaps your God will have mercy upon us, but I will not abandon my sister."

Negasi's face turned to stone. "So be it. May God have mercy on you." He nodded to two of his guards who led the twins away.

Boshet was devastated. She buried her face in her hands. Batshua laid her arm around her shoulder. Nada and Omar were staring at each other, saying something with their eyes that only they understood. They excused themselves and left the judgment hall.

-:--o--:-

Two of Negasi's guards traveled much of the night so they could abandon the twins on The Anvil in time to escape most of its heat themselves.

The younger man turned to his veteran buddy, "So why aren't we just throwing these two onto the pyre with the others? This doesn't make any sense, we're not going to get any sleep tonight." He complained in the same way soldiers have complained to each other for all eternity. To the younger man's way of thinking, a soldier's main concern was to be as comfortable as possible as often as possible for as long as possible. This situation was impossible!

The older warrior scratched thickly muscled ribs that bore the scars of many battles. The ancient wounds itched under his hot leather armor. "Whatsa matter? Didn't your momma ever put you to sleep at night with poems? This is poetic justice boy! Shut up and soldier!" He grinned at the kid who was probably only sixteen. The grin faded when he glanced at the two condemned prisoners on the camels in tow behind them. Such a pitiful waste. Where is the poetry in that?! *"May God have mercy on their souls"*, he thought, *"for the desert will have none."*

-:--o--:-

Nada and Omar did not show for breakfast. Everyone figured they had discovered a secret place to practice their fighting arts, something they had not had much opportunity to do lately. Negasi noticed five camels were missing from the stockyard. And Labid, the younger of the two guards he had sent to accompany the twins to the Anvil had not reported for duty this morning.

Negasi informed Batshua about the discrepancies. She asked him to hold his peace about it, but she had a good notion what Nada and Omar were up to. She did not approve, but had little control over them now. She hoped they realized the scorpion's nest they were digging into.

-:--o--:-

The soldiers had kept a grueling pace during the night, they stopped when Orion's belt touched the horizon. Dawn would come in only an hour. They unbound their prisoners and remounted their camels to go without saying a word.

B'jin begged them to leave a skin of water. She offered her body but was laughed to scorn. The two men claimed they stank of camel dung and still laughing, they rode away. As B'jin watched, something slid from the younger soldier's saddle and dropped unnoticed to the sand. She ran to it and discovered a half-full water bag! She ran to her sister excitedly.

"Look! A gift from the young man!" she said, holding the bag toward her sister.

B'jal was less enthusiastic. "It will make no difference."

B'jin loved her sister, or at least for the moment, she remained loyal. Her feelings toward the woman with whom she had spent her life as a mirror image did not seem to mirror her own changed character. Her sister B'jal could not see life, truth, grace and hope in those who had ended Ba'al-Hanni and Harun reign of terror. B'jin herself however could see that the new lords of the temple were fair and just men and women. Where B'jin saw hope of a new life, her sister saw the demise of her road to personal power. B'jal was blind because she refused to see, she refused to hope.

"Perhaps it will make no difference, my sister, but if we are to die, a little water will allow us to talk awhile longer on our journey toward death. Walk with me and I shall tell you a story as we go." B'jin had decided she would lead her sister instead of follow for once.

"Which way?" B'jal's compliance was a sign she had begun to resign herself to a delirium, pain and death. She may as well humor her sister.

"Northwest, back toward Tariq. Why not?" They started a slow walk, conserving their strength. The ground was hard-packed powder-sand. It had the consistency of fine flour mixed with gravel. The land was infinitely flat in every direction. B'jin had noticed the stars on their right side as they rode, she now kept the same constellation on their left. When the sun rose it would provide an easier point of reference until it rose high at noon. But by then, she thought ruefully, they would no longer need to know their way, for they would surely be dead.

"Tell me your story. I do not believe I have ever heard you tell a story. First, tell me where you learned of it? I thought you did not know anything that I did not know." B'jal's arrogance had blinded her to her sister's qualities.

"Ba'al-Hanni sent me to accompany... to be the consort, of a Phoenician trader." She choked up somewhat at the thought, "You were otherwise occupied observing shepherds in the north, remember?"

"Ah yes! I had forgotten. Please continue with your story." She said as she placed her arm within her sister's.

B'jin began, "The trader said this story came from a faraway land and is very ancient. He told of a thief who was caught stealing a king's prize horse."

B'jal interrupted, "That sounds like something I would do, only I would not get caught!"

B'jin laughed, "Be still and let me tell the story!"

Her sister sighed, "You tell it very slowly."

"Only because you are interrupting! Are you going to listen or do you want to tell it yourself?!"

B'jal loved getting her sister angry, it was always entertaining. "No, you are doing fine. So a thief was caught stealing the king's prize horse. Was the thief put to death by abandoning him in the desert like we are?"

"No! He was killed immediately because the king choked him to death, the same as I am going to do to you if you do not be quiet and listen!" B'jin wondered why B'jal always did this, it was a constant game that B'jal always won.

"Okay, I am sorry. Please continue." B'jal had scored her winning points, so she quieted down.

"The king condemned the thief to death by beheading, but the thief surprised the king. He said, 'Oh noble king, I only wanted to steal your horse because it is the one of most magnificent horses in all the land. However, if you spare my life for a year, I shall teach your horse to sing! Then you will have a horse like no other in all the world!'"

B'jal laughed and said, "That is foolishness. A horse cannot ever learn to sing."

B'jin continued, "The king also laughed, but he granted the thief a year. He said, 'You shall have your year, thief. If my horse sings, I shall spare your life.' The thief moved into the stables and spent every day singing to the horse."

B'jal said, "Is that your story? The thief is a fool, the horse will never sing, it is a hopeless task."

B'jin replied, "That is what all the thief's friends said. They came to the stables and laughed at him. They said, 'You are a fool! What you are trying to do is impossible!' The thief replied with a wise smile however. He said, 'Ah my friends, that may be true. But I have a year and who knows what may happen in that time? The king could die, the horse could die or I might die. And who knows? Maybe the horse will learn to sing.'"

B'jal laughed and her sister joined in. "Oh, that is a wonderful story! I think I see your point – one should never give up because while you are striving toward an impossible goal, something else may come to the rescue. Is that right?"

B'jin smiled. "Very good. That is about right, yes."

The sun peaked over the horizon just behind and to their right. The stars had disappeared about a half hour before. B'jin was relieved to know they were still heading roughly toward Tariq.

B'jal felt the sun's heat immediately on her neck. She pulled her shawl over her head as did her sister. They were pampered women and unused to physical exertion. They both knew that in the featureless expanse of the Anvil, without better clothing and more water, they would succumb to heat exhaustion, delirium, stoke and death within the next few hours.

B'jin took a sip of water and handed the skin to her sister. "Have a little water to wet your tongue, sister. We will be able to talk a little longer. I think I saw a large rock on our way here. If we make it there, we can rest in its shade until night."

Taking only one swallow, her sister's voice was hoarse after only two hour's trudging in the sun. The temperature had already reached a blistering one hundred twenty degrees, their bodies were baking dry quickly. In only another hour, the temperature would soar to one hundred thirty.

B'jin's legs were already trembling with weakness and she felt the first waves of nausea. She tried to see her rock of comparative safety on the horizon, but her eyes were already difficult to focus. The distance shimmering waves of heat danced like a liquid mirror of water beckoning to immerse herself in its cooling welcome. She blinked and shook herself free of her mind's dazed meandering. She must remain strong for her sister as long as possible!

They walked along another two hours. The sun was almost at its zenith.

"B'jal, do you remember our mother?" B'jin asked.

"Odd that you should say that, I was just thinking of her. She was a beautiful woman..." B'jal's voice trailed to a whisper.

"Yes. Very beautiful. And very proud of her twin girls, I think." B'jin regretted that her sister B'jal had never gotten as close to her mother as she.

B'jal stumbled, nearly falling. With great effort, her sister helped her to regain her balance. They stood for a moment, disoriented. B'jin eyed the sun, it was high noon, and she had lost her source of direction, but soon it would not matter anyway. She doubted they would last another hour. She reoriented and started pulling her sister along in what she hoped was a northwesterly direction again.

"She died before knowing that her twin girls lived a life that would have brought her shame." B'jal stated this flatly, but her own sense of shame was evident.

"Father followed Ba'al, but mother did not, did you know?" B'jin asked.

"No, I did not. You were always closer to mother. I was jealous." B'jal smiled weakly. Her lips cracked and started to bleed.

"Mother told me she believed in the same God as those who have sent us into this desert." B'jin looked straight at the horizon. Her sister stared at her, disbelieving what she had just heard. Feeling her sister's eyes on her, she turned to look directly into her mirror image. "It is true. And now the judgment of our mother's God grinds his justice upon us out here on the Anvil. It is justice come full circle is it not, my sister? Soon, I will join our mother, do you not wish the same?"

B'jal's eyes would have filled up with tears, but she was far too dehydrated, in fact she had stopped perspiring. Her face was flushed and blotchy red, she did not have long to live. But her eyes spoke years of pain and rage and unbridled passion. Yet she longed to wipe away the wrongs she had committed. In this place of dust and dryness, there was no fountain to cleanse her dirty soul. What was left to her? Only a sister who had not given up, someone who loved her enough to stay with her even if it meant death.

She realized she was looking at her own reflection, a hopeful self that had been hidden from her own eyes her entire life – the secret of a Godly mother, a sister with a seed a grace. Why had she allowed B'jin to follow her here? Why? Her sister should have lived! Her heart ached with remorse for her own worthless, wasted life. If only she could impart some gift to her dear sister before she died, some blessing that would at least show B'jin she was grateful for her love and loyalty... Casting her eyes above B'jin's shoulder, she thought of something.

"B'jin, water..." But the water bag had run dry hours ago. "Turn around, look at the sky, B'jin. See the small cloud there? I say that is your God's cloud coming to your rescue, to give you shade. I call upon the God of the Anvil, the God of my sister and mother to grant my dying wish. Hover your hand over my dear sister, be her shade for her this day that she may reach safety tonight. I am worthless and I would gladly give my life that she may live, for she is more worthy than me."

B'jal hiccoughed, then vomited dark bile from the corner of her mouth. Her knees crumpled and she sprawled unmoving on the searing hot dirt. Her eyes were too dry to close. B'jin knelt beside her, determined to die with her sister.

Unnoticed, a shadow moved across the women. The shadow darkened and B'jin heard a splat in the dirt beside her, then another. Her fevered mind could not make sense of the smell of large hot droplets falling around her in random, rapid succession. Several hit her head and shoulders, then began to attack her sister. In her delirious stupor, she moved to protect B'jal, but then sat back to enjoy her dream. For a dream it was! There was no other explanation. She had died and her soul was being ushered to an eternity where it rained in the desert!

She looked up as warm rain drenched her parched face. She opened her mouth and drank in its refreshing coolness. If this was heaven, she wondered what other wonders were in store! But when she looked at her sister, B'jal's face was half buried in mud! She quickly pulled her onto her lap and washed her face with rain. She allowed the water to wash over all her clothing to cool her sister's overheated body. She funneled water into B'jal's mouth and watched her swallow reflexively but still she did not wake. What sort of heaven was this?

Abruptly, the rain stopped. The sun began to burn again, turning the wet sand steamy. B'jin understood. God had answered her sister's dying wish. The rain had been a gift from God's own hand. Unconscious, B'jal lay with her head on her sister's lap, her knees drawn up. By chance, they were in a slight depression so the heavy rain had filled it with nearly eight inches of cool mud.

B'jin looked up at the clear sky and said aloud to the sky, "God, thank you for your grace. I surrender my worn-out soul to you. I am sorry I have nothing more worthy to give other than my gratitude and praise for your gift of rain. They say God shows no mercy to those abandoned on the Anvil. Now I know that those who say such things are wrong, for I have seen your mercy. Thank you, thank you for my life." She lay across her sister's knees, with her sister's head on her own knees. The two women curled in perfect symmetry under the merciless noon sun.

-:--o--:-

"I found them!" Omar shouted back to Nada and Labid, the young guard whom they had roped into guiding them. "I told you that cloud was a sign!"

-:--o--:-

B'jin awoke on a comfortable mat with her head resting on a silk pillow. Everything ached, her face burned like she was standing next to a bonfire. She knew she was awake, but she could not open her eyes, they were encrusted and felt as if they were sealed shut. She moaned and writhed in pain. A voice murmured soothingly. She realized her hand was held by another. She felt a gentle squeeze and somehow knew it was her sister's. How? Where? She sighed and surrendered herself to sleep that could not be resisted.

Hours, perhaps days later, she awoke again with a raging thirst. She moaned, "Thirsty." A cup was immediately at her lips. She sipped refreshment into her body and soul. "Where?"

"We are back at the temple. Nada and Omar found us. They said we were lying in a puddle of mud, but that is impossible. Do you know what they are talking about?"

"Hmmm." B'jin twisted her mouth into a sly smile. "Your fault."

"What?" B'jal stroked her sister's forehead.

"Your cloud. Your prayer. Everyone is wrong you know."

B'jal laughed. "You are still feverish and not making any sense, my sister."

"Oh yes I am." She struggled to sit up but groaned in pain. She opened her eyes and looked at her sister. "B'jal, we found God's mercy on the Anvil. Your prayer was answered. God brought the cloud to bring us shade and to cool us with rain. I saw this myself. I will never doubt God. We live in a holy land."

"I have my doubts about that." B'jal patted her sister's hand lovingly, "But I believe you, my sister. I believe you."

B'jin shifted on the bed. Her ordeal had so weakened her, this small movement sapped her remaining strength. Sleepily, she squeezed her sister's hand. "Good enough. Believe me then, my sister and perhaps sooner or later you will believe in God as I do." She dropped off to a normal night's rest.

-:--o--:-

"What will you do with them?" Batshua asked Nada. Omar stood next to his wife, but somehow Batshua sensed their rescue of the twins had been at Nada's urging.

"As you know, master Job has made a gift of lands in the Chaldean city of Mari to me and my husband. It is very distant, perhaps far enough away from all that the twins have known."

Omar interjected, "We will offer them an opportunity to become lifetime bond-servants to Nada and me or face the Anvil once again. Perhaps they will accept our offer graciously and not reject it as disdainfully as they did Negasi's?"

Batshua laughed heartily. "I love both of you! You are learning the ways of leadership. I expect to hear that you have become the Emir and Emira of Chaldea one day!" They all laughed.

"And now, I believe our business here is complete. I wish to begin the journey home to my husband." She smiled as if she was not afraid, but she could not hide her misgivings from Nada.

"We shall accompany you." Omar stated emphatically, not waiting for an invitation.

"Bless you Omar. Your company will be most appreciated. It will be difficult to leave Negasi behind, though I do not regret my decision. Tariq needs a man such as Negasi to judge fairly and continue to purge the corruption from this awful place. But he has led my caravans for many years, I am at a loss..." Batshua left an opening for suggestions.

Omar looked at Nada and they shared a knowing smile, he turned to Batshua, "Ah! We may have a suggestion for you, if Negasi will give his permission."

-:--o--:-

21

Reunion

"But those who suffer he delivers in their suffering;
he speaks to them in their affliction."

The Book of Job 36:15

-:--o--:-

Labid, the young soldier who had been out to the Anvil twice, once to abandon the twins and then again to assist in their rescue, stood timidly before his boss. Omar and Nada stood to either side as all three faced Negasi's stony stare. They had gathered this morning in the temple's great hall of judgment with Labid's fellow soldiers in the audience. Batshua sat beside Negasi as usual this morning. She looked very grim.

Omar began, "Master Negasi, I beg your indulgence in the matter of Labid..."

Negasi held up his hand impatiently, "Silence!" His look bore none of the usual camaraderie he shared with his friend, Omar. "Master Omar, you disappoint me, sir. Perhaps you think you were acting as an agent of God's mercy with your impetuous search for those abandoned to his grace. But I do not believe God is honored by the deceptive way you have gone about your task. Especially when it involves undermining the discipline and conduct of one of my guards. Noble as your intentions may have been, I cannot allow your actions, or Labid's actions to go unpunished."

Omar and Nada looked worried. Labid looked terrified. All three stared at the pile of stone that used to be the temple's altar.

Negasi conferred with Batshua. Negasi shook his head and looked angry. The two whispered together as the three miscreants began to fidget and sweat. At last Negasi agreed to whatever Batshua was saying, but he looked disgusted.

"Omar and Nada!" They looked at Negasi, surrendered to their fate. "Step back from Labid." They obeyed. "B'jin and B'jal are remanded to your custody. I dust my hands of them." He figuratively gestured with his words. "Much as it pains me, you are banished from the city of Tariq for a period of one year. Do not tempt my patience further."

They knelt to one knee in acceptance. Negasi's glare focused on Labid, causing him to nearly buckle under its intensity. "Labid!"

"Sir!" Labid did his best to stand fully erect. If he was to die, he would die as he had witnessed other men die.

"You are a young fool." Negasi barked.

"Yes sir!" Evidently he would be ridiculed before Negasi's blade fell.

"I have no need of young fools, but apparently madam Batshua does. Your obligation to me would have been completed in five years. You will now complete your service to madam Batshua, adding an additional five years. She will either drive the foolishness from your addled brain or drive you to an early grave, but you are no longer any concern of mine." He stood abruptly and strode from the hall.

Labid was so stunned at still being alive he almost followed Negasi. Omar touched his elbow and whispered, "Follow me."

As they left the temple Nada said "That went well, I think."

Omar replied, "Yes, Negasi played his part well."

Labid said, "What?! What are you two talking about?!"

Omar answered, "Bah! Madam Batshua needed a new camel tender. Negasi needed to show that we did not get away with rescuing the twins. Everyone is happy. Relax."

Labid was very confused, "I thought Negasi was your friend."

Nada spoke, "He is indeed. He is a very good friend."

"Then why the punishment? Why wound your friendship by banishing you from the city?" Labid was very confused.

Omar slapped Labid on the shoulder, "Labid, we undermined Negasi's authority by rescuing the women. He has wounded us by banishing us from his city, but we have been treated quite fairly. The wounds of a friend are true."

-:--o--:-

Labid turned out to be an astute camel man with a natural affinity for the knobby-kneed, obnoxious creatures. He seemed awkward and self-conscious around people, but he and camels seemed to understand each other as if they spoke the same language. He knew their moods and needs, and they knew that he knew they could not bluff him.

Forty camels were lined up obediently, waiting for their human and cargo burdens. Labid was amazing. With a commission from madam Batshua, he had scoured Tariq all morning searching for the most sturdy, healthy and trained mounts in the city.

Negasi had hand-picked a dozen additional guards and assigned them to escort his Emira to Hareb. Besides their precious human passengers, the caravan would be carrying about three hundred pounds of gold. A large portion of Ba'al-Hanni's stash would remain in the temple's protection, but the treasury of Hareb would now be replenished sufficiently to begin restoring its herds. The extra dozen guards, along with Naaman's eight would not be enough to repel a raid coming after the gold, only enough to discourage thieves seeking targets of opportunity. Negasi thought a larger force would attract too much attention. A normal-looking caravan with abnormal cargo should be safe enough.

They left without fanfare, Negasi bid farewell to his friends privately. His smile was back as genuine as ever. He promised a grand reception upon their return next year.

-:--o--:-

B'jal and B'jin had made the beginnings of peace with Boshet. Boshet herself had started things off with a simple, yet sincere apology to them. She did not make excuses or expect forgiveness. She simply stated that she had been a wicked woman who was now attempting to live right in the eyes of her Creator. She said she knew she had a lot to learn.

The twins asked what she planned to do with herself. Boshet responded that she did not know yet, but hoped to find employment with the Emira. She wished them long life and success with Nada and Omar wherever they wound up in Chaldea. Boshet told both the women how pleased she had been that their ordeal in the desert had turned out so miraculously. Each promised that they would hold no hard feelings for past deeds. It was a start.

At their first camp, the six women had a few moments alone while the men set up camp.

Nada stared into the flames of a small campfire. The tinder had burned away, a few of the larger twigs had started to catch in the gentle evening breeze – shooting small jets of flame into each other like a nest of wooden fire-breathing serpents. She played with her dagger idly, the blade and hilt sparkling in the firelight as it danced between her hands.

"So much bloodshed in Tariq." She mused. "I have bathed many times, but I do not feel clean. I do not feel that I will ever be clean again." She flipped her knife into the sand, it slid into the ground to the hilt. She gathered her knees to her chin, wrapped her arms around her ankles and stared at it with baleful eyes. Nobody said anything until the fire's crackling quieted.

Batshua said, "Nada, may I see your knife?" Nada handed it to her with a curious expression. Batshua accepted it gingerly and tapped the sand free.

"You have maintained it well. Very clean and sharp, my compliments." She smiled at her former handmaiden. The two friends eyed each other with respect.

"May I see your belt?" A slight frown crossed Nada's visage but was quickly erased with a conscious effort. She handed the ornately carved leather piece to her former mistress.

"Tell me, Nada," Batshua said, as she slid the blade into its hidden sheath and folded the belt into her lap, "how do you feel just now?"

"You mean now that you have disarmed me?" she said with a smile and a nervous laugh.

Batshua raised one eyebrow, "Yes, now that you are disarmed."

"I feel strangely small." She thought for a moment. "The night sky seems darker… would you return my weapon? You are making me uneasy."

Batshua tossed it, Nada caught it smoothly and wrapped the belt around her waist as if she had practiced the move for endless hours.

"Nada, what killed Ba'al-Hanni?" Batshua asked.

With her face screwed up into an ironic smile, Nada pulled her knife out of its sheath and held it by the blade for all to see by the firelight. "Does anyone doubt?" she asked. She was getting smiles from Boshet and Frayda.

"You can be proud, but be mindful of the truth. Ba'al-Hanni was led to his execution by God's own hand. Evidently he had been self-deluded into thinking he could restore himself to power by suddenly making his presence known. I feel quite certain that if the toss of your dagger had missed, God could have easily killed that evil man by any other means. His heart would have burst or his brain suddenly melted like wax or a piece of stone could have fallen from the ceiling of the temple onto his head. God chose you to be the instrument of his death and you can rejoice in that, but do not be so proud that you are blinded to God's hand."

She paused and inhaled deeply of the night air. She let it escape slowly as she felt herself totally relax. The others sensed the import of her words and also sensed what Batshua now perceived – God's own hand had covered their camp.

An awed reverence wrapped the women in silence. A meteor streaked noiselessly across the night sky. Its beauty flared only briefly and drew attention to the brilliance of God's eternal creation in the heavens. All around the campfire's gentle glow were the low sounds of their camels and the men making their beds ready for the night. It was all so ordinary but expansive in a way that was very unordinary.

Batshua spoke clearly, but just above a whisper. "In our haste, we forget to give God the praise he is due. I feel that I am bringing a child home to my husband, but it is not me, it is God's gift to my husband. I feel that it is our victory in Tariq that yields the gold that will restore the fortunes of Hareb, but that again is God's doing. God gathered the gold in Tariq with Ba'al-Hanni's own hand. I have been blind."

She continued. "My father brought me to the potter's shed in Goshen. He wanted me to learn something but I failed to see it until now. The vessel the potter made was House Hareb and when the vessel was marred, the potter selected a bit of mud to repair it. He blended the bit of mud into the vessel until it became whole again. I was thinking that the 'potter' was using bits of mud to make *me* a better vessel, but I know now that I am the bit of mud, not the vessel.

"No one will ever speak of me or even know my name. But God knows. He is the Potter and will have used me like a bit of mud to make House Hareb a better vessel suitable for his purpose."

Nada's eyes glistened with tears in the firelight. "Madam Batshua, this does not seem fair."

Batshua laughed and relaxed at a young woman's inevitable conclusion. "Ah Nada! I love you so! You are right of course. It is not fair in the short span of a human lifetime, but God is not human. It is therefore very fair to him. God is fair and he is good. He is very good."

She looked around the circle of her closest friends. "I think we will make a small detour on our journey. There is a priest in Rosh-Ramen. We will visit him and present ourselves for ritual cleansing. He is a wise man, perhaps he will have insight as to how I might best present myself in reunion to my husband. I fear to arrive in Hareb as a conquering warrior, for that is not what I am. I am a run-away wife who is humbly returning to her husband whom she has wronged."

-:--o--:-

The temple in Rosh-Ramen turned out to be an elaborate tent. Nada was disappointed, she expected to see a magnificent stone temple like those she had seen erected for Ba'al. Her God should receive more homage than Ba'al! His temple should be as big as a mountain!

The man attending the doorway to the temple recognized Nada. She recognized him too. It was the E'mat's servant from Aqaba!

"Nada, you have come a long way. Or should I call you 'madam Nada' now? My name is Raziel." he spoke with a sincere smile.

"I am very surprised to see you here, sir. Whatever brings you to Rosh-Ramen?" Nada could not believe this was the same man.

"There is a proverb that says, 'I would rather be at peace keeping watch over the door of my God's house than live in distress within the tents of the wicked.' That is why I am here." Raziel would not explain further.

"I have wanted to thank you for the gift from mistress Leah." Nada said with a subdued voice.

Raziel nodded. "It was my pleasure to pass it along. That day was so chaotic. I did not get a chance to give you a message from mistress Leah. She had asked me to tell you something before she passed away, but in all the confusion of the breakup of master E'mat's household, I never got the chance. The message makes no sense to me, perhaps it will to you. She said to tell you, 'Look under the fisherman.' She said you would know what she means. Do you?"

Nada pondered this but responded only, "I do not know, master Raziel, but thank you for passing it along. May God bless you, sir."

Later that day, Nada spoke secretly to Omar that they would have to make a trek to Aqaba before heading off to inspect their inheritance in Chaldea. She would not say why.

-:--o--:-

Eli-Ramen, priest of Rosh-Ramen was a direct descendent of Melchizedek, the former king of Salem who had been honored by father Abraham two centuries ago. Batshua presented herself to Eli-Ramen on behalf of her household. She explained the recent events in Tariq and her own despair in returning to her husband who may have already died without knowing of her repentance. She begged for his wisdom. Could she find peace with God? If not for herself, she wanted peace for her companions whose fealty and love should be sung by the angels themselves. She emptied her soul to Eli-Ramen, surrounded by all her friends who, with the exception of Nada, had not known the true depth of her grief and inner turmoil.

When Batshua ended her story, she expected Eli-Ramen to be shocked by her betrayal. But he merely nodded as if he heard stories such as hers every day.

The priest surveyed the scene before him. Whether by design, happy circumstance or the hand of God, Batshua's friends surrounded her in a semi-circle. Naaman and Frayda to her left, Omar and Nada at her right. Boshet had assumed the position previously occupied by Nada, just off her mistress's right shoulder. Omar and Nada had assigned other duties to the twins, they needed time to ponder their new circumstances.

Batshua spoke into the silence, "Is there no hope of redemption for me? I fear that I have run too far from my husband and I have run from my God. There is no way back."

Eli-Ramen looked at her curiously. His eyes were marvelously deep and shone with loving compassion. "Madam Batshua, look around you." He waited while she turned self-consciously and acknowledged the presence of her friends. "Your friends are here to support you in your hour of need. They sought you out -- they stood by you when you were in danger. Is this not true?"

"It is true. They are more dear to me than I can say. I am honored and humbled to be called their friend."

"Tell me, madam Batshua, do you believe that their qualities exceed the character of God? Do you believe God is less loyal than your friends in your hour of need? Do you believe God did not seek you out when you ran or that he did not stand by you when you were in danger?"

"No, I... I know my friends. But..."

"But you do not know God. You trust your friends because you have given something of yourself to them, so there is less of a surprise when they give something of themselves in return. But what can you give to God that will make a difference? What can you do to keep God motivated and on your side, eh? How can a man or a woman know this God who does not even let us know so much as his name?"

Batshua remained silent. She had struggled her whole life with these questions.

"Have you ever wondered why God has no name? I cannot answer many of your life's greatest questions, but I can give you an answer to that one." He smiled indulgently.

Batshua was intrigued, but this priest was beginning to sound like her husband – always teaching! "Please satisfy my curiosity. I have always been frustrated that I cannot know God by name the same way I can know a friend or anyone else by name."

"Think of this. When you assign a name to a person or a thing, you have set boundaries around it. For example, my name is 'Eli-Ramen'. By that name, you know something of my boundaries. For instance, you know that I am not 'Batshua' or 'Naaman'. Given the characteristics of my name, you might deduce that I am a man and not a woman. My name implies many boundaries and borders -- attributes that determine what I am and what I am not. But our God is boundless and infinite. Therefore how can he be named? The pagan gods that are worshipped by the rest of humanity have boundaries. They are spirits of the air or sea or animals and so on. They have names because they have boundaries. Do you see the difference?"

Batshua's eyes lit up in epiphany. "Ba'al is not a god then, he may be real, he may in fact be a demon at work in the world, but he does not have limitless power. That is why we were able to overcome him, because our God is infinitely greater!" Batshua's head was swirling with new ideas. "But if God is so powerful, why does he rely on mere human beings to do his bidding? We are weak and so often fail." Her eyes showed pain when she remembered her own failings. "Why doesn't God work around us instead of through us when we might fail him?"

Eli-Ramen laughed. "Ah, my dear, if you figure that one out, please return and tell me your answer for it will be you that teaches me!" Batshua joined in his laughter.

The priest grew sober, "But you must be on your way soon. You do not wish to linger here to listen to the musings of an old philosopher."

"I must say that you are a wonderful teacher. But I fear the ritual you may ask of me. Whatever sacrifice you demand, I am prepared to give. I have no pride or self-worth, no dignity that I yet struggle to preserve. I hope to see my husband before he dies to beg his forgiveness, whether or not he deigns to forgive me is not my main concern. I ask only that I be allowed to bear his child before I pay whatever final penalty imposed upon me by him or you." She bowed her head in complete acceptance of Eli-Ramen's judgment.

"Well spoken, madam Batshua, Emira of Edom, grand lady and mistress of Hareb, friend of the conquerors of Tariq." He used all the titles without a trace of irony. "God's spirit has spoken clearly to my spirit concerning you. There are only two words: 'go home'."

Batshua's head snapped up to look the priest in the eyes. Was he taunting her? "That is all? No ritual, no payment, no sacrifice? I have come prepared..."

Eli-Ramen held up his hand and interrupted, "There is nothing more or less from the Lord. His ways are simple, but simple does not mean easy. 'Go home', madam Batshua. That is a simple commandment from God to obey, I suspect it will not be easy and will demand from you sufficient sacrifice."

"But I thought surely you would request... payment of some sort..." she looked around the enclosure. It was not very richly appointed.

"No. God requests nothing else except your obedience and loving devotion. God is not honored by meaningless sacrifices, empty rituals or gifts of gold dug from the mountains he himself has created." The reference to gold stung Batshua deeply. She had thought the tent needed repair and was hoping to endear herself with a large offering. Evidently the priest read her mind.

Eli-Ramen started to turn away and go about his business but had a second thought, "There is one thing you could do as a personal favor to me. I ask this as a personal favor, not as priest of the Lord."

Batshua thought, "*Now we are getting down to it, I wonder what he really wants?*" She said, "I will help you in any way possible. What is your request?"

"Since you are bound for the province of Hareb, you may as well accept a passenger on my behalf. He is a leper who presented himself to the temple more than a week ago for observation. He stated that his leprosy had abated and wanted to be pronounced ritually clean, a task I accomplished for him only yesterday. Since he is now cleansed of his leprosy, you could give him passage to his home if you think it is not too much trouble or too far out of the way for you. I do not believe he can offer much in the way of payment."

Batshua's heart shrank at the thought of a leper among them, especially given that she was pregnant, but she did not hesitate. She bowed graciously, "I shall be more than happy to accept your passenger. He will be welcome in our company and we shall conduct him safely home, no matter how far out of the way it may be."

"Ah, very good. Come this way then, I shall introduce you. I believe he is just outside in the north garden." Eli-Ramen led the way, Batshua and her friends followed.

-:--o--:-

Eli-Ramen walked a short distant down a beautifully groomed garden. To the left and right were fruit trees growing on mounds of loam with small streams of irrigation water trickling between them. The air was heavy with the smells of ripening fruit and their sweetness filled Batshua's senses deliciously.

The priest stepped toward the left onto a side path and gestured with his hand toward a man seated on a stone bench under a pomegranate tree. He wore an ochre robe with a cowl draped over his head which was bent low over folded hands held between his knees. He was obviously meditating. His leathery hands were very thin and pale, almost skin over bones and very dry. Batshua followed the priest's gesture and approached the decrepit man.

"Good evening sir. I am Batshua. I understand you need passage to Edom." She felt so awkward. She had expected Eli-Ramen to do some sort of introduction.

The man spoke down into his hands. His voice was a hoarse whisper, but clearly audible in the dusky stillness of early evening. A shaft of golden light broke through the trees from the setting sun to light up his head and shoulders. "Good evening, Batshua, my love. It is so good to hear your voice again. It has been a long time…"

Batshua heard the words, but…?

The man sat up and slid back his cowl. With eyes bright, clear and strong with love, A'dab Ben Hareb lifted his arms to his wife, "Batshua, my dear wife, come home."

Batshua ran to her husband, her shocked face full of pure joy. She fell at his feet, making an altar of his knees. She wrapped her arms around his thin body and began to sob in relief. A'dab wrapped his arms around her shoulders, pulling her to his chest and bent low over her, murmuring soft words that were lost in the flood of emotion. Their quiet sobs were punctuated only by the joyous chatter of Batshua's friends as they waited only a few seconds before joining the two in their embrace.

Only a moment passed before Naaman caught Omar's eye. He motioned with his chin back toward the tent. Omar got the message and touched Nada's shoulder gently. She disengaged herself from Batshua and A'dab. She whispered encouraging words as she pulled away. The group of friends followed Eli-Ramen back into the tent.

Once inside, they exploded in questions. How long had he known master A'dab had been here?! Why hadn't he told Batshua right away? Had he traveled here alone? Is he indeed well? How could he have healed so quickly? Would he be alright now?

Eli-Ramen held up his hands in a 'please slow down' gesture. He was smiling broadly. He began to answer their questions.

The priest said, "Master A'dab arrived alone just over a week ago disguised as a humble wayfaring man of no means, dressed as you now see him. He rode a tired old horse, carrying only dried meat and fruit, nothing that anyone would steal should he encounter thieves. I can assure you that he is completely sound in both body and mind, though he is weak from his ordeal. He came here to be pronounced clean, as I have stated. A'dab and I are old friends, you see. He required my affirmation of his health when God begins to restore his fortunes, which I am certain God will do."

Eli-Ramen spoke a calm assurance that no one could doubt. Everyone felt a giddy excitement and a heightened, unreasonable feeling of well-being very similar to the sense one has when a storm has passed and the atmosphere is charged with the passage of lightning and damp with the promise of peace and life springing from refreshing rain.

A'dab and Batshua strolled into their company with their arms around each other's waists. Their faces bore uncomplicated smiles. A'dab's cheeks were stained with tracks of tears. They traced a glistening path from his grinning mouth to his laughing eyes. He looked physically strong and happier than anyone could remember. A'dab's face and whole body also had a hint of something else. He looked like a man in love!

Batshua reflected her husband's demeanor. Nada had a strange thought – she wondered if the lamps in the tent suddenly flickered out, would her two friends glow in the darkness? She smiled at her own imagination, but her former master and mistress appeared to be on fire with renewed passion.

Eli-Ramen spoke, "Well, from your appearance, it would seem that you have come to some sort of decision. Perhaps several decisions…" His eyes questioned and offered an opportunity for A'dab to fill in the rest of the statement.

"Yes. I am grateful to you, my friend Eli-Ramen. Your wisdom is God-inspired." He turned to his friends. "To each of you, Nada and Omar, Naaman, Frayda, and Boshet, and also to Negasi who remains on guard in Tariq, I must express.." he closed his eyes and drew a deep breath, struggling to contain his emotion. When he spoke, his voice was barely under control, "I must express my deepest thanks. You have risked your very lives to save the love of my life. I do not believe you fully understand the extent to which God will use what you have done. But I know your accomplishments will prosper and that you will live to see the fruit of your labors and the risks you have taken together will not have been in vain. Long life and peace to each of you, may God's own hand hover over you... over us, the new foundation of House Hareb."

-:--o--:-

For three days, the entire crew rested. Rosh-Ramen was a fairly safe city, with shops and cafes for travelers who visited the temple.

Batshua and Job took another stroll through the temple's garden the day of their departure. "I heard you have changed your name, or added a name." She prompted her husband.

"Yes, I think 'Job' is more fitting, given what I have been through. Easier to say, too. In fact, if you need to yell at me for any reason, 'JOB!' has a much more delightful echo than 'ADAB!'. Just a thought."

Batshua rolled her eyes. "I shall try to remember that. To me, you will always be 'Dabby.'" She giggled.

"And you are my beloved 'shua, though you may consider changing your name now that you have conquered and largely purged the city of Tariq. Not a bad accomplishment... for a woman."

Batshua elbowed him in the ribs hard enough to make him grunt. "It was Nada, Omar, Naaman and Negasi who took the temple of Ba'al. And that could not have been done had it not been for the men you sent from Hareb. I was merely their... inspiration. I acted mostly as a lady in distress along with Frayda who showed surprising courage. I did not have to strain my acting ability to play my part. I am certain that had you been there, we would have conquered the entire province." She grinned at his compliment but she would not allow him to tease her this way.

They rounded a corner to where Labid had gathered their mounts for the trip home. Batshua was shocked to see a full complement of at least sixty camels lined along the road with two dozen horses. There were new recruits among the warriors as well!

Batshua estimated at thirty. Where had these additional men and animals come from?!

Job read his wife's mind. Reading her mind was a favorite hobby of his that he had missed for many months. He knew this talent both frustrated and amused her.

He spoke into the back of her head as she stared at the street scene. "You are perhaps wondering where all these men and animals came from, hmmm?"

Batshua snapped around to glare at him, "Yes! You came to Rosh-Ramen as a pitiful beggar! It seems impossible that you rounded up guards and mounts by flashing your smiling face around the city!" She scowled in confusion and not just a little accusation. Their reunion was only a day old and already they were back at their old playful banter, each vying to get one up on the other. Batshua enjoyed the challenge though she almost always lost.

"Perhaps I should have consulted with you, but I did not want to spoil the enchantment of our rest with the droll humdrum of business. I needed to make preparations for our trip westward. The additional guards are necessary for that direction is dangerous and plagued by thieves."

Batshua raised one eyebrow at her husband, examining her husband's face for signs of illness. "My husband, are you quite certain Eli-Ramen was accurate in his assessment of your health? Our home lies northeast of here."

"Yes, my love. But The Great Sea lies west. Within a week, Phoenician ships carrying a thousand sheep and several hundred camels will be arriving at the Port of Ashdod. I think it would be wise to replenish our herds and give the remaining shepherd, Zahur at Serenity Rock something to do, hmmm?"

"We will be home in time for the birth of our child. I have sent messages to all my relatives and your father as well. They will arrive this spring to celebrate. It will be quite a gathering, I assure you!"

"How do you intend to pay for this?" Batshua thought of the camels packed with gold. Did her husband already lay claim to it? They had not discussed it.

"Who killed Ba'al-Hanni, you?" Job's playful banter was back, he was enjoying this.

"As I have described the fight several times already, Nada threw her dagger into Ba'al-Hanni's heart and Omar struck the death blow." The scene replaying in her mind took some of the playfulness out of Batshua, she struggled to regain her enjoyment of this time with her husband.

"Well then! Ba'al-Hanni's gold belongs to me", he said triumphantly.

"Oh!?" I have you now, she thought, "How do you figure? Omar and Nada are my servants..." her voice trailed off as she realized she had freed them in her mad dash away from Hareb. "Oh... I had forgotten that I had set them both free."

"Ah ha! And so while they were free, they requested that I marry them, which I did, and then they requested that they become servants in my employ which I also did. I hired them as special agents on my staff with full authority to act on behalf of House Hareb. So when they killed Ba'al-Hanni, it was as if House Hareb killed Ba'al-Hanni. You freed Negasi before sending him to me. I also took the liberty of hiring him before sending him to rescue you with the soldiers. Therefore the gold belongs to House Hareb." He looked down his nose with drooped eyelids, daring his wife to refute the logic.

She laughed so hard it made her belly hurt. "Okay, okay. Have it your way! The gold is too heavy for me to carry around, you may as well get some use out of it." She sighed with a deep, exaggerated girlish sigh that made her husband laugh. He loved winning arguments because she gave up in a most delightful way.

He suddenly stopped walking, turned and held his wife's face cupped tenderly in both hands. He looked deep into her eyes, the eyes that looked back into his own with confidence and a fierce loyalty he knew would never waver again.

"Batshua, my love, my heart's desire... I have missed you so." He swallowed back his emotion, he was struggling to find the right words. "Lands can be inherited. Gold and wealth can be acquired by conquest and hard work. But a good wife... a wife a noble character, who can find? Can a good wife be acquired by hard work or conquest? No. A wife of noble character is a gift from God."

Arm in arm, the great Emir and Emira of Edom strolled forward into history.

-:--O--:-

Epilogue

The birth of Job's new heir delighted her parents, but Batshua had desperately hoped for a son. She had spoken of this often to Job whose reassuring face remained philosophically non-committal. When the squalling cries of a girl-child were heard echoing throughout the tiled walls of Batshua's birthing room, Job's relatives were politely congratulatory, but inwardly scandalized. They felt Job must still be under God's curse. As Batshua nursed young Jemimah atop her watchtower during the early weeks of spring, she looked at the morning star and thought she could see God winking.

Job proclaimed that any daughter born to his household would have the same inheritance rights as a son. His brothers and sisters had no choice but to acquiesce to Job's unusual wisdom. Each of Job's siblings honored his new heir with a gift of silver and a gold ring. These gifts became a yearly tradition as Batshua produced nine more children, one each year with a set of twins thrown in by a God who had a sense of humor. Job and Batshua's children -- seven handsome sons and three beautiful daughters -- were a great consolation to each of their parents in different ways.

-:--o--:-

Asher's crops failed to take root that spring in Goshen. For the prior seven years the crops had been exceptionally good, but the Pharaoh's regent, Zaphenath-Paneah had taxed the people mercilessly. Certainly the land had produced abundantly, but what good was that when Pharaoh kept it all to himself?! Asher decided to spend his twilight years with his daughter and grandchildren, so he migrated to Edom with his only unmarried child, Ruben.

-:--o--:-

Rueben and Boshet were overjoyed to see each other! Boshet, the Emira's new handmaiden, became an odd kind of tutor for the young genius lad. God had answered Boshet's prayer – that she be useful rather than used.

She began to discover that the training and education she had endured at the temple of Ba'al could be useful in ways she had not previously seen. Where she had viewed her prior life of slavery as only 'take, take, take', with God-cleansed eyes, she picked through her skills as a gold miner panned for treasure from a muddy stream.

During her years of slavery, Boshet had been forced to learn four languages in order to communicate with her temple clients. Temple prostitutes were also required to learn a musical instrument and all manner of courtly etiquette. These nuances were required to serve the high and mighty at the temple's feasts. She discovered that her knowledge of courtly manners and skill as an intercultural colloquist were rare and highly valuable. Ruben, as well as the Emira's children and grandchildren became adroit in the arts of trade and international diplomacy, largely due to Boshet's influence.

Boshet knew in her heart that her shame had at last been taken away. At master Job's urging, she selected a new name – Ephrata, meaning 'fruitful and honored'. Always carrying a tiny satchel of dried hyssop leaves tied to her sash, Ephrata poured herself into her new life – it felt so good being useful.

-:--o--:-

Job enjoyed conducting another marriage ceremony between the most unlikely couple in his memory: Naaman and Frayda. As the towering dark tree that was Naaman stood next to the delicate pale flower that was Frayda, Job thought this may not be so much of a marriage as it was a grafting. He hoped they would take root together, but only God knew what attracted people to each other. No one would have matched him with Batshua, after all…

After the ceremony, Batshua hugged Frayda in congratulations. She whispered, "Try teaching him some new songs!"

Frayda whispered back, "Perhaps next year, for this year, I will settle for him shouting only my name and not the names of his old pagan gods when he stubs his toe!" Batshua hugged Frayda again and both women shook together vigorously in silent laughter. Everyone thought they were crying.

-:--o--:-

After the birth of Jemimah, Nada and Omar left Hareb to find their fortunes and destiny in the land of the Chaldeans. Unknown to the lords of Hareb, they diverted their small entourage south toward the Gulf of Aqaba. Raziel's cryptic message delivered to Nada during their last journey through Rosh-Ramen had itched in the back of Nada's mind like an insect bite. She would have no rest until she checked it out.

They found the dock, house and other features of master Amal's holdings in complete ruins. E'mat had said he had sold it, but apparently misfortune had come to the buyer, for the scene looked as if raiders from land, sea or both had taken anything of value and burned the rest. The only company they had were gulls screeching their eternal complaints and the sifting sound of waves cascading on the beach, dragging the loose gravel back and forth in its restless rhythm. Nada felt desolate and forlorn seeing the place in such condition.

Nada dismounted. Omar had taught her to ride a horse and now she never wanted to return to a stinking camel again! Camels were more practical in the desert, but horses smelled much, much better.

She and Omar approached the remains of the dock. Omar asked, "What was it the doorman said?"

Nada paused, closing her eyes in thought. "I think he said, 'Look under the fisherman.' I do not know for sure what he meant."

"I am a fisherman, perhaps I can help you!" A sarcastic voice came from behind the large rock where Nada and Leah used to sit and chat. He staggered down toward Nada, a mean-looking knife in his hand. Scruffy-looking, with spittle and the remains of last night's ale apparently dried on his gray-black beard.

"Who are you?" asked Omar politely, he still sat casually astride his stallion. The 'fisherman' was moving menacingly toward Nada. She had moved down to the water's edge near the remains of the fish-skinning docks.

The man stopped, waved his arms, twirling around and gestured with the knife. "Who am I?! I am master Herem and I am lord of these lands!" He continued his way to Nada and presumptuously wrapped an arm around her shoulder.

Omar remained where he was. He caught his wife's look and raised an eyebrow. She scowled and turned her head sideways in a motion that communicated clearly, *"Omar, you big, dumb, leather-armored warrior, are you going to do something about this?!"* His answering look was a tease, *"I am perfectly comfortable sitting here on my horse, my dear..."*

Herem caught none of their non-verbal exchange. He pointed up to Omar with his knife. "You there! I tell you whaaaat!" 'What' was punctuated with a very loud belch. "Come down off that horse and fight me! Winner gets the girl!" He squeezed Nada to his side in a most provocative manner.

Omar smiled fiercely and leaned forward in his saddle. "I have a better proposal for you, master Herem." He nodded with his chin toward Nada. "Fight her."

Herem looked confused as he responded, "Eh?" Anything else he might have said was physically impossible because his lower jaw was suddenly pinned to his upper as a six-inch dagger drove upward through his chin into the base of his brain.

Nada backed away quickly before her clothing was soiled and turned to Omar in a huff, "I would think you could trouble yourself just once! This is the second time this week…!"

Omar smiled at his warrior-wife, "Have you any idea what blood and wet leather armor smells like as it dries in the desert sun? Besides…" he displayed his three foot sword he had silently withdrawn from its scabbard the moment they heard the voice. "You were never in any danger."

"Harrumph!" Nada expressed her opinion of the logic of men. She cupped her hands and threw two fistfuls of sand onto her blade to absorb most of the mess so she would not stain her own clothing as she retrieved it. She washed the blade and they decided to let the tide take Herem wherever the tide decided it wanted to take him. That triggered a memory…

"Omar! I think I know what mistress Leah meant!" She ran to the remains of the skinning docks and pondered the location. Omar followed querulously.

She began to dig in the loose sand and gravel. "When I was a slave in mistress Leah's household, I killed a fisherman here."

Omar yelled, "What?!" He stood up and withdrew from his wife. "You have spoken nothing of this!"

Nada stopped digging and kneeled beside the small pit she had started. She looked toward her young husband in pain. "My love, there is much about me that I have not shared only because we have not had the time. The same can be said of you. I know almost nothing of your life before you came to Hareb. Tell me something."

"Huh?"

"Tell me something of your life before Hareb. Then I will tell you the story of the fisherman." She looked down at the pit. "I will tell you about the fisherman who died here."

"Alright. My village was slaughtered by Sabean raiders, same as yours. But they wanted to recruit me and make me a fighter like them. When I refused to kill innocents I was beaten and nearly executed, but the boss thought he could make a profit by selling me in Tariq. I… was about to be sold to the temple of Ba'al. That is when madam Batshua saw me. I understand the price she paid for me is still a laughing matter among the traders. She bid very high…" Omar seemed lost in thought.

"I am saddened to hear of your village. You are an orphan… like me?"

Omar peered deeply into his woman's soul and said, "No longer. I am of House Hareb."

A slow smile grew on Nada's face. She understood his wisdom. "And I am of House Omar Al-Hareb." She winked. "Now I will tell you my story. I was on alone on this beach one Sabbath day of rest when a drunken fisherman discovered me. He intended to rape me and dragged me under the docks that used to cover this place. I had been practicing with a skinning knife that he had not seen, so I used it to kill him. Madam Leah found me and helped me hide it all. No one ever found out."

Omar stared at his wife wide-eyed. "You are an amazing woman. That's two."

"Two?"

"Two fisherman. I think you and fisherman do no get along. I will give you a wide berth if I ever take up the profession." They both laughed. Nada found Omar's humor to be good medicine for her soul.

Nada said, "When madam Leah said 'Look under the fisherman', I think she must have meant to look for something buried where I killed the fisherman."

They both began to dig with renewed energy. After they had a hole about three feet deep they came upon a thick leather bag! They dug around it and slowly hauled it out, being careful not to tear it. It must have weighed over twenty pounds.

With their hearts pounding, they untied the top and rolled back the leather to reveal… a cache of gold, silver and jewelry! They faced one other in stunned surprised. Then wrapped their arms around each other in a warm embrace over their treasure!!

They figured the bag contained Leah's personal treasury, something she had hidden from her husband. The new wealth provided the foundation they needed to restore the gardens in the Kingdom of Mari and establish the respectable household of Trader Omar Al-Hareb.

-:--o--:-

Negasi and Wajib developed an unlikely friendship. Negasi was a man of passion, Wajib a quieter man of thought. The professor and the warrior discovered neither of them had any misgivings about the other: they could be themselves in each other's presence. In fact, they were always themselves in anyone's presence. Negasi and Wajib were genuine, one-faced men.

Negasi told Wajib about the papyrus and vellum sheets he had seen used by scribes in his homeland. Wajib was nearly beside himself with enthusiasm! He *must* learn this technology! During the next few years he and Negasi traveled to Egypt, allowing Wajib to import the new writing skills to his school. He developed a fine library, his students recorded observations of all types of drawings and astute observations regarding the life and climate of the land surrounding Tariq.

Tariq flourished for awhile as students came and then dispersed throughout the land with the knowledge and wisdom of God instead of the corruption of Ba'al. But anger is the longest lasting emotion in the human species. Those who had been displaced by the conquest of the temple of Ba'al never forgot their hatred. They taught their sons to hate until there was enough hatred within enough men to form a raid on the city.

The old friends, Negasi and Wajib escaped with their lives. Wajib was able to rescue many of his parchments. Negasi went home to Ethiopia and died among his family, old and satisfied with a life well-lived. Wajib served his remaining years in view of the great pyramids of Egypt, telling stories about Job, the Great Emir of Edom.

In their wrath, the raiders razed Tariq to the ground, utterly destroying it. No one lived there for a thousand years. The winds swept over the ruins, completely blowing down every old building and covering the remains with sand. Boshet's drowning pool was no more, she would have been pleased.

-:--o--:-

God restored Job's fortunes with twice what he had before his troubles. God also blessed Job and Batshua with abnormally long lives -- they lived to see their great, great, great grandchildren!

Batshua at last knew complete contentment and peace. She disappeared one morning after sharing an early breakfast with Job. He went looking for her and found her atop her watchtower. How she had climbed up there by herself was beyond his understanding. She was sitting on an old pillow, a gift from Nada, leaning back against the railing. She looked asleep with the sun in her face, but Job knew she had at last gone to meet God. Feeling lightheaded from the climb, he sat down beside her with a sigh and took her old, dry-skinned hand. He patted it and murmured, "Me too." The watchtower shuddered slightly as the hand of God carried his dear child to his honored, eternal home.

Job's fame spread throughout the world – the man who had remained faithful to God even though it seemed that God had turned on him. But Batshua's prediction came true. No one remembered her name, or ever knew the story of Job's wife.

-:--o--:-

About the Author

Don Arey's favorite color is plaid. He says his personality type usually turns up as an asterisk on any personality test he has ever taken.

He has a B.A. in Chemistry and an M.A. in Religion / Spiritual Formation. He has run a construction business, served as an interim pastor, recorded a Nashville album, and wrote large volumes of disposable software for the semiconductor industry over the past twenty two years.

Lately, he has been interviewing applicants for the State Fuel Assistance Program, an occupation that keeps him entertained daily and provides plenty of time to write in the evenings.

God is good and so is life.

Cast of Characters

The meaning of names can be interesting. Some characters of this story
live up to their names, others do not.

Abel (vanity)
Nada's father

A'dab Ben Hareb (hope) a.k.a **Job** (oppressed)
The Emir of Edom.

Amal (aspiration)
Nada's uncle

Anna (favor)
Nada's aunt

Aqil (wise)
Ba'al-Hanni's waterman

Asher (happy)
Batshua's father

A'jin (gold) a.k.a **Naaman** (be pleasant)
A'dab / Job's bodyguard, formerly a Sabean warrior

Ba'al-Hanni ("Man of Ba'al", root of modern day "Hannibal")
High priest of Ba'al at the temple in Tariq City

Batshua (daughter of prosperity) **Al-Nahdiyah** (delicate)
Job's wife, the Emira of Edom

B'jin and **B'jal** (Jin – gold, Jal – wanderer)
Twin sisters, agents of Ba'al-Hanni

Boshet (shameful thing) renamed **Ephrata** (fruitful and honored)
A shrine prostitute and captive wife of Ba'al-Hanni

Ephrata (fruitful and honored) a.k.a. **Boshet** (shameful thing)
A shrine prostitute and captive wife of Ba'al-Hanni

Gera (pilgrim)
Donkey cart driver

Frayda (joy)
> Nada's friend and kinsmen

Haran (mountaineer)
> Ostrich farmer in El'Hajar

Harun (strength)
> Leader of the Sabean raiders

Herem (destroyer)
> A fisherman, Gulf of Aqaba

Jabal (glides away)
> Young beggar of El'Hajar

Jamal (grace)
> Priest of Ba'al

Job (oppressed) a.k.a. **A'dab Ben Hareb** (hope)
> The Emir of Edom

Lamech (ancient name of unknown meaning)
> Priest of Ba'al at the temple of Tariq

Labid (ancient name of unknown meaning)
> Young soldier in Negasi's service

Leah (delicate, weary)
> Nada's mistress in Aqaba

Miriam (bitter) **Al-Belial** (worthless)
> Nada's mother

Naaman (be pleasant)
> A'dab / Job's bodyguard, formerly a Sabean warrior

Nada (glistening with dew)
> Batshua's handmaiden, kinsman of Frayda

Nadim (drinking-partner)
> A friend of Job's eldest son

Negasi (royalty)
> Batshua's camel driver

Omar (speaker)
>Batshua's bodyguard

Raziel (secrets of God)
>Doorman for House Amal in the Gulf of Aqaba

Ruben (behold, a son)
>Batshua's youngest brother

Tahir (pure)
>A camel trainer from El'Hajar, province of Hareb

Udi (love, diminutive version of "Ehud")
>Donkey cart driver

Wajib (merciful)
>Priest / scholar in the temple of Ba'al

Zahur (a flower)
>A shepherd from Hareb' northern pasturelands

Made in the USA
Charleston, SC
07 November 2011